"We'll get a couple of people on this today. They'll be the best, Mr. Morgan. Very costly, but then you appreciate the best. I can tell."

"I like results."

"We try, and that's all we assure you. Don't speak about this to anyone. When your wife returns home . . ."

"How do you know she will?"

"If she doesn't, that's abandonment, and we have three-quarters of the case won. But I think she's gone to blow off some steam and she'll come home. At that point, you mislead her. Forgive her for all the terrible things she's done. Make it seem that you're mending the fences. Fuck her a few times, and tell her that you love her. Say that she can bring a few discreet friends to the house. Fucking a non spouse at home is *prima facie* evidence of depravity . . . our best grounds for the divorce. One more thing, Mr. Morgan," the attorney said. "If you ever repeat to anyone what I've said here, I'll deny it. Furthermore, I'll get you for slander." Bob Booth paused. "Still with me, Mr. Morgan?"

"Absolutely."

"You'll win, Mr. Morgan . . . you'll win this divorce."

Bob Booth was the right man, Kent thought. No doubt about it.

THE DIVORCE—A shocking novel of marital scandal

THE
DIVORCE

ROBERT P. DAVIS

ace books

A Division of Charter Communications Inc.
A GROSSET & DUNLAP COMPANY
51 Madison Avenue
New York, New York 10010

THE DIVORCE

Copyright © 1980 by Robert P. Davis

An ACE Book, by arrangement with
William Morrow and Company, Inc.

First Ace Printing: January 1982

Published simultaneously in Canada

2 4 6 8 0 9 7 5 3 1
Manufactured in the United States of America

ACKNOWLEDGMENTS

The author wishes to express special gratitude to those who assisted in the preparation of this work, especially the participants in the actual divorce action who requested not to be mentioned by name. Others who supplied their wisdom and understanding of the law were: Mr. Justice Franklin M. Stone, Jurist Emeritus, United States Federal Court of Claims; H. Bryant Sims, Esq., and Jeffrey C. Howard, Esq., of the Federal District Court, North Carolina.

AUTHOR'S NOTE

This is the story of what might be one of the most brutal divorce actions ever recorded by an American judiciary. It happened recently in the climate of divorce reform where the no-fault provision of the law is supposed to evoke a calm and rational solution to the irretrievable marriage. Instead, greed, hatred, subterfuge, vengeance and self-pride took over, all of which ignited a path of horror and death.

It would be reasonable to assume that this divorce took place in a dark, airless ghetto where violence and insensibility might prevail as weapons of social revolt. It did not. The family identified as the Morgans were rich and cultured. They had everything, and that compounded the overall tragedy.

For reasons which will become obvious, I had to establish this work as a novel; still, I must add a few disclaimers. The people I call the Morgans are still alive, but there is no such place as Menlo Head; however, in most ways my fictitious town is similar, in attitude at least, to the community where these people lived.

The Morgans' divorce action was not heard in the state of Connecticut, and the judicial system and civil procedure referred to in this writing are a composite of the legal process in six other states.

Those involved directly or indirectly with the Morgans may look upon this writing as a gruesome reminder; but I hope they find my work fair, balanced and accurate.

Palm Beach, Florida
June 1980

7

CHAPTER ONE

The divorce began the day they were born. They were two unique and accomplished people who placed their human and financial inventories into the common bond of marriage, a logical progression, it seemed to them and to all those who knew Kenneth Morgan and the former Louise Upton.

It would be almost impossible to say exactly when the tide turned on the Morgans. There were imperceptible hints from the beginning of the marriage, and more portents were there before they began as man and wife; but if one day had to be selected, it probably would have been the eighth day of October, just as autumn began its long slide into winter and the winds of Long Island Sound began backing, backing, backing from south to east and finally settling just north of east.

After sixteen successful years of marriage, their love appeared firm and steady. Perhaps their sex life suffered from the passage of time. The adventure was old now; the orchestra had thinned out, and the love tune had dulled to the clicks of a metronome. There was no offending or fumbling during their bedroom act, but it had slipped into a dreary, seldom-practiced routine. The same situation was probably a cross-grain of most Menlo Head marriages, those which had survived the trial years.

Bringing up three children, all girls, ages seven to fifteen; the back-to-back parties to promote Kent's career as a naval architect; the three big "C's" of involvement—church, charity, community—the grueling yacht races they sailed to help prove that Kent's designs were highly competitive, evoked chronic exhaustion. They often drank too much, and the Morgans would have been termed "social alcoholics" by some definitions, but no more so than most of the Menlo Head "set."

In the early years when they lived in New York and Kent was learning his profession at the distinguished yacht-design firm of Sparkman & Stephens, there had been tensions and squabbles. But time, the queller and adjuster, smoothed out the edges of their marriage, so when they moved to Connecticut, the Morgans had a union grounded in mutual esteem.

The children had much to do with that, and while there were boats and parties, their daughters came first. Both Morgans joined the First Episcopal Church, where Kent at the age of forty became the youngest warden. Most marital observers, of whom there were many around Menlo Head, called their marriage a "rosy Gibraltar," a stunning illustration of storybook love.

Perfect love in a storybook town probably should have been suspect from the beginning because nothing in Menlo Head was quite real. It was a town of props, and its passions dealt with correct old money, correct old schools, plus the correct club affiliations. The local tests for acceptability and success were shallow.

Louise Upton Morgan was from an old established Chesapeake family. Her husband, Kent, was distantly related to the J. P. Morgans, and he came from a Locust Valley, Long Island, family who through generations of quietude and sound planning had managed to survive wars, depressions, liberalism, popularism, progressive income tax and all the rest.

She had graduated first in her class from Ethel Walker, and he was an honor student at Choate and president of the sixth form. (Kent was best remembered by Choate football historians for making a 102-yard touchdown run against Deerfield to win a critical game in the last thirty seconds of play.)

Louise Upton and Kent Morgan didn't know it, but even in prep school they were establishing points on the Menlo Head rating list. More pluses were added because they both went to Yale, where they met; they both held postgraduate degrees: Louise, an M.F.A. from the Boston Museum School of Fine Arts, and Kent, an M.S. from M.I.T. They topped the social scoreboard by what happened after college, for Louise gained a silver medal in sailing in the 1964 Olympics, and Kent went on to become one of the world's most admired yacht designers whose hulls furrowed the oceans faster than anyone else's in the prestigious offshore races.

They shared sailing, education, breeding and money, and everyone said that the Morgan marriage reproved the shopworn theory that birds of a feather must stay together to protect themselves.

On this October morning with a dry easterly blowing, Kent was shuffled out of his sleep at 6:10 A.M. by a shrill buzz which had nothing to do with his dull hangover. He didn't have to look from the second-floor window of Pigeon Hill, their *Town & Country*-type home which girded Long Island Sound, to know that a chattering wind was ruffling the cove. His wife, the true basement tinkerer, had the wind data on the wall beside their bed, a small weather station hooked up to an alarm clock.

"The only one in the world," Louise used to say.

If the wind was blowing ten knots or over, the alarm would go off; if not, the clock merely ticked on until the sun was higher and the time came for young voices to echo about their nineteen-room house.

Kent blinked sleepily. He glanced at the slight mound of his stomach and decided that today he would halt his luncheon martinis. (He thought of himself as a thin-boned aristocrat, which he was, in a way, and his kind, as if by ordination, were flab fighters.) Louise and Kent had agreed that age was a shipwreck, but they were not going to smack the rocks until the very last moment. He knew he was aging because he had started to read the obituary page of *The New*

York Times before turning to the sports section. Growing old was inevitable; being old wasn't, Kent used to say.

While many Menlo Head matrons over thirty-five had secretly slipped away for eye nips and temple tucks, Louise was more fortunate: she had a classically sculptured face with bushy amber brows, heavily lidded brown eyes—the kind one sees on lady prime ministers—high cheekbones, a perky, expressive mouth and a complexion which revealed that she kept constant company with the sun.

If you took each of her features separately and rated them, the score would be low; but as a whole, each of the parts, the ridges and hollows of her face, came together exquisitely. Her face indexed character, discipline, breeding and a background where hard work and well-rubbed values were the unspoken rules of thumb. She smiled frequently through her eyes because Louise had slightly bucked incisor teeth. Her Baltimore coming-out party had conflicted with the orthodontist's silver cap work, and she had learned to spread her lips in a smile rather than let people in on her toothy mistake. Finally, though, as her early embarrassment passed, Louise began opening her mouth more; she thought that her two teeth heading a little out rather than straight down were interesting marvels, and having a quipping sense of humor, she would say, "Well, if female vampirism is in next year, I'm ready."

The advantage of her sort of face, of course, was that she appeared old at twenty-five and young at forty. Nothing much changed. Her skin rode tightly over her pronounced bone structure, and she was fortified against the usual failure of a middle-aged face. Most of the Menlo Head matrons were tuned to lankiness through breeding or tennis or diets, or all three. Louise was slightly chunky, and she could have used an extra two inches in height. She appeared a little top-heavy even though her breasts were only bumps, and she walked a bit duckishly. There was a little extra flesh hanging about her midships section, but her body was far from fat, just well developed. Her hands were large; they blended into particularly strong forearms, muscular from years of sail yanking. Some said she looked like a rich jock. Others, mostly thirsty men, and a few thirsty women, too, said that Louise Morgan was an exciting hunk of sex, that she could probably kill her partner between the sheets.

"There is no one . . . no one in Menlo Head . . . that I'd rather have crush my ribs or bust my balls than Louise Morgan," claimed Matty Holt, a local lawyer. "Anytime she wants to clamp her thighs around me for an extracurricular dunk, I'm ready," he added when he was tittering from too much booze one night.

On this morning, Kent, two years older than Louise, rolled over and looked at his wife's broad, mahogany shoulders. She was sitting with her elbows resting on her drawn-up knees, studying the wind gauge which was illuminated by a tiny night light, another one of her ideas.

"Are you going out?" he asked, pushing his words through a yawn.

"Sure . . . it's gusting twenty. That's my kind of weather . . . mine and *Kerry Dancer*'s."

She jumped out of bed and pulled on a pair of bleached sailing pants, and a few minutes later she was gone.

The broad lawn of Pigeon Hill eased down to a breakwall banked by moss-covered rocks whose craggy green heads were exposed only at low water. To the sides of the lawn like great curtains were batteries of tall elms, the New England variety which always seemed to border shaded walks on college campuses. The trees were swaying and creaking as the wind sliced through the branches, flipping the leaves inside out. From the breakwall a gray-and-white wooden pier ran seventy feet to deep water. At the end was a summer-house, a mock pavilion, with a wide entablature scrolled into curlicues and decorative posts with fluted caps. Here, ladies in their crinolines sipping lemonade had once promenaded. The dock and the carriage house were the only remnants of the original Pigeon Hill, an 1889 home of a Tammany Hall politician who wanted the breeze while City Hall grew cob-webs from June to September; it later drifted into the Morgan family, powerful New York real estate people, to settle a debt, perhaps, or for other unmentioned reasons.

At the water end of the old dock was a new fiberglass float approached by a gangplank. On each side of the dock was a "his" and a "hers" yacht. Louise's was a small, ancient 1929 Atlantic Class sloop, and on his side, starboard, of course, was a pristine thirty-seven-foot racing yacht, a type which Kent's design firm sold to marginal skippers—mostly long in the tooth and heavy in the pocket—so they could maintain some sort of respect at the men's bar of the Menlo Head Yacht Club.

Louise had a keen eye, and with particular clarity, she froze moments in her mind, as if her imagination were a continual click of a camera shutter. For instance, when she came from the kitchen door of their white brick regency house, she stopped to see the lawn from the bow of the flagstone terrace. The grass was glistening from the night dew; the blades stood stiffly, and with the low sun behind them, the green was silvered. She had read Ruskin at Yale with blood-coursing aliveness. He talked about ascribing human attributes to inanimate things—Pathetic Fallacy, the man called this poetic device—and Louise, with a quick and fervid mind, became intoxicated with these human ascriptions.

As she stared at the damp, verdant carpet before her, she imagined that the argent blades were really millions of Russian soldiers standing at attention during an ice storm, a scene clipped from *Zhivago*. In a split second that visual slid away, and now the grass tips were actually porcupines freshly dipped in shining paint, and that fantasy eclipsed. She noticed troops of brown wrens paddling about the lawn pecking for worms, and beyond, on the lip of the breakwall, were gulls, puffed and white. The water was too furrowed for fish dunking, and not being worm fanciers, the gulls jealously watched the breakfasting wrens. But Louise would never let the gulls be gulls, or wrens wrens. No. The gulls were really fat British officers in India stuffed into their summer whites reviewing the native troops, played by the darkish

14

wrens, just before they marched into the Khyber Pass at dawn.

Nothing wrong with these whimsies, she thought; at least they were cheaper and more convenient than the real thing, not that Louise lived idealistically in a made-up world. It was just that she liked to mesh the real with the unreal at some pleasant intersection, and, too, it was a way of barging through the downs, while embossing the ups.

The float bobbed gently under her feet, and the water slapped the sides. Underneath there were loud, metallic sucks of escaping air being squeezed out as the pontoons lifted and fell deep into the frothy water.

"Mrs. Morgan—Mrs. Morgan—" Carrie, the black maid, called halfway down the lawn. "Laurie and Cathy want to know if they can go with you."

"All right," Louise yelled back over the peal of the wind. "Tell them to hurry. Mrs. Lunsford is picking them up for school right at eight. She's very punctual."

Louise looked at her waterproof Patek Philippe: one hour and ten minutes to tack around Humble Cove, and maybe, if it wasn't too sloppy, they would swing the sloop around buoy forty-one, a mile and a quarter out in Long Island Sound, marking the entrance to the Menlo River.

Cathy, her fifteen-year-old, galloped across the lawn and clacked her way down the gray pine boards of the finger dock. She was a big-boned girl who looked eighteen; in many ways Cathy resembled her mother, with strong forearms, straight amber hair and a grouping of facial features, pronounced and distinctive, which insinuated a long path of selective breeding. At times people confused Cathy and her mother. They were about the same size, and both spoke in deep, raspy tones. To the males of Menlo Head, including the boys at Country Day School, the bass notes of the Morgan females were mysterious and sensuous—lady spylike. However, those of the same sex believed all the Pigeon Hill females were just plain tough.

Part of this assessment was speculative gossip, but there

was direct criticism, too: from Kent Morgan himself and also from the headmaster of Menlo Head Country Day, a dandyish fellow who was continually entertained in those Menlo Head homes which had children at his school. Louise called him the "pansy poke."

"Mrs. Morgan," he said one day with a flourish of his thin, waving arms, "your daughters are feared at school. They bat the other girls on the knees with their field-hockey sticks. We at Country Day don't mind aggressive action on the playing field . . . but sportsmanship comes first. Knees, as you know, are important, very important, and anyhow, the parents have complained."

"I never saw life in terms of knees," Louise shot back. "My girls aren't tough per se . . . they're tough-fibered, and I taught them to win. That's it! Tell the other parents to pump a little guts into their daughters. God knows they'll need more than you dose out at this school."

He looked at Louise and could not digest what he was hearing; the schoolmaster and many others in Menlo Head never understood Louise Morgan.

She was a fully stamped-out product of her upbringing, a true "Bay daughter," and a direct descendant of the manor days. The women's movement along the Tidewater began in the seventeenth century. Historically, the Eastern Bay people suffered from acute insularity, and the Bay women, young and old, were expected to pull almost equal weight with the men.

Some called the Chesapeake the "noblest Bay in the world." It was one of the few geographies in the United States where water work blended into fieldwork, where plows were parked next to drying fish nets. Bay people were continually in motion and, above all, they were not imitators. They were themselves, as themselves, and they did not fancy transformations anymore than a self-respecting loblolly pine wishes to become a daffodil.

There was a saying which Louise had learned early: "If a Bay daughter can get her pinky through the dainty handle of a teacup, she's without a rope-storied hand." Translated, it meant that a girl was a traitor to Tidewater traditions if her fingers were uncoarsened or unthickened by work. Further translated, a pearly-white, soft hand meant dilettantism. Not good.

The Bay people raced fine yachts; they showed horses, and they bred thoroughbreds for Pimlico, Belmont and Churchill Downs. Tidewater people were proud to remind their fellow Virginians, especially the pompous horsemen of Middleburg, Virginia, that the first fox hunt ever held in America took place in Queens County, Maryland, in the year 1650.

So Louise Upton hacked it out in the fields, on the tractors, in the barns, on the big Bay, pulling just as much weight as her two brothers. When Louise and her husband moved to Menlo Head, she was certain that a typical Bay upbringing in Connecticut was not only advisable but a strict exigency for her girls. She looked around at the local matron-mothers and thought they were soft, useless pawns of the male ego, especially those men who had dribbled out of Ivy League colleges to continue the activities of their fathers.

Louise was her own woman, and her daughters were to be molded into self-reliant individuals. She knew just what they needed, and it was not the mushiness of Menlo Head. (The only reason they located there and not on a Tidewater plantation was because of Kent's profession. Marketing a seven-hundred-thousand-dollar racing yacht was a tough sale in Bay country, but it could be done in "yachtie" communities such as Menlo Head. And Kent did it with aplomb.)

Louise Morgan, in attempting to raise her daughters correctly, slid one arrogance over another. In doing things her way, she became at times too strident, too single-minded for her husband. Once when there was a minor argument on how her girls should be brought up, Louise said, "One difference between you and me is our viewpoint of motherhood. While your mummie was chipping her manicure

17

playing the piano and writing social invitations, my mom was boning whitefish and shooting ducks and deer."

Kent fumed. It was a cruel put-down, and when Kent Morgan sizzled, he usually pouted in his room, failing to fight back.

This morning, when Cathy arrived on the swaying float wearing only cutoff jeans and a weather jacket, Louise said, "Honey, this water is icy and lumpy . . . go back and get your 'funny suit,' and tell Laurie *not* to report without hers."

The girl sprinted back to the house.

The "funny suit." Louise thought about it. If their marriage had had a first crack, it might have commenced with the "funny suit" the year before, and it was a portent of the violent collision yet to come. Louise was a horse-and-hounder, a farmer. Yet her single-hearted gaze went to the sea, and that transfixion was fine in Kent's eyes except for one element: The Bay people went to sea—really to the Bay —all year long, while the Long Island Sound watermen or yachtsmen surrendered their territory at the first sign of ice. The lower New England fishing craft and the yachts were yanked upon the ways to sleep until the warmth returned.

It seemed sensible to all but Louise Morgan. She was an all-year water person who, maniacally, some said, *enjoyed* frozen strands of hair during one part of the year and burned shoulders during the other. To Louise, the act of working and enjoying the Sound all year long was a metaphor of her life. She told her daughters, "Life is hot and cold, good and bad, comfortable and painful . . . so let's get our asses ready."

They went along with their mother: After all, she had beat out ninety-two men in the 1964 Olympics, and Mom could do all sorts of other things, like shoot a bouncing buck right through the heart with a sixty-pound bow and arrow, carve the best duck decoys in New England and pluck out of the air mallards, blacks, pintails and mergansers with a well-balanced, underpowered twenty-gauge shotgun (a feat

18

judged by *Sports Afield* as a true test of sportsmanship and waterfowl gunning).

To her daughters, Louise was the best, and she knew what was best. This led to a growing breach in her marriage which she did not size up properly at the time. Louise built a boat to fetch the rich white meat from the bottom of the Sound. There were plenty of lobsters crawling around, and the waters were all hers in winter since very few, if any, commercial takers were out to trap them.

Louise recognized the dangers of winter lobstering and dragging. One could fall overboard and die within minutes from hypothermia—cold water reducing the body temperature too quickly—and wearing a life jacket meant one merely died on the surface, not on the bottom. The lobster boat could run into a sudden winter gale and belly up because the oncoming water would turn to ice before it rushed out of the gunwales; the additional weight could press the craft down or under, depending upon the run of the seas.

So Louise went to the United States Navy and told them that she wished to fish and sail in the worst weather without peril to herself and her daughters. How could they get through the worst? The Navy told her to order arctic hypothermal suits.

They looked like jump suits with thin layers of flotation padding, and one could plunge into the twenty-degree water and drift about in perfect comfort and safety for days. (The seawater entering the flotation suit was warmed by body temperature and formed an insulation shield.)

Louise had three such suits custom-made for her daughters at a cost of $290 each. (She paid for them out of her Baltimore-based trust fund.)

The suit might have been life-giving in the frigid water, but if one wore it in the boat, the bulky garment restricted free movement while turning one's entire body into a bath of sweat, even on the coldest days. Louise then devised a plan for herself and her daughters. They would fold the flotation suits into knapsacks and wear them over their shoulders. If they went overboard, or the workboat or sloop was swamped, they would enter the water, remove the flotation suits from the backpacks and get into them while bobbing about.

This took practice, and Louise started with her daughters during the last weeks of September, as the Sound water cooled gradually to its winter temperature—about forty-eight degrees.

They began after school by jumping off the workboat in their weather gear, which was removed and replaced by the "funny suits." Louise eased her daughters into this routine slowly with three practices a week to overcome their fears and improve their techniques of changing clothes in cold water. The air and water temperature curves tilted downwards as the practice sessions went on into December, and on a blustery afternoon Kent returned to Pigeon Hill to see the workboat anchored about forty yards from the finger dock. Clumps of ice speckled the steel-gray Sound; three-foot breaking waves were foaming and flopping over the miniature bergs; and in the middle of this freezing pandemonium, Kent saw his wife and their three daughters jumping into the frigid water, changing into their Day-Glo flotation suits.

He ran to the float and bellowed: "All of you . . . get in here! Have you gone insane!"

They yanked the hook and motored the lobster boat to the dock, which was being washed with icy water driven by the howling northeaster.

"What the hell is going on?"

"We're practicing getting into our flotation suits," Cathy said.

"Louise, damn it . . . it's dangerous!"

"Why?"

"For a lot of obvious reasons. The girls could drown."

"We've been practicing for months. We know just what we're doing," Laurie spoke up.

"Yeah, it's fun, Dad," little Jody, six years old, piped.

"Fun!" Kent exploded. "Fun!"

"We haven't had any problems, Kent," Louise told him as she stepped on the whipping float with an iced-up dock line in a rubber-gloved hand.

"Well, I forbid it. What will the neighbors think . . . my daughters jumping in the water in the middle of winter? It's damn embarrassing!"

"Now, Kent, you'll just have to bear with us."

"I don't want our girls growing up like explorers or hunters. They should be ladies."

"We don't want to be just ladies, Dad," Cathy said.

"Yeah, that's boring," Laurie added, making a face.

"I want you to stop this immediately."

"No, we're not," Louise said.

"Mom has a good idea," Cathy said. "Anyone can fall into the water, Dad . . . so now we know what to do if it happens."

"That's right . . . Mom's ideas always make sense," Laurie nodded.

"So no one is going to listen to me. Is that it?"

Louise and her daughters simply stood looking at Kent, and he thumped back across the finger dock to his room, shaking his head all the way. The girls went back to one more practice session.

Kent knew he was no longer the patriarch of Pigeon Hill.

CHAPTER TWO

Louise usually sailed alone at dawn, but at times some of her children were signed on as rope pullers. Each of them enjoyed the sport to varying degrees, and they looked up to Louise, trying to be as agile as their mother.

Louise glanced out towards the Sound, away from the lee of the land. The wind was knocking off the wave heads, splintering them into long white streaks; the brows of the breaking waves were rimmed with pure gold. It was a day, she thought, for spirits to soar. The *Kerry Dancer* was an old rebuilt racing sloop which she had deftly restored, scraping and varnishing each of the matched mahogany planks, but the cigarlike yacht was tender to the breeze: that was the challenge of a gusty day. If you didn't sail her right, she would lay over so far that the cockpit would swamp. Louise knew that at times a sharp-edged gust could claw her before the main sheet could wheeze through the wooden blocks. She didn't want to sail *Kerry Dancer* under on a day when most of the Menlo Head yachts were safely snatched to their mooring buoys. Louise decided that since the children were coming today, she would tie a reef in the mainsail to keep *Kerry Dancer* on her feet.

Once, during a late November sail off Menlo Head, when the wind was cutting thirty in the gusts and a slight snow was falling—a day every sensible fish duck was grounded—an angry burst of wind had knocked the sloop down, and the cockpit suddenly became a big bathtub of icy water. Louise

had driven her beloved sloop downwind—the thing to do—
and once in the lee of Barton's Island, she hove to, shivering,
and bailed out the sloshing cockpit with a galvanized hand
pump.

Kent told her later that she was crazy to have gone out on
a day like that, when all the other yachts were fast asleep
under winter covers.

"I knew what I was doing," she said.

"What would have happened if you had driven her under?
God, you would have lasted ten minutes in that water. I'd be
a widower with three kids."

She didn't answer that day. She knew he was right, but
Louise flicked on her gadgeteering mind, and in two weeks
the problem of a sudden knockdown was solved. First, Louise
went out and bought an outsized electric bilge pump which
operated off a twenty-four-volt system; then she wired up
two secondhand batteries which she purchased from a junk
dealer—she was a thrifty woman—and finally she went shopping for a used battery charger with a stepdown transformer.
She made cardboard patterns for the battery holder which
she planned to bolt down under the foredeck. She cut out
marine plywood to fit the patterns with the band saw in the
cellar of Pigeon Hill, fastened in the supports, then the
pump. Finally, she crisscrossed the two twelve-volt car batteries with waterproof cable. (The power to recharge the
units came from the 110-outlet on the dock.) When she had
completed her jury-rigged bilge pump, she filled the *Kerry
Dancer* with hose water. As the old sloop was literally foun-
dering, she flicked on the waterproof switch which she had
screwed under the aft rail coaming.

With noisy bubbles, gulps, swishes of escaping air, the
electric pump sucked the sloop almost dry in minutes, and
the bilge water gurgled back into the Sound through the
discharge line.

One morning shortly afterwards, she decided to play a
practical joke on Kent. Louise should have known better.
His usual response to gags was a small pout, rather than a

good-hearted laugh. She bounded in that day just as he was getting ready to go to his design office in Menlo Head.

"Kent, Kent . . . *Kerry Dancer* is sinking by the dock! Help me!" she wailed.

He leaped from his bed, raced across the lawn in his shorts and halted with an oval mouth and wide eyes, seeing the sloop about to slip under, taking his expensive float down, too.

"God damn it!" he yelled. "Why the hell didn't you keep the cauling up? Shit!"

Together they tore out along the Victorian dock, through the summerhouse, down the gangway to the float. She threw back her broad shoulders, stiffened her well-formed legs and looked up into the sky.

"Alla Kazoop, Alla Kazoop . . . save my sloop!" she cried.

"Have you gone nuts!" Kent yelled, grabbing her by the arm.

"No, no . . . Alla Kazoop . . . save my sloop," she chanted once again. "He'll do it, I know."

Then she hurled herself over the low gunwale, landing squarely in a geyser of water. She touched the pump switch and continued her prayer to the god of half-sunken boats. The pump sucked and sucked; the water level came down; the sloop came up. She burst into a belly laugh which in the end pained her stomach.

"Very funny," he said dully.

"Oh, come on . . . don't be such a hard-ass. I thought it was a rare joke." Her husband did not smile.

Louise thought of that incident now. Waves are often deceiving, and when she hauled in the sheets going upwind to clear the head of Barton's Island, the bash of the breaking sea rattled and shook the sloop; water jumped over the low lee rail. On came her ticking bilge pump.

Laurie was a strong eleven. Her face was tanned; her forearms were already well developed from tennis and mainsheet pulling. She sat on the aft cockpit boards with Cathy, and the two grasped the mainsheet, playing it in and out as

Louise slugged her yacht tight to the wind. None of them were at loose ends. They knew what to do, and Louise had wiped the fear of rough water out of their heads years ago with the aid of the "funny suits."

To Louise, sailing on a bad morning was like an open-air gymnasium. You had ropes to pull, winches to wind, legs that had to be stiffened and flexed hard for balance. And there was crisp, salted air that poured into the lungs, while all the blood and juices ran wild.

"Laurie, take the tiller!" she yelled over the clap and smash of the crests.

The young girl slid over, taking the helm.

"Anticipate . . . anticipate. When you feel the gust, bring her up into the wind beforehand, *never* after. Ride the rudder. Come on, Laurie, get that feel . . . ride her up!" Louise screamed over the shriek of the wind.

They spent almost forty minutes tacking about the sloop. The girls were soaked and laughing. Louise finally let the sheets run, and they tore downwind towards the Pigeon Hill dock. The sun had lifted by then, and it put a fine light on the facade of their home, etching out the details, even the slats in the dark gray shutters flanking the upstairs windows. The house had almost perfect proportions. It was large, but not opulent.

The second Pigeon Hill had been built in 1932 from the foundations of the first structure, which had burnt to the ground in 1924 during a party Jimmy Walker was said to have attended. The new house was hidden purposely in great gatherings of greenery—high rhododendron, trees hauled in to smother the size of the place, making it appear smaller— a discreet move during the Depression.

The interior of the regency structure did not reflect the presence of three children, their parents or two in help. Carrie, who had been with them since the girls were born, was permanently settled in the carriage house, and the second maid came in at eleven each morning. Toys were always picked up and put away. When one or several children chipped the paint by a doorsill or a chair rail—normal attrition—Kent, who couldn't stand blemishes on people, yachts or houses, would run to the garage where he stored rows of paint cans labeled to match the color of every room in the house. Taking his light sandpaper, he would smooth off the chip and then apply the paint, feathering the edges out so the patchwork blended into the previous coat as if nothing had happened. He was steeped in the rule of appearances: his own and those associated with him.

As she watched their place looming closer, Louise felt that the world was hers. How extraordinarily well things had gone. They were financially secure; their children were loving, unspoiled, adjusted and healthy. Aside from mumps, the various pox, the usual colds and a few flips off bikes, the Morgan children had glided easily through the beginning years, and they moved into life's stuff with hard work fused into the pride of accomplishment and self-reliance. They were beginning to be good "Bay daughters."

Louise rounded up the sloop and came to a halt just beside the mooring cleats, good sailing on a blustery day without auxiliary power. After tying up *Kerry Dancer*, she ran across the lawn, skipping and hopping with her arms draped over the shoulders of her two drenched girls. Forty minutes later, after warm showers and bran flakes, Bunny Lunsford's station wagon rolled upon the crushed bluestone driveway of Pigeon Hill, and the three children climbed in. Bunny, a buxom blonde, stuck her head out of the window and reminded Louise of the racquet ball game that day at the Menlo Head Field Club.

Louise returned to the highly mechanized kitchen through the side door and glanced over at Kent, eating his melon and reading *The New York Times*, the financial page as usual. Those were his people, his potential clients, and he always knew who was sinking or swimming. She leaned over and kissed him on the cheek.

"Darling, I'm sorry about this morning. I really should have taken my boat ride in bed, instead of out there."

26

"It's all right. So you prefer your sloop and your daughters over me," he said, his eyes fastened on the paper. "I know where I stand."

"You adore martyrdom . . . you ought to study the dangers of self-pity."

She walked across to the kitchen drawer and pulled out a stack of school report cards packed together with a rubber band.

"Kent, you haven't even looked at these," she said, returning to the breakfast table with a cup of coffee.

"I've been very busy. And I don't have time to do it now . . . have to be in New York for a design conference at twelve-thirty today."

"Who are you meeting?"

"Roger Halston. We're showing him preliminary designs for a fifty-five-foot yawl. A very important job, Louise."

"Well, just put the paper down a minute, please. I'm not satisfied with Cathy's work. She's slipped in math again, and Laurie could be doing a lot better in social studies and history."

"What the hell do you expect . . . you've put duck shooting, lobstering and every other pursuit around here over normal education."

"That's unfair!"

"Hell it is. They can carve decoys, blast mallards, but can those little girls—your creations—take nine to the cube root?"

"We've had this discussion before, Kent. I'm bringing up these girls the way I was brought up. I would hope it was our way because you've always emphasized physical courage. And there's not one damn bit of inconsistency between adding up figures and learning how to survive in life."

"It's all one-sided, Louise . . . top-heavy. I'll tell you the solution. Those girls should go away to school."

"What you're saying is they should get away from me."

"Yes. They should have a solid, well-rounded education, a balanced education, and that Country Day is for losers."

"Cathy's old enough . . . but you're not suggesting that

we send Jody and Laurie to boarding school? If you put both their ages together, it would only equal eighteen."

He nodded. "In fact, I think I'll call Choate-Rosemary Hall tomorrow."

"I've already mentioned it to Cathy. She doesn't want to go to Rosemary or Ethel Walker. She'll be away at Yale and graduate school long enough."

"And do you think she'll qualify for New Haven with those marks?"

"We're going to work on it." Louise paused and then continued, "Besides, I've made a decision. She should go to Sacred Heart. The Sisters of Charity will shape her up."

Kent recoiled in anger, and his tidy face became furrowed, as if Louise had suggested sending their oldest daughter to a public school in the black belt of Alabama. He shot a hand over the smooth blond hair that was beginning to creep back from his forehead and said finally, "The girls *aren't* Catholic."

"What's the difference? The Justines and Monroes aren't Catholic, and their daughters are over there. Yes, I think I'll speak to Mother O'Brien tomorrow. I've met her. She's very well-educated and a strict school mistress."

Kent pushed to his feet and locked his knees like a racehorse, shifting his weight backwards without losing his balance. Then he pointed his finger in Louise's face.

"First the girls are drenched in your Chesapeake philosophy. Now you want them propagandized by the Catholic Church. That's *not* going to happen. I won't pay the bills!"

"Then *I* will!"

The look on his face was fierce. Louise knew she had gone too far this time, and she wanted to say she was sorry, but he was gone before she could arrange her thoughts.

Ten minutes later Kent drove his sparkling green Maserati through the town of Menlo Head and reflected as usual that the facades of Main Street, actually U.S. 1, abraded his sense of design and taste. The village, incorporated in 1623, had served originally as a trading center for coastal schooners

28

coming up the Menlo River to load lumber and grain from the gristmill, which once stood near the place where the New Haven Railroad bridge now spanned the river. Like many Connecticut towns rooted in early history, Menlo Head soon lost most of its colonial flavor. Main Street was wrecked by the explosion of late-nineteenth-century building: dull brick fronts topped off by cornices which looked as if they had been carved by a second-rate cookie maker.

Then the prideful town fathers decided to scrape up history. They found sepia photographs and drawings of the original Menlo Head, and a firm of Massachusetts architects was given the job of recreation, or reincarnation, as some put it. Down came the late-Victorian Main Street, and up went the new-old, quaint little shops with simulated old windows, split shingles weathered by a special factory process and fake colonial signs announcing the nature of each business.

To Louise, Kent and many others, it all appeared like a medium-budget movie set with the art directors on strike. Clumsy imitation. About the time Main Street was yanked backwards, Kent established his design firm in Menlo Head, and at Louise's urging, they bought a *real* building, an old sail loft which had stood by the muddy slope of the Menlo River since the early 1800s. (There might have been previous deeds, but they had been lost.)

The dove-gray structure leaned a bit outwards, and Louise insisted that the cant be preserved to prove that one building in the made-up town she detested had survived the awkward progression. The outside shingles were actually weathered by weather; the panes of glass, eight over eight, were filled with tiny airholes, proving that the job had been handblown rather than stamped out of Owens-Corning. After commercial sailmaking ended, the building had been used as a feed grain loft, an Elks' meeting hall and a warehouse for the Honda dealer next door.

On the first floor were the offices of the eleven-man firm, and upstairs, where they used to sew the sails, was a large room of hand-hewn beams and wide pine boards, pegged instead of nailed. Not much of the original character of the old loft could be appreciated: rows of drafting tables with stools stood upon the mellowed boards; boat models hung from the cross beams; and it was hard to see the tiny cuts of the adz, marks of true heritage, which even the slick colonial copiers up on Main Street couldn't quite duplicate in their "look-alike factories."

To the back of the design room was a skinny loft with a sling hoist overhead and a double door to the side, where bags of feed grain used to be lowered to the flatbed wagons. Louise decided to turn this space into an apprentice's loft. She found a retired sailmaker who knew the skills of rope and canvas, and four days a week, groups from the high school, the YMCA and other organizations would come to learn the lost art. The Menlo Head parents approved of Louise's sail school; at least their children would grow up realizing that needles had other functions besides shooting it up—a town problem. And the yacht designers in the next room savored the smell of beeswax; it gave them a sense of the sea, when all they were doing was drawing remote lines on tissue paper.

That contribution from Louise Morgan was appreciated by the town mothers more than her homegrown educational patterns. Teaching her girls to kill and skin wildlife was an endeavor better left to others, they thought, particularly lamebrained male hunters who slept in their undershirts and drank beer in the woods.

Bunny Lunsford understood. The other Menlo Head matrons were shocked to see Louise out on the Sound on frigid, snow-swept mornings with her three girls, plucking lobsters from their homemade traps. But these same antagonists were not so maddened that they wouldn't buy fresh lobster from Louise at four dollars a pound, instead of paying seven dollars at Fredrick's Fish Market on Main Street.

Kent wore his special rumpled blazer that day. (He always appeared at design conferences slightly uniformed, and this blazer was instantly respected.) His dark blue coat, of deliberately poor tailoring, would have marked Kent as a third-rate sailing bum trying to make an impression if it had not been for a tiny gold emblem stitched into the left breast pocket. The emblem was small and stingy compared to that of the New York Yacht Club; it was the badge of the Royal Yacht Squadron, one of the oldest, most honored clubs in the world. (Kent had spent one year at Christ Church College, Cambridge, between Yale and M.I.T., and he had come home with a slight English accent which he kept well lubricated at appropriate times.) That and his cheap blazer with the small "R.Y.S." gave him a boost with those who knew. And those people were the only ones who counted. Kent was a classic snob, but he didn't know it because he moved for the most part among those of identical rank and privilege.

Kent entered his office, and Buddy Foster, his senior man who wore rope belts and wanted nothing more in life than to design and sail yachts, rushed up to him.

"Morning, Kent . . . the preliminary bluelines for the Halston job are ready!" he announced with pride, knowing that Kent realized they had worked late the night before.

Buddy spread the prints out on the drawing table, and they reviewed the interior arrangement. Kent made a few corrections, and they hurried the tissue upstairs for the last-minute work.

Kent started a little late for New York. The dry easterly had turned foul, making the going even slower as the pounding rain brought traffic to a crawl on the approaches to the Triborough Bridge. Halfway across the bridge, the Maserati's left front tire blew out with a muffled bang and a gush of air.

Kent stopped, opened the back trunk and took the two-hundred-dollar hydraulic jack from its black leather holder. He placed it on the wet cement and brought out his chromium lug wrench, also a product of fine Italian craftsmanship. The rain pelted down, and already his pockets were becoming small swamps; his waterproof Burberry admitted water like an old sponge. He was jacking the car up, working by the steel separation barrier between the bridge walkway and the vehicle thoroughfare, when a hefty tow truck marked "Triborough Bridge Authority" crawled into the space in front of the Maserati and backed up towards the front bumper.

Two plump, half-shaven men, each about six feet tall and wearing grease-stained slickers and boots, climbed out of the cab. "Hey, you. No changin' tires on the bridge. We're towin' yuh."

"I prefer to change it right here," Kent shot back, pumping in a bit more of his Lloyd George accent than usual.

"We don't give a shit what yuh prefer, mista," the second man said. "We're haulin' yuh off."

They returned to the back of their truck and drew out a chain and tow bar. Kent raced after them and clamped his arm around one man's slicker.

"I don't want you wrecking my car with that thing! I've heard of front ends being destroyed with that tank of yours. This is a forty-two-thousand-dollar sports car."

"Get yuh fuckin' hand off me," the man said, shuffling his arm away. "If yuh got a fifty-thousand-dollar toy, mista . . . that don't change the rule. Get the hell back."

"I happen to be Kent Morgan from Menlo Head. The city doesn't take liability for tows, so I'm not allowing this."

Kent said those words in the same lofty British-toned accent, and to one of the two men, he suddenly seemed a rich, privileged gay. The rain fell madly, and the tow man's temper was shortening.

"We don't have time for fags. Get lost."

"What did you say?"

"You heard me."

"Apologize."

"Get lost, queenie."

"Don't go near my car."

"What are you going to do about it?"

32

"Break your jaw."

Both of the hulks winked at each other and burst into laughter. The man who had insulted Kent said, "Which one are you goin' to drop, that guy or me?"

"You."

"Go drop him," the other nodded, shifting the cigar in his mouth. "I'll just watch. Won't interfere, fellow."

A spell of rage, hot and uncontrolled, swept over Kent Morgan, dissolving his restraint and rational thought. He moved swiftly to the cab of the truck and before they could stop him, Kent yanked open the door, reached in, pulled the microphone out of the transceiver and tossed it over the walkway of the bridge structure and into the East River. One of the men started a long windmill punch. Kent halted it with his right hand which he crossed with his left, tapping the outstuck jaw. He then snapped a fast uppercut to the man's jaw and double-crossed with a stinging punch which caved in his opponent's belly. The man fell in a lump, splashing into the muddy puddle. The fellow worker came towards Kent who stopped him with a square punch on the upper jaw, and the second man sprawled unconscious. Kent rubbed his knuckles and continued to change the tire, but first he unlatched and removed his Connecticut license plate. When the men recovered, they did not approach Kent again but ran down the bridge towards the tollgate for help.

Kent did not bother to attach all the lug bolts. With three of them secured, he hopped into the Maserati and drove off the bridge, down the 125th Street ramp. After several blocks, he pulled to the curb and attached the remaining bolts. Then he was on his way to meet Roger Halston, looking into his rearview mirror for the police he knew would be after him for laying out two city employees and tossing city equipment into the river. (A Maserati, even one missing a license plate, would not be too difficult to trace through the Department of Motor Vehicles.)

Kent gloated, thinking about his escapade. And as he

swung his racing machine down the East River Drive, he told himself that history did repeat itself. It had just happened on the Triborough Bridge.

Years before, when he was attending day school in Locust Valley, a bigger and older boy demanded sex from Kent Morgan. Kent rebelled. He was beaten up twice, but he never succumbed. Still, the incidents brought dark thoughts to the youth's mind: he could not defend himself; and was he a homosexual? Was that the reason the older boy had made repeated moves? Kent took up boxing at the New York Athletic Club where he was personally trained by Arthur Donovan, ex-fighter, ex-referee of heavyweight championship matches.

Kent went on to become captain of the Yale boxing team; he also boxed for his college team at Cambridge.

He had just been called a fag on the bridge, and he had summoned his skills which had, at times, been the response to his explosive temper. The thought that he might still sound and look gay, an impression he had tried to eradicate all his life, haunted him.

CHAPTER THREE

Five years before, as the design business progressed, the Morgans had bought a duplex on the corner of Sixty-sixth Street and Fifth Avenue, which they used mostly during the winter when staying in town for parties or the theater. Kent had turned one room into a drafting studio where he could make quick design corrections for New York clients. As he drove up to the Plaza, Kent wondered if he should go over to the apartment and change, or enter the Edwardian Room looking like a yachtsman just plucked from the sea. His pants were now stinking and itching; his knuckles were skinned and one was bleeding, but he was already forty minutes late.

Roger Halston, a man who suffered from too many semesters at Harvard and too many years in the estate and trust department of the Chemical Bank where he served as a senior vice president, was a clock-watcher; his tolerance for lateness and other slips of conduct was confined by an acute sense of propriety.

Kent grabbed his drawings, gave the car to a doorman and proceeded into the Edwardian Room, trailing tiny drops of water like a duck paddling up the slope of a pond.

"What happened, Kent?" Roger Halston asked, standing to shake hands.

"Sorry to be late, Roger. I was smack in the middle of the Triborough when my Maserati's front tire blew out. It isn't even a year old, and look . . . I skinned my knuckles on the jack."

"You sports car people. Well, sit down. We'll fix you up with a drink. This is my daughter, Babs."

Kent looked over and smiled at the girl sitting at the table. He remembered meeting Babs long before; at that time she had had a Band-Aid on her knee and scrapes on her shins and about the longest coal-black hair he had ever seen on a young girl. Now she was grown and the Band-Aids were gone, but the long shining hair remained. She was radiant and already mysterious. Her dark eyes were steady and unblinking.

"How are you, Mr. Morgan?" she said in a low-pitched voice which was mellow but unchanging, like a one-note organ, reminding Kent of Louise's love of bass notes.

"Well, fine. I remember you over at Pigeon Hill. Didn't you come to a Fourth of July party?"

"That was five years ago."

Roger signaled the waiter. "What will it be, Kent? You need something or you'll catch pneumonia."

"I could go over to the apartment and change . . . make myself more presentable."

"Nothing of the sort, and anyhow, sailors are supposed to be wet. Your usual superdry vodka martini?"

"Ah, I had planned to give them up today."

"Make it tomorrow," Roger said, easing a smile onto his soft lips. He wore a dark banker's pin-striped suit; he would have been a handsome man if it were not for the fact that his ebony hair had thinned and departed, leaving a shining skull which was flecked with sun blemishes, some pink, some brown.

Kent's first martini wasn't enough; his second was too much. His third left him wanting another, but he didn't slip to the fourth, knowing that he had to remain coherent. He rolled out the drawings, explaining the progress of the design. Babs Halston kept silent, only bobbing her head in agreement when asked by her father if it wouldn't be better to arrange two heads on the yawl instead of the large one aft, and what about a 110 electrical circuit and the bar?

"But, Roger, you can't have everything. For instance, the AC generator will go nine hundred pounds, the hi-fi one hundred, and weight doesn't win boat races."

"I'd *like* it all," said the man who was used to everything.

"But an entertaining yacht is one breed . . . a racing machine another."

"Isn't it a heartache when people have yachting problems, Mr. Morgan?" Babs said, breaking a long silence.

The remark jolted Kent and angered her father.

"Unfortunately, Kent, you can see that Babs has that haughty sense of humor which comes from spending too much time in the south of France with her mother."

"Well, Babs, all designs have problems," Kent said, changing the subject. "Solutions are found in compromises."

"Even Kandinsky had design problems, Mr. Morgan."

"Who? Babs, what the devil does that have to do with our sailboat? Besides, it'll be yours as much as mine," Roger Halston snapped.

She didn't answer, and the table was still for a time while Kent thought through the alternatives.

"Roger, I'd like to propose something a little crazy . . . a design never attempted," he said finally.

"No experiments, Kent. Nothing unproven."

"It's not an experiment, just an idea to give you two boats instead of one."

"I can hardly afford the one," Halston laughed complacently, sipping his Chateau Lafite Rothschild.

"You'll tough it out, Father," Babs interposed, with no expression or change in her voice.

Kent spoke hastily, losing a bit of his adopted British accent. (It always happened when his mind raced ahead of his borrowed demeanor.) He explained his two-for-one theory: the yacht would be convertible, a hollowed-out cabin for racing, and one stuffed full of accoutrements for cocktail parties and comfortable cruising. Kent's resolution: the heavy bunks, the AC generator, the fireplace, the air-conditioner and the hi-fi and other refinements would be designed

37

in such a way that they could be unbolted quickly and lifted out of the yacht when she was entered in an important race. (This was more to please Roger than anything else because the man's skill at boat handling was marginal.)

"Kent, you're a genius, but will it work?"

"I think so. But I need some time on the drawing board. I'll have to come up with sketches and give you a schedule of weight reduction to see if it's worthwhile."

"How fast can this be assessed? I want to let the construction contract this week."

"If I go back to my apartment now and get started, I can have the preliminary drawings this afternoon."

"Fine. I'll send someone over for them. We can talk by phone." He turned to his daughter. "Don't you think it sounds like a good idea, Babs, or aren't you interested?"

"Father, I'm always interested in everything you do," she said in the same muted voice in the identical octave. Obviously, she didn't mean it.

Roger shook his head and smiled sardonically at his beautiful daughter, who seemed to have nothing else to say during the luncheon.

The dampness and depression still clung to Kent when he left the Plaza. The martinis hadn't soaked up his clamminess, even though it had stopped raining by the time he arrived at the front of One East Sixty-sixth Street. He went up to the duplex and was surprised to find the door ajar.

"Hullo . . ." a voice called.

A pudgy, paint-splattered worker in overalls waddled out to the upstairs balustrade and looked down at Kent.

"I'm the painter," he said.

"I wouldn't have guessed."

"I'm doing the library for Mrs. Morgan."

"It's been done."

The man shook his head. "Nope. She changed her mind . . . wanted mist white instead of ivory buff. Had to re-order."

"Of course. She's a mist-white. Definitely."

The downstairs was broken up into three areas: the design studio which also served as a dining room; the living room with a working fireplace engulfed in pilasters and inset panels of cherrywood which ran to the ceiling; and a small kitchen and a downstairs powder room. Upstairs were two large bedrooms, one fitted with a bookcase which technically made it a library or a place to have after-dinner coffee.

The duplex was more Kent's domain than Louise's. In a way, the apartment was a visual parchment of Kent Morgan. On the walls were his diplomas from Choate, Yale and M.I.T. Shined-up sailing trophies, some used as flower vases, were about, along with yacht models, mostly vessels which Kent had designed, and pictures of himself being awarded prizes and at the helm of various ocean-racing yachts. Spotted through all this were old cracked photos of the outsized family estate in Locust Valley, a model of the Cup defender that his father had helped finance and a sepia of Kent's great-grandfather who had served as an under secretary of state during the Wilson administration. On the Queen Anne table was a medal in a flat glass case, the Croix de Guerre, given to his father "for valor" in World War I, and his own decorations for having served as an adviser in the early days of Vietnam.

To some, the museum indicated that the curator or tenant was a socially nervous person who needed the reassurances of his identity through props. Kent didn't see it this way. Louise, a modest woman, so sure of herself that she stored her Olympic medal under her old unused bras in the lower lefthand drawer of a bureau, said when she noticed Kent's museum filling up, "Kent, isn't this too much puffery?"

Kent simply reminded her that sportsmen stuffed their trophies to prove that their shots didn't miss.

He entered the kitchen, made himself a hefty Irish coffee and then shuffled to the upstairs study as the rain started once more. Looking out the window, he saw Central Park obscured by a grayish veil and people scrambling for cover.

His spirits were ground down, and he felt depressed. Kent carried his mug into the bathroom, ran a tub and, a few minutes later, was relaxing in the warm bath, sipping his drink. Later he changed into fresh clothes and went downstairs for another Irish coffee, which he hoped would improve his spirits so he could make some sense on the drawing board.

But he was restless and couldn't concentrate. For a while he studied the rain on the windows, the beads of water falling off into rivulets, and he realized that his head was too mushy to draw well. He called the office, and they read off the approximate weights of the gear that could be lifted out of the Halston yacht. Then he made a few clumsy drawings of an enlarged hatch, through which the nautical junk would travel, and scribbled a tiedown bolt arrangement.

Time passed, and finally Kent threw down his pencil and watched the traffic move down Fifth Avenue, and the small fights for cabs. The doorbell's peal jerked him upright. He crossed the hall and swung open the door hastily, thinking that it was Roger's messenger, but the messenger was Babs Halston.

"Oh . . ." he said, "I didn't expect you."

"I'm going to take the stuff back to my father, but I thought I'd come over early and watch you draw. Do you mind?"

"No . . . no . . . course not," Kent said slowly, shielding the blur in his voice. "Come in."

She followed him into the design studio where he settled on the stool again, pretending to draw.

"Are you going to offer me a drink?" she asked after a pause.

"Why don't you make your own? Everything's in the kitchen."

The girl disappeared, and Kent's eyes followed her. He noticed that her legs were unusually long and well shaped and that her ass was small. Her shoulders were broad and her breasts nicely developed; she wore no bra under her light dress. He wiggled his pencil, trying to clear his head; from the corner of his eye, he could see her taking inventory of the living room, moving her long fingers across the boat models. Once in a while, she lifted her glance to catch his stare. She remained silent, meandering around, gulping a vodka.

"Lousy day," he said finally.

"Yes."

"What did you do in Europe?" he asked casually.

"Sucked and fucked," she said flatly, never arching her brows or changing the steady look in her eyes.

Kent spun around on his drafting stool. "What did you say?"

"I sucked and fucked my way through Europe. Mother and I spent a lot of time on the Riviera. What do you want me to tell you, that we went to museums and took pictures of the old ladies and pigeons in the Paris parks?"

"You're trying to shock me."

"Why should I?"

"Does your father know this?"

"No. But don't report us. You see, Mother's kind of horny. She was an original subscriber to *Screw* . . . plain brown envelopes . . . and we're both kinky as hell. Actually we're charitable hedonists. We do terrible, sensual things, but we also help support a French orphanage run by impoverished nuns. . . ."

As the girl continued smoothly, Kent wondered if she could be drunk already. What was Roger going to say? Then he thought about Babs's mother, Gwen Halston, a large woman with a near-perfect face who came from an old, upper New York State family. She seemed, like so many Menlo Head matrons, to be a totally proper female, and Kent *couldn't* believe that Gwen Halston was horny. Yet the town's facade, its outward gleam of respectability, did not always agree with its concealed nakedness.

Kent didn't see or hear Babs approach his drawing board; the scent of jasmine preceded her. With her elbows on the table, the girl bent over so that her deeply cut V-neck fell away and the soft flow of her bronzed left breast was exposed almost down to the nipple. He shot a glance sideways and felt the press of excitement.

"I have to explain," she said.

"No, you don't. I'll have these drawings finished in a minute, and then you can take them back to your father."

"I want to explain anyhow," she said, just as mechanically as before. "I'm going to be a doctor."

"You!" Kent said with a laugh.

"Me. I have straight A's in science up at Columbia, and I don't want to be an average doctor who sneaks through medical school and passes the boards by a squeak. But Mr. Morgan, I don't want to miss anything in life at the expense of studying my ass off. I know that you can't be plugging the medical books and plugging every cock in town at the same time. One or the other. So I said to myself, 'I'll get it out of my system beforehand . . . I'll fuck everything that stands still.' Everything . . . if you know what I mean. I've been into every drug known, and I've had about all the scenes except . . . well, there're still a few on my shopping list. Then comes the day when it's all over, but at least I'll have no regrets. When I enter Cornell Med, I'll be a very good little girl."

"I need a drink," Kent said, getting up from his stool.

"Fix me one, too, please."

Kent entered the kitchen and built two stiff vodkas. She leaned against the doorjamb, watching him. Kent's mind was wobbling back and forth. He'd never heard that sort of commentary from a girl her age, or anyone else that he could recall.

"Are you annoyed?" she asked.

"A little stunned is more like it. I keep remembering you with Band-Aids on your knees."

"I'm sorry," she said with a quick smile, and for the first time her voice lifted a bit and vibrated with feeling.

Then she came towards him. He stood rigidly, and she moved until her breasts were pressing against him. Her thighs followed, landing against his groin. She slipped a soft kiss on Kent's cheek and whispered close to his ear. "You were so funny today . . . running into the Plaza like a wet Labrador."

"Why did you come to the luncheon? You were so damned sarcastic to your father."

She shrugged. "We trade sarcasms. Why was I there? Well, I tire of giggly roommates up on 116th Street. Should have gone to Smith . . . Columbia's tacky. I just wanted to drift downtown today. No, that's kind of a lie. I really wanted to see if you had changed."

"Me?"

"I had a mad crush on you when I was younger."

Her firm body remained clamped against his. He looked straight into her eyes, trying to clear his head and mentally screw her in the same instant. She moved her face towards him very slowly, bringing her mouth nearer to his, and her expression . . . no expression . . . remained constant. Their lips came together, softly at first, but the passion rose within him, and Kent widened his mouth and slid his tongue in. She was in front of him and, now, the little kid with the Band-Aids drove her knee deep into his groin and kept moving it there as her tongue met his in a wild exchange.

"This isn't right, Babs," he said, bringing his head back slowly. "You know that."

"Ummmm . . . do you want me to leave now with the idiotic drawings, or should we continue?"

"Maybe we'd better sit in the living room and talk."

She sat on one couch in front of the Chippendale coffee table spotted with sterling silver plates, the least obtrusive of Kent's trophy collection. Actually, Babs partly reclined in a seductive way, with her arms back and her legs crossed.

The hem of her dress, rising higher than it should have, exposed much of her tanned legs. He sat stiffly on the opposite couch. She continued to stare at him, or right through him, with a slight smile of self-mastery and self-assurance fixed on her face. He suddenly hoped that she would burp or fart just to trim her confidence, which nagged and excited him at the same time.

"Do you feel your life's work is satisfying, Mr. Morgan?" she asked.

"Yes . . . probably not so much as being a doctor in a jungle full of disease."

"Oh, I don't want to be in a jungle full of disease. In fact, I'm going to be on Park Avenue specializing in the female sex machinery. I'd rather deal with the start of life; the end is kind of troublesome. There's no way a doctor can win. The best you can do is go into extra innings and relieve the pain, but it's always a defeat."

"I never thought of it that way."

"You *do* like me just a little, don't you, Mr. Morgan? I'm not asking for a large dose."

"I'm sort of fascinated, Babs. I keep thinking that you're only a few years older than my daughter, Cathy."

She fell silent again and brushed her leg as she lit a cigarette. Her dress was higher now, and she watched Kent's eyes.

"Sit over here," she said.

"Am I being ordered?"

"A suggestion."

Kent didn't move, and she leaned forward to flick the ashes off her cigarette. He could see the display of young, full breasts, and he cursed himself for letting this stretched-out vamp draw him on. He wished he had the grit to shake her and give her a fast boot through the front door. Kent thought of Louise, but not too clearly; his head was still misted, and his emotions were straying from one wild extreme to another. For a second he considered asking the girl to leave. The thought wasn't entirely resolved when Babs stood and crossed over to his couch, standing at the end, gliding her longer fingernails across the back of his neck.

"If the drawings are ready, I'll deliver them to Lord Nelson."

He reached up and touched her soft hand. She leaned down and slowly pushed her tongue along his cheek; the trip ended at the corner of Kent's mouth.

"You're so uptight. What do you think I'm going to do . . . run back and tell my father, or send a juicy item to the *Menlo Head Herald-Statesman?*"

She swung her body towards him, and they kissed passionately. He pulled her down next to him; his tingling hand explored her thighs and found its way towards her juiciness. He pressed his finger deep inside her.

"Mr. Morgan," she laughed, "we're not at the drive-in . . . those stairs go someplace."

Kent took her hand. They started upstairs, and right ahead of them, waggling a fat brush around, was the painter whose presence had slipped Kent's mind. They stopped, and Kent said, "Ah . . . I have to go over some things with my client's daughter. We need to use this room."

"It's still wet, and the smell's bad, Mr. Morgan."

"That's all right. You can leave now."

"But I can't come back until late tomorrow afternoon. The manager wants me to work on the downstairs hall."

"*All right* . . . tomorrow afternoon, then."

The painter picked up his drop cloths, placed the lids back on his cans and started to wipe his brushes. Babs moved into the bedroom, leaving the door open. A few minutes later Kent heard the downstairs door close, and he entered the bedroom; Babs sat on the edge of the bed, moving her hands over her thighs.

"Mr. Morgan . . ."

"Stop calling me that," he said, cutting her off.

"I was only trying to be polite. Mother always told me

45

to address older men by rank or title."

"Call me Kent, or Mr. Kent, or Louie, or George Washington."

"How about Noel Coward? You look like a young Noel Coward."

"Fine. Anything but Mr. Morgan."

The common grammar between them in that moment was a primitive desire which, for Kent, overwhelmed his deep sense of imposed values. Babs had few values to dispose of, and all she wanted was a sordid satisfaction, a triumph between her legs. Particles of fear and regret continued to confuse Kent; it was like a killing thunderstorm racking his head, the first one he had been exposed to during his married life, which he then decided had become barren and functional.

"You're nervous and I'm panting wet," she said as she continued to stroke herself. Then she took over, seeing the hesitation locked into his pure blue eyes.

"Go downstairs and bring up two dining room chairs."

"Why?"

"Because I like it that way, to begin with. Go ahead . . ." she said in a voice which had become slightly brittle and rasping.

He stood still, as if he were stuck. She waved him away, slipping her tongue out of her mouth, and stretched back on the bed, already enjoying herself. His internal temperature was so high, it dulled his mind. He spun around, descended the curving stairs two at a time, went into the kitchen and poured out a vodka. He grasped two banister-back chairs from the dining room, and, balancing the load, he moved upstairs. By the time he returned to the bedroom, her dress was off, and she stood fondling herself. A steely look had entered her eyes, offering no hint of the warm gorgings she was already feeling between her legs.

"Throw the drink away . . . you don't need it. Put one chair facing me and the other alongside it, and then dispose of those Brooks Brothers clothes."

The drink was put aside; his clothes were stripped off. He felt himself throb and stiffen as he arranged the chairs. She eyed him and finally crossed to kiss him deeply.

"Blow me first, and get your tongue all the way up there."

Babs settled back on the two chairs, raised her arms over her head to hold onto the banister backs. She rested her hips and buttocks on the second chair, and her long legs dipped to the floor. As Kent knelt before her, his tongue moved up her thighs, and soon his spinning head was in a warm darkness. He didn't remember when she came, except that he heard a great breath being forced out of her lungs, and her legs wrapped around his head like a quick, tightening vise.

How he got to the bed and just how soon he was on top of her, forcing himself deep inside her, was also blurred. But he knew it was happening, and he pumped away until he exploded with her. She brought her lips down on him, and soon he was stiff once more and felt the silkiness of her hair tingling his genitals, and when he was ready again and disgusted again at this bourgeois horror, Kent locked into her once more. Babs moved under him with small thrusts, and finally in a heave their juices met, and he stayed within the young fire for a time until things went blank.

When he awoke, she was standing fully dressed at the window looking out, and she turned and said, "How do you feel?"

"Guilty."

"Don't be. You're better than you look. Somehow, the Eastern Establishment men don't screw well, but your rod blew like it had been capped for years. I felt it all the way up to my deep throat. Lousy pun . . . right?"

He leaned back in the bed; he was in a terrible void, still fiery, perhaps still a little drunk, and the obvious conflicts upset him. His first thought was to call Louise, confess, but then he reflected that that might be unwise and certainly not chivalrous.

"Mr. Morgan . . ."

"*Don't* call me that."

"Sorry . . . it's the way I've always known you. Anyhow, I realize what you're thinking."

"Then tell me," he said quickly.

"This is the first fling you've had since you were married, isn't it?"

Kent didn't say anything; instead, he lit a cigarette and stared at the ceiling, thinking that it, too, had to be repainted.

"You didn't answer me."

"Yes, it's the first time."

"You've thought of it before?"

"Every man thinks of it."

"I mean . . . did you ever go out of your way to try it?"

"God damn it, stop this!" he howled.

"I'm sorry . . . really sorry," she said with genuine feeling. "I know I come on too strong. There's *nothing* to feel guilty about. I made you. I *came* here to make you. You were a little drunk . . . defenses were down . . . don't let it get to you. Tell your wife if it'll make you feel better, or I'll call her and apologize. It was my fault, but I wasn't trying to hurt you."

"We're not calling anybody, but why did you pick me?"

"It's like I tried to tell you before. I've been turned on by you since I was fifteen years old, and don't ask me why. I always thought that you were handsome . . . bright and rich. You had everything, and I used to sit in that fucking Country Day School with the idea of balling you someday . . . a schoolgirl's fantasy."

"Babs." He stirred restlessly. "What happens to people like you . . . what's next?"

"I gave you the game plan. Someday I'll be a Park Avenue doctor, a good one, I hope, and maybe your daughters will be my patients. Who knows? I realize that's hard for you to swallow."

"Frankly, it is."

"Well, we'll just forget this. You won't say a thing . . . I won't say a thing. It just never happened, Mr. Morgan.

It was one very small mistake . . . *not* to be continued."

"I was here, too, Babs, so don't be that sorry."

"All right. Just tell me you're not going to get the gloomies."

"No, I won't."

"And good luck with my father's yacht."

"Thanks."

She was gone.

CHAPTER FOUR

It rained in Menlo Head. Louise spent part of the afternoon buying Cathy a new dress for a party she was attending later that week.

At four that day Louise remembered that she wanted the cornice leading to the library of the duplex to be painted the same color as the room, and she dialed the number at One East Sixty-sixth Street. (All calls went through the downstairs switchboard; the co-op was run like a small hotel, offering maid, valet and meal service.)

"Sorry, Mrs. Morgan . . . there's no answer up there," the operator said.

"There has to be. Mr. Korvick was supposed to be painting all day. Where is he?"

"Oh, he's down here, working on the hall. Do you want to speak to him?"

The operator called the painter over, and he wiped his hands, taking the phone. "Yes, Mrs. Morgan?"

"Is the room finished?"

"No, ma'am. Mr. Morgan came up there with a client. He told me to come back later . . . tomorrow afternoon."

"A client? You must be mistaken My husband does his drafting downstairs."

"Yes, ma'am, but they came upstairs."

"Who?"

"He . . . ah . . . was with a young girl."

"A *young girl?*"

The painter knew he was about to wade in over his head, if he hadn't already, but he continued, "It was somebody's daughter . . . I believe he said, ma'am . . . ah . . . I left when they asked me to."

"What was the girl's name?"

"I don't know, Mrs. Morgan."

There was a pause, and then Louise heard herself asking almost unwillingly, "What did she look like?"

"Ah . . . tell you the truth, Mrs. Morgan . . . I don't remember too well. I mean, I was cleaning my brushes, but she had very long black hair."

"Are they up there now, Mr. Korvick?"

"No, I saw her leave, and then a little while later, Mr. Morgan left."

Louise trembled as she slowly placed the phone back on the cradle. She stood looking into air. Was there anything to worry about? Her imagination grabbed her, and her thoughts spun around like the pictures on a one-arm bandit. Louise had heard idle gossip, rumors about Babs Halston, her relations with married men around Menlo Head, but that could have been local gobble.

She jerked up a sweater and walked outside, trying to tame her fears. There was a tiny pool rimmed by small red maple trees near the house. The rain had stopped, and the friendly frogs were at peace in their pond. Louise sat down on a damp moss-covered rock and peered into the water.

"What does one do?" she asked herself. "Did he make love to her? Will he tell me? How long has this been going on?"

The pitch of her emotions rose; she felt as if she were on the edge of a sheer cliff. She was looking over, trying to see what was far below, but she couldn't lean that far out and still maintain her footing. Suddenly she had an acid taste in the back of her mouth.

As a rule, Louise Morgan thought logically and in orderly fashion. She never permitted her panic to run out like a fishing reel gone wild, and in those moments sitting by the frog pond, she remembered again what her father, a country taskmaster, always said, "*Never* come apart. There's very little to come apart about."

She was carried back momentarily to the eastern shore of Maryland on a therapeutic mind trip. Maybe the odyssey was evoked by the sounds of the Menlo Head frogs. Their Chesapeake acreage had been full of natural tidewater ponds where the toads lived and flourished. Her father, Matthew Upton, a ninth-generation son of the Bay, had once told her, "There's street sense and field sense, Louise. The difference between the two is that the person with street sense reacts like a bolt of lightning; he has to because the knife might be coming at him. Survival is decided in seconds. The person with field sense, on the other hand, acts more slowly, understands the problems—if they really exist—sifts the solutions, then takes action."

As an example of good old field sense, Louise remembered the summers when the corn wasn't as high as it should have been, when the ancient Ford tractor seemed to lose power as it ruffled the rich earth. There had been time to study each problem, and the solution usually followed. The rule primarily meant: "Don't act too quickly."

She could confront Kent that evening; yet her information was shallow, and what would she accuse him of . . . having Babs Halston in the apartment? Keep it calm and cool. That was the Upton motto for survival.

Her family had lived on Annock Creek, a winding body of sluggish water which entered the rich flatlands between a canyon of weeds and their house. Westerfield, built in 1690, once had had a hundred slaves working the crops planted on the 678 acres which bordered the creek on one side and the Bay on the other. The place was of salmon-colored brick eighteen inches thick, and it had four chimneys, revealing *true* affluence in manor days.

On the Virginia side of the Chesapeake the old homes were backdropped with formality. Boxwood gardens and undulating brick walks partitioned one bank of flowers from

52

the next. But on the Eastern Shore there was no formality, and the houses were not so perfectly proportioned, nor were there great gardens. Had the Upton family by chance been launched on the more privileged side of the Bay, Louise might have been a different woman, but as a product of the Eastern Shore, she was totally informal and resourceful. (The original difference between the savants of democracy on either side of the Bay was their relationship with the English overlords: the Eastern Shore rebels advocated forceable ejection; the others, being closer to Williamsburg, wished for a less violent solution, a status quo.)

Louise always thought that if Kent had been a Tidewater son, he would, naturally, have been from the opposite side of the water. He had a Virginian's pomp and demeanor, the aristocratic stance which hinted at watching the field hands for generations without once exposing one's fingernails to dirt.

Westerfield had outcroppings of great bay trees, and from any window there could be seen pure stands of loblolly pines, water oak, southern tupelo and wax myrtle, sometimes a bald eagle would build a nest in these trees.

For generations the Upton family had lived at Westerfield. Few knew how the Upton fortune had been established, but that mattered little because it all came to an end shortly before Louise Upton was born. The Depression wiped the family out, which suggested that they had lived on dividends from stocks and bonds. By 1940, the Uptons were land-poor, but her father declared, "We must hold onto the acreage at all costs."

The family's field sense came into play. Matthew put four hundred acres into corn and five acres into vegetables. He bought a secondhand hothouse, restored it, and they went into winter tomatoes and flower production. But prices for produce were down in those days, even as the war approached, so Louise's father took up other ventures to satisfy the Baltimore mortgagees.

He began carving duck and geese decoys which he sold

53

at Abercrombie & Fitch, and with homemade lines, the family went crabbing during certain times of the year when the fields were buried under light blankets of snow. Sometimes they clammed from flatboards or went oyster tonging—anything and everything to save Westerfield, while feeding themselves.

Louise was brought up knowing how to fix a tractor because they could not afford a new machine, even if one had been available during those years. She learned to pole crabs, crack oysters, paint decoys, furrow a field, and in the picking season the whole three-generation family—her two brothers plus aunts, uncles and grandparents—turned out at dawn to fill the row boxes with vegetables.

When Louise was seven her uncles, who used to sail in Marblehead, helped her build a Snipe sloop from a set of seven-dollar plans, and she learned to sail her creation. As times improved and the family recovered, Louise began entering yacht races, and she went all the way.

The frogs croaked and that, plus the fading light, transported her vacationing mind back to Pigeon Hill and to what could be the first acute crack in her marriage. (She realized, of course, that a war of attrition based primarily on her control over the children had already existed for some time.) She dreamed of the best situation: Kent would probably come home, take her into the study after dinner, close the door and tell her what had happened at One East Sixty-sixth Street. (Louise also knew that Kent was secretive, that he sealed his joys and hates and fears within himself.)

His expression that night was singular, and when he spoke at dinner, their eyes didn't meet as usual. He wore no sheepish mantle of culpability, but his mind seemed to be residing someplace else.

"How did the meeting go, Kent?" Louise asked.

"All right. Roger wanted a few design changes."

"Were you able to do them?"

"Yeah. I had a lousy day though . . . flat tire on the Triborough Bridge this morning . . . got wet changing it . . . and, to be frank, I got into a fight with a couple of tow men. They called me a fag, and I cracked them."

"Tell me about it."

Kent went through the events, impressing Louise with how clever he had been to heave the microphone into the river so they couldn't contact the tollbooth for help; how he had quickly removed the license plate after belting the pugs.

"Kent, why do you worry about being called a fag? You're not a fag, and one time—where was it—oh, yes, in Bermuda after the race, that man came up to you and made a perfectly innocent remark, and you kidney-punched him. Said he made a pass at you. A couple of other times you got out of hand with your fists. Children act that way, Kent . . . not adults."

"Do you think I look gay?"

"No."

"Well, I'm certainly *not*," he said, thinking back momentarily to the afternoon in the apartment with Babs Halston.

"I just said that." She paused and then said slowly, "But you don't make love to me much anymore."

"I'll tell you why. Do you want to know? Really want to know?"

"Sure."

"Louise, half the time you smell like a fish . . . just a faint odor, and every time I think of fucking a fish, I'm turned off."

"Then I'll shower ten times a day, and I'll pour perfume all over me. Or do you want me to pour it on the fish, too?"

"Just stop fishing."

"I don't think I want to continue this. So what happened after you floored the guys on the bridge? And what an insane thing to do; they'll come after you, Kent. How many green Maseratis are there?"

"There're nicks in the paint, anyhow. I think it's time for a red Maserati. That's the Italian racing color. Deep green is the English racing color . . . I don't know why the Italians chose green for this car in the first place."

"All right . . . paint the car over like some common criminal."

"I'm not a common criminal, but I won't be called a gay guy by a couple of hoods. That really ticked me off!"

Louise gazed at her husband's smoldering face. She knew that the one thing Kent could not stand was being embarrassed in front of others.

"You're much too sensitive in that area. Everyone is embarrassed now and then," she said finally.

"I *won't* be."

"Okay. Now tell me about the rest of the afternoon."

"I sat alone in that apartment all afternoon, trying to satisfy Roger's crazy demands. He wants a heavy boat and a light boat, all at the same time."

"Wasn't the painter there? He was supposed to be finishing up."

"Oh, yes. He was upstairs for a while, but then he took off."

The two lies nicked her mind: the painter didn't just "take off"; he was told to go, and Kent had not been alone in the duplex. He said nothing more about the afternoon. Later that night, Louise went down to the Victorian dock, lit her kerosene lamps which she lashed to the shrouds of the *Kerry Dancer* and went for a quiet sail across the cove which was speckled with a dull moonlight.

She sailed back and forth in the darkness, tacking easily between patches of gray and black water, and when she returned an hour later, she had succeeded in putting suspicion behind her.

CHAPTER FIVE

The first crispness of deep autumn, the new slant of the wind changing and freshening to the east, the trees turning russet and giving up their summer uniforms evoked a snap of activity at Pigeon Hill. Homemade lobster pots, the markers of which were newly painted, were stacked on the breakwall. The expansive vegetable garden was plowed under as new seedlings were planted in the greenhouse; shrubs were put to sleep under blankets of burlap-sack cloth until they became sodden by the spring rain, the alarm clock to get up and change to green again.

All this—the harmony, the work of the seasons—was Louise Morgan's idea. Thinking of her Chesapeake background, she had announced one night that it was far better to hear the lark sing than the mouse squeak. The remark, a typical Tidewater saying, flew right over Kent's head, but it meant that a family gained more from living outdoors than indoors, although there were no small animals with long tails inside Pigeon Hill, or larks outside.

Louise had decided that her family should exist from the land and the sea as she had done, never giving up that elemental contact which she believed was both spiritual and practical. It was not only much cheaper in times of maniacal inflation to gather free harvests, but it taught independence, resourcefulness, survival, knowledge and pleasure, all lessons the children could use and lean upon in future years.

She told Kent that there was no reason they could not grow their own vegetables, fish for their seafood, shoot the flights of ducks that visited Humble Cove in the late autumn months, go deer hunting and pheasant hunting and take care of the grounds themselves.

Louise's recipe for the do-it-yourself existence was written many years before the incident of the "funny suits," and Kent, after a few shallow protests, let his wife have her way, to check discord, if nothing else. He concluded later that this had been a grave mistake, a surrender, a switch of authorities. He was soon to realize something he suspected from his first visit to Bay country: her bash of home activities underlined the disparities in husband and wife.

It was not right versus wrong because Kent knew that varied philosophies, reasons for living, could meet and co-exist while buttressing each other. But varied living themes had to be pliable for the proper blend. Hers, in basic terms, was physical and moral survival—the Robinson Crusoe thrust without trappings. His theme, drilled in generations before, was to prevail and reap material reward through excellence; the Morgan family had left Crusoe on his beach long ago.

After they became engaged in 1962, Kent visited Louise Upton's country. Westerfield, in a sense, was a survival compound, scarred and shabby by Locust Valley standards. It was old and strong and used, as if many wars against many enemies had been waged from this old manor. Yet it was majestic in the way that an Irish Georgian country house reveals that lived-in look of ages past. Some call it shabby gentility; others, particularly the Anglo-Irish, describe it as the edginess of country people who are forever screwing or nailing things together, opening the earth, pulling fish and shelled meat from the water, thinning the air of ducks, geese and game birds.

Kent was an apprentice sportsman, having shot a few pheasants with his father at one of those game farms where the corn-fed bird is set out of a gunnysack, and he enjoyed casting for salmon in a swift, bubbling Irish stream where his uncles went each year. (This was play. Kent never cleaned or ate what he took; Louise Upton did.) As far as Kent was concerned, sport remained outdoors and far away from the civility of the home.

Not so in Bay country; here the outdoors was brought inside as a modality of life. And it was not a feigned assessment of Kent Morgan's. The dirt of the mired fields and the mud slime from the marsh were delivered straight into the old manor houses on the pads of dogs. And every place he visited in Tidewater seemed to be dominated by canines of all kinds: knee-high dogs to chase the fox, medium-sized dogs to point out the hidden field birds and big, dampish dogs to dive into the icy Bay water to retrieve what had been killed by sprays of pellets.

In Kent's mind, there was nothing wrong with working dogs as long as they stayed outside or, more properly, in the kennel under the direction of the gamekeeper. When visiting estates in Pennsylvania horse-and-hound country during Yale vacations, Kent had noticed that each big house had a mudroom where boots were changed and neatly hung on pegs with a name above each dowel. The dogs were kept outside, and the boots were segregated from the living quarters. The outdoors remaining outdoors seemed to insure cleanliness indoors.

The Bay people were not so concerned. They had no mudrooms. The doors were swollen and slightly ajar, never locked because the tumblers were rusty, and robbery was almost unheard-of in these low counties. While the open-door policy of the Eastern Shore might have been commendable on one level, it shuffled Kent's equanimity on another. The dogs in twos and threes pushed their wet noses against the chipped door panels; they entered the Upton house from the rear, exited from the front, galloped and wailed as they circled the side to start their roundabout journey again, as if the house were set down in the middle of a greyhound track. The cataract of dogs went through not only Westerfield but other manor places nearby, and Kent, who was fluttered over with engagement cocktail parties given by the Uptons and their friends, was shocked by the enervated attitudes of the Bay people with whom he was about to be linked through marriage.

The guests came in old station wagons and pickup trucks, and their heels were worn and their shoes were dull. Worst of all, in Kent's mind, their footwear, men's and women's, spread additional Maryland dirt on the thread-exposed carpets.

Kent noticed their necks first. Not one of them enjoyed the smoothness of a Locust Valley neck. Even the young men and women had grizzled, coffee-colored flesh beneath their jaws; the skin on their foreheads and around their eyes was going to hell, too, as if Bay people were continually straining their faces towards the sun and things they could never reach. They were *too busy* carrying on hoary traditions. Had Kent lived among them, he would have assessed the place as a junkyard. They believed it was a museum, and the grim, streaked reminders of lost attainments resided in their fields as heritage, not forgotten waste.

They stood about in chilly, bog-odored rooms sipping cocktails from Waterford glassware, while the canine stampede cascaded through the halls. The Uptons and their neighbors never eyed the dogs, and when the animals yelped louder, all the Bay people did was notch their voices one note up to be heard.

Kent arrived at Westerfield on a cold autumn day when the pale sun was afternooning in a blanket of hazy gray clouds. As he got out of his rented car and walked up the unweeded drive, the first thing he noticed was the carcass of a gutted buck swinging to the Bay breeze from a hook driven into the mellow brick of Westerfield's side wall. The limp hoofs clacked against the hard surface like a meager warning.

His eyes went further. Far off, almost overtopped with marsh weed, the saw the rotting remains of a skipjack eaten into by the sun, rain and salt wind. As his eyes panned on, he noticed the rusted frame of an old biplane which Louise's father had found in a barn and fixed up to become airborne during the thirties. Nothing had been tossed away. The past existed simultaneously with the present, and the whole place seemed to be lonely, mysterious, as rueful as an Andy Wyeth painting. In fact, Kent thought, the Bay umbers and siennas and shallow reds might have been clipped directly from the artist's palette. The joy, the laughter of life, the warm bath of visual pleasures seemed raped from these staunch people, and if they were getting along at all, it was not evidenced by their gaunt surroundings.

What the hell was he walking into? he asked himself. But the worst was yet to come.

All the Uptons in the rambling house were pleasant enough, but even dressed in their best, stiff, frayed threads protruded from their clothing like porcupine spindles. The huge family living under the roof of the manor was *never* out of cheap, crumbling tweeds that held onto the oily smells of the marsh and the dogs, as if a trip to the tailor or dry cleaner was unknown.

And this was all the more curious to Kent Morgan because these people were rich with very old money, though they never talked about it. The riches were buried someplace, but apparently the vault was locked, as if having money and showing it was evil.

Engagement parties were planned for the new couple. Kent continued his Locust Valley comparison. He knew *his* people for what they were: neat, fleshy, materialistic, addicts of heritage, habitual name droppers, achievers. Most of them were purposely vague unless they were closeted with their very own, when inside jokes could be told with perfect impunity.

The Uptons and their Bay neighbors were distinct antipodes of the Locust Valley and Menlo Head Americans. They were an austere race—practical, precise, systematic, resourceful—and they did not bounce social names about.

These might have been good and appropriate qualities, except for one Bay attitude which abraded the young man from the soft suburbs.

In their own way the Bay folks were magisterial. They could train dogs better than anyone; they knew just how to take a duck with a small-bore shotgun; they downed deer with bows and arrows. They built better; they scraped the bottom seas better; they farmed better. They made babies better; they cooked better; they laughed better. They educated better; they said prayers better; they were better because, to Kent, they were all Aristotles conversing in the language of absolutes.

Kent suggested that they postpone their marriage to size things up, but Louise said that the invitations had already been sent out, and many guests were arriving from faraway states. She accused Kent of being frightened by commitment. He gave in with the hope that Louise Upton could learn to adapt to another social geography.

He was wrong. He thought she needed a Locust Valley refinement, but she believed that Kent required his soft edges honed with a sharp rasp or, at least, a flow of icy water beneath his hull. Louise was not about to change. The dogmatic Bay attitudes prevailed in Connecticut. She turned Pigeon Hill into a northern Westerfield, but at the beginning Kent was unaware of this transformation. He was away most of the time, sailing ocean races in tepid waters, and the introduction of Chesapeake ideas occurred with a subtle invasion.

One of her enterprising moves at Pigeon Hill was to divide the property into grids based on the survey supplied by a civil engineer. The Morgan girls were to be responsible for their own grids, keeping the grass free from weeds, trimming the hedges, raking up the fallen leaves from the masses of trees which ornamented the small estate, lending the eye every imaginable shade of misty green. Gardeners were barred from Pigeon Hill; yet it was one of the finest-kept places on the Menlo Head shore, with alcoves of rusticated stones, steps leading from one lawn level to the next, small yews and bunches of hydrangeas—Louise's favorite flower. While the Pigeon Hill gardens were not rococo or trumped-up versions of French palace gardens whittled down to suggest elegance, the Morgans achieved a luxurious effect of multi-plantings: roses, climbers, lilacs, outdoor vegetables and herbs. Backdropping the mass of colors were high boxwood hedges which the local tobacco-chewing gardeners—botanists, they called themselves—said would *never* exist in Connecticut.

And then one day the first firearms arrived. It was on a Saturday, and Kent had to sign for the box which was insured. There was a bright red sticker attached: "Dangerous! Contains firearms!"

The box was addressed to Louise, but Kent began to tear into it, wondering who could have shipped firearms to them. Louise came into the carriage house just as he had succeeded in opening the crate. Inside were five shotguns—four twelve-gauge and a 410—over-and-under and side-by-side guns; and three bows and arrows, the steel-tipped kind used for killing animals.

"What on earth . . ." Kent said, staring at the arsenal.

"Kent, you had no right opening that . . . it was addressed to me!" Louise cried, snatching at the box.

He later realized he should have stood his ground right there and then and shipped every weapon back to Westerfield, every bow and arrow. But he didn't. And a short time later, the delivery man returned with six more boxes containing ninety-one ducks and geese decoys which Louise said she had carved with her father.

Kent knew what was coming, and they had a big argument, Louise insisting that the girls learn to use a shotgun and to cook and clean what they brought down, Kent protesting that the idea was too dangerous and unladylike.

But a month later, the first blast went off.

Kent was sitting in the dining room at Pigeon Hill, eating his usual breakfast—poached egg on rye toast, fresh orange juice and Colombian coffee with a vanilla bean—and perusing *The Wall Street Journal* and *The New York Times* when the sudden roar caused him to leap out of his chair. Carrie ran outside immediately, thinking one of the girls had shot herself, and Kent ran after the housekeeper. And there was his wife, crawling along a slimy rock after some duck she'd just shot.

Considerably shaken, Kent returned to the dining room and picked up his fork from the floor. He poked at his egg, which was cold by then, and a couple of minutes later, Louise bounced into the room and tossed down a bloody duck right in front of him on the table.

"How do you like that fellow? Feel that plump breast."

Kent looked down into the dead eyes, at the blood coming out of the duck's beak, and went straight upstairs to the bathroom where he vomited the egg and orange juice. As he flushed the toilet, he kept thinking about the gutted deer hanging on the side of the house at Westerfield.

Her reformation progressed. Louise, an amateur boat builder, sent away for a set of lobster workboat plans from a small Maine builder. Kent was insulted that she had not asked him to design the boat, but she convinced her husband that it was a matter of expediency since the plans cost only thirty dollars. If Kent's firm had drafted the lines, the out-of-pocket costs would have reached over a thousand. (She did not tell her husband the real reason she had sent away for the stock plans. Kent could design a fast yacht, but he knew nothing about commercial craft, and the folks up in Maine did.) Louise had miscalculated Kent's reaction, however; despite her coming up with a tested workboat and saving design money, he stayed chronically offended.

His big warehouse of pride had been punctured.

That and his assumed British diction were the only facets of Kent's character that Louise abhorred, for she had always likened human pride to the attic of a house, the highest point and usually the emptiest. Kent was hurt, and when he

64

was hurt, he withdrew. It was a portent that Louise should have taken seriously.

For a time, Louise thought of scrapping the workboat idea to save Kent's self-esteem, but being an extremely determined woman who never retreated, she decided that she would build the boat anyhow. It was not too soon for her children to learn about wood and nails. She taught them each step, from selecting the seasoned oak and yellow pine to the use and care of fine wooden hand tools. With the help of workmen from a local yacht yard, slipways were built on the small beach to the far side of the Pigeon Hill breakwall.

Kent never went to their boat yard on the beach, nor did he discuss the progress of the craft. He said only, "It's enough that we operate a vegetable farm and a duck-shooting range; we don't need a commercial fishery, too."

The workboat took shape. The oak ribs went up fastened to the shaped keelson, and over the skeleton, yellow pine planks were steamed and bent and secured by galvanized boat nails. The racket went on for almost a year. Then the twenty-six-foot boat, with the sharp sheer to keep the water out and the cuddly cabin to provide warmth and protection, was put overboard with a launching party attended by almost everyone in Menlo Head, with the exception of Kent who looked out of his upstairs window with the bedroom door locked.

No one was more gladdened than their next-door neighbors, the Craigs and the Potters. They thought the ear-shattering noises were over. Wrong. The pounding had just begun. Louise, a practical traditionalist, found out that most Maine fishermen used a two-stroke diesel, or a "one-lunger." She could have slipped in a yacht engine or an expensive four-stroke diesel to run the workboat, but those power plants were less reliable. And they burned expensive number two diesel oil, a distillate blend costing ninety-one cents a gallon. Instead, Louise searched for a "one-lunger," which she turned up on the Chesapeake; it was a worn-out piece of machinery built in 1915 to power an oyster dragger.

The only disadvantage of the one-lung diesel burning its black muck was the constant throbbing. Slow revolutions of the engine went thump, thump, thump, and the sound reverberated about the rocks of the cove. The Potters and the Craigs never escaped the noise from Pigeon Hill.

Workboat—that was the official name—was then equipped with a power winch for hauling lobster pots, and with a commercial fishing license, Louise and her girls started to clean the seas near Pigeon Hill. They set the lobster pots, dragged for bottom fish, and in the first year the Morgan fishery landed 942 pounds of fish and hard shells. Kent, in a show of defiance, only picked and poked at the pure white fish. The rest of the household under the direction of Louise Morgan enjoyed priceless duck, lobsters, whiting and occasionally the one or two deer she plugged with an arrow each season. Her grasp on Pigeon Hill and the children tightened.

CHAPTER SIX

During the busy autumn following Kent's meeting with Roger Halston's daughter, Louise gradually erased the memory of Babs having been at the duplex for whatever reason. Then a course of events in the weeks before Christmas rekindled Louise Morgan's thoughts about the dark-haired girl.

About three weeks before Christmas, Kent came home very late for dinner, saying that he had been down inspecting the Halston job. Actually, he had been in New York, secretly Christmas shopping. Louise didn't believe him, and she called Williams' yard in Mamaroneck and spoke to the secretary.

"Sarah, did my husband leave his sunglasses there yesterday afternoon?"

(Kent's affectation for wearing sunglasses year-round was well known.)

"Mr. Morgan wasn't here yesterday afternoon," the woman said.

"Are you sure?"

"Yes, Mrs. Morgan. He came in last Thursday, but we haven't seen him since."

Louise was suspicious, and she abhorred the new but compulsive emotion. A trusting woman, Louise had never been wary of people, especially of her husband; now she checked his pockets for confirming clues, his shirts for lipstick, the mileage on the Maserati, but she found nothing.

She wondered if she should talk to Kent, get it out, because the accumulation of doubts and distrust was beginning to take its toll. She drank more and more vodka martinis during the day to wash away the fears that were enveloping her.

Down on the Chesapeake and up to the time they moved to Connecticut, Louise had needed no propping up from a bottle of liquor. She drank like everyone else at Menlo Head's frequent parties. Kent wanted her to look great and join in. For his sake, Louise spent enormous sums on her going-out clothes and on her hair, which Kent had redesigned in the "rich girl coiffure." It was the chameleon qualities of Louise Morgan which amazed most women in Menlo Head: from the sea-slimed slicker to the *Harper's Bazaar* look in a matter of hours. And Louise brightened parties with her quaint homilies and quick and frequent laughs. She was not quite understood in the regiments of identical Menlo Head women—Foxcrofted, Wellesleyed and Radcliffed—usually collegiate dropouts because of the coming-out parties which had nipped at their educational rigors. Louise began to like drinking the friendly cup, and slowly, almost unnoticeably, she had been drawn into the category of a social alcoholic.

Now she was afraid she was turning into a bona fide alcoholic. Kent had already slipped into addicted drinking a few years before as a necessary adjunct to business life. Louise realized that she had to reverse the trend before it was too late. Just before Christmas of that year, she made an appointment with Dr. Thomas Driscoll, a kindly social physician, the rich "Dr. Welby" of Menlo Head who had delivered her babies and sent over prescriptions when the girls were sick.

The gynecologist, who wore bow ties and pastel-colored shirts under his white coat, greeted her with the usual benevolent smile. "Hello, Louise. How's your fishing this year?"

"We've landed a hundred and eighty pounds so far."

"Beth and I enjoyed those last four lobsters. Very tasty.

And you're looking very fit and well . . . so what brings you here? Anything wrong with the kids?"

"No . . . no . . . everyone's fine. A little personal problem, Tom." She paused, then blurted it out. "I'd like to drink less."

"So would we all," the well-tanned doctor said. "Ha, ha. Well, it's up to you. You're drinking too much these days . . . is that it?"

"Yes."

"And why is this?"

"Well, I think Kent is having an affair with Babs Halston."

The doctor smiled and leaned back, tugging at his starched white jacket.

"What are you smiling at?" Louise asked.

"Those Halston women are something else. I think I can remember about five wives coming in here and saying that they thought their husbands were having affairs with either Babs or Gwen."

"Were they?"

"I don't think so, because the women never came back. But I always wondered about something. How can Roger Halston exist in this town with all the rumors going around about his wife and daughter?"

"Do you think they're true?"

"I don't know. But Louise, a lot of people are having affairs around here . . . it's not uncommon . . . and you can understand that. Middle-aged men reach a certain point where it seems that most of the good times are behind them, so they have a bit of a revolt to prove they are still virile . . . as young and forceful as they once were, but these things pass. So I wouldn't take it too seriously."

"But I do. Maybe it's my fault. It shows I'm inadequate or guilty. I don't know . . . seems the only time he talks to me anymore is to complain about something. I'm getting a complex."

The gynecologist laughed. "I've heard that before, too.

Listen, Louise, marriage does get monotonous after a while . . . for all of us. Now, you've got a husband who's rich . . . handsome . . . charming . . ."

"Yeah, I know. Of course, I see a side of him that nobody else knows is there. Kent broods for days sometimes, and the children and I won't even know what's bothering him. Or he flies into god-awful temper tantrums, and I always end up forgiving him, feeling sorry for him, because I see the little boy inside who's hurting. He's really very insecure, which most people don't realize. Oh, Christ, he'd kill me, too, if he knew I was telling you all this."

Tom Driscoll smiled and glanced at his wall clock. "Well, I wouldn't worry about it. Give your husband a little freedom, and things will work themselves out."

"But I don't have affairs, Tom. I think it's wrong."

"Of course it is. But we're all human." He paused and then said, "How often do you and Kent have intercourse?"

"Oh . . . well . . . lately he seems to work out in the carriage house a lot after dinner. And then I'm usually asleep when he gets to bed. But, as you say, Tom, after sixteen years . . ."

He leaned across the desk. "My advice is to calm down and forget all this nonsense. And do something constructive. Go out and buy yourself a sexy new nightgown."

"I don't *want* a sexy new nightgown, and it wouldn't work, anyway. And I don't want to calm down. I think about Kent and that Babs all the time."

"Do you *know* they're having an affair?"

She was silent for a moment. "I hear things . . . and why won't he talk to me?"

"Why don't you talk to him?"

"I don't have to. Why should I? He has to come to me . . . not the other way around. I'm not having the affair."

He sighed. "You're a very uncompromising woman, Louise Morgan."

"Well, damn it . . . I'm in the right here."

"I see. Well . . . three rules. Try to cut the drinking

down to a couple of cocktails before dinner. Then take three of these Valium a day"—he was busily scribbling on his pad as he spoke—"but *not* while you're drinking. The third rule is to forget this situation, because right now you don't know anything, do you? Tell me the truth."

"I'm not sure."

"See? I thought so. Suspicion is a defense mechanism . . . an alert. That's OK, but keep it in perspective. You're a very practical, sensible woman. You'll be just fine."

She went by March's Drugstore with the prescription and had a cup of coffee while she waited for it to be filled. Then she remembered that Jody needed some new tiebacks for her ponytail, and she bought a package of the brightly colored yarn pieces and a couple of other items for the medicine chest. But all the time her mind was churning, thinking about Kent, about the interview she just had with the doctor.

When she walked into the house with the small vial of yellow pills in her purse, she felt no different. No better. If anything, Louise Morgan was more riled up; why had this doctor, a friend, taken her pleading so casually? He had almost chuckled as if he were saying: "Having a little affair? So what else is new today or tomorrow or next year, or in the aggregate of all the years which make up our history?"

She remembered the local doctor down in Queen Annes County, Maryland, a typical grizzle-necked graduate of Johns Hopkins whose father, as an intern in the same hospital, had ridden the horse-drawn ambulance hanging off the back platform in his flapping white gown, just like policemen used to ride the back of paddy wagons.

He would have said in his clipped, gutsy way, "Halston women? They're no good. They're weak. They're a curse around here. Their hounds should bite them. Kent? Well, you go get him by the scruff of the neck, and I'll tell him a thing or two. And if he doesn't believe me, I'll fetch the Reverend Doctor Harley, and he'll force some sense into that husband of yours. We don't take affairs lightly 'round here, Louise. I'm damn disturbed to hear it . . . if it's true. Now you go on home and get your claws around that man's neck . . . right now, you hear?"

There was little for Kent to say up to this time except that he had been to bed with Babs in one isolated incident. He believed that this was not infidelity as much as a drunken slip on a bad afternoon. There had been no further contact with the young girl, with the exception of the note he had received at the office three days after the episode at the duplex.

> *Dear Kent:*
>   I am truly sorry about the other afternoon. I acted very badly, and I hope you will forgive me. I was a little high on coke, but I did dream of you in class at Country Day. Everything is all over now, and I hope you are not bothered by the mean guilts. Good luck with Lord Nelson's yacht. I know it will float well until His Honor hits a dock with your magnificent winning machine. Will you rescue him for the sake of the Chemical Bank, if for no other reason?
>
>   *Sin-sincerely,*
>   *(and love)*
>   *Babs.*

Kent did not answer the note, but two weeks before Christmas she wrote again:

> *Dear Kent,*
>   Yesterday I went up to the yard to see my father's yacht, and they showed me the enlarged hatch and how all the heavy lollipop stuff could be lifted out in case my father wants an ego trip at the starting line. He's delighted with your solution, and I'm sure it will make him a bigger man at the yacht club. Regardless, you have made him quite happy, and the builder told me that he thinks your idea could very well start a trend

until the yacht-racing rules committee catches on. Whatever, I think you're clever and creative.

I've been working very hard this semester, spending most of my time in labs instead of beds, and my average in all the sciences is now running A+. Good news came the other day after my interview with the director of admissions for Cornell Med. He said there was very little doubt that I would have a seat next fall, and that's given me new incentive.

I've moved to a small apartment on the upper East Side in the nineties, furnishing it with a loan from Mom, and although I can't cook well, I wonder if you would like to come for lunch next week if you're in New York. We'll have a Christmas drink, and who knows what's for dessert at this time of year when love's the theme? (My number is 800-8990.) Call me if you like. And if you feel we need a chaperone of older and wiser years, there's just such an ancient one downstairs. She retired from the Short Hills school system in 1932!

Sin-sincerely,
Babs.

The invitation seemed gracious and intriguing. At first, Kent considered asking Louise to accompany him to the apartment; that idea was discarded almost immediately, but it might have been the coup of his life if he'd followed through on it. Then he thought of not calling Babs; but she *was* the daughter of an important client. Realizing she was a girl full of contradictions and not too predictable, he told himself she might be upset and tell her father what had happened at the duplex, coloring the facts, of course, to suit herself. The simplest solution, Kent concluded, was to call her and accept her invitation to drop around for a Christmas drink, which he did.

The snow had begun very early that Tuesday morning; it was the kind that covered the ground quickly, changing the whole face of Main Street from storybook to real.

Through the windblown snow, the quaint buildings looked authentic.

When Kent reached New York, he immediately felt the pleasures of Christmas: chestnuts were being sold on the corners; people padded through the snow with presents; and sidewalk Christmas trees, resting against ropes, were sprinkled with the fresh whiteness. Bells were jingled by Santa Clauses; richly colored store windows bulged with expensive toys of the season. The dirt and grime of the city were veiled temporarily.

Kent was joyous. What a feeling to be driving a warm, well-tuned Maserati, now blood-red, about New York at Christmas with the first snow falling; and to be heading for the apartment of a young girl who was beautiful, sexy, smart and crazy. What man could ask more? Even a married man. It was an urbane flourish.

About halfway up Madison Avenue, Kent stopped to buy Babs a present. He had no idea what the girl needed, if anything, but a Christmas cake set into a forest of liquors could always be used. He spent fifty-one dollars for a large basket sealed by a shiny red and green ribbon which said: "Joy and Enjoy."

Ninety-first Street between Madison and Park was lined with identical brownstones; some had their stoops removed; others did not. Number 145 was a neat sandstone building with Christmas hangings or candles in almost every recently washed window. Kent took his present from the trunk, made his way up the stoop, rang the inside-hall buzzer and started climbing the five flights of stairs to Babs's apartment on the top floor.

"Keep at it," came a voice. "It's only Everest."

Kent looked up and saw her.

She was different, and he studied her as he moved up slowly, trying to conserve his breath. Her hair had been cut shorter, with bangs, and she wore a pleated gray skirt with knee socks and a simple white blouse. With the addition of a jumper and a school emblem, the outfit could have passed as the uniform of a girls' school.

He halted on the landing of the fourth floor to gain his breath.

"Any of your boyfriends ever die on the stairs?" he panted.

"Nope . . . hey, is that box for me?"

"Yes, I'm playing Santa today."

"How do you know I've been a good girl?"

"Well, I don't."

"I haven't been that good," she laughed. "Good is dull, you know."

The way she stood exposed her long legs, and Kent could see all the way up to her bikini pants.

The three-room apartment, when he finally reached it, was neat and well-furnished; about the walls were Chagall prints and bookcases jammed with science books. In the living room was a working fireplace, and a fat log was crackling. Christmas music was on the hi-fi, and a trimmed Christmas tree stood in the corner.

"How are you, Babs?" Kent asked. "You look great."

They kissed on the lips lightly, and he turned and inspected the room. "So this is where the future doctor does her scene?"

"A few scenes, Kent; you can't imagine how great it is not to have three sloppy roommates anymore."

They exchanged presents, and Kent was rather shocked by what she gave him: three old steel engravings, British naval architectural drawings of nineteenth-century yachts.

"Where did you find these?" he asked.

"In an antique store down on South Street. Figured you might like them."

"It's much more thoughtful than my present."

"No, it's not. The basket is beautiful. Thank you," she said, opening the package. Then she came towards him and kissed him. This time she lingered a bit on his mouth and pulled away, holding his hand.

·"I told you we could have someone here for lunch if you like . . . the old lady downstairs."

"We don't need her."

"Good."

They made drinks and settled by the fire, talking about what had happened since that day at One East Sixty-sixth Street. She seemed to be a different person. Her wackiness was toned down, and she was much more serious, talking about chemistry and advanced biology. She could be bright and studious one moment, silly the next, and as seductive as a man could wish for, Kent decided.

They had a cheese soufflé which Babs cooked, and they were filled with wine and laughter. Babs suggested that they take a walk in Central Park to clear their heads.

They walked hand in hand through the snow of the park, making snowballs and laughing and stopping for short kisses.

"Getting cold?" he asked her finally.

"Yes. Shall we get warm again?"

They ran back to the apartment, and Kent was breathless when he reached the top of the stairs again. They fixed hot buttered rums in the tiny kitchen and then sat looking into the fire for a time, saying nothing.

Finally Babs stirred and said, "How are you getting along with your wife?"

He shrugged. "Status quo . . . not a particularly good one."

"I was asking my mother about Louise."

"And what did she say?"

"Your wife's something else . . . all this lobstering . . . fishing. Some people around Menlo Head are scared of her. Is she butch?"

"No . . . no . . . she only appears that way."

"I remember her very well over at Country Day. One time she complained about the green-colored seats on the swings being rotten. The headmaster told her, 'Oh, no, Mrs. Morgan, they're strong . . . just need a bit of paint.' Do you know what Louise did? She brought one of those. karate punches right down on the seat, and it broke into a million splinters."

"Sounds like her."

"I was standing right there . . . with the Band-Aid on my knee. What a chop! I wouldn't have wanted to be that seat."

Kent's clear blue eyes, which had been crinkled by his new happiness all afternoon, suddenly drooped and showed sadness.

"What's wrong . . . something you want to talk about?" Babs said, reaching over and touching his hand.

Kent forced a smile through obvious gloom and shook his head as if thinking back over the painful memory of his life with Louise Morgan. Finally he began to vocalize his thoughts.

"You think karate chopping the seat was something . . . I'll tell you another one. For years Louise used to say, 'Kent, why don't you join in the family fun?' "

"What was the family fun?" Babs asked.

"Besides the lobster traps, Louise taught the kids to set rabbit traps in the Catskills. So one day I drove up with them. We spent an hour tramping through the woods on snow shoes getting dead bunnies from the traps, and then they *ate* them that night at Pigeon Hill. But not me . . . I went to Burger-King."

"Why did you ever marry her, Kent?"

"We met at Yale—the young, gay hearts—she was a fine sailor, beautiful . . . good in bed . . . a great sense of humor. We spent a year in England together . . . had a ball. Louise never mentioned one damn thing about rabbits or deer, or this fascination with lobstering. I didn't get the first hint until I went down to her house in Maryland . . . and then I wasn't sure if my wife was really one of those rural people or not. I thought she wanted to escape that. Then it came to me—very slowly—Louise was *never* going to give up her former way of life."

"Well, let's just relax and enjoy ourselves," she said. "Forget everything else. This is Christmas . . . the season for renewals . . . and love . . . and making love."

He moved his head into her lap and looked up at her, and the stare held. The passion was there and she knew it. Babs slowly lowered her head and kissed him; he felt the smothering heat of her moist lips all the way down to his groin.

"Hello, Mr. Yacht Designer."

"Hello, Miss Blowtorch."

"Is that what I am?"

"You're a turn-on, Babs . . . even in knee socks."

She smiled and stretched out alongside him by the fire. Their arms were about each other, and their bodies pressed tightly together. Their legs entwined as his hand explored her thighs.

"Should I stop?" he asked.

"You'd better not," she laughed. "I'm dripping like a waterfall."

He felt her moisture, and then he wanted to kiss her. He pulled off her pants and buried his mouth between her legs as she reeled up, presenting all her sex to his flashing tongue and lips.

"I think I'm coming," she whispered. "No, I don't think I'm coming . . . I just came. God, you turn me on."

Kent stood and pulled Babs to her feet; they moved towards the bedroom. He unbuttoned her blouse and saw her sugar-white breasts standing out from her light bra. They were the full breasts of youth, and he pressed his tongue over her stiffened nipples as she slipped out of her skirt and stood before him, hips back, pelvis out.

"Make me explode again, darling."

He undressed quickly. She took his genitals in her mouth and slid her tongue around in faster circles, and he felt a great pumping and throbbing deep inside him. Then he came in her mouth, and he cursed himself because he wanted this to go on all day.

"Stretch out on the bed, Kent, and sleep for about fifteen

minutes. That's all you need. I'll warm the motors up."

He did that. When he awoke from a short dreamy sleep, she was fondling him, and he soon stiffened again.

"Drive it into me, Kent. As deep as you can."

She edged under him, spread her legs and guided him inside her with a series of movements going two ways at once, something he had never experienced. He felt himself getting harder, and then he climaxed with her in one single burst.

They held each other for a long time, saying nothing. Then she whispered, "Is it going to be three months before I see you again?"

"I don't know. I'm afraid to start this . . . afraid not to."

"Kent, let's be practical," she said, sitting up. "We have something to give each other. I'm not in love, but I'm kind of hot for you. Couldn't we handle this harmlessly?"

"How?"

"Little Babs is no home wrecker, but it sounds as if your marriage is shot to hell, anyway. You and I can have our special thing . . . we'll be kinky and crazy."

"You sound very European, Babs. Is that what you learned abroad?"

"Well, I can tell you one thing. People over there understand sexual variety, and their divorce rate is one tenth of what ours is. They must be doing something right."

There was a pause, and then Kent said, "How discreet could we be?"

"Very," she grinned. "But I must warn you . . . I believe in *anything* that makes me feel good."

"Well, I've never been involved in anything lewd," Kent said.

"You just don't know how stimulating life can be. We'll try it. I'm going out to Aspen for skiing. Why don't we plan to get together on the sixth of January, when I get back? I'll write you at the office."

They made love again. When Kent left the apartment, the snow had thickened, and the windshield of his car was packed with whiteness which he mopped off with quick sweeps of his forearm.

He drove back to Menlo Head believing he was entering a new world, without having to demolish his old one. With this approach, possibly he could survive in the aridity of Pigeon Hill.

CHAPTER SEVEN

A week after Christmas, a letter arrived from the Motor
Vehicle Bureau of New York, and since Louise paid the
family speeding tickets for the Maserati, she opened the
envelope:

CITATION

Having failed to appear or remit the fine as prescribed on enclosed copy of your citation issued on
December 18 for illegal parking on the north side of
91st Street between Park Avenue and Madison Avenue, you are hereby cited for a violation of the New
York City Code 190086, as amended.

You or your counsel are ordered to appear at 106
Centre Street, Department 8A, on February 18 for a
hearing before the magistrate. Failure to appear may
result in a contempt-of-court citation, fine of $500, im-
prisonment for twenty days and/or both.

Louise knew immediately where Kent had been. She
laughed. Was she married to a totally dumb man? Twice
he had failed to cover his tracks. (The traffic ticket had
been under the snow on the windshield that day, and it had
been brushed away by Kent's forearm. He knew nothing
about the citation.)

A moment later, Louise was boiling with anger, her
usual cool and collected demeanor completely cracked. She
reached for the phone and was about to call Kent at his

office and say, "You son of a bitch, you've been seeing that Babs Halston again. You dumb asshole, I know *all* about it!" She detested her own violent rage which the daily doses of Valium did not quell, but she checked herself immediately. Louise knew that anger led to action, and like a hot steed, it often stumbled.

She felt herself trembling, though. Louise had to talk to someone, and that person was Bunny Lunsford, her best friend in Menlo Head. Bunny was a bit older than Louise, and the two women enjoyed a kind of gentle revolt against the rituals of their town, especially the lady lunches where the matrons got dressed up, sipped drinks, ate salads and played poor bridge. Like Bunny, Louise never attended these affairs, except when Kent's design business required her presence. Instead, she and Bunny dressed in dungarees and heavy Irish sweaters and took *Workboat* out, even in the worst weather. They heated the small cabin with hickory chips which they burned in the Franklin wood stove, pulled lobster pots, boiled and ate the fresh meat soaked in butter and drank smoky old whiskey, the kind that warms and makes one cough at the same time.

The two women were alike in other ways. Bunny had skied for the Vassar team, and she was a big-boned, outdoor type, having been reared by a hardworking lumber family. She was also attractive, if one appreciated a solid, gutsy woman. Like Louise, Bunny was field-wise and practical. She had not been too lucky with her marriages, but Bunny knew husbands and lovers and divorces, and she had recently re-wed, this time to a retired Army general. Louise called her, saying that something had come up and she had to talk.

It was the third of January, and the cove was as still as polished chrome; rime ice had formed around the heads of exposed rocks as if each of them had suddenly grown glassy beards. (Sometimes Louise saw people's faces in the rocks, and she had names for them: Old Jeff, Old Ned, Old Sawtooth.) The temperature was hanging in the twenties when Louise went down to *Workboat* and started the diesel to warm it up. She dumped a bag of hickory blocks into the black four-legged stove, and within minutes there was a glow and warmth in the cabin.

Bunny arrived on time, carrying a pumpkin pie she had baked the night before; the two women climbed aboard and headed out to the point of Barton's Island where the line of lobster buoys stretched in a long slow curve. The first two pots were empty, but the third had two four-pounders inside. Louise grabbed them and wiped the slime and weeds from the green-brown shells. In ten minutes they were at anchor, and the big pot on the wood stove was boiling.

"What's wrong, Louise?" Bunny asked finally. "You look pissed."

"Kent's having an affair," she said without a hitch in her voice.

Bunny stared at her for a minute, and the same smile that had appeared on Dr. Driscoll's face came over hers, as if she were thinking: "Well, so what? Who isn't having an extra trickle now and then?"

"Who is it?" she asked Louise.

"Babs Halston."

"Well, that must be keeping him busy. Her cunt's the hottest number from here to Boston."

"I've heard that."

"How did you find out?"

Louise told Bunny about the parking ticket and what the painter had said when she called the duplex that day.

"Honey, you don't know a *damn* thing! There might be any number of explanations. Isn't Kent building a boat for that sour ass, Roger Halston?"

"Yes."

"If you found out Kent was having an affair, would you forgive him?"

"I guess so."

"All my husbands had affairs, and I found out about each one of them."

"Did you forgive them?"

"Twice I did. But my marriages broke up for other reasons."

Louise thought a moment and sipped her drink, wondering if she would really forgive Kent. She didn't know. Then she said, "If I'm going to forgive him, I have to know what I'm forgiving him for."

"Now you're talking, honey. You have a couple of choices. You can ask Kent about it, but it's been my experience that men always lie about such things. They won't admit they're doing anything wrong unless you catch them right in the old saddle."

"I don't really want to catch anyone."

"You want to be sure of what's going on, don't you? You could be wrong."

"I realize that."

"You won't be satisfied until you know. And there's only one way to find out."

"What's that?"

"Private investigator."

Louise doubled up in laughter.

"I know what you're thinking, Louise. Even to hire one of these second-rate Sam Spades is an admission that you don't trust your husband. Frankly, you don't, at this point. I've used these boys for years . . . never sorry. There's an old man named Hughes in New York who's especially good. He'll find out what you want. Now come on, Louise, stop screwing up your face. I know it's tacky, costly bullshit but look at your options. Do you want to go on imagining the worst, or do you really want to *know* the worst? Sometimes the pictures you build in your mind are worse than reality. I've suffered through this kind of thing, and I wouldn't trust any man as far as I could kick him. And most of them need a kick in the balls—not the ass."

"That sounds so brittle. Why do you keep marrying, then? What about the general?"

Bunny nodded. "He's a lovable doggy, but the general is

too old for extra cockmanship. Now you're an imaginative gal, and that's good sometimes, but it can also eat you up, Louise."

"Don't tell me. I lie awake nights looking over at the man next to me, thinking of him and Babs Halston . . . I get up and pace. I go look at the Maserati's mileage when I've just done it five hours before. He says nothing. That makes it worse. Then I get depressed and ask myself where I've failed. What did I neglect to do? Should I be a sex maniac? Is that what men need and demand, or is Kent seeing his life slip by? He's made his mark, but maybe it's not enough, and he wants the satisfaction of screwing a rich little whore. Oh, Christ, Bunny, I'm so confused."

Bunny slid away from her side of the settee, put down her lobster fork, and sat next to Louise, placing her arm about the younger woman. "Listen . . . it happens to a lot of women. The roof starts to cave in suddenly, and you don't know why. You mistrust yourself . . . your husband. Right now you're trapped by suspicion, and that's a killer. Find out! I'll give you Hughes's number."

"Detectives, shit!"

"I know. I couldn't accept it at first myself. One word of warning though . . . *never, never* let Kent know what you're doing. I made that mistake once, and it backfired. My husband found out I had this investigator, so he hired an investigator to tail the investigator. It was wild. In the end, all we did was laugh."

"What happened?"

"We got quite a civilized divorce. Louise, I want you to know something. I'm your friend. I'll never say anything about this, but you can come to me anytime. Call me in the middle of the night if you want to."

"Thanks, Bunny, you're a dear. I might have to."

"Now eat your lobster, and let's forget it," Bunny said briskly, returning to her seat.

They exchanged smiles, but Louise Morgan couldn't forget it.

Three days after Louise's talk with Bunny, Kent moved out of the main house to his drafting-studio setup in the carriage house, which he called his "upstairs back."

"Why are you moving?" Louise asked him.

"I have design problems. Sometimes I wake up with a new idea, and I want my drawing board near me."

"Why don't you move the drafting equipment in here?"

"It would only disturb you."

For two nights Louise knelt at the window with her five-powered night binoculars resting on the sill. She was certain that Babs, who often came to Menlo Head, would stop over to see Kent.

A five-hundred-watt floodlight bathed the entire carriage house in a dull glow, outlining the groomed poplar trees which girded the bluestone drive. There was only *one* entrance to the building besides the double garage doors. From her position at the upstairs bedroom window, Louise could see that door.

She listened to the all-night radio talk show and drank heavy Cuban coffee, trying to stay awake while squinting through the eye side of the infrared glasses. Louise saw a raccoon, a field rat, two neighborhood cats, but no person entered the carriage house, and at the end of her second sleepless night, she chided herself for being suspicious. Then she succumbed to exhaustion, waking up about ten the next morning when the phone rang.

"Louise, this is Bunny."

"Oh . . . hi, Bunny."

"You sound sleepy . . . did I wake you up?"

"Yeah. It's okay, though."

"I have an idea. Chug that boat of yours around Humble Cove . . . I'll meet you at the club. We'll eat at the pier . . . get some of that hot bisque from the kitchen and do our own thing."

"Good. I'll bring the booze and try to pull a lobster trap."

Louise yanked on her Levi's and fumbled for a heavy

Irish wool sweater inscribed, "Waste time, not energy," a gift from Cathy. When she shuffled into the kitchen still moving in that soft border between wakefulness and sleep, Kent sat the breakfast table with an engineer's calculator and a set of hull lines before him. She was surprised to see him still home.

"How's it coming?" Louise asked as she poured a cup of coffee.

"Didn't know you cared."

"Sure I care . . . boats are my life."

"Your life?" Kent mused, his eyes still on the hull lines. "That's a long way from your livelihood. Sometimes I think I'm like a baseball pitcher who's only as good as his last season. He can pitch a no-hitter one year . . . win the series . . . all of a sudden, the guy goes into a slump . . . and where is he? At some dumb outback ball club. The yacht designer is always on trial. I've had big race winners, so people expect me to design next year's racing machine . . . it's always this search for speed and more speed. I have to go faster each year so my clients can pick up additional silverware. Maybe I have a bad year, and do you know what they say? 'Kent Morgan has passed his prime. He's lost his magic.' "

Louise saw in her husband's eyes a fleeting desperation, the pinched look of a man before a harsh jury, and she reached across the table and took his hand.

"I know what it must be like," she said.

He shook his head slowly. "No, you probably think that the design office runs like a well-greased diesel. I draw up a few lines . . . they pop out of my head . . . and the money bubbles in."

"Kent, I've *never* thought that. I know it's competitive and tough."

"Damn right. For three fucking nights I've been working with a little curve of the hull near the rudder. Do you realize that the slightest turn in a line can make a big difference? I deal in hairlines."

"I can imagine."

"There're five stages to a yacht designer's career. The first . . . someone says, 'Kent Morgan? Who's he?' Years later, 'Kent Morgan . . . oh, yeah . . . he's coming along.' Then, 'Kent Morgan? Great! Do you think we can get him?' Finally, 'Kent Morgan . . . is he still designing?' And at the very end, 'Kent Morgan . . . who's he?' "

He went on, banging his pencil on the table for emphasis. "When they ask . . . 'Kent Morgan, who's he?' . . . when my hulls don't go as fast as they used to, or I have no commissions, I've decided I'll design bowling balls. There's a challenge! The ultimate fast bowling ball. I bet it could be done. Don't you think I could design a faster bowling ball?"

"What's wrong with you this morning?"

"Oh, I don't know."

She studied her husband flicking his hands over the calculator as if replacing one thought, one problem, for another. Louise felt that he was on the edge of telling her something which, for some reason, he could not push up through his throat. She wanted him to know that she understood.

"Kent . . . something's on your mind. . . ."

"This," he said, pointing towards the congestion of rough hull lines crisscrossing the tracing paper.

"I don't mean that. Is there anything else, more important, maybe, that you want to tell me . . . or discuss with me?"

"Of course not. What would it be?"

"You're sure?"

"I'm sure."

"We used to be able to talk everything out," Louise said.

"You mean *you've* always been able to talk . . . I've listened mostly. Yep, I've learned to listen and obey around here . . . just like one of the kids. Only the kids get a reward when they're good, and Daddy doesn't."

He picked up his papers and left the house without saying good-bye. She heard the deep reverberations of his Maserati echo off the carriage house walls and then the spit of pebbles being shot back as he snapped the machine into gear and disappeared between the overhanging trees which canopied the drive.

Louise sighed and looked down, noticing that the quarter-round molding on the baseboards had been slightly scuffed by the rompings of her children. Kent must not have worked on them lately. The scratched baseboards were another clue that Kent was suffering some sort of mid-life crisis. Louise promised herself that as soon as she returned from lunch, she would go to the garage for the sandpaper, prepare the surfaces and repaint them, a signal to her husband that she was pitching in and helping.

Louise grabbed her weather clothes and went out on the lawns of Pigeon Hill towards the dock. It was cold, and the wind tore through the bare branches, bending and twisting them into tight curves. Dark clouds were sailing in from the east. A light rain fell.

The stiff boat chugged over the mounding seas, spray shooting back and turning to thin layers of ice on the deck. From a point beyond Barton's Island, she could see further out into the Sound; it was being whipped into more whiteness all the time.

She throttled back with ice-covered gloves which cracked and snapped. Louise yanked up four traps, rolling them to the surface on the barrel winch; the last one was heavier than the others, and she knew that two lobsters had taken up residence in the slatted home with the door locked forever.

Forty minutes later she rounded *Workboat* up to the dock of the Menlo Head Yacht Club. Bunny was waiting there, dressed in her bulky, orange weather suit. They ate their meal, drank their vodka, and Louise told her friend about that morning's conversation with Kent.

"Sounds like he's all tensed up over the job for some reason, Louise. He may not be having an affair at all."

Louise shook her head. "I know my husband. After sixteen years, you develop an instinct . . . know when something's different. I think he is having an affair."

"But you won't force the issue?"

"I have my pride."

"You're letting pride destroy you and the marriage, Louise. Come on . . . give Hughes a call."

"I can't see myself hiring a detective . . . talking to one or paying one."

"Then what will happen?"

"I think it will pass," Louise said, thinking of Dr. Driscoll's words. She went on to explain about her visit to the gynecologist's office. "Don't you think he should have had something better to offer than . . . get a new nightgown and some Valium?"

"Sure, but that's good old Tom . . . always ready with a Band-Aid when you need a transfusion."

"He implied that I hadn't pleased Kent . . . that I should seduce my husband to keep him at home."

"Of course," Bunny said sarcastically. "It's always the woman's fault when a man starts looking around. We're supposed to keep 'em happy . . . tie their shoelaces . . . cook their food . . . rub their backs . . . and despite all that, if they're unhappy, *we've* failed."

Louise was silent for a moment; then she started giggling. "Can't you picture me popping out at Kent when he opens the front door in a peekaboo outfit like . . . what is it? Fredericks Of Hollywood . . . with the cutouts for boobs and the fanny, standing there with a martini in one hand and a leer on my face, beckoning him to the bedroom?"

Bunny laughed and threw a pillow across the cabin at her friend. Louise ducked. They were both getting a little drunk now. They had two more martinis, and then *Workboat* seemed to become a hollow ashcan being bombarded by pellets: hailstones. They decided to leave the craft at the yacht club dock, and Bunny drove Louise back to Pigeon Hill.

In the driveway she said, "You're sure you don't want me to call Hughes?"

"I'm sure. Thanks, Bunny," Louise said.

She got out of the car and entered the house.

CHAPTER EIGHT

That night Kent burst into the kitchen. His face was sallow, and she wondered if his design problem, the inching of a curve one way or another, was still baffling him. But she thought again and decided that plain old guilt was eating away at her husband.

"Kent, I have a surprise for you," she said quickly. "I painted the baseboards . . . I mean, where they're scuffed."

"You did what?" he snorted as he took off his wet Burberry raincoat, slinging it down.

"The baseboards," she said again, smiling.

"Who told you to do that?"

"I saw they needed some tidying up, and I knew you were very busy. . . ." Her voice trailed off as she noticed the expression on his face.

"All the time you've been out there making a commercial fishery of our home . . . some damn duck-shooting range or vegetable farm . . . I didn't complain. All I wanted to do was sand the baseboards and paint them. That was *my* job!"

"Kent, I didn't mean to take your job, but this morning . . ."

"What about this morning?" he snapped, cutting her off. "What about this morning?"

"Well . . . ah . . . you seemed so down . . . talking about bowling balls."

"Yeah. Well, I'm no longer talking about bowling balls. I

found out how to fix the stern. We're tank-testing the model next week at the Stevens Institute."

"Then shouldn't you be happy?" she said.

"I'm not, God damn it! You fuck . . ." He stopped just short of unfolding the word.

Louise reeled back, her hands on her hips. "Never talk to me like that, Kent!" she boiled. "You ever use that word to me, or anything like it, and I'll be out of here in a second." Her face was cherry-red, and her breath came in short heaves, but she caught enough air to say crisply, "I don't deserve that kind of language from you. I've done nothing."

"Nothing?" he laughed. "You have so."

"What?"

"You're not supposed to paint the baseboards without my permission. It's my house."

"It's our house."

"No . . . no . . . it's not *our* house; it's your fishery, duck-shooting range, vegetable truck farm, shipyard . . . and what else . . . I don't know what else. Oh, yes, a cannery."

"I'll tell you what else, too," she snapped. "It's saved you about ten thousand dollars in food last year. We eat fresh duck, fresh fish, fresh lobsters and fresh vegetables. And the kids are resourceful, and that kind of food is better than beef and one hell of a lot cheaper. Better . . . cheaper."

"And I vomit thinking of duck. I hate duck! I only like roast beef and veal, and I've eaten so many lobsters I feel that I'm growing claws one minute . . . and mallard feathers the next."

"Is that what you're mad about?"

"No."

"Then what? Stop acting like a spoiled kid. The money I saved lets you run that Maserati . . . what does it get? Four miles to the gallon? Three hundred ten dollars for a carburetor tune-up . . . I know, I pay these bills."

"Don't start in on the car. You use it, too. I'll tell you what just happened. I've *never* been so embarrassed. I get this call from the commodore of the Menlo Head Yacht Club, Ogden Barnes."

"Oh, yes, dear old soggy Oggie."

"That's a tired slur. It was amusing five years ago, Louise."

"What did he want?"

"Ogden is well connected in yachting circles, my love. He's put five design commissions into my office indirectly. Roger Halston was going to Sparkman & Stevens, but Ogden told him to keep the business local. He's my silent salesman. So he says, 'Kent, I had a very important client up from New York, and I was proudly showing him our yacht club. There at the dock was your wife's lobster boat smelling like a fish. Below decks there were whiskey bottles, dirty glasses, weather gear not even hung up.' He said the boat was a slobby eyesore."

"It's not supposed to be a yacht. Bunny and I were aboard for lunch."

"Then why didn't you move the boat back here?"

"The seas were running high . . . it was hailing."

"I thought you were the rough-weather goddess," he snarled. "You were probably too drunk to find your way around the cove. *You* were high, not the waves."

"All right, Kent," Louise said, a warning note in her voice.

He chattered on. "The commodore reminded me that boats were not allowed to be tied to the dock."

"That's in the summer when the launch operates."

"*Anytime.*"

"Who the hell is out now? The launches are up."

"It's still the rule. And then Ogden says that a commercial lobster boat at the dock wasn't in keeping with the proper club image. Louise, it's a yacht club, not a fish wharf."

"I didn't land lobster there."

"But you used the dock. For Christ's sake, you made a fool out of me. He said, 'Kent, why do you send your wife out to lobster? Are things that bad?' He laughed, but he wasn't making a joke. I could tell. He was mocking me. That's beside the point. He still thinks I'm a hell of a designer. But I grabbed the hint, so I promised to move the boat immediately."

"It's still blowing out there."

"You can handle it . . . quit stalling. Get in your gear, and I'll drop you by."

"I don't want to," Louise said. "Not tonight."

"Okay, then, I'll untie the boat and let her crack up on the rocks."

"You'd get a sadistic pleasure out of that!" Louise stormed.

She grabbed her jacket and "funny suit" and stomped out of the house with Kent trailing her.

The icy rain was being slung sideways by the snap of the gale. The Menlo Head trees creaked; their vacant branches had become rigid spindles, and everything looked mournful. Kent and Louise did not speak during the ten-minute ride to the club. She was so angry at her husband that she spent the entire time trying to think up appropriate ways to get back at him.

Kent's "business fountain" was dark, and the sprawling, white, one-story clubhouse was totally deserted when they arrived. Suddenly Louise burst into high-pitched laughter as she stepped out of the Maserati, pulling the hood of her sailing jacket around her head and clutching the packed "funny suit" to her chest.

"What's so hilarious?" he asked.

"There's no one here."

"Of course not. The club's closed on Tuesday."

"And you still think my boat's a blemish at a shut-down club on a crazy night in January?"

"I don't want to talk about it."

"That boat might be the only real thing at this club. Think of that one."

"I'll wait for you at the Pigeon Hill dock," Kent said, leaning out the Maserati window.

It was just at the end of cocktail time in Menlo Head, the "fuzzy" hour, when the bulbous commodores, finished with their clumsy jibbing, weaved into the dining rooms, martini-heavy, to eat what Cook had braised, baked, roasted, sautéed or dumped into boiling water.

On *Workboat,* Louise decided to construct a birdbath cocktail for herself. The imported English vodka gurgled out of the bottle over the ice, launching the cubes onto their little white lake. She liked the sound of the boxlike iceboats banging the side of the glass in a chorus of funny clicks and clanks. Each time *Workboat* heaved and nipped at her dock lines, the chorus was different, offsetting the rattle of the wind.

Finally Louise opened her mouth and gulped a cataract of booze; she decided to take a Valium, too. The mixture, while hardly recommended, did give a slightly different boost. She raised her glass and toasted the Gilbert and Sullivan commodores, some of whom lived on the hill, the only high place in Menlo Head. Their Gothic estates looked down upon everything of importance: the historic river, the historic town and the historic yacht club. The residents were an exalted bunch who preferred to be seen from below, and the estate lights, illuminating the gardens and docks, sent a Kafka-like stage glow over the harbor. On calm, dry nights when the wind wasn't hissing, the buttery lights seemed to twinkle, proving that even in the dark, wealth and position should not be totally hermetic.

On this night, though, Louise thought that the rocky mansions on the hill, part of a vanished era, looked like a series of small prisons, or blockhouses, and the powerful, energy-wasting illumination was really to deter the prisoners from escaping.

"Do you know who you are up there?" she yelled. "You're a perverse colony of socially nervous, feebleminded weaklings. That's what you are. You're all rotting away, and your breaths are foul, and not one fucking one of you has had a new idea since your old great-granddaddies deeded you those puff houses."

She had another drink, trying to decide what to do. She

could take *Workboat* down the river and tie her alongside the boat yard dock for the night, then call Bunny for a meal at Ye Olde Beef & Brew, where they would get drunk and talk and stuff their bellies with artificially flavored and dyed red meat. Or she could simply remain aboard *Workboat,* crawl into the bunk and booze herself to sleep while listening to the "Larry King All-Night Radio Talk Show." But then, of course, Kent would simply race his play machine back to the club, and the mania would be twice as aggravated.

The wind friction had begun to lump the seas into solid seven-footers. She could tell just by the pitch and roll of the boat.

"I'll show you," she shouted out. "Mr. Yacht Designer, sweat this one out."

It would be a neat revenge, she thought. She cranked up the diesel and tossed off the dock lines, letting them fall into mucky water instead of resting the ropes on the tidy dock for the next admiral to come alongside in his ego tub—not until the weather warmed, still four months off.

Over the wallops of the one-lunger, she heard a high-pitched voice, "Hello . . . hello there. . . ."

Louise looked around and saw Ralph-somebody; she never did know the dockmaster's last name because it was a compound Scandinavian mishmash.

"Hello, Ralph."

"Mrs. Morgan . . . is that you?"

"It sure is."

"I heard the diesel start up. You're not going out in this stuff, are you?"

"Oh, yes, Ralph," she called. "Commodore Barnes complained to my husband about my lovable *Workboat.* I was instructed to move it back to our parking lot."

"Not tonight, Mrs. Morgan. The anemometer in my boat house says it's gusting forty."

"That's nothing, Ralph. You see, I enjoy balmy nights in

96

the tropics with the moon sliding in and out of the ghostly clouds and the sea a glimmer of stardust."

"What?"

"I was just mushing a few sea poems together, Ralph. Practicing."

Ralph, who ran the launches in the summer and revarnished them in the winter, was not abundantly cognizant, and he stood looking at her, his dripping mouth hanging open in a pouch.

"There hasn't been a boat at this dock for weeks now. You can leave it here, Mrs. Morgan. Bring her around in the morning."

"But the commodore said to move it. So did my husband who has passionate love spasms for commodores. And if I don't move it, you will be sacked, Ralph, and they'll tie you to the flagpole, strip off your shirt and lay ten cat-o'-nine-tails over your back. I'm doing this for you, Ralph, and the commodore and my husband and the image of the Menlo Head Yacht Club."

"What did you say, Mrs. Morgan?" he yelled over the wind.

"Call Commodore Barnes for me, Ralph. Tell him that Louise Morgan has just removed her squalid, stinking lobster boat from his clean dock and that she is now heading out into a wild icy Sound. There is no doubt that Mrs. Morgan will be lost to the eternal seas, and the burden of guilt, Ralph, will be placed squarely on the commodore's plump shoulders, and he will suffer from these pains and others for the rest of his life."

Ralph came towards *Workboat* and called over the hiss of the wind, "Mrs. Morgan, please . . . just keep it tied up here safe and sound. Only a fool would go out there tonight."

"It's the rule, Ralph."

"Do you want me to come with you?"

"That's very kind of you, but I'll handle it."

Before the man could continue his pleading, Louise jerked the one-lunger into gear, and *Workboat* arched around, pointing her head towards the open Sound. The diesel ran at full throttle.

The sea was up. Louise felt it just as she inched past the outer marker buoy. The little bow dug in; hard water splashed back, running into the cockpit and out along the scuppers. She retarded the throttle and began whistling the Yale boola-boola song as the hearty little craft settled down, pushing the sloppy water out of the way. The ice built up, layer upon layer.

Almost a mile offshore, Louise saw the back-lighted town appearing as a red glow on the horizon. Instead of swinging around to port, Louise decided to stay out. There was nothing to collide with her this night, so she flicked off the navigation lights; she was going to give Kent Morgan and a few others, she hoped, a little time to ponder.

Running dark, Louise headed *Workboat* into the lee water of Hawk Island, a rocky outcropping half a mile from Humble Cove. Once behind the natural breakwall, the erratic motion of *Workboat* diminished. She was bobbing easily. Louise throttled back just to keep the bow to the wind, tossed the hook and made herself another drink. She turned on the portable radio and pushed a hunk of cold lobster meat into her mouth.

Kent returned to Pigeon Hill, and the children asked for their mother.

"She's bringing the boat around from the yacht club."

"In this weather?" Laurie asked.

"There's no weather too much for Mom," Kent said in a singsong. "If this were a hundred years ago, your mother would be out there harpooning whales with Moby Dick."

"Dad, Moby Dick was the whale," Cathy said. "You mean Captain Ahab."

"Little smart ass," Kent said to himself, looking over at the image of Louise. "It was a joke, Cathy . . . your mother likes tormented weather. She wanted to bring the boat around all by herself. I offered my help, but of course she doesn't need help . . . *ever*."

Kent put on his weather gear and, hauling a fresh drink, he meandered across the lawns to the breakwall and out along the pier to grab the docking line when Louise pulled in.

The course from the harbor to Pigeon Hill, even in a howler, would take no more than twenty minutes. Yet forty-five minutes went by as Kent stood drinking under the portico of the summerhouse, looking at his watch and smoking cigarette after cigarette. He decided that Louise had *not* taken the boat around; he plucked the phone out of its wooden box on the pillar and called the yacht club.

"Menlo Head Yacht Club . . . Ralph speaking."

"Ralph, this is Mr. Morgan. Did my wife remove that lobster crock about forty-five minutes ago?"

"Yes, sir."

"Which way did she head?"

"Out to the Sound," the dockmaster said. "Couldn't figure it out, Mr. Morgan."

"What?"

"You see, I noticed the boat there all day. Mrs. Morgan brought it in about lunchtime, and I was watching it . . . with this gale and everything. . . ."

"Ralph, get to the point."

"Well, I was in working on the launch tonight, and I saw a car in the parking lot."

"That was my car."

"Yes, sir. Then I walked out and heard the lobster boat start up. Thought it was being stolen. Who would go out on a night like this? I was saying to my wife. Then I went over and saw Mrs. Morgan."

"Well?"

"Mrs. Morgan asked me to call the commodore and say that she would be lost to the eternal seas, and it was all his fault."

"Are you kidding me!" Kent blasted.

"I never kid. My job is serious, Mr. Morgan. Believe me, that's exactly what she said, and she sounded funny. I thought she sounded real funny."

"Why didn't you call me?"

"It's not my place, Mr. Morgan."

"Well, for God's sake, I hope you didn't call the commodore."

"No, sir . . ."

"*Don't*, Ralph. Are there any fishing boats tied up in the harbor?"

"Not tonight."

"How about the boat from the shipyard?"

"She's up on the ways."

"You mean that harbor has nothing in it?"

"Only a few yachts in wet storage. I could call the Coast Guard."

"It would be hours before they came across the Sound, even if those bastards would leave their poker game on a night like this. Get in your car, Ralph, and drive to the end of Woods Lane; see if you can pick up the running lights."

"I'll do that."

"And call me back at my dock number. Do you have it?"

"Yes, sir."

A rising panic leaped through Kent Morgan. Still, he rationalized: What could happen to his wife? She knew these waters; her boat was sound and hammered together with the best fastenings; the wood was dried yellow pine, almost bulletproof; and the rebuilt diesel was totally reliable. Louise was the best small-boat handler in Menlo Head, and her specially designed lobster craft could tame any sea outside of an ocean. Long Island Sound was hardly an ocean, and the wind, Kent estimated, was no more than forty knots—still in the gale range, hardly a fully developed storm.

But uncertainty clung to him. Kent looked at his watch once more. It had been fifty minutes now and still no running lights. Maybe her pal, Bunny, had some information.

Kent picked up the phone and called Bunny Lunsford and told her what had happened.

"You mean you sent that woman out on a night like this, you creep!"

"I didn't call for a lecture, Bunny. Was my wife all right today?"

"Yes, she was all right, in spite of everything."

"Everything?"

"Forget it . . . I'm driving over there right now."

"It's not necessary. There's nothing wrong."

"Nothing wrong! The woman's offshore alone in a hurricane. All the trees are icy, and you have the fat-ass gall to say nothing's wrong! There's something wrong, all right . . . with your head. You have marmalade in there."

There was a click. Kent swore and put the phone down.

He paced back and forth in the confines of the summer-house, now turned into a miniature ice palace. He knocked at the ice with his bare knuckles, and small slivers fell to the deck. What the hell had happened? Louise had her "funny suit" with her, and she could probably exist in it if *Workboat* was driven under.

Something was inching its way up in Kent's mind, and he was almost ashamed to admit to himself that overriding his concern for his wife was another anxiety: How would it look to the town, to his children, if Louise Morgan was lost at sea simply because he had sent her out to bring the boat around on the worst night of the year? His judgment would be called into question; even more than that, his courage. Why had he not accompanied his wife in the boat? Nothing could be concealed. Too many people knew just what had happened, including Ralph, the dockmaster, who was a born tattler.

CHAPTER NINE

Twenty minutes later, Bunny, trying to hold an umbrella against the wind, raced out on the finger pier. Cathy and Laurie followed her.

"Dad . . . Mrs. Lunsford says Mother's lost at sea!" Cathy yelled.

"She's *not* lost," Kent said, glaring at Bunny. "Maybe she had engine trouble. Now get back in the house . . . you'll catch cold."

"Carrie said we could come out and wait," Laurie protested.

"*I'm* saying get back in the house! Now run. Mother will be in soon."

"How do you know?" Cathy asked.

"Because I know."

"We're staying here," Cathy said, holding her sister.

The phone rang. "Ah . . . Mr. Morgan . . . this is Ralph. I looked out there. Couldn't see no running lights."

"How hard did you look?"

"Very hard. And I called Commodore Barnes."

"I told you not to!" Kent screamed.

"Well, I'm sorry, Mr. Morgan, but I thought it was time. Your wife did tell me to call."

"And what did the commodore say?"

"First I explained that it was all right with me if we kept the boat at the dock just until the wind died down.

He agreed, and when I told him that Mrs. Morgan had headed out because she was told to, he said he was sorry. Very sorry."

"Oh, God, I'll call him. You ride along Elbow Road and continue looking, Ralph, and I'm not forgetting that you called the commodore when I forbade it."

Kent hung up the phone and dialed information. Once on the line with Ogden Barnes, Kent softened his hard-edged voice to a lighthearted tone.

"Hello, Ogden, this is Kent Morgan."

"Yes, Kent," came the stiff reply. "I just received a very disturbing call from Ralph over at the club."

"He told me."

"Kent, when I talked to you this afternoon, I didn't necessarily mean that you were supposed to move your wife's boat tonight. I understand she went out alone in this weather."

"Yes, Ogden, but you know Louise. She can handle weather. That boat of hers is an eyesore, I agree with you. I've been against it from the . . ."

"Kent, that's not the problem. Ralph mentioned that Louise said good-bye to me. But maybe Ralph has it wrong. He's getting a bit long in the tooth, I'd say. Has Louise been okay lately . . . I mean, is she all right?"

"Of course. But she's a free spirit, Ogden, very liberated."

"But something appears to have happened, Kent. I feel partly responsible."

"Just a mix-up. I'm sure she's fine."

"But where is she?"

"I don't know."

"Well, if she's still missing . . . what are you going to do about it?"

"I could call the Coast Guard, of course; that would take time. Ralph says there are no boats in the harbor. I was thinking of going out to look, but how?"

"Ummm . . . there're two tugs down at Stamford, working on the dredging. I can call Phil Ashinwald who heads up the club . . . fine man . . . belongs to Metropolitan and New York Yacht. He might be able to get the tug men to go out."

"But how much would that cost?"

"No idea. I'll phone and get an estimate. What else can we do, Kent?"

"To put tugs out on a night like this . . . overtime and . . ."

Bunny, who had a firm, tough body, pushed Kent aside with one hand and pulled the phone away from him with the other.

"Ogden, this is Bunny Lunsford."

"Oh, hello, Bunny."

"Now, listen," she bellowed. "God damn it . . . all this fussy talk. Louise Morgan might be in trouble . . . hopefully with her head still above water. Now you get onto those people with the tugs. I don't care what it costs . . . I'll pay for it if Kent won't. I'm going to phone the Coast Guard myself. This thing is cruel and creepy. Creepy, Ogden. You realize that?"

"Bunny, relax. There's probably a simple explanation. I'm certain she's safe."

"Do what I say!"

Kent stiffened with rage. He grabbed the phone from Bunny's hand.

"Ogden . . . Bunny's a little upset. Of course, I'll pay for the tugs."

"Fine, Kent. If I can get through to the right person, I'll have him call you."

Kent gave the commodore the number at his dock and put the phone down. He walked towards the far side of the summerhouse, his fists curled in knots and his breath heavy. Suddenly he whirled around as if his body were attached to a spindle.

"Why the Christ did you speak to him like that? Giving the man orders. Shit! I can handle it. I don't require your assistance."

"You were talking about the price of the tugs."

"Why not? It's a consideration."

"Like hell it is. Louise's safety is the consideration."

"You just stay away from my wife, and don't come over here anymore. We don't need you!"

"I think you do."

"What does that mean?"

"Someday I'll tell you."

The towboat operator called the Pigeon Hill dock twenty minutes later. He told Kent that he could put two tugs to sea for a flat sum of five thousand dollars for the first six hours and two thousand per hour after that. Kent swallowed stiffly, looked at Cathy and Laurie and Bunny who stood staring at him and agreed.

The tug operator put in a fast qualification: He wanted the fee upfront, and he was sending one of his associates to Pigeon Hill by car to collect the check.

An hour later Louise, who still had her workboat back behind the lee of the island, looked south and noticed the powerful beams of the tugs coming closer, their searchlights sweeping the dark waters. She thought it might be the Coast Guard, and a feeling of culpability and shame gripped her. She spun *Workboat* about, eased up the throttle and headed back towards Pigeon Hill.

Bunny picked her up first.

"Kent!" she yelled. "I see running lights coming in! It's Louise . . . I know her lights!"

"That's Mom's boat!" Laurie cried out. "She's okay!"

All of them galloped out to the slick pier to wait as the red and green lights from *Workboat* grew larger.

"You *will* adjust the price, won't you?" Kent said to the collector of revenues for the tug company, who had remained at Pigeon Hill after pocketing the agreed-upon fee.

"No, sir. We had a deal."

"Five thousand dollars for coming up here? That's an hour's work . . . no more."

"It was the price."

"I'm canceling that check."

"Yeah, you do that, Mr. Morgan . . . and you'll be in court. We performed a service. Glad your wife is okay, but our tugs put to sea."

The workboat rounded up to the dock, and Kent took the lines.

After securing the vessel, he stepped aboard.

"What happened?" he asked his wife.

"Nothing."

"What the hell do you mean . . . nothing?"

"I just decided to stay out there awhile."

"For what?"

"To think."

"And why didn't you radio in?"

"And why did you make me take this around tonight?"

Kent's anger swelled again. "It cost me *five thousand dollars* for tugs . . . and you made a fool out of me again with Ogden Barnes."

"Mom . . ." Laurie yelled as she and Cathy ran down the dock towards her.

It was just then that Kent Morgan, his fury boiling, clenched his fists once more, drew back his arm and struck his wife with one short snap punch which landed on the side of her face, knocking her to the bulwark of the after cockpit.

"Dad! Mom! What's going on!" Cathy yelled.

The two girls grabbed their father, fearing that he would continue to strike Louise. Bunny and the tug man, seeing what had happened, scrambled down to the dock.

"You're out of your mind, Kent!" Bunny yelled.

In a second the big tug man had wrapped his meaty arms around Kent Morgan, who struggled to get away.

"You're crazy, fellow," he said. "You ought to be glad your wife's okay."

"She . . . she . . . she was never in trouble . . . she did this on purpose."

"Yeah, well, but you act like a goon."

Bunny picked Louise up. "Are you all right?"

"I think so."

Kent started walking back through the ice storm to the house, and Cathy, slipping and sliding on the slick grass, ran up behind him.

"Why did you do that!" she screamed, beating her fists against his back. "Why did you hurt Mom?"

"Get away from me!" Kent turned and yelled at his daughter.

The girl ran around in front of him, blocking his way, and he pushed her aside. Cathy slipped on the wet grass and went down.

"You hate Mom . . ." she shouted, the tears streaming down her face as she struggled to get up. "You hate her!"

Kent drew in a large breath and screamed maniacally over the zinging wind, "She did it on purpose, Cathy! Don't you understand . . . one of her sick little jokes!"

Cathy knelt there, eyeing her father's tortured face. He whirled around and went quickly up the steps. The girl sank to the wet ground, sobbing, as behind her, Louise and the others slowly made their way up the ice-laden finger dock.

CHAPTER TEN

Kent moved back to the carriage house studio. He said that he had an important design problem to solve and needed to be near his drafting table at all times. On the second evening after the tug incident, he arrived at the dinner table, his snarl replaced by a bright look.

"I have something to say. I've been thinking out in the carriage house. Sometimes, when I get up at night, I think things over clearly. Anyhow, I want you all to know how sorry I am for punching your mother. There was no excuse for that, but I was desperately worried about her being out in the storm. I also know I was wrong to have her move the workboat in such a gale. It was rather inane of me to listen to the commodore. I never meant to put club rules over Mom's safety, and I misunderstood what the commodore meant. I thought he was saying that your Mom's boat had to be moved that instant . . . but that's not what he meant. I love your mother and each of you very much . . . and I ask your forgiveness. Let's all forget it. Nothing like this will ever happen again."

There was a long pause after the speech, and the girls traded suspicious looks. But Louise bowed her head, then leaned over and kissed her husband.

"Apology accepted. Everything's forgotten . . . right, girls?" she said.

They were realists, and they nodded slowly.

About three weeks later on a Saturday, Louise was in her study, going over the household accounts. Most of the bills seemed to be overdue, and she had a hangover from the night before.

Jody suddenly burst into the room without knocking, followed closely by Laurie.

"Mother . . . Laurie ate all the lemon pie."

"I did not! She's lying, Mom."

Louise looked up irritably. "I'm very busy . . . can't you see that? Laurie, you're too old to pick on your sister."

"But I didn't eat all the pie, Mom. Leopold ate it."

"What are you talking about? Who's Leopold?"

"Mrs. Potter's cat. Carrie gave it to him and . . ."

"Laurie!" Louise snapped, putting down the stack of bills. "I don't think cats eat lemon meringue pie, but just get out of here . . . both of you. Go somewhere else and play."

Jody started chanting, "See . . . I told you . . you ate it."

"Out!" Louise stood up and shouted. "Right now."

"Gee, okay, Mom," Laurie said. She paused at the door as Jody flew past her down the stairs. "Do you have another headache?"

Louise, who had gone back to work on her accounts, looked up.

"What do you mean . . . another headache?"

Laurie shrugged. "Well, I noticed the liquor bottles out this morning, and every time they're out, you have a headache."

She turned and ran down the stairs, leaving Louise staring after her. She shoved the bills away and lit a cigarette, a habit which she had given up a long time ago and recently begun again. She was still looking out the window when Cathy came in a few minutes later.

"Hi, Mom."

"Oh, hi, dear." Louise roused herself. "Did you have a nice sail?"

"It was okay."

Cathy collapsed on the couch with a big sigh, eyeing her mother. "What are you doing?"

"Oh, just paying a few bills."

Cathy hit her sneaker against the rug, pinning her eyes on the scuff mark as she said, "Why doesn't Dad ever pay any bills?"

"Why, Cathy . . . what a thing to say. Your father and I share the responsibilities for the house."

The girl shook her head. "I don't call it sharing. We bring all the food in . . . and I've seen those account books. You support Dad."

"Cathy, this discussion will cease this minute. You don't know what you're talking about."

Cathy stood and walked over to the desk. She picked up a letter opener and turned it idly in her hands as she spoke. "I know that things aren't going well between you and Dad . . . even Laurie and Jody know. And they're very upset. Ever since he hit you on the dock that night . . ."

"Let's not go into that again, Cathy. I was wrong that night, too. I shouldn't have stayed out so long and upset everybody."

"But, Mom . . . that's not the only thing. We haven't pulled a lobster pot for ages. You sleep all afternoon, and you take pills. You never did that before."

"Oh, darling." Louise pulled the distraught girl down beside her and brushed the hair back from her forehead. "The pills were given to me by Dr. Driscoll . . . it's perfectly all right to take them. They do make me sleepy, that's true. I tell you what . . . I'll stop taking them, and then I won't sleep anymore, and we'll start taking *Workboat* out again. Okay, that make you happy?"

She hugged her daughter and felt the girl nod. Then Cathy pulled away. "I'd like that, but it won't solve everything, will it, Mom? I mean, you and Dad aren't ever going to be the way you used to be . . . everything's changed."

Louise stared at her for a moment and then said slowly, "Cathy, your father is going through a rather difficult time in his life right now. It's sort of like the thing women go through when they have menopause. It'll pass, but we have to be patient."

"Is he fooling around?"

"Cathy!"

There was a long pause; then the girl said defiantly, "Well . . . lots of men do. Dad's good-looking . . . he could probably find plenty of girls."

"Why do you bring up such a thing? Do you have any reason to suspect your father of 'fooling around,' as you put it?"

Cathy shook her head. "No . . . I just . . . well, let's forget it, Mom. I just want you to be happy. I gotta go take a shower. Catch your later."

The following Monday Louise talked to Bunny Lunsford, telling her of the conversation she'd had with her oldest daughter. "It's beginning to get to the children, Bunny, and God knows, I never wanted them to be affected by all this."

Bunny nodded. "They always know when things are going wrong . . . can't hide it."

"You should have heard Cathy. She's right about one thing . . . I do support Kent. Look at the prices in the stores . . . the gas pump lines. I think we all need to go back to a simpler time. Anyhow, I thought it was right to put on my scene at Pigeon Hill. We eat the freshest fish of anyone in town. My ducks have less grease than those served at Lavandou for sixty dollars a plate. I have sixteen recipes for bluefish, along with nine for lobster, eleven sauces for swordfish, all sorts of vegetable cookware, clay pots from all over the world. Do you know that I own eighty-nine cookbooks, some in French?"

"Maybe you're overstocked."

"Maybe. But my children were taught to enjoy this kind of life . . . killing the ducks themselves, preparing them creatively. Okay, so we're subsistence hunters; that's the truth of it, but Kent is extravagant, spends every cent he makes. When the girls helped me with *Workboat*, they learned how to handle tools and not cut the shit out of themselves. Cathy came to me after that and said she'd like a joiner so she could build furniture. Kent thought it was dangerous for a young girl to be operating power tools, but I bought it for her. And she and her sisters built their own furniture, good copies of Adams and Hepplewhite."

"But Kent never appreciated it?"

"Not only that . . . he hated it. And I never realized that until recently. Oh, I knew he wasn't enthusiastic about what we were doing, but all these years he's sat at the table, nibbling at the duck and the fish like some stoic martyr. I guess the legacy I was trying to build was too imperious. Sometimes I think Kent should have married a different kind of woman . . . a fragile little flower who'd lean on him and make him feel strong and masculine."

"Kent Morgan's not strong enough to support himself and somebody else, Louise. He'd collapse without you."

"Bunny, you never said anything like that before."

"Well, it's none of my business, but I've always thought Kent was like one of those cardboard cutout dolls, smooth and weightless. Anyway, why didn't he just open up his little mouth and tell you he didn't like what was going on?"

Louise shook her head. "That's not Kent. He's a brooder. He seethes inside . . . keeps all his little frustrations to himself. And then . . . bango, one day, there's an explosion."

Bunny said wryly, "Yeah, I know . . . like that night on the dock when he clobbered you."

"I stayed out there for my own little revenge, Bunny. You know that."

"You had a right to. The whole incident of removing that boat was sick, and you know it. Damn it, Louise, *don't* do this to yourself . . . don't take all the blame for everything. Let me tell you something. All this soul wrenching and chastisement doesn't mean a fucking thing. You want to know whether Kent is screwing Babs or not, right? That's what it's all about. Until you find out, you're just going to come apart more and more each day."

"You're talking detective again."

"Damn right."

"It's not for me, Bunny."

"Well, think of the children then . . . and in the meantime, you're flopping through all this shit. Have you looked in the mirror lately? You've got brown pockets under your eyes; you're haggard. It's the *not knowing* that's doing it. Oh, Christ, Louise, do what you have to do!"

Still Louise refused to consult a detective, and Bunny knew there was no point in pressing her further. Once Louise's mind was made up, that was it. Over the next few weeks, Bunny watched her friend's gradual deterioration.

Louise began taking the Valium again because when she tried to discontinue the drug, she found that her habit was stronger than she'd realized. She couldn't sleep . . . her hands shook . . . and she felt strange and disoriented. She told herself that it was all right to take the Valium because it was harmless and it had been prescribed for her. Anyhow, it was only for a temporary situation. But the booze and the pills were taking their toll, and Louise began to lose weight. She and Bunny continued to eat their lobster lunches together whenever possible, but the old joys and the confidences, the laughs and the craziness were gone.

Towards the middle of February, Bunny made her move. If Louise Morgan would not confront her husband or find out what was going on, she would.

Rod, her twenty-year-old son by a first marriage, was taking a photographic course in New York City. Bunny called him in and asked him if he wanted a domestic relations job at a hundred a week to improve his camera technique. She explained the situation to her son, who went down to Babs's brownstone on Ninety-first Street. Within a couple of hours, he had found a way to reach the roof through a back fire escape on the adjoining building.

After punching off a roll of test shots through the skylight of the girl's top-floor apartment, Rod blew up the shots in the cellar darkroom. He was satisfied with the detail, and he began his snoop assignment with a kind of youthful, fumbling zeal.

At precisely eight-ten in the morning, Rod would go into March's Drugstore, two blocks from Kent Morgan's design office, and buy a takeout coffee and two jelly Danish. By eight-thirty, the junior agent had his rust-pocked Volkswagen parked either across from the office if he could find a place, or around the corner where he could see beyond a vacant lot to the double doors leading into the former sail loft.

When Kent arrived at his office at exactly 9 A.M., Rod would unlatch the cardboard cover from the soggy, lukewarm container and begin to gnaw away on the sticky Danish.

Usually Kent Morgan would arrive at his office in a casual but explicit uniform: a Brooks Brothers buttoned-down shirt from which floated a yacht-club tie to reveal his proper affiliation; and a dark blue blazer, one of four with a gold-embroidered yacht-club emblem over the heart to reinforce the tiny markings of the tie, in case the smaller clue was missed. This formality was abridged by Kent's pants—baggy, ill-fitting, soiled denims in various hues to prove further that he prowled the decks of fast, self-designed yachts. In one sweep of a knowledgeable eye, Kent Morgan's social stance and his profession could be delineated. He wore this quasi-uniform so that no one could ever be caught short of the right impression.

On the twelfth of March there were two abrupt changes in the surveillance pattern. One involved the weather and the other, Kent Morgan's dress.

Traces of winter had lingered on in Menlo Head that year. Pockets of piled-up snow, gritty and ash-gray, remained about the curbstones and on the north sides of the clapboard houses. During the night of March 11, an inversion covered southern New England. Warm air was sandwiched above the cooler surface temperature, and from the flushed clouds a gentle rain fell, easing the evidences of winter.

At dawn, Menlo Head was nested in a flow of warm air. The snow was gone, and so were the dour, cold looks of the villagers. Smiles bloomed, the chrome on the cars sparkled and people moved along the streets jauntily, realizing that soon the tarp coverings of their sleeping yachts would be peeled back. The air would be choked with the buzzing sounds of electric sanders as owners prepared their yacht bright work for summer sailing, not so much to shield it from the salt air, but rather to underscore the fact that these were "Bristol" sailors, neat, clean, caring, diligent.

On this bright day, Rod noticed that his subject wore a neatly tailored glen plaid suit, a stiff white shirt, and a blue tie which might have been speckled with a yacht-club emblem. Rod couldn't pick that up through his binoculars.

Kent was going someplace; Rod was sure of that. At ten minutes after eleven, Kent jumped off the steps, sprang into his freshly washed Maserati and headed the twelve-cylinder power pack towards the New England Thruway. Rod floored the accelerator of his Beetle to keep up with his subject.

Kent had called Babs several times in January, hoping to see her when she returned to New York from her western skiing trip. But it was exam time, and Babs told him that it was all books and no "sport fucking" until the tests were over. And then she had had to take some extra courses, so it was March before she finally called.

"The green light is on, and is it *on*," she said. "I'm pooped from studying and ready for a celebration. I hope you are."

"I'm goddamn ready," Kent said.

"Hey . . . have you gone crazy?"

"What do you mean?" Kent asked.

"I heard you popped your wife. What happened?"

"I'll explain it sometime. It was a mistake on my part, but the bitch is getting so goddamn self-centered, I've been eating Swanson frozen dinners for a month."

"Why is that?"

"Louise and the girls went hunting . . . killed a small buck with bows and arrows . . . and they've been fixing it a different way every night. I hate the damn stuff!"

"Poor Kent. I think you probably need some recharging, a real experience, and a long way from the primitive scene."

He did not know exactly what she meant, but he wanted to find out.

CHAPTER ELEVEN

Kent arrived at Babs's upper East Side apartment at twelve-ten, and Rod, who had zigzagged from lane to lane to keep up with the sports car, pulled in five spaces behind Kent.

"How's the Philip Johnson of the watery world?" Babs yelled down the stairwell.

Kent looked up and thought that his clock had slipped ahead five hours. Babs was peering down at him from her usual greeting place at the banister of the top floor; she was dressed for a six o'clock cocktail gathering with the opera set. Her hair seemed darker, and it was pulled tightly back along her head, advancing her girlish features in age. She wore a slim black dress, a diamond necklace glistening above the deep plunge of the neckline, and very high black heels with sheer black stockings. She had an expensive, silky shine, even under the dim hall light.

"You look like you're about to swing into Sardi's on Rex Harrison's arm," Kent said.

"Who goes to Sardi's, and who's Rex Harrison? I'm simply dressed for an *occasion.*"

"What occasion?"

"Come on up here, Methuselah, and find out."

Kent bounded up the last flight, and she stood staring at him, head tilted back. Her mouth was slightly parted in a smothered smile, and her tongue slipped around the edge of her lips.

The invitation was obvious. Kent embraced her swiftly, and he felt her tongue on its well-charted voyage. They parted, and he said, "I feel like I'm kissing a *Cosmopolitan* cover."

She took his hand and guided him through the open door to the apartment.

Kent froze.

Before him was Babs's mother, sitting on the couch in a brief purple cocktail dress with a slit which traveled from the hem almost to her pelvic bone. She wore a small hat, and at the nape of her neck rode a cluster of diamonds, mimicking her daughter's, but three-tiered instead of two. Her hair was pulled back to match Babs's.

Gwen Halston looked at him through the bowl of a Steuben glass, the birdbath martini she had almost finished. Her stare was fixed and incontinent.

"Don't stand there like a petrified rock, Kent. Aren't you glad to see me?" Gwen asked.

"Yes, Gwen, I'm just . . ." His words trailed off.

"Surprised to see me?" she said, finishing his sentence. "Well, come over here and give me a welcome hug."

Kent shuffled forward and bent over to give Babs's mother a polite kiss on the cheek. His eyes slipped down to her perfectly formed breasts as he was enveloped in a cloud of perfume, the sort rich women bought, never asking the price. It might have been that his aim missed, or that Gwen hooked her head at the final moment of their union, but the corner of her lips met his. There was no doubt that the greeting had turned savory, for he felt the flick of her tongue whip across the far borders of his lips.

He had known Roger's wife as a dowdily dressed conservative woman. Everyone had said, "Menlo Head needs a stubborn voice like Gwen's. No permissiveness when the Halstons are about." That claim or boast excluded Babs, who was judged by the town's social corner as simply a sophisticated student of her liberalized generation.

"Why the hell is she here?" he asked himself.

As he stood away from Gwen, his mind was crackling, imagining the indignation that was about to be heaped upon him. He cleared his throat and moved to the bar, waiting for her motherly lecture.

"Kent, you haven't noticed my second surprise," Babs said, stretching out her arms so widely that her breasts almost took leave of her snaky black dress.

He looked around, and the second shock wave hit him.

It was not the same apartment.

Babs was in her cocktail dress; her mother was in her cocktail dress; and the apartment had swung from a Salvation Army testimonial to the best from Bloomingdale's. In place of the old stained couch was a buttery-white set of modules, deep, sensuous and expensive. The cockleshell rug was like soft sand, and the walls still smelled of resin from the recent paint job. Persian-silk pillows of delicate umber and black were tossed about, but the newest accoutrement was the portable stereo deck, a collection of electronic dials, lights and brushed chrome knobs set on a modular tower which could be wheeled about.

"Do you like it, Kent?" Babs asked.

"Quite a change. Yes, I like it."

"I think she's done a fine job with a little help from Roger and me," Gwen said, looking at her daughter admiringly. "Kent, have a double something. You look like you need a pepper-upper."

Kent poured out a solid vodka on the rocks, hoping that the chilly white liquid would mollify his curious mixture of fear and percussion.

Gwen, seeing him fumble with the ice cubes, pressed up out of the soft sofa and crossed to the French maitre d' cart converted to a rolling bar. She clasped his hand in hers.

"We're sorry, Kent. We thought you'd laugh."

His mouth was pinned shut, and he continued to alternate his bogus smile between mother and daughter, but his face was clearly drained.

"We thought it would be a little joke," Gwen said. "Just

the idea of you romping down here for a little afternoon fuck . . . and seeing old Mom here as a chaperone. That's a switch, isn't it?"

Kent, who was slow on fast comebacks, did not ride with the gag. Instead he said slowly, "You know all about us?"

"Of course. Didn't Babs describe our . . . ah . . . rather unorthodox relationship?"

"She said something about *Screw* magazine and enjoying mutual lovers . . . but, Gwen, I thought it was merely talk. Babs loves shock talk."

"But it's true, Kent. Now *don't* be a stiff."

"I'm trying to handle this."

Gwen guided Kent back to the sofa where she settled him in the middle and then continued. "Let me explain a few things. Then we can all relax. We all like excursions in life . . . double lives . . . hidden lives . . . playing various roles. I'm one woman in Menlo Head, quite another beyond our quaint borders. I have two vocabularies, two wardrobes, two hairstyles, two of everything."

"I can see that," Kent said, running his eyes along her body. He had never seen this Gwen Halston.

"You're intrigued with the British. Do you remember the patter song, 'You can do at the sea side what you can't do in town'?" Gwen said.

"I think I remember it."

"Regardless, we're all rather animal in nature. Only the hypocrites say we're not. We need erotic explorations now and then. It's kept my marriage together. Roger *is* chilly. He used to get his rocks off inside me . . . now he counts money and comes more frequently."

"He's my client and friend."

"Of course, but, Kent . . . you have double desires?"

Kent thought a moment and nodded in perfect agreement. He broke into his first genuine smile.

"I'm here . . . you're here . . . we're both married. We're both on the Menlo Head morals committee, figuratively speaking, of course," Kent said.

Babs and Gwen broke into laughter.

"You get a smack for that one," Gwen said, leaning over and pressing her soft, open lips against Kent's mouth. This time it was no near miss.

"You see, Gwen," Babs beamed. "I told you he's not a stiff; his cock graduated from Vic Tanny's. Wasn't your cock on the honor roll, Kent?"

"It graduated summa cum laude."

"So we agree that a little reconnaissance trip into erotica builds up the mind and body," Gwen said, clapping her hands.

"As long as no one knows," Kent said.

"Darling, no one does know. No one will. As Wellington said, 'Be discreet in all things, and so render it unnecessary to be mysterious about any.' And how is your marriage coming along, Kent?" Gwen asked. "I heard something about a little altercation on the dock one night. You're not intending to murder poor Louise, are you?"

"I lost my head, and I've apologized. Everything's fine at Pigeon Hill. But Gwen, there's something else. What did you have in mind for this afternoon?"

"Sex."

"Oh."

"You see, Kent, I didn't bring Babs up to be selfish. When she told me that you were good, I decided that I should share. We both want you."

"Together?"

"Yes. Aren't you flattered?"

"Of course. And I'm not quite the prude you think I am, Gwen."

"But you've never been into a group scene, much less a momsie-daughter group scene?" Gwen said. "After all, my love, that's lesbo incest. Shame. The *last* taboo!"

Kent was wordless; he communicated by bobs of his head, smiles, agreement, but mostly he snuggled his face down to his martini glass, hoping to shield his flushed cheeks.

"Rest at ease," Gwen said. "But what interests you most,

Kent . . . and I can see it in your face . . . is how did all this begin? The etiology, as they say."

Again he nodded, urging Gwen to continue.

"Well, I was into horny excursions just after I married Roger, and I had Babs when I was only eighteen . . . she's more my age than Roger is. As I said, he's as lifeless as the money he rents. So I started to spend my summers in Cannes. It was my health spa; I needed Cannes in the summer to face Menlo Head in the winter. Yes, Kent . . . I did have affairs with women, beautiful, warm, loving, passionate women. Men, too, of course. Now there was this sexual leader along the Riviera for a while . . . a half-white, half-black mystic from some fucking mountainside who wore Gucci clothes with real gold chains. He was the erotic tour guide. We called him 'Sweet Daddy Joy.' "

Kent chuckled out loud for the first time, feeling the flow of the icy vodka.

"Sweet Daddy Joy," he repeated.

"And he had a fourteen-inch cock," Babs said. "Unbelievable."

"Is Sweet Daddy Joy still operating?" Kent asked.

"He disappeared," Gwen sighed. "He might have been grabbed for drugs, but some say he returned to his mountainside for more of the truth. It was a sad day when the horny prophet suddenly dropped out of sight. What sensuous summers we had . . . the game was never played exactly the same, and that made it creatively exciting. Now, Kent, with Sweet Daddy Joy's approval . . . wherever he's meditating . . . you're hereby invited into our elegant sporting club."

"I think the coffee-colored mystic would approve," Babs nodded.

"Sure. He's busy thinking now, Kent, so he can't approve you personally."

"What's he thinking about?" Kent asked. "Sex is sex."

"Hell, no!" Gwen blurted out. "It's an art! Or a form of art. That's what's wrong with most marriages. The partners

122

aren't sexual stylists or creators . . . they're just dull old humpers. Barnyard regulars. Sweet Daddy Joy is up in the Himalayas, trying to find an answer for all of us. Is life a fountain or a mountain? When he finds out, he'll return to Cannes."

Kent Morgan, the staid designer, chuckled to himself. "A mountain or a fountain?" With that, he got to his feet and moved to the bar. He thought that these women had lost their minds years before, but he was interested. One brain wave told him to get back to Menlo Head quickly, and the other said to stay for the sport.

His second urge prevailed.

CHAPTER TWELVE

It was the best of lunches, and the set, props and costumes were just as they should have been. The room was bathed in a dull white glare, and as the sun swung to the west, dropping behind the cluster of higher buildings towards Madison Avenue, the room lost its luminosity in the afterglow. The music was haunting, throaty, the words of a Frenchwoman crying for new love. The pictures on the wall were impressionistic nudes, some photographs, others steel engravings and mezzotints, but the center prop, Kent thought, was the most igniting.

They sat about a glass-topped Casa Bella Italian table. In the middle was a hexagonal marble base settled deeply into a lush carpet, but it was the thick glass which rested upon the foundation that fascinated Kent. He could see a lower erotic gambol, missing nothing, and yet on the table and above the table there was more to watch.

The wine glasses were crystal, and the napkins and plates were bone white. The accent of color was introduced through bowls of berries: blueberries, blackberries and raspberries. (Kent wondered where they had found them at this time of year.) The other offsetting color was the deep purple of Gwen's dress and matching spike heels, neutralized by the ebony of Babs's dress.

They had prepared the meal for effect, dressed for effect, moved for effect. Perhaps even the table had been selected for the views it offered. It was elegant foreplay, a well-designed stage set.

And Kent thought how exquisitely the women were turned out, with smooth, perfect hair, flawless complexions, revealing neckline plunges. Their diamonds seemed to lead the eye to their pearl-white breasts, which were not restrained by modesty. Gwen still wore her hat, and the entire impression was one of succulence.

"Both of you look like dreams . . . beautiful dreams," he said. "But you're dressed so formally."

Gwen reached towards a plump raspberry; she dipped it into the whipped cream, opened her glossy mouth and, with her tongue making small gyrations, reduced the berry as she spoke.

"Sweet Daddy Joy . . . used to say, 'Most people get undressed for sex.' His theory was much more stylish. He taught us to dress for passion."

Gwen moved her hand over her breasts quickly and sensuously to show Kent she wore no bra. She tipped her large pink nipple with the point of one fingernail; she parted her slit skirt, showing Kent that her stockings were held in place by a high-fashion garter belt. The inner assembly did not include bikini panties. She was bare.

She winked at Kent. "Deception, my love."

They began eating the thinnest crêpes Kent had ever seen. That course was counterpointed by the sucking and licking of the berries and very small bananas, which they pushed in and out of their mouths, playing out the delights to come.

CHAPTER THIRTEEN

Rod, whose head was reeling as much as Kent Morgan's, returned to Menlo Head; he went directly to his darkroom in the cellar to develop and blow up his negatives. He put them through the dryer and invited his mother into the darkroom.

"Mr. Morgan went to the brownstone today," Rod said sheepishly. "And I took some photos through the skylight."

He placed the twelve-by-fourteen blowups out on the darkroom table, and Bunny bent over and studied them.

"That's Babs and her mother."

"Right. They're having cocktails here; then they had lunch with Mr. Morgan."

"I hope they didn't see you climbing around on top of the building, Rod."

"No."

He showed his mother an entire set of shots, none of which revealed the true tease and expectancy of the lunch, except that each of the women, Bunny noticed, was seductively over-dressed for that time of day. She became aware that her son was tapping the side of the darkroom table and fidgeting with the chemicals, placing them upon the shelf and taking them down again.

Finally she said, "What's the matter with you, Rod?"

"I saw something else, too, Mother. After lunch I went to the second skylight . . . the one that looks down on the bedroom. The light was fading by then, and the bedroom was kind of dark. I didn't have my tripod for a time exposure . . . I was out of business photographically . . . but I looked through as best I could."

"And?"

"I don't know exactly how to say this . . . but they all went to bed together."

"Gwen and her daughter?"

"Yeah . . . and with Mr. Morgan. They all got involved."

"It was a group screw . . . that's what you're trying to tell me?"

"Yes, and, well . . . Mrs. Halston made love to her daughter and Mr. Morgan watched, and then he made love to both of them."

"Are you sure of this, Rod? You said the light was bad."

"No, I saw it, Mother, and I wish I hadn't. It was . . . ah . . ."

"Gross," Bunny said flatly. "I believe that's what the kids say. Incest . . . a threesie with a little incest stirred in for a kicker."

"What are you going to tell Mrs. Morgan?"

"I don't know yet, Rod. But promise me that you won't mention this to *anyone*."

"Christ, who'd believe me? Do you want me to keep taking pictures?"

"Yes," Bunny said, looking down at the blowups again. "I'm going to talk with Louise, but until I tell you differently, you continue with the pictures. And for God's sake, take along the proper film and tripod next time."

"I will, but this is kind of heavy, Mother. Maybe we shouldn't become involved."

"I'll decide that. You just do what I tell you . . . you're being paid for your services, not your advice."

Bunny went upstairs and tried to think. Ironically, she was the one who had nagged Louise to find out what was going on, but she never expected anything like this. That sanctimonious Kent Morgan. Shit! She was almost certain that if she told Louise what Rod had discovered, it would push the woman over the edge completely. Her friend was slipping further into regression each day, withdrawing from all but her pills and her booze.

Bunny decided upon a partial explanation; she would shelter one bit of information with another. It was the only humane thing to do, she rationalized, and it would give Louise Morgan a much-needed tonic, more helpful than all her tranquilizers.

She called Louise and told her to get right over there. Bunny used a facetious approach, explaining how she had hired her son to take the place of Mr. Hughes.

"I don't think you had any right to do that, Bunny. Frankly, I'm pissed," Louise said.

"Don't get pissed yet."

Bunny took out the photographs showing Kent, Gwen and Babs having lunch.

"And that's all there was?" Louise asked.

"That's all."

Rod was called downstairs, and he amplified upon the harmless luncheon without betraying in his voice or face what had gone on in the bedroom. Rod was excused, and Louise Morgan burst into tears.

"Oh, Bunny, why was I so distrustful? God, I fouled up! Do you think this is the extent of it?"

"Of course, dear. Put two and two together. A man doesn't screw a young girl and then join her for a family luncheon. You know how prim and prissy Gwen is . . . how could Babs and Kent keep a straight face in front of her? What happened, I think, is this. Babs did see your husband . . . and maybe it had something to do with the design commission. Perhaps they met one day in New York for lunch, but I can assure you nothing else went on. If it had, Gwen would never have been at that brownstone."

Bunny convinced Louise Morgan there was nothing to fear. That night, Louise's attitude changed, and it notched precisely into Kent Morgan's plans for the weekend.

Years before, Kent had mentioned his disdain for big,

sloppy dogs that rampaged through a house. After the ducks started coming down, Kent stamped his foot in that same direction when Louise was about to buy a team of prize Chesapeake retrievers.

"If you have to shoot ducks, you can get them yourself from a dinghy, but I will *not* have big working dogs around here."

"But the girls have been asking for a pet."

"They have goldfish and turtles . . . nice, neat little things. Why do they need a dog?"

Louise explained the difference between those creatures and a dog that would help make Pigeon Hill more of a home, not merely a house. Louise gave in on the working dogs, and Kent agreed that they could have a small watchdog. Louise chose a fine taffy-colored Lhasa apso puppy, and the little fellow, called Chairman Mao, soon won the hearts of all at Pigeon Hill, including Kent, who walked the dog late at night and played with him before he went to the design office.

Once a year, Saint James Episcopal Church in Menlo Head conducted a Saint Francis of Assisi service when the children brought their dogs and rabbits and pet raccoons to be blessed by the Reverend Alcott, a man who spoke in English tones as counterfeit as Kent Morgan's. The two men enjoyed a close relationship on a social, rather than a spiritual, level.

On the Saturday following Bunny's "disclosure" to Louise, Kent said to his wife, "Tomorrow we take the Chairman to be blessed."

And Louise, who was quickly emerging from the agonizing stall in her life, agreed: Mao would be brushed and groomed and made ready by the girls that day. He had a bath, and the combing went on until late that evening; even the children recognized the sudden new brightness at Pigeon Hill.

The Sunday service was scheduled for nine o'clock; it was a unique event, and even those who usually attended other churches in Menlo Head came to see the rites and to hear

129

Reverend Alcott conduct his inspiring service. To the blare of the great organ, the assembly of boys and girls holding dogs, cats, rabbits, altered skunks, tamed porcupines, turtles, lizards, tropical fish in bowls and fifteen other varieties of animals, including one baby leopard, stood about in their very best outfits, ready for the processional. The prelude consisted of the choir singing J. S. Bach's "Sheep May Safely Graze"; then Reverend Alcott mounted the steps to his pulpit and intoned: "Grace to you and peace from God our Father and the Lord Jesus Christ." The response came back: "Let us be glad and rejoice in the Lord. Songs will I make of your Name, O Lord Most High."

The Reverend Alcott continued: "Everyone who has an animal or plant or statue for the procession, please line up in the garth before the service. The procession will circle the nave of the church and return outside, where you can give your pet to someone or tie it in the garden for the duration of the service, if you wish. The procession will continue down the center aisle to the chancel, so that you may follow it to your seat. Well-behaved pets may remain in the pews with you during the service."

On signal, the processional theme began: "Marche Militaire," by Charles Gounod, "Where E'er You Walk," by G. F. Handel and "The Cuckoo," by Louis Claude d'Aquin. The children waddled up the aisle to the whimpering of puppies, woofs of dogs and meows of cats. As they passed the altar, they received a double bonus. In the spirit of Christian unity, Father Dominick Visconti of Saint Mary's Catholic Church in Menlo Head was the assistant blesser, or cocelebrant.

The Morgan children had drawn straws that morning to see who would have the honor of escorting Chairman Mao up the aisle, and Jody won. Louise dressed her very carefully in a dress of bright blue, her favorite color, with a matching ribbon to hold back her blond ponytail. Mao had a blue ribbon, too, which was coping unsuccessfully with his own flopping blond hair.

Suddenly Laurie, who was sitting between Louise and Cathy, nudged her mother and pointed. The Chairman wasn't used to discipline, usually running free around Pigeon Hill, and about halfway up the aisle, he'd begun straining at his leash and trying to duck under the pews. Jody pulled with all her strength, but it looked as if the Chairman was going to win out. Jody glanced back frantically for a moment, trying to locate her mother in the crowd. Then she turned around and yanked determinedly on the leash, and Mao knew he had had it. From then on, they proceeded placidly up the aisle.

As Louise gazed at her youngest daughter—she looked more like Kent than the others, with his light coloring and deep blue eyes—she suddenly felt tears stinging her eyes. She had been so selfish, wallowing in her own preoccupation all these weeks, and she knew the children had suffered, too.

After the pets had been endowed with God's grace, the rest of the service took on a slight animal tinge. Psalm number eight mentioned, besides people, sheep and oxen, birds of the air and fish of the sea; the collect of the day included Saint Francis of Assisi and his animals of the realm. The sermon delivered by the rector was appropriately full of the right syrup as the Boy Scouts moved up and down the aisles with pooper-scoopers and bottles of pine-scented Lestoil.

Reverend Alcott said that he wished he could speak to animals the way Dr. Doolittle did. Then he became serious, reminding everyone that there were two incidents in the Bible that mentioned talking animals: the snake with Adam and Eve and the donkey in the Book of Job. He summed up his oratory by telling everyone that he had watched two robins that week building their nest, taking turns sitting on the eggs and bringing the babies food. "Maybe we should learn from the birds how to make our lives more manageable."

Louise smiled to herself. There were no robins in Menlo Head that early in the year, and besides, the father robin never sat on his wife's eggs. Other species did, but not robins.

Even the pastor was phony, she thought, but he took his license from those around him.

After the service, everyone came outside to pet the animals. Bunny greeted Kent in his long black robes with a conciliatory smile, but she wondered just who were the true animals. At least Louise looked reasonably happy as she herded Chairman Mao and all the kids into the station wagon.

For Louise, it was a time of rebuilding trust, in herself and in their marriage, but the repair work was sluggish because she felt guilty and ashamed. How could she ever have brought herself to doubt Kent just on the basis of a few false vouchers? Her sense of inadequacy and failure continued through the first weeks of April, but at least Kent had moved back into the main house, and they had made love once, although on a night when they were both doused in alcohol.

Each April, the Menlo Head Yacht Club held its new members' party. It was more of a look, see and size-up affair, so that the old guard could check on the decisions of the membership committee. The no-charge Bash 'n' Buffet, as it was called, was also billed as the official opening of the club for the summer months. The club burgee was hoisted on the jackstaff; there was a prayer by Reverend Alcott, invoking the Lord's protection for all those who went down to the sea in yachts (at least those flying the Menlo Head Yacht Club flag); and, most importantly for Kent this year, the club also chose this day to present its new flag officers.

And he was now one of them.

For years Kent had dreamed of becoming a commodore of the Menlo Head Yacht Club, a position usually reserved for older and fatter members who were honored for their devotion to club affairs.

Commodore Barnes had called Kent over during December of the previous year, saying that the vice commodore was gravely ill. Would Kent take his place on a pro tem basis? In the meantime, the senior man died, and Soggy Oggie asked if Kent would continue the duties of vice commodore.

But after the incident of the lobster boat and the unleashing of Kent's fist against his wife's jaw, the commodore again talked to Kent to make sure that things had been patched up at Pigeon Hill. Kent assured Ogden that everything was settled, and the commodore upheld his appointment of Kent Morgan as a club officer. Still, Oggie was uneasy, but he rationalized Kent's actions to himself by saying that it all began when he asked that the lobster boat be removed from the club dock.

So on opening day Kent Morgan, in a new tailored uniform, stood in a line with the dignified commodores as the flag was ceremoniously hoisted through the squeaky pulleys by Ralph, who was turned out in a secondhand officer's uniform of the Swedish Navy.

When the gold-and-white burgee hit the spring breeze, a gentle round of applause rippled about. The club was open. Oggie stepped up and said, "I want to welcome Menlo Head's brilliant naval architect to our ranks as vice commodore. You all know Kent Morgan. Good to have you aboard, Kent. So that's it, and let's start our fifty-fourth season with happiness and encouragement. Once again, it's great seeing you all. The bar is open . . . the cocktail flag is hoisted!"

Throughout the invocation and Oggie's remarks, Gwen and Babs, in their most conservative and high-necked dresses, stood in the front row. The Halston women eyed Kent with easy, smug looks.

One of the more attractive couples accepted for membership that year were the Bianchis, and everyone agreed that the membership committee had done its job well. The new members were rich, and they drove a Ferrari.

No Italians had ever been admitted to the club. In fact, Irish Catholics had only broken the barrier in Menlo Head just after World War II, but Antonio Bianchi was a noble Italian, a slender, aristocratic man who headed up the New York office of the Bank of Milan. His wife, Jill, a former model, was from an entrenched Saint Louis family, a stunning woman who looked every inch her profession: a fashion editor for *Vogue*. Jill had served on the magazine's Italian-edition staff before being transferred to the home office in Manhattan.

The chattering party finally broke up at ten o'clock that night, and Louise, with the laughter still ringing in her ears, said to her husband, "Let's have a party for the Halstons. I like Gwen and Roger . . . also, we could include the new members, the Bianchis."

Kent sobered quickly. "Why the Halstons?" he asked.

"Well, the yacht's going to be launched next week, you said. Why don't we have it towed up here . . . put it at the dock? It'll be a great advertisement for you and a chance to express your appreciation to Roger."

Kent agreed reluctantly, thinking that somehow there would be a wrong gesture, an ill-conceived joke or a slip, that would expose the Halston-Morgan group affair. He called Gwen the very next morning.

"Gwen . . . ah . . . Louise wants to give a party in your honor."

She did not answer at once; then slowly her slight laugh swelled into a hilarious outburst. "Is she honoring our sport fucks?"

"Not funny," Kent said. "Listen, I hope we can play it cool, and, goddamn it, you two almost made me break up at the club yesterday."

"Just bite your lip, dear heart. Anyone who can screw like a midnight cowboy can certainly contain a little laughter. And we're putting you down on our calendar for another action afternoon. Are you ready?"

"More than ready," Kent said, "but I'm uneasy about this party."

"For Christ's sake, grow up. No one's going to say anything. I told you the rules . . . discretion all the way. How the hell do you think we've pulled this off for so many years? We're never clumsy. Cheer up. And by the way, watch your slick Italian friend there . . . he has a hard-on for Louise."

134

"Don't be ridiculous."

"Keep an eye on him. He's a ladies' man. All Italians are."

During that week when Louise usually would have been preparing for spring—scraping and painting *Workboat*, furrowing the ground for vegetable planting, mending the nets for dragging and nailing the lobster pots—she postponed the rituals and organized the biggest party in the history of Pigeon Hill.

There would be two orchestras, a huge tent, an extravagant buffet. While the party was supposed to honor the Halstons and the new couple, Louise was striving for another effect; she desperately wanted the entire community to know that the Morgan marriage was never stronger. After all, husbands and wives in the middle of marital disputes do *not* throw large, costly parties if a breakup and a court battle are tentatively scheduled.

CHAPTER FOURTEEN

The second Pigeon Hill had been built on the heavy stone foundations of the old house, and the landscaping followed the lines of the original terracing. The house was rectangular, except for the bow of the dining room placed between the kitchen and living room, all of which faced out on Long Island Sound. To each side of the dining room there were two doors leading to a flagstone terrace where tables could be set up for a summer dinner party, allowing the guests to reach the dining room for the buffet in an orderly traffic pattern: in one door and out the other. The terrace was raised seven feet from the lower grade level, and one had to descend eleven steps set in a quarter circle to a perfectly flat lawn measuring ninety by one hundred and ten feet. On the eastern border of this expanse, the grade rose to a brow of rhododendron plantings and fell away again to an easy sloping lawn of some four hundred feet, where it met the water in a large, gently scalloped curve of concrete, the seawall.

When the Morgans bought the house, they could not understand why such a large rectangle of tightly woven grass bordered their terrace. For two years after they moved from the apartment in New York, Kent and Louise believed that the grass plateau beyond the terrace must have been a croquet course; that easy afternoon sport had seemed popular in the time when Pigeon Hill was going through its halcyon days.

One Sunday afternoon in the summer of their second year in Menlo Head, an old, shiny Buick, a four-holer, arrived in the circular driveway. It was driven by a gaunt chauffeur who opened the door for an old lady in a white brocade dress. She introduced herself as Mrs. Marjorie MacAllister, of the New York and Southampton MacAllisters.

She said she had come to Pigeon Hill as a young girl just before World War I, and since she was driving up to Hartford to visit friends, she thought she would simply swing by and see the place to which she had not returned since 1919.

"I hope you don't mind my nostalgia journey, Mrs. Morgan. I heard the old house burned down sometime in the twenties."

"I believe it was 1924," Louise said. "At least, that's what several merchants in Menlo Head told us."

"Oh, yes. Well, I had many happy times here, and Pigeon Hill was filled with important guests . . . Swope, and I don't mean young Herb, and the other newspaper people were always around and literary people, too. Sinclair Lewis came here when he was young, and so did Eugene O'Neill. I remember that dear man, Flo Ziegfeld, arriving with seven of his Follies girls, and while we all sat out there on the terrace with a stand-up piano, the girls went through their kicks on the tennis court. His wife, Billie Burke, was provoked as usual."

The words "tennis court" touched Kent's ear with a reassuring bounce; his early Locust Valley life had been linked to fine tennis courts and yachts, each maintained without regard to cost.

"Where was the tennis court?" Kent asked the old lady who was still keen, despite her ninety-odd years; her porcelain skin was stretched across her bony face as tightly as the gut on a snare drum.

"Right out there," she said, pointing to the terrace. "The steps were built like a Greek amphitheater's . . . we used to sit and watch the lawn tennis games, and we all played with the pro who was invited to hit balls with the guests every Sunday."

The old lady left, and that night Kent and Louise walked

over the even expanse beyond the terrace; the mystery was solved.

"Let's resurrect the tennis court," Kent said. "I can see it now . . . a beautifully manicured grass court . . . and all of us sitting up on the terrace, sipping drinks in quality white ducks, of course, and those floppy FDR tennis hats . . . watching the games. Who else has a grass court around here?"

"There're six at the Field Club," Louise said in her precise way.

"Of course, darling . . . but I mean a private grass court. That's true class, Louise . . . just like having a home squash court or one's own polo field."

"I didn't know you liked tennis, Kent."

"We played it all the time at Piping Rock. Frankly, Louise, it would be good for business. I'll have my blueprints in the library along with the yacht models, and we'll entertain. That's the only pitch a yacht designer has, a certain look."

"Darling, I know how much you'd like a tennis court, but I think we should use the ground to raise vegetables."

"Vegetables?"

"Yes, we can feed ourselves. Certain types of vegetables like the salt air. That's what we did on the Bay."

The argument—the tennis court versus the vegetable garden—continued for weeks. It was another symbolic thread of their disparate upbringings.

Kent, among others, felt that these divisions were residues of the Civil War: the Northerners being clean, correct and highly intelligent, while the Southerners were land disciples, propagating horses, crops and acreage as gentlemen farmers. Hay people.

When Kent argued on behalf of the tennis court instead of the vegetable garden, he used inverted logic, claiming that the home court was really an outgrowth of Eastern thinking and heritage. "Our way of life," he said.

But Louise's logic ran straighter than Kent's, and she spotted his inbred snobbism at once.

"You're giving me the New York establishment line. That's

138

a fable. Thomas Jefferson, who wrote the great paper, lived in Virginia . . . Washington was a Southern planter . . . and Atlanta's come a long way from the day Sherman reduced it to ashes. I'm not a Scarlett O'Hara . . . some giddy dreamer. I want the vegetable garden to teach the children survival, and you play your tennis at the club."

"But you miss the point. It's not for me. The grass court is for *us* . . . not my business . . . *our* business."

Louise prevailed. The garden went in.

Kent withdrew. It was another incident like the ducks and the "funny suits," a defeat of purpose and principles. He asked himself again: Was he the master of Pigeon Hill or the well-dressed prisoner within?

Kent never played tennis after that. He politely rebelled.

When it came time to decide where the party tent was to be battened down and yanked up, where the wooden floor panels were to be laid, the fusty argument flared up. Louise said that late April was the time to get the seeds in the ground because of the rain, but Kent responded that there was no sense in putting up a tent anywhere except over the leaf-covered earth of the garden.

"It's the only flat place we have. If it's set on the other lawn, it will have to be jacked up and leveled. That will cost us a lot more . . . and, besides, we need the tent by the kitchen so we can serve the buffet."

Louise, who was well into her mending mood by this time, trying to please Kent, said uncharacteristically, "Darling, if you think the tent should go over my vegetable garden, then that's where it will go."

They came in three large stake trucks a week before the party, and from Louise's upstairs window, she watched the caterer lay down the eight-by-ten wooden panels.

"What about our garden?" Laurie asked her mother one afternoon.

"We might not get it in this year," Louise said. "Other things are more important now."

Her daughter did not understand, but Louise sensed that

certain changes were coming to Pigeon Hill, invasions.

And she was correct.

It was a Saturday night party.

"Scott and Zelda would have loved this," Betsy Potter said in her ethereal voice borrowed, it appeared, from the age of Elizabeth Barrett Browning.

Kent Morgan looked at his vaporous neighbor. "How do you know, Betsy?"

"It's a beautiful night. All the stars are out, and the moon is sending dancing patterns across the ripples of Humble Cove . . . those were the nights Scott wrote about. He detested foul weather. And do you see those beacons?"

"Yes," Kent said patronizingly. "Those are the buoy lights marking the entrance to the Menlo River."

"Maybe not. They could be on the dock of West Egg, and this could be East Egg. And all the people here look like Scott's crowd."

Kent agreed with a nod, and the woman, who hummed continuously, glided off across the terrace in the direction of the great candy-striped party tent.

Upon considering it, Kent thought perhaps Betsy was right; it was a Fitzgerald night, if that meant laughter springing from sure, trouble-free merriment. The women in long, floating dresses and the men, mostly in white flannels and dark blue coats, strolled about the damp, glistening lawns of Pigeon Hill with self-satisfied grins; the music played on amid their tinkles of light chatter. It was a page out of the past, or out of a present issue of *Town & Country*—timeless. This must have been the intent of the man who conceived Pigeon Hill: an elegant assembly of well-mannered, well-bred, well-dressed, well-moneyed guests enjoying themselves in a sylvan setting.

Kent forgot what it was costing; the memory of the Morgans' delightful party would linger on long after the bills were paid, and, too, several important Menlo Headers had spoken to Kent about possible design commissions.

"I'm moving to sail," one of the guests told Kent. "I'll be

damned if I'm going to pay a dollar forty for that diesel oil . . . hell with motor yachts. At least, the wind is free."

For Kent, the party was a compound victory. His success in the community was delicately balanced. Designing yachts during a deep, aggravated recession, or at any other time, was truly the most frivolous of occupations. Even a toy designer was more important, Kent thought; at least, nowadays they made educational toys for young people, but he was furthering the egos of grown-ups who required million-dollar playthings, the most luxurious extravagances in the world.

But to secure commissions for these unnecessary accoutrements was, as Kent told his wife, "like going uphill on a snowy afternoon." And to reach the brow of the incline demanded the right image of breeding and behavior. Talent on the drawing board was not enough in a socially knit community such as Menlo Head.

To own a Morgan custom-designed racing yacht was a status symbol to the local yachtsmen, and they, in turn, spoke to others over lunch. But to achieve a contiguous pattern of referrals, Kent knew his demeanor and image counted as much as his design skills. And the party proved, just as Louise had known it would, that there were *no* seams coming apart at Pigeon Hill; the bashing on the dock, a rare aside of conduct, was now forgotten.

The social parade at Pigeon Hill that night was akin to a gallery opening for Kent Morgan. His new Halston yacht, the state of his art, was tied to the dock, and the guests, some of whom were prospects, walked out to look at Roger's seven-hundred-thousand-dollar bauble. Kent stood there to receive the congratulations as a painter would during the first night of his one-man show.

Louise, in a simple long white dress, a new one she had ordered from Bergdorf's, looked radiant as she moved among the guests, laughing and talking. She had based her food on three varieties of gourmet cuisine: Oriental, French and northern Italian. In New York she found three chefs in each of the disciplines.

141

For the Oriental menu, she engaged three chefs from Benihana's. She even went so far as to rent three hibachi tables so her guests could sit down and watch the cook go through his flourishes, rapidly slicing the filet mignon and the tempura shrimp and twirling the salt and pepper shakers in the air. The Morgan girls, turned out in their best frocks, carried the food from the kitchen, where five secondary cooks lined up supplies for the professional chefs in the tent.

It was about ten o'clock, as the laughter rang deeper and the band played louder, that Cathy came up to her mother who was weaving slightly from her drinks, poured down now out of thanksgiving rather than despair. The children were confused that such a party would be given by their mother and father. The atmosphere at Pigeon Hill had been noxious, and suddenly it had blended into a spirit of instant joy; Cathy, speaking for her two sisters, wanted to know why. And being as direct as Louise, she asked, "What happened, Mom? Why the party?"

"I found out something, dear . . . I misjudged your father. There was nothing wrong . . . yes, yes," Louise slurred slightly. "There *was* something wrong . . . it was me . . . I caused myself . . . well, all of us, a lot of trouble, dear. I was unjustly suspicious."

She smiled at Cathy who still did not understand what had happened, only that it must have been extremely positive and auspicious.

Shortly after the hasty conversation with her mother, Cathy picked up two signals: her mother was being fawned over by the guest of honor, the Italian banker, who was dancing and smiling and whispering to Louise; and her father had also caught the drift of the man's moves.

"I've heard that you were an Olympic medalist," Antonio said to Louise, holding her closely as they danced.

"Oh, that was many years ago."

"But your children must be very proud of you," he persisted. "Do they not brag about their mother?"

Louise laughed. "We never really talk about it."

She tried to remember where she had put the silver medal she had won. Yes, now she recalled . . . under her obsolete bras in the bottom left-hand drawer of her dresser. In that moment Louise decided to take the medal to the local silversmith for polishing; then she would have a plaque made to house the piece of silver with the inscription underneath:

SILVER OLYMPIC MEDAL
Awarded to Louise Upton of
the United States Sailing Team
Olympic Summer Games
Japan, June 16, 1964

The only reason she had buried the medal was to avoid overriding Kent's honors: the cups, the plates, his pictures— all hymns to himself. But why shouldn't she show her honor?

After the long pause which Antonio interpreted as modesty, Louise said, "Yes, I was a silver medal winner in Japan . . . 1964."

"That's quite an accomplishment. I also sail in competition. I raced Dragons for ten years in Italy . . . and I'm thinking of commissioning your husband to design an offshore yacht for my account. I'd love to see the Halston sloop."

She smiled, nodding her head, and they left the tent immediately, heading across the lawns towards the finger pier. Louise believed that Antonio's request was sincere; being a yachtsman, he naturally wanted to see the latest in racing machines. She took his hand and led him towards the seawall. To Antonio, her hand was a hint of acquiescence.

The moon was beginning its swing across the lower sky, evoking a dim evanescent glow behind the long pier; the two sailboats, *Kerry Dancer* and Roger's prize named *Gwen*, slowly rocked to the rhythms of the incoming tide, their tall sticks picking up flecks of light.

Both the father and the daughter noted the wobbly

journey to the dock. First Kent moved out along the slope of the grass; then Cathy walked after him with a sense of foreboding.

Louise's head was fuzzy, and her eyes were slipping from focus to focus. She did not recognize the potential of Antonio's stares or the tighter grasp of his hand.

"What do you think of it, Antonio?" she asked, gesturing at the slick, cherry-red yacht.

His eyes scanned the deck hardwood, and they stepped aboard.

The tide was dead low. The sharp pinnacle rocks of the cove were high above nut-brown water; their slim sides grabbed the light from the moon, a beacon hanging indefinitely just over Oyster Bay, the notch of land directly across the Sound from Menlo Head. It was so bright that the Japanese lanterns strung out along the pier did not provide their intended flush and twinkle; they could not compete with the lunar glow.

Kent followed Louise and Antonio, tiptoeing towards the middle of the dock. The clacks of his English leather heels hitting the slat boards echoed against the exposed rocks, and he removed his shoes quickly with a flick of his wrists.

Cathy saw it in the backglow of the moon.

Kent knew that Louise had become a paradox, a contradiction in Menlo Head. She was an eccentric, yes, but no one forgot, or let it be forgotten, that this transfer from the "noblest Bay" was anything but a totally straight, dutiful wife who would never think of an extramarital affair, much less enter into one. The woman was a voluntary exile: above, beyond, outside, far away from the inner circle of Menlo Head "fun," meaning giggling, good-hearted affairs, totally unmessy.

Kent, a premier rationalizer, went catlike along the dock with mounting relish. To catch his wife with another man was a supreme conquest; it would affirm that the virtuous Louise was just like everyone else. He sought a tawdry scene. It would engender for him a tit-for-tat stronghold; the "you-do-it-so-I-can-do-it" relief.

What Kent saw did not disappoint him. He could view everything from his position within the shadows of the summer pavilion, and he smiled to himself; what fools they were. The forehatch of Roger's sophisticated, convertible sloop was plexiglass, designed that way to admit sunlight to the sail-handling area. The cabin light was on. Louise and Antonio had moved to the narrowest, most uncomfortable part of the hull where it flared towards the sharp, water-cutting bow. Kent reasoned they must have thought they would be safe since there was only one access to the craft, and that was far aft by the galley, some thirty feet from their nesting position.

Kent stood high above them, looking down at the two soft figures locked and unlocked in a series of swift embraces. His gaze was riveted on the couple with such passionate satisfaction that he was unaware of the rumble behind him. By the time he snapped his mind from profitable voyeurism to the noise, Cathy had whizzed past. She bounded down the gangplank, leaping onto the bow deck of Roger's yacht in one catapult over the lifelines.

The girl yanked up her pale salmon-colored party dress, her first, and knelt on her knees, pounding on the deck with her fists.

"He's looking . . . he's looking. Mom, he's here!"

CHAPTER FIFTEEN

Kent was off the dock and once more mingling with the guests under the tent by the time Louise and Antonio came back from the sloop. Cathy, after thumping on the fiberglass deck, ran, too; she did not wish to face her mother with the banker, and about twenty minutes later, Louise, considerably sobered, approached her daughter.

"Cathy . . . I had too much to drink, but there was nothing going on between Mr. Bianchi and me . . . just a harmless flirtation, that's all. But thank you, darling."

She reached out and touched the girl's cheek.

"I realize that, Mom. I didn't think anything else, but I saw Dad walking out there after you, and I was afraid."

"Afraid?"

"Well . . ." Cathy's eyes were fastened on the ground. "I knew you were celebrating with a lot of drinks and everything . . . and why not?" She looked up. "It's been so gloomy around here . . . I was glad you were laughing and having a good time. But I thought Dad was going to punch Mr. Bianchi . . . ruin everything."

"Sweetheart, don't worry." Louise pressed the girl close to her. "I shouldn't have been out there. It was dumb, but everything's going to be fine. I'm quite sober now. Thanks for coming to the rescue of your old mom, though."

She smiled and locked her arm in Cathy's, and the two of them strolled back to the party goers.

Kent felt a certain smug glow when he entered the bedroom at twenty minutes after one that morning. He turned to his wife and snapped, "How drunk were you tonight?"

"I had a few too many. But it was a celebration."

"I'm goddamn disgusted with you!"

She remained quiet, knowing how explosive Kent's temper could be if he thought his image had been tarnished. She was determined to be reasonable. She crossed to him and put her arms around his neck, ready to explain what had happened on the sloop; he tossed them off with a hasty fling and began to talk in a more strident voice which the three children heard through the bedroom door.

"You ought to be ashamed of yourself."

"Kent, don't wake the children. Can't we be civilized?"

"Civilized? What's civilized . . . you on the Halston yacht making love to some fucking Italian . . . and your own daughter trying to warn you! How in hell do you think that looks! Your own daughter breaking in on a fast screwing session!"

Louise reeled about with her fists loosely knotted and shoved her chin forward, the hard cords in her neck standing out. Kent's shirt was off, and the taut muscles of his stomach twitched with each jab of her voice coming at him in staccato waves. Her words were toned down to a deep guttural whisper, and that made her wrath all the more piercing.

"I wasn't making love to him, you fool. He kissed me and told me how beautiful I looked. I was drunk . . . yes . . . if I hadn't been drinking so much, I would *never, never* have gone to that yacht with a man I hardly knew. Now do you get that, sir? And why were you on the dock?"

He was backing slowly away from his wife. He felt the wall by the door and flattened himself against the jamb.

"You love those whys. I'll tell you. I wasn't going to allow that Italian bastard who should never have been allowed in the club to enter my house . . . fuck my wife . . . at my dock . . . on a yacht I designed . . . at a party I paid for. Is that enough?"

"You're on the wrong trip. I told you he wasn't fucking me. It was *nothing*."

He could see the madness in her eyes, the heated ignition. She kept her voice smothered, but the bass notes were clearly audible to the three children who were now outside their bedrooms, expecting the worst.

She started, "Now I'm going to lay it out for you. I hadn't planned to, but you've put me through a bloody hell for months! I know I'm drinking too much . . . taking Valium. I can hardly eat, and I've lost fourteen pounds . . . and it's all because of you. Just how dumb do you think I am, Kent? You didn't marry an idiot. I might be a country coarse-head, fellow, but I'm not feeble or barn-crazy."

"Listen to you. You're still high on pills or booze. You ought to hear yourself. For God's sake . . . stop it . . . what are you trying to say?"

"Guess!" she bellowed, breaking her low octave.

Kent moved himself out from the wall. He shuffled to the far side of the bed where he folded his arms and looked at the ceiling, thinking that his wife, the placid, sturdy one, had gone crackers. Her look in those seconds reminded him of Olivia De Havilland's stiff-necked scowl in the movie, *The Snake Pit*: the dissembling facade of a stunted mind.

Louise recited slowly, "You were in the duplex with Babs Halston on October eighth. You were with Babs on December eighteenth at One Forty-five East Ninety-first Street. You were with Babs and Gwen at the same address on March twelfth. Now, should I continue?"

His ego, his superior position, were demolished. He felt the first real alarm of his life, for here was the presence of a devilish spirit. His next move was conjured out of self-defense to give himself time to think clearly.

Kent threw his hands in the air and said, "I give up. I give up. How did you find out? Don't shoot."

Louise opened her smile. "You're terrible at affairs. The painter told me that Babs was in the apartment October eighth of last year. He didn't know her name, but he described her . . . long black hair . . . and since you were working with Roger, it didn't take too much acuity to put that one together. You lied to me, Kent. You said you were alone that afternoon. Now, on December eighteenth, the next visitation, something occurred quite by accident. You got a traffic ticket; the day the summons arrived from the police department, I opened it. I knew where you'd been and who lived there, because Lady Gwen blabbed it all around Menlo Head that her daughter bought a brownstone co-op on Ninety-first Street. Then we come to the interesting part. You and Gwen and her daughter met for lunch on March twelfth. How am I doing so far, Kent?"

Kent knew he'd lost the round, but very carefully he kept his expression and voice neutral. "How did you know about Gwen?"

"Simple. Very simple," Louise said.

No one, Kent figured, could have been in that apartment or known about the gymnastics inspired by Sweet Daddy Joy. He had to test Louise, but he thought it likely that either she or a detective had seen him enter the brownstone and, perhaps, Gwen ahead of him. Kent, on that foggy afternoon, dismayed first by Gwen's appearance and then gulping martinis to quell his surprise, had not noticed the two skylights. In any case, his mind had been occupied with the performances going on at eye level.

"You're putting me on, Louise," he said finally. "You don't know a damn thing."

She decided to bluff her way, and she strolled about the bedroom, thinking of how she could exploit Rod's photographs.

"You think so?" she said. "Ask me anything."

"All right . . . what does the apartment look like?"

"Let's see . . . it has a series of white modular couches . . . there's a coffee table in front. There are bookcases between the windows, and on the far side there's one of those hi-fi units up on a rolling cart . . . plenty of dials and lights. Now, towards the other side, I mean back by the kitchen, we have a glass-topped dinner table on a pedestal. Just beyond, there's a rolling maitre d' cart that acts as a bar. You and mumsie and daughter ate lunch there, and Gwen kept her hat on. Shall I continue?" She laughed suddenly, harshly. "Close your mouth, Kent . . . you look ridiculous. Didn't you realize that someone could peep through the skylights . . . and see what you were up to?"

Kent believed then that Louise had hired a detective and that she knew the entire gambit of that afternoon in the brownstone. He exhausted his lungs of air and felt a great hollowness and debilitation. His pride, his command, his composure had been looted, and he stood in the bedroom naked, having been, in one salvo from Louise, stripped of his offense. Kent could not refute the facts, and there was no way to squirm out of it. His own anger boiled like a cauldron. How could he be caught three times, during the only three times he had experienced extramarital sex? Was he that doltish, or was it plain bad luck?

"Why didn't you come to me and discuss this, instead of holding it in?" he asked, attempting to resecure his position.

"Oh, I tried to. Remember the morning I said to you, 'Is there anything you want to tell me?' "

He frowned. "Not really. You mean . . . confess? I had nothing to confess. Yes, I did see Babs and Gwen . . . it was quite harmless."

On the word "harmless," Louise believed that he was talking about a simple lunch with a mother and daughter, and it was an ironic gulf in their communication. She truly thought that Kent had merely been visiting with Babs; she had seen only dim photographs of the luncheon, and she remembered what Bunny had said: "Do you think a man who's screwing a college-age girl would invite her mother to lunch with them?"

Kent, on the other hand, believed that Louise knew everything, and he did not elaborate.

"Did you ask yourself why I saw Babs and Gwen?" he asked calmly.

"No."

"I'll tell you because *that's* the heart of this . . . not that I saw them. I was forced out of my own house, Louise. You have taken over the children . . . you never listen to me or my wishes . . . I'm just a tenant at Pigeon Hill . . . a rent-paying nonessential. You've brought up formidable females. They're tough and not even respectful or courteous. I won't go back and talk about the workboat . . . the farming . . . the ducks. Forget that . . . I don't have to travel back that far. Take tonight. My new sloop for Roger Halston, one of the best I've ever designed, with plenty of new ideas, was towed up here from the yard at four o'clock. Your daughters never so much as said to me, 'Dad, it looks great. Congratulations.' And I saw that superior attitude on your face when you looked at the sloop this afternoon, as much as to say, 'Here's a waste of money; the only vessel worth anything is my lobster boat,' or dragger, or whatever you call that goddamn thing of yours."

"I was going to mention Roger's yacht . . . but I've been busy planning for the party."

"See? See . . . you were planning for the party. Was I asked once about anything?"

"Yes, you were . . . the placement of the tent."

"That wasn't a concession on your part. There was no other place for the tent but just beyond the terrace. Oh, the facts are clear. It's obvious what you've done to our daughters and me . . . and I keep asking myself, what's it for? Where is it going to end? I don't get you, Louise. I never got you . . . ever since that day I went to Westerfield for the first time. So now you know what I did. What are you going to do about it?"

"Nothing."

"No divorce?"

"I don't believe in divorce. I guess we have to begin by talking to each other . . . not sending messages through silence and hurt looks."

She was speaking to him in a guttural monotone, as if

her thoughts were sapped of meaning or the slightest sense of regret. To Kent, she was just as monarchical as always, living in a fortified chateau with mullioned windows so sinewy that an assaulting arrow could not get through. And he felt his anger come alive again, the bristle of a caught man.

"You didn't trust me . . . you wouldn't talk to me . . . and you hired a detective to watch me. Not for a divorce action . . . just to pile up some more cards so you could have a little fun yourself."

"Take that back!"

"It's the truth!"

He began pushing his stiffened fingers into her sternum, bobbing her back a little on each of his words, "Isn't it? Isn't it? Isn't it? Tell me . . . can you admit something? *Go ahead . . . go ahead . . . go ahead!*"

His voice shrieked, and his eyes were moist. As Louise backed away, seeing his rage, her heel caught the delicate leg of a Hepplewhite side table crowded with silver-framed photographs of his family and the Morgan yachts, including JP's *Corsair*. The overloaded, top-heavy table went over, and the pictures plunged to the floor where the plush oyster-white carpet ended and the parquet floor began. There was a resounding crash, a crunching of glass as her heels continued back, pulverizing what remained of the family photograph collection. He continued to force her through the sea of splintered crystals, still shouting: "Isn't it! Isn't it!"

To the children, it sounded as if Kent had smashed their mother once again. In a body, they leaped at the door handle and entered the bedroom to protect her.

"Get the hell out of here!" Kent howled.

The faces of their parents were red, and their brows were drenched in beads of sweat. Cathy sprang towards the back of Kent's belt, hoping to drag him away from Louise; Laurie and Jody snapped their small arms about Kent's elbow, holding back what they thought would be another un-leashed fist.

"Out!" Kent screamed. "All of you!"

They did not let go, and with all the might in him, Kent spun around, trying to shake off his children; he sent them sailing into the air in a violent twist of his body. Cathy flew towards Louise's feet. She put her hand out to break her fall, but her palm came down upon the splinters of glass, and her flesh was mangled and ripped. Laurie, the eleven-year-old, being lighter, went in the other direction over the velvet-covered window seat, and her head crashed through the bottom pane of the window. When she brought it back, the jagged glass had etched gashes in her face. Louise saw the instant spout of blood. Little Jody was knocked into a sprawl across the chaise longue, and all the girls started screaming. Without a split second's thought, Louise notched her fist, took aim and delivered her knuckles into Kent's mouth with such velocity and power that his lower teeth shuffled on their roots and his mouth filled with blood. He stumbled, swallowed blood and then spit it up in a great hacking cough.

Carrie, who slept just under Kent's design studio in the carriage house, heard the breaking glass and cries from within the big house. She immediately thought that an in-truder had forced his way in; perhaps one of the caterers had returned to rob them.

She sat up quickly and dialed 911.

"Menlo Head police," came a yawning answer.

"This is Carrie, the housekeeper over at Pigeon Hill. Someone's broken into the house . . . there's a terrible fight going on!"

"We'll be right there."

Four squad cars and the paramedics were immediately dispatched with the instruction: "Felony in progress."

Four minutes later, the police arrived, parking their cars on the main street leading into the curved driveway of

153

Pigeon Hill. Taking shotguns, eight officers fanned out along the grounds to prevent the "burglar" from escaping. The paramedics drew their mobile intensive-care unit to the far side of the road, and the three men waited, ready for orders over their walkie-talkies.

Sergeant DiMaggio, called the Clipper for his namesake, was in charge of the operation. A burly, second-generation Italian, he was one of the few members of the sixty-two-man Menlo Head force with a college education. He heard indistinguishable screeching from the upstairs, a low hum of crying and muted talk. The Clipper circled the house, trying every door; there was no evidence of forcible entry, and the sergeant had heard—the drums in the town beat wildly—that Kent Morgan had recently smashed his wife in the jaw. The Clipper sized up the howl at Pigeon Hill as a domestic quarrel. (It was the practice of the Menlo Head police *not* to become involved in such altercations; he was about to withdraw when Carrie came across the lawn in her bathrobe.)

"I heard the children scream . . . somebody's in there."

"I don't think so. The doors are all locked," he told her.

"What are you going to do?"

"Well . . . ah . . . I don't think we have to worry about it," the Clipper said as the other officers gathered about him.

"If you won't do something, I will!" Carrie screamed out, taking a wad of keys from her pocket and shaking them in the face of the tub-bellied sergeant. "Why don't you go in?"

"You called and said there was an intruder. We don't have probable cause to enter the house without some suspicion of a crime being committed."

"Officer," Carrie said, losing her patience, "I heard screams . . . I can still hear those children crying. Isn't that enough?"

(Technically, it was not enough to enter a premise, but the Clipper waved the others forward and made his way towards the kitchen door, following Carrie.)

"Leave those shotguns outside," the Clipper told his men.

DiMaggio climbed the stairs alone, and when he reached the second floor, there was no doubt in his mind that he had every legal right to enter Pigeon Hill forcibly early that morning. Two of the children were huddled in the hall. Cathy was crying softly, a large, blood-soaked towel wrapped around her hand, and Laurie had a reddened pillow over her face. The inside of the bedroom was a mass of wreckage. Kent clasped another towel to his mouth, and Louise was sitting on the bed, holding Jody, and they were both sobbing.

Carrie screamed, rushing towards Louise. The Clipper was frozen as his eyes swung about the room. There was so much splattered blood over the carpet, the turned-back bed, the curtains and even the walls that the Clipper without hesitation pushed his walkie-talkie to his lips, saying, "Paramedics . . . get up to the second floor . . . quick!"

"We don't need you," Kent said, pulling the towel from his mouth so he could speak. "This is a family problem."

"The children are under age, Mr. Morgan . . . it's a police problem. If you and your wife want to kill each other, that's one thing, but these children are injured, and I'll have to ask you and Mrs. Morgan to come down to headquarters."

The paramedics had arrived by this time, and they began looking over the children.

"These two will need some stitches," one of the men said to Louise, indicating Cathy and Laurie. "I believe the little girl will be okay."

"Yes . . . yes . . . get them to the hospital," she said. "I'll call Dr. Driscoll."

"What happened here?" one of the paramedics asked her.

"Don't say a goddamn thing, Louise!" Kent yelled, gurgling the words through a mouthful of blood.

"Just tell me something, Mr. Morgan," the Clipper asked. "Was there an intruder in this house?"

"No."

"I want you to come down and make a statement."

"Like hell I will. You can't force us out of here."

"Do you want me to go back for a warrant?"

Ignoring him, Kent walked out into the hall and leaned down to Cathy.

"I'm sorry, darling. You should have let your mom and me solve this."

The young girl said nothing.

Kent continued downstairs. He stopped in the kitchen to spit the blood from his mouth, wondering just how much force Louise had in her sinewy wrists and forearms. Still holding his towel, he went to the library where he looked up the number of his attorney; Phil Cummings, a Harvard-trained lawyer, handled the Morgans' private work, plus that of the design firm. Kent dialed, and Irene, Phil's wife, awoke from a deep sleep.

"Is Phil there?"

"Who's this?"

"Kent Morgan, Irene . . . I have to speak to Phil right away."

She nudged her husband, who took the phone.

"Kent, are you still partying?" the lawyer said. "What time is it?"

"I don't know. Listen, Phil . . . we had a little argument over here. The children were involved . . . a couple of them are cut, and I have a bleeding lip. Louise slugged me."

"Oh, Christ."

"Carrie called the police, damn it! I have a houseful of cops, plus the paramedics. Clipper's here . . . that ball buster . . . he wants me down at the station to make a statement."

"Did you say anything, Kent?" Phil asked, his voice becoming clearer and more defined.

"No."

"For God's sake . . . don't, but what happened?"

"I caught Louise aboard Roger's sloop, making a little love with the Italian . . . Bianchi. I want him out of the club, Phil. Out! I'm going to talk to Ogden about him."

"Forget that now. Go on."

"Well, I accused Louise of being with him. I had a right to, didn't I?"

"I suppose . . . but, Kent, get to the point. How did the fight start?"

"Louise tripped over a table full of stuff. Everything broke, and the kids must have heard the glass break because they all rushed into the room and grabbed my hands and feet."

"Did you hit the children? Think, Kent . . . it's very important."

"Of course not. I merely tried to get them off me."

"You said they were cut?"

"Laurie put her head through the window, and Cathy accidentally pushed her hand into some broken picture glass."

"Listen to me carefully. Go get Clipper. Put him on the phone, and tell Louise not to say a goddamn thing. I'll hold on."

Kent went upstairs as the paramedics were helping the children out of their nightclothes while holding compresses over their cuts.

"Louise," Kent whispered. "Don't say anything to the police. Phil Cummings is on the phone. He wants to talk to Clipper."

"I'll tell them the whole story," she blurted out.

"Louise, don't do that. Take Phil's advice. I'm sorry for what happened . . . but don't make it worse. I beg you."

Clipper overheard the conversation in the hall and said, "Mr. Morgan, are you ready? We'll take the children over to the hospital. You can join them later."

"I want Dr. Driscoll there," Louise said.

"All right," Clipper nodded. "Call him and say you'll meet him at the emergency room. First, though, I want a statement."

"My lawyer, Phil Cummings, wants to speak with you, sergeant," Kent interrupted. "Pick it up there."

"I don't have to speak to him, Mr. Morgan."

"And we don't have to leave with you."

Clipper stiffened. The sergeant was a man of intelligence and fairness who abhorred working among the rich of Menlo Head. He knew that anything from drugs to murder could be covered up in the town with the right money in the right pocket. And when the wealthy killed each other, it was somehow dismissed on the grounds of mitigating evidence. What frustrated the sergeant was the dreary excuse: "I thought my husband was an intruder, so I shot him." That had been the defense in two killings during the years the Clipper had served on the force, and it had revolted him each time.

He picked up the phone in the bedroom. "Sergeant DiMaggio."

"Sergeant, this is Mr. Cummings. What's the trouble over there?"

"We were called to Pigeon Hill on the complaint of the maid. When we got here, everything upstairs, at least in the bedroom, was in a shambles. Two of the children are bleeding a lot . . . and Mr. Morgan's face, around his mouth, is twice the size it should be. I simply want both the Morgans to make a statement."

"Did you actually see anyone being hit, Sergeant?"

"I saw the aftermath, Mr. Cummings. I know the law, too. There was violence, and I can smell the whiskey a mile away."

"The Morgans drink vodka, not whiskey."

"They're drunk, and the children are hurt . . . might be serious. I want a statement."

"You don't have probable cause, Sergeant. You saw nothing with your own eyes. How do you know the children didn't strike each other?"

"I've been in law enforcement nineteen years . . . I know what I'm looking at."

"I've been a lawyer twenty years, and I know you're inside a premise where you don't belong. Illegal trespassing, Sergeant DiMaggio."

"I acted upon a complaint . . . the housekeeper called."

"She's not a parent . . . she's not the legal owner of Pigeon Hill. There's no probable cause for you to be there, or for the Morgans to make a statement. Let me put you on notice. If you arrest Mr. and Mrs. Morgan, you'll be exceeding your immunity as a deputized officer. You'll be wide open for disciplinary action within the department. You'll also be open to civil suit. I plan to advise my clients that there's a cause of action. So decide if you want to take that kind of exposure."

"I want a statement," the Clipper said crisply. "I heard that Mr. Morgan hit his wife in the jaw sometime back."

"That's hearsay, and it has no bearing on this matter. I don't believe anyone is lodging a complaint. Is there a complaint?"

"Wait a minute."

The sergeant put down the phone, walked out into the hall and asked Louise, "Mrs. Morgan, do you want to file a complaint?"

She did not answer. Kent heard the question and said quickly, "She tried to kill me. Look at my mouth."

The sergeant returned to the bedroom.

"Mr. Morgan will file a complaint. He says his wife tried to kill him . . . and he's got a big lip to prove it, so I'll act on a pro forma complaint."

"For Christ's sake . . . put him on the phone!" Phil yelled.

"Mr. Morgan . . . your lawyer, sir."

Kent took the phone again.

"Kent, forget the complaint. Get hold of yourself. Both of you are in trouble. The sergeant knows he can't arrest you unless he gets a bench warrant from Judge Shallaway. I doubt if he'll issue one because the police didn't see anything. But that's not where it ends. The Clipper will make a detailed report . . . he has to do that under law. This complaint could be turned over by the chief to the social service people and the juvenile authorities. Shallaway will hold a preliminary hearing; then the report becomes a public document . . . and in two minutes, *The Herald-Statesman* will print it."

"Print what? No one hit the children . . . it was simply an accident."

"I'm talking about appearance, Kent . . . the way it looks. You had an argument . . . it turned bloody. Now listen . . . first we have to prevent Clipper from making his report. The newspapers will devastate you, Kent, and the juvenile authorities will snatch it up. I'm going to call Walt Turpin. He was at the party tonight."

"What's he going to do?"

"The mayor has certain ex-officio privileges. He appoints Chief Caramati and the judges. We'll meet in Walt's office . . . he owes me a couple of favors. Now make *sure* you get Louise over to Town Hall, and comb your hair and wear a tie. Put the Clipper back on."

Kent handed the phone to the sergeant. Phil Cummings spoke in a soft, cooperative voice, "Sergeant, my client has agreed to go downtown. We'll meet at the mayor's office . . . I'll have the chief there."

"Why not meet at the police department?"

"Sergeant, let's be reasonable about all this. We want to help the Morgans if there's a dispute. We wish to be co-operative. If we adjudicate this through regular channels, we'll only injure the entire family. These are intelligent, worthwhile people, not common criminals. We have one duty, Sergeant . . . to help them solve their problems, not cause more problems through mishandling. Now you wait there . . . the chief will call."

"Mr. Cummings," Clipper said, "I've seen children abused . . . neglected . . . I'm seeing it right here in this house tonight. Now you get the mayor, the judge and the chief in one room and try to smooth this over, but even if I'm fired, I'm going to push it towards a hearing."

"Then you do it at risk," Phil said as he put the phone down.

CHAPTER SIXTEEN

The Menlo Head Courthouse was both an anachronism and a symbol of Menlo Head's vision of itself. In one sense, the old sandstone building was a relic of a much older judicial system, built during the years when Connecticut, like most other states, ran local magistrates' courts, the comfortable and democratic system of hometown justice.

The court of first impression in Menlo Head was to convene early that morning in the mayor's office, two doors down from Judge Shallaway's chambers, to make certain that this matter did not swell into the Superior Court of Stamford for all to see and hear.

Phil Cummings made these facts known to a still boozy Mayor Turpin. After explaining the situation the best he could at that point, he said, "The Clipper is out to hang my clients, Walt. We'd better put a call into Shallaway and meet right away."

"Do you know exactly what happened, Phil?" the mayor asked. "Sounds devastating to me . . . and didn't Ogden Barnes tell me something about Kent hitting his wife a while back?"

"I'm afraid it's true, Walt."

"What's wrong with that guy?"

"I don't know . . . but there's no sense in having the Clipper force it over to the juvenile authorities."

"Of course not. I'll call Caramati and Shallaway . . . have them meet us in my office. You know, we could get our

161

heads handed to us for squashing something like this. The judge might demand a hearing in the morning."

"Walt, if it goes into sessions, the Morgans . . . all of them . . . will be permanently damaged. We have to make *sure* there's no probable cause for a hearing."

There was silence for a moment as the mayor thought it over. "Well," he said, "Kent and Louise have always been our friends. They tossed a great party tonight . . . too bad it had to end up this way. I'll have Chief Caramati call the sergeant at Pigeon Hill."

Chief Caramati had already been awakened once and informed that a felony was in progress. Fifteen minutes later a second call had come to his home in Menlo Head's one marginal section, saying that his men had found a domestic dispute instead. The fifty-five-year-old man was just slipping off to sleep again when the mayor phoned and explained the situation.

"Sounds like a case of aggravated assault," the chief said, yawning. "We'll have to have a hearing . . . that's the law."

"Of course it's the law. That's why I'm requesting that all parties meet right now . . . while their recollections are clear. I'd suggest calling your sergeant. Tell him not to go back to the station . . . bring everyone involved to my office. I'm going there now," Mayor Turpin instructed, hanging up the phone.

The chief capitulated, grumbling to his wife as he pulled on his pants, "People . . . people . . . people . . . always in the middle of the night."

Dr. Tom Driscoll had also been informed of the incident by Louise, who simply said with a shrug in her voice that the children had fallen over a table holding glassware.

"Children will be children," she explained, hoping to slip a cliché past the doctor.

And then Phil Cummings called the Morgan home once more, after the sergeant had finished speaking to his chief.

"Kent, it's all arranged. Here's what I want. Have Louise

get dressed in something conservative . . . a suit of some kind . . . are you both sober now?"

"I'll say we are."

"Tell the paramedics to wait until she jumps into something quick. Then have her ride with the children in the ambulance, and make sure all of them go over to Memorial for a checkup. Then you put on a coat and tie . . . drive over to the hospital with the maid. Does she drive?"

"Yes."

"She was the one who called the police because she thought a burglar had entered?"

"That's what she said."

"Tell her to stick to that story . . . no tales about a family fight."

"She didn't see anything, and the only one who hit somebody was my wife."

"Will your oldest daughter attest to that?"

"Phil, are we bringing the children down to City Hall . . . and Carrie?"

"Just to prevent a hearing, yes."

"It's very late . . . and the kids are still upset."

"Kent, they'll be all right. We *have* to halt that hearing. Don't you understand what will happen if Shallaway convenes this in his courtroom? You'll be finished in Menlo Head. We have to get to work fast . . . damn fast. Please listen to me."

"All right . . . anything you say."

In the emergency room of Menlo Head Memorial Hospital, a highly endowed, 230-bed facility, Dr. Driscoll sewed up Cathy's hand with twenty-two stitches. He asked the girl, "How did this happen, Cathy?"

"I fell into some broken glass."

"Oh . . . who broke the glass?"

"A table went over . . . it was an accident."

"And your sister . . . did she put her forehead in the same glass?" the old doctor asked.

Cathy hesitated a minute and said, "Yes."

When the physician came to the other Morgan child, Laurie, he probed the deep cut in the young girl's forehead, plucking out pieces of glass.

"What does that look like to you?" he asked the assisting resident.

Fingering the small triangle of glass, holding it up to the light, the young doctor said, "Windowpane."

"That's what I thought."

Dr. Driscoll turned back to Laurie. "Young lady, you do know that I brought you into this world?"

"Yes," she said, still fighting back her tears.

"Are you going to tell me the truth?"

"About what?"

"How did you get this glass in your head?"

There was a pause as the girl thought over what her mother had said earlier. When they reached the hospital, Louise told them, "No matter who asks you . . . say it was an accident. You fell on some glass in our bedroom. Glass from picture frames. Please do this for me," she pleaded.

"It was an accident, Mom . . . that's all it was," the young girl said.

"Of course," Louise answered. "Just wanted to remind you."

"I fell on some glass," Laurie said again in answer to Dr. Driscoll's question.

"What kind of glass?" the doctor asked.

"From a picture frame."

After sixteen stitches had closed the lacerations in Laurie's head, the doctor approached Louise in the waiting room. He noticed her hollow eyes and trembling fingers.

"Come around to my office tomorrow, Louise."

"Why?"

"The glass in your daughter's head came from a windowpane . . . not a picture frame."

"How do you . . . ?"

164

"It was much too thick to cover a picture. Louise, how many years have we known each other?"

"Oh . . . ever since we came to Menlo Head."

"And we've always dealt in the truth, haven't we?"

"I guess so."

"You're not telling me the truth. Both your daughters are going to be fine . . . very small scars . . . and thank God, no physical impairments." He paused. "I should have taken your problems more seriously than I did the last time we talked, but in any case, we have things to discuss now."

She nodded numbly as he strode off in the direction of Kent Morgan.

The doctor asked Kent the same question he had asked the children as he stitched up the mess of tissue inside the designer's mouth.

"It was an accident," Kent said, echoing the family's rehearsed story.

The doctor grunted. "I've asked Louise to stop around to see me tomorrow."

Kent didn't respond; he thanked the doctor, and at four-fifty that morning, Carrie took the children in the station wagon and drove off towards City Hall. Kent and Louise, who had to prepare for what they were about to say, sat in the Maserati, thinking.

Kent spread his thickened lips to talk, feeling the ting of the novocaine plus the heaviness of his mouth; he turned his face to his wife and kissed her awkwardly on the cheek.

She laughed and said, "I'm sorry, Kent . . . it was just a lucky punch."

"You sure let me have it . . . but I deserved it."

"No, perhaps I did."

"Louise, I suppose we evened up the score. I saw something unpleasant, and so did you."

The "so did you" bewildered Louise. What had she seen? A picture of Gwen, Babs and Kent having lunch, or did he mean that the mutual spying had been equalized? The communication gap, their misunderstanding, was still continuing, even into the halls of the courthouse.

The Clipper had been adamant, and Kent realized there was just so much the mayor could do to control Judge Shallaway. The jurist had taken an oath of office to serve and uphold the laws of the state of Connecticut, and one of those laws said that: "The State shall have jurisdiction over the well-being of minors under the age of eighteen and the State shall take whatever appropriate steps as may be determined to protect the interests, physical, mental and moral, of those minors whose rights under law have been abused, neglected, or abdicated by parental conduct."

"We're in trouble," Kent told his wife.

"I know," she sighed. "That sergeant is pissed. He's one of those honest-to-God protectors of the unfortunate . . . he's out to save our children."

"Here's what Phil said," Kent began. "If this goes to a hearing in Stamford . . . maybe . . . we might as well sell Pigeon Hill and take off for Acapulco or someplace."

"I've always wanted to go there . . . maybe we should."

"Not this way, Louise."

"No . . ."

"Phil suggested that you take the rap, and that will calm everyone down."

"*Me?*"

"Just tell Shallaway what happened. Antonio kissed you . . . I happened to see it, as well as Cathy. We had an argument in the bedroom . . . the children entered to protect you. Then you smashed me in the face, and the children were cut accidentally. Say that you're going through the change of life and . . ."

"I'm not," she said quickly.

"Just *say* you are. You were upset and acted irresponsibly tonight by becoming involved with Antonio, and then you tried to, ah . . . teach me a lesson because I saw what happened and condemned you."

"Jesus Christ! Why should I take the whole blame?"

166

"Because we have to bullshit our way out of this . . . tell Shallaway what he wants to hear. In absolving me, the whole incident will be forgotten, and I have the puffed-up face to prove the story."

"What about the Clipper?"

"He'll have to go along with Shallaway and the chief of police. Louise, darling . . . we can mend the fences our own way . . . in our own time. I just don't want the fucking state of Connecticut telling us how to run our lives. If we can't handle our affairs, we don't deserve to be parents!"

Louise Morgan dropped her head. She thought of the total injustice of her becoming the sacrificial lamb in front of people she had known for at least fourteen years. Only a few hours ago, the judge, the mayor and Phil Cummings had been guests at their home to celebrate the earnest mending of the Pigeon Hill family.

Kent waited; finally she gave a slight nod of acquiescence.

CHAPTER SEVENTEEN

The Menlo Head Courthouse and City Hall were combined in a thick, blockish, two-story building constructed in 1921; the architecture was civic modern for the day, and the heavy facade facing Main Street was complete with six Doric columns and an entablature which said in Roman niched letters: Menlo Head Town Hall and Courthouse. To the left side of the pale-gray sandstone building was a driveway and a sign at the entrance:

POLICE DEPARTMENT, SHERIFF'S OFFICE,
CLERK'S OFFICE
PARKING IN REAR

The two musty courtrooms were located on the ground floor, off a wide hall which was constantly being wiped with foul-smelling antiseptic. The municipal offices, including the town council's meeting room and the division of deeds and records, were located on the second floor.

The lights were already on upstairs when Kent and Louise drove into the empty parking lot. Carrie had arrived first and was waiting with the children, her arms stretched around them as they all leaned against the station wagon, more apprehensive than ever.

"Hey, gang, we have a surprise!" Kent said to the girls, trying to evaporate their shock.

The exhausted children, feeling their pains—physical and emotional—merely looked up at their father with blank, gaping expressions. None of them needed additional surprises, but when Kent told them they were all flying to the Virgin Islands in a private jet later that day, they broke into slight smiles, not because they were escaping school, but because at least their mother and father had seemingly talked things over and arrived at another truce.

"Why are we here?" Laurie asked her mother.

"We just have to explain some things to the people in City Hall, darling . . . nothing to worry about."

"How do we say it?" Cathy asked, crossing to her mother.

"Tell the truth," Kent said.

"The truth?" Cathy asked.

"Yes. All of you know that I did not hit you. It was an accident. All of you saw your mother hit me. She didn't mean it, of course. She was angry."

"Am I supposed to tell them about Mr. Bianchi, Mom?" Cathy whispered into her mother's ear.

"No. I'll tell them exactly what happened."

"What will they think?" Cathy asked.

"I don't know, Cathy," Louise sighed. "Your mother made a mistake . . . it led to a dreadful misunderstanding."

Carrie stood apart, listening to the family rehearsal; she wanted to tell the police that Louise Morgan had been driven to madness by her husband. The maid, who had been with the Morgans for over eleven years, had seen the gradual deterioration of the marital relationship and Kent's growing disinterest in the children and life at Pigeon Hill. She, too, had been rehearsed, and realizing that jobs such as the Morgans' were not easy to come by, Carrie had planned to repeat precisely what Kent had told her to say. Still, she felt deep concern for the children she had helped raise; Carrie could see the insidious devastation attacking them, wrenching their sense of well-being and the protection they sought.

Judge Shallaway, a plump, easygoing man of fifty-seven, remembered when the Morgans had first arrived in town. The jurist was disturbed and unable to associate the physical eruption at Pigeon Hill with the people who lived there, knowing, as so many others, Louise and Kent Morgan as a dignified, respectable couple.

As long as he was arriving at town hall with the first blush of light just beginning to seep through the darkness, the judge decided to hold the meeting in *his* chambers, not the mayor's office. He walked through the upstairs hall, and in the dim light he saw the cluster of others: Mayor Turpin, Sergeant DiMaggio, the lead paramedic who had responded that night, Phil Cummings and Chief Caramati. They were all huddled in a circle, drinking coffee from cardboard cups which they had picked up at the all-night truck diner on Route One, which ran through the center of town.

Walt Turpin, the Menlo Head mayor, was not compensated for his elected, part-time duties. He ran the local lumberyard and had served in his official post for the past three terms, two of which were unopposed at election time; few Menlo Headers wanted the headaches of serving as mayor without salary. The only privileges of the office were freedom from traffic tickets and the right to attend the yearly convention of Connecticut mayors held in Hartford, a three-day family affair paid for out of the fiscal budget.

Walt, whose family had arrived in the town in 1901, was a highly decorated veteran of the Korean War; he walked with a limp, smiled often and was about as ordinary a man as there existed in Menlo Head. Walt had never finished college, but the lumberyard operator was accepted in the tight Menlo Head social circle, including the Field and Yacht Clubs, merely because he was an updated George Babbitt, a town booster who served his community untiringly. He was not against getting dressed in the middle of the night and coming to City Hall if he was needed. Judge Shallaway did not share the same willingness. He knew he was being pressured, and his head was aching from too many drinks downed at Pigeon Hill earlier that evening. As soon as he reached the knot of men outside Walt's office, he said gruffly, "Let's get this over with. I have a hearing at ten-thirty and five stipulations to sign."

170

"Judge," Phil Cummings spoke up quickly, "I appreciate your coming down here at this hour. This is just an informal fact-finding session. Nothing official . . . we're not taking notes or recording this."

"I understand. Are the Morgans here?"

"On the way."

"Phil, tell your clients to wait outside until we get a grasp of what happened. The whole matter upsets me . . . so does the hour."

The counselor stepped outside and saw the Morgans coming down the hall; he forced a smile on his face, trying to soften the embarrassment of the session. The Morgans approached as if they were already condemned and the only due process left was the punishment.

"Is the judge in a good mood?" Kent asked, shaking hands with Phil Cummings.

"How could anybody be in a good mood at six-fifteen? I hope you have your stories lined up," Phil said, half under his breath.

"We're all set. I'm telling the truth . . . a version of the truth."

"Sound contrite. Wow, that's some mouth, Kent."

"My wife has good aim."

"Now, kids," Phil said, turning to the children, "there's nothing to be afraid of. Mom and Dad are friends again . . . we'll have this over with in a few minutes."

He smiled at the battered Morgans and asked himself: why? And that was the core of the early morning meeting; not what, but why? As the lawyer looked at the family, he could not comprehend that these had been joyous, celebrating people only hours before. Phil then stepped inside.

"Are the Morgans here?" the judge asked.

"Yes, Your Honor . . . all of them, including the maid."

The judge patted his bald head, glanced at his watch and said, "What's the story? Why are we here at just after six o'clock in the morning?"

The jurist did not direct the question to any one person,

but since he had been called to his office by the mayor, Walt Turpin responded haltingly, almost diffidently.

"Well . . . ah . . . we've had a little misunderstanding here, Judge, and . . . we . . ."

The Clipper, who was leaning against the wood-paneled wall, stepped forward and interrupted the mayor with a raise of his hand.

"Sir, there was no misunderstanding . . . not in my eyes."

"Sergeant!" the chief said in a cracking voice, "I'll handle the department's point of view. We talked about that. You just answer the questions, and don't interrupt the mayor or the judge until you're asked to speak."

Chief Caramati was a squashed-face Italian who smoked cigars and appeared to many around Menlo Head as an ex member of a Midwestern crime family. When he spoke, his dark, heavy eyes and his thick lips which curled over tobacco-stained teeth seemed to suggest a highly paid hit man; but he was honest and appeared to handle his job well, making as few political ripples as possible.

"Go ahead, Mr. Mayor," the judge said.

Phil Cummings was restive, uneasy with the punctilious tone of the meeting. They were addressing each other as Mr. Mayor and Judge; these men, all close friends, were usually on a first-name basis, at least outside of council meetings and the Menlo Head courtroom.

But it was turning into a courtroom, Phil thought. The judge wasn't wearing his robes, but everyone else was dressed as if this was, indeed, a judicial hearing, an adversary proceeding. Even Phil himself had worn his trial suit, a three-piece gray worsted, tailored by J. Press in New York City.

"Your Honor," Walt began once more, picking up his pace, "what we have here is a slight misconception. The Morgans had a party last evening, and we all enjoyed their hospitality . . . I especially enjoyed the tempura shrimp. Now, as things will happen, some of us had a little too much to drink . . ."

"Speak for yourself," the judge interrupted.

"Well, the Morgans must have celebrated a little too much. There was an argument, and a few of the children cut themselves . . . by accident, of course. That's the truth, and the Morgans, including the children, will tell you just how it happened."

"Your Honor," Phil Cummings said, "we all know the Morgans to be solid, contributing citizens . . . talented and educated people from fine old American families. We only came down here—and we apologize for meeting at this hour— to prove that what occurred last night was a misunderstanding. In fact, the Morgans have already apologized to each other."

"Everyone has made up?" the judge asked.

"Yes, Your Honor," Phil Cummings nodded. "There's no problem."

"I'm glad of that, counselor . . . so why are we here? Are there complaints being filed?"

"No, Your Honor," the chief said.

"Then, counselor, if you assure me that there won't be a repetition of this situation over at Pigeon Hill, then I think we can adjourn. Are the children all right?"

"Yes, sir," Phil said. "They were cut a bit . . . nothing very serious."

The judge looked up and noticed that the Clipper and his chief were staring at each other. The judge said, "Sergeant DiMaggio, you want to say something?"

"Yes, sir. I responded to a call from the Morgans' maid at two-twelve this morning. She informed the dispatch desk that a felony was in progress. When we arrived at Pigeon Hill, there was no evidence of forced entry, but we entered the house anyhow because we heard screams."

"How did you enter the house, and on what basis?" the judge asked.

"The maid suggested that we enter . . . she had a key. We thought people were in danger."

"You just said there was no evidence of forced entry."

"But the children were crying."

"I don't think, Your Honor," Phil said, "that this was probable cause. The entry into the Morgan house could be construed as illegal trespass without a warrant."

"Forget the technicalities of entry. What did you see, Sergeant?" the judge asked.

The Clipper recited each detail of the upstairs bedroom and what he had come upon; the officer read from notes which in no way embellished the facts. The responding paramedic backed up the sergeant's report, and finally Phil Cummings said, "There is no dispute as to facts, Your Honor, but the important point is the intent of these acts. We must be sure that the children were not struck by the Morgans, and they are prepared to tell you that."

"What am I being asked to decide?" the judge asked.

The chief of police pushed out of his hardwood chair and lit a cigar. He padded about the judge's chamber as he spoke, blowing long funnels of cigar smoke towards the creaking cooler fan which revolved lazily from a ceiling mount.

"You see, the sergeant here thinks there should be a hearing and maybe the situation should be turned over to the juvenile section in Stamford."

"*No* complaint has been filed, and the sergeant did *not* see the children being beaten," Judge Shallaway said in a machine gun-like rattle.

"They were bloody, Your Honor," the Clipper added.

"But there was an explanation," Phil said. "There's no sense in conducting a hearing; nothing will come out that's not being said right here."

"We haven't heard from the Morgans or their children," the sergeant said.

"Are you telling me how to run this?" Judge Shallaway cracked, resenting the Italian sergeant's intimidation.

"No, sir, but I feel we should hear from the Morgans."

"I plan to. Ask Mr. and Mrs. Morgan to come in."

"May I hear this myself?" the sergeant asked.

Judge Shallaway pushed back his roller chair and lowered

his heavy jowls towards the sergeant. The jurist tapped on the large wooden desk with a letter opener.

"All right. There's nothing to hide, but Sergeant DiMaggio, I don't like being told how to handle this matter. I've sat on this bench twenty-one years, a long time before you joined the force."

"I am not instructing you, Your Honor, but I was shocked and fearful for the Morgan children. I thought I was performing my duty by making my opinions known."

"Yes, you've carried out your duties. No one's denying that."

Louise and Kent entered the chambers. They sat before the judge who explained to them that the meeting was being conducted under the normal rules of a closed courtroom in order to protect the children; none of those present would be allowed to discuss the conversation or quote from it to other parties, including those in their own departments. After there was general agreement and an expressed pledge of confidentiality all around, Judge Shallaway asked the Morgans, "Mr. and Mrs. Morgan, what happened at Pigeon Hill after the party tonight?"

Kent nodded to Louise. He held her hand in a show of solidarity and love; Louise drew a deep breath and began slowly, "I've been on prescribed medication to ease certain discomforts. I was warned *not* to mix it with alcohol . . . but after spending a week preparing for the party, I felt I needed something . . . and I had few drinks before the party to settle my nerves. I had some more vodkas during the party. Mr. Bianchi asked me to show him the yacht my husband designed for Mr. Halston, which, as you remember, Judge, was docked by our pier. I hardly remember going out there . . . but I do recall that Mr. Bianchi and I kissed each other. We were sitting in the sail locker on the forward end of the yacht. I . . . ah . . . didn't realize my husband and Cathy, our oldest daughter, saw us. After the party . . . I mean . . . well, after everyone, including the caterers, had left, my husband confronted me. I was still drunk . . .

or feeling the effects of the pills, I don't know which. I accused him of spying on me. I can't remember exactly what I said. We argued. I stepped back, and my leg caught a small table . . . it went over, breaking the glass on some picture frames. We were arguing so loudly the children heard us and came into the bedroom. They thought that Kent had hit me."

"*Did* your husband strike you, Mrs. Morgan?" the judge said.

"No, but the girls thought differently. They grabbed their father's arms and legs, and Kent spun around, trying to unloosen them . . . ah . . . so he could put them back to bed. The children fell into the broken glass and cut themselves. Then I exploded. I . . . ah . . . lost my head and hit Kent. That's it. I lost my head."

"You sure did," the judge said, edging the first smile to his lips.

"I'm terribly embarrassed . . . and in a few hours, we're taking the whole family in a private jet to the Virgin Islands for a vacation. I'm sorry that I caused all of you so much trouble and . . . well . . . what else can I say?"

Judge Shallaway stood and walked around the end of his desk and extended his hand to Louise Morgan.

"Thank you. I appreciate your candor. That wasn't easy to say in front of others. Kent, do you have anything to add?"

Phil Cummings felt relieved. The judge was satisfied; he had used the word "Kent," and the formality of the hearing was over.

"I, too, must apologize, Your Honor," Kent said, "not only to my wife and our children, but to everyone who had enough interest in our problems to come down here at this hour. Because of my work pressures, I let my wife handle the entire party by herself, when I should have been by her side. Her indiscretion with Mr. Bianchi was a simple mistake. I overreacted. I love Louise and my children very much, and I'm certain that Mr. Bianchi will apologize. My mistake was not realizing that Louise was going through physical and psychological problems. I understand now that we should have postponed the party until she was feeling better. You know how we all get so caught up in our own lives . . . we don't fully realize things that are going on right next to us. I'm sorry for this."

Kent finished and kissed his wife on the cheek. He smiled through his fattened lips at her, and all of them in the room shared the grin, except the sergeant who stood stony-faced against the wall.

"Louise," the judge said, "do you mind if I just ask the children a couple of questions?"

"Not at all," she said.

The children were brought into the room. They stood shyly before Judge Shallaway who bent and put his arms around them.

"We just want to be helpful to your mom and dad," the judge said, looking from one child to the other. "Did anyone hit you this evening?"

Jody stared at the man, and Cathy said, "No, sir. It was one of those things . . . we fell on some glass."

Laurie bobbed her head, and the judge continued, "But you thought your mother and father were hurting each other . . . that's why you entered the bedroom?"

The children said yes in a chorus, and the judge went on, "So you entered the room and tried to hold your father's arms, and he tried to shake you off, and that's when you got hurt?"

"Yes."

"Well, now, I want to tell you that your mom and dad love each other . . . and all of you very much. This will never happen again, and, in fact, Dad is taking all of you on a wonderful vacation. I want you to help Mom and Dad . . . and everything is going to be fine."

The children were not convinced, anymore than they had been on the previous occasions when they thought Kent had hit their mother, but they left the judge's chambers with

Kent and Louise. Cathy said to the judge, "Thank you."

The maid was summoned, and Judge Shallaway continued his interrogation.

"You called the police because you thought there was an intruder in the house?"

"Yes, sir."

"From what you have observed, have the Morgans ever beaten their children?"

"No, sir. They're wonderful people, and tonight there was just a lot of confusion with the party and all. Ah . . . I thought one of the caterers or somebody like that had come back to rob the house. I've heard of that happening before . . . that's why I called the police."

"You did the right thing. Thank you."

Carrie left the chambers, and the judge returned to his desk.

"Sergeant DiMaggio, there is *nothing* that has to be heard in addition to what these good people have said. Nobody, not even the Juvenile Division, can do anymore with this situation. I have faith in the Morgans. They are totally capable of handling their own affairs. This session is closed. No further depositions are necessary."

Phil Cummings rose and thanked the judge and everyone else for responding so quickly.

"Can I ask you something, Mr. Cummings?" the sergeant said.

"Of course."

"Why were you against this being heard in summary proceedings . . . in the court, I mean?"

"Because such a thing could create serious emotional trauma for the children. Sometimes discretion is the best way to solve a problem."

The judge nodded. "Mr. Cummings had the foresight to settle this correctly. We've done our duty as concerned neighbors . . . even though I won't think so when I fall asleep on the bench later this morning."

Everyone laughed, and Phil finally said, "Judge, I don't

178

feel that the police blotter should reflect the situation any-more than a courtroom hearing."

"I understand. Chief Caramati," the judge ordered, "put down on your record that the police responded to an emergency intruder call, but that no intruder was found at Pigeon Hill."

"Sir," the paramedic said, "what do we put down?"

The judge raised his voice for the first time, and it broke into a yawn as he paused, staring icily at the paramedic. "You took the Morgan children to the hospital for first-aid treatment. The cause of their cuts was accidental . . . you just heard what the Morgans said."

The Clipper, no longer able to hide his concern for the Morgan children—a tableau, he thought, of parental abuse and neglect—lingered behind in the chambers, his stark eyes pinned on the judge.

"Sergeant, you're satisfied, aren't you?"

"No, sir."

"Now, Your Honor," Chief Caramati said, with a stretched smile to signal *his* concurrence, "as a department, we're satisfied with the Morgans' testimony. There was no dispute as to facts. We agree that nothing further has to be done."

"No, now . . . wait a minute," the judge said. "We want everyone to feel at ease around here. I'd like to hear what you have to say, Sergeant. Talk as an individual . . . not as a departmental officer."

"Well, sir," the Clipper continued, shooting a quick glance towards Chief Caramati, "I think this situation should be referred to the juvenile authorities for counseling. This family has to be straightened out . . . or next time, we'll find one of them dead . . . and we'll look at each other and say, 'We could have prevented it.' "

The judge pointed his hand towards a chair. "Sit down, Sergeant . . . everyone sit down. Let's talk about marriage. We deal with a right of privacy older than the Bill of Rights . . . older than political parties . . . older than our school system. Marriage is an association that promotes a way of life, not causes. It's harmony in living, not political faiths, a bilateral loyalty, not commercial or social projects. Marriage has a constitutional dimension; it embodies constitutional guarantees to privacy, the pursuit of happiness and self-determination not to be interfered with by the state law unless there is strong evidence of child abuse, neglect or depravity on the part of the parents. But it has to be asked, given the need for state involvement in child rearing, what levels, what methods of value inculcation, are acceptable within the framework of a democratic society? If I refer this case to Stamford, I'm interfering with the Morgans' right to privacy and self-determination. They are financially stable, reasonable and intelligent people. They not only are *able* to solve their own problems in my judgment, but *should* be allowed to settle their private affairs under the constitution of the United States. I have faith in the Morgans and faith in our system. That's all we need."

CHAPTER EIGHTEEN

The children, chauffeured by the maid, rode back to Pigeon Hill in the station wagon; they were mute, aching, confused, still devastated by the bedroom collisions, the hospital emergency room and having to appear before a judge when the sun wasn't even up yet.

Kent led in the Maserati. His mouth was swollen into a fleshy lump, and he tasted the brine of blood flowing out of the sutured gash. His speech was thick, as if he were talking through big bubbles. Every time he sucked in a short breath, a trickle of blood entered his throat, and he wondered if the doctor had run out of thread along the way. Louise's heart was still pounding, and she needed a drink. She deserved a drink, she thought, and she was planning to build the tangiest, heaviest bloody mary possible as soon as they reached the Pigeon Hill kitchen.

"Why didn't you let me ride with the girls?" Louise asked. "They need me."

"We have some things to talk about," Kent gurgled.

"I thought it was all talked out at Town Hall."

"It was, dear, and you were absolutely magnificent."

"Thanks," she sighed. "Anytime. You know, I adore taking all the blame."

"All right, Louise. It hasn't been easy for me, either, but we're all going to fly away."

"Why are we going to the Virgin Islands . . . spending all that money for a private plane?"

"I'm doing it to get you and the children out of here, to prove that we're still a unit . . . a caring family . . . with love and respect for each other."

Louise chuckled in her stomach and glanced over at Kent. He looked like a gorilla; his lower lip protruded out beyond the line of his pointed jawbone. His well-bred, or over-bred, features—she never knew which—had collapsed into the transitory illusion of an ape, but perhaps her punch had worked a real and sudden truth.

Kent had been right about the strategy, Louise thought. Making her the sacrificial glob had worked; the ghoulish episode was explained and excused. But none of those present in the sterile chambers that morning would ever look upon Louise Morgan in quite the same way. And she was sure that these men, despite Judge Shallaway's pledge of strict confidentiality, would talk to others and rake over the domestic concussion.

There was no such confidentiality in Menlo Head.

"I think we're going to the Virgin Islands for other reasons," she said after a while. "You don't want to explain your fat lip . . . or why your children are bandaged up. And when your lip goes down and the children's bandages come off, we'll come back to Menlo Head, all sun-tanned, as if *nothing's* happened. We're going to the Virgin Islands to uphold the image of the vice commodore of the Menlo Head Yacht Club. Forget the children . . . it's the commodore."

"That's part of it. We have to heal things . . . you know that."

The small caravan turned into the driveway. A pale, haloed sun was already high enough to crisscross the bluestone drive with bluish shadows. There was a sudden sharp exclamation from Kent as he noticed a squad of trucks clogging the far end of the driveway.

"Goddamn caterers . . . why are they here so early?" Kent said. "I don't want those guys seeing our mess . . . the kids banged up."

Kent got out of the car just as Carrie arrived in the station wagon. The girls were asleep in the back seat, and Kent leaned in, saying to the housekeeper, "Bring your car to the rear door, Carrie . . . get the children upstairs to bed."

"Aren't we going on a trip, Dad?" Jody asked, stirring.

"Of course. But I have to arrange things, dear. It'll be a few hours. Now I want you to go upstairs and get rid of all those bloody nightgowns. Throw them away; the blood won't wash out. You help Carrie with the children, Cathy . . . your mother and I will clean the bedroom. And Carrie, get the children's clothes packed, and prepare to go yourself."

"I'm afraid of those private planes, Mr. Morgan."

"It's just like a small airliner. I want you down there to assist my wife. And Carrie, don't answer the doorbell or the phone."

"Yes, sir," she said.

Kent returned to the Maserati and continued to inch around to the front door. A man in green work clothes was standing under the small portico, ringing the doorbell.

"Louise, get him out of here!"

"Why don't you tell him?"

"With this mouth? Aw, shit!"

Kent jumped from the car, trying to hide his face. He edged back along the far side of his sports car and told Carrie, "Carrie, talk to that man. Tell him not to disturb us."

Kent climbed in the car again as Carrie went up to the front door; Kent watched in the rearview mirror.

Carrie returned to the Maserati. "He says they'll just be here about three hours . . . but they have to get in the kitchen to pick up the dishes and silverware."

"Then go around and open the door," Kent said. "We'll take the children in."

When the way was clear, Kent and Louise hurried the girls inside the house.

They stood in the hall, dumbfounded. Traces of their

human bombardment looked like amber potholes etched into the white marble of the gallery. A trail of dried blood—spots and long thin lines—led across the hall and up the sienna carpet of the formal stairway.

In the bright light, the master bedroom looked like the aftermath of a gang killing. The precision of the large white room with the tray ceiling was gone. Pieces of Hepplewhite antiques—the nightstand, the small lady's chair—were scattered over the deep-pile rug as if they had been detonated by gelignite bombs. There were bits and splinters of glass everywhere, and blood dotted the wall and soiled the sheets of the turned-down bed. There was a large dried lake of crimson on the silk window seats just under the shuttered windowpane where Laurie's head had entered. Scattered about were wads of reddish compresses which had been used by the paramedics and hastily discarded.

The Morgans stood surveying the shocking mélange. It was worse than they imagined.

"Louise, put the children to bed and then have Carrie come up here with ammonia. Get my tool case," Kent ordered, as if he were commanding one of his racing sloops.

"Tool case?" she asked.

"We can wash the blood off the walls, but these curtains and rugs are coming up. I don't want reminders. We'll never get the blood off the coverings."

Kent began by ripping the splattered curtains down; then the sheets were peeled off the bed. He hauled the stained remnants out into the hall and went down to the kitchen to make a cup of coffee. Louise was already there, making herself the tall bloody mary which she had looked forward to for some hours.

"That's not going to help," Kent said.

"I think it is."

"Your drinking started all this last night. Now go get the tools."

"After I have this drink . . . and maybe a second."

184

"We don't have much time. The phone's going to start ringing . . . and I want to be out of here."

Kent thumbed through the telephone book and found the number of Executive Jet, a company based at the Westchester County Airport, just over the New York line from Menlo Head. He called, explaining his need for a plane that morning.

"How many passengers?" the operations manager asked.

"Six."

"Um—that means a Gulfstream Two . . . don't have any at the moment."

"Find one."

"I'll try to borrow one of Union Carbide's. They charter out to us now and then. But it'll cost you over eight thousand, Mr. Morgan, round trip."

"I believe our firm has credit with you. Send the bill to the office."

For the next thirty minutes Kent worked furiously, ripping up about ten thousand dollars worth of rugs, and with the help of Carrie and Louise, the evidence was rolled up to be taken outside. They dragged the heavy materials downstairs across the driveway to a position by the potting shed. After three trips, a five-foot-high pile was lumped up on the west end of the carriage house where the fertilizer and mulch for the garden were stored. Kent grabbed two cans of gasoline from the garage, and, splattering the liquid over the coverings, he tossed a match on the rugs and curtains. A high wall of fire, sending up ugly black smoke, rose between the hardwood pines.

At that moment Betsy Potter was sitting in her breakfast room, drinking tea. She happened to look over towards Pigeon Hill and saw the plume of ebony smoke; she ran to the phone and dialed the Morgans' number. There was no answer.

"Lane! Lane!" she screamed upstairs. "I think Pigeon Hill is on fire!"

"What?"

She repeated her words. Lane Potter, with shaving cream covering his face, walked through the bedroom and looked out. The flames were reflected in the four upstairs windows of the carriage house; it appeared that the fire was inside.

"It's the carriage house! Did you call Kent?" Lane asked.

"Yes . . . there was no answer."

Lane quickly phoned the fire department, telling them that the Pigeon Hill carriage house was burning. Realizing the age of the clapboard building, five trucks from two Menlo Head companies responded immediately.

Kent was inside, cleaning up the glass in the bedroom, when he heard the sirens; a minute later, the trucks rolled into the driveway.

"Louise . . . get out there!" Kent yelled. "I can't be seen like this."

"How much more do I have to do?" Louise screamed back as she trotted out to the driveway where the fire marshal met her.

"What's the matter?" she asked.

"Mrs. Morgan, we got a call from your neighbors. They said the carriage house was on fire."

"I was just burning some trash."

"You're not supposed to burn trash. The town provides a pickup."

"I'm sorry. I forgot."

They all walked toward the pile of rugs. The firemen had already smothered the flames with spouts from their CO-2 extinguishers. Betsy and Lane Potter and two of their children were standing on the border of the fire, watching.

"Louise, we thought the carriage house was burning," Lane said.

"It was none of your business! Can't you tell a trash fire when you see one?" Louise said.

Lane was stopped short, expecting to be thanked for his efforts.

"I tried to call you," Betsy said. "There was no answer."

"We were sleeping late because of the party."

"What were all the police doing here last night?"

"How did you know they were here, Betsy? Spying out the window again?"

"Mrs. Morgan, you said you set the fire . . . and now you tell the Potters you were sleeping," the fire marshal said.

"What difference does it make?"

"There's a fire violation here. I'll have to give the citation to the right party. Was it you?"

"Yes!" Louise barked.

The fire marshal finished writing out his citation and handed it to her. "I'm sorry, Mrs. Morgan, but there's fire rules in Menlo Head."

Louise turned and barged her way through the cluster of firemen and caterers, eavesdropping. She entered the house and slapped the citation down on the kitchen counter.

"What happened?" Kent asked.

"You got a summons for starting a fire. Kent, let's get out of here. I can't stand this!"

Louise had not seen or heard of the newsman early that morning; he had arrived after she returned to the house, when the rug fire had been reduced to an acrid whiff of smoke. His name was Marvin Eddleman, a twenty-one-year-old junior reporter for *The Menlo Head Herald-Statesman*. He was fresh from the Columbia University Graduate School of Journalism. Because of poor grades, Marvin had failed to land a berth on the twenty-two respectable dailies to which he had applied, including *The New York Times, The Baltimore Sun* and *The Charlotte Observer*.

At the bottom of his list, and finally accepting him, was the local Menlo Head paper, which had long ago given up competing with the New York dailies to become a society, obituary, real estate and shopping gazette, poorly edited and poorly reproduced.

Marvin was the son of a kosher butcher from Queens, and he was determined to become a great investigative reporter.

So far, the young journalist had only been handed marginal assignments by *The Herald-Statesman*: police and fire stories and a few obituaries.

The rug fire at the Morgans was another such bland assignment. Marvin took out his pad and asked the fire marshal what had happened. The story, Marvin thought, was not worth writing until the man said, "There's something strange going on here."

"In what way?" Marvin asked.

"Well, I guess the Morgans had a big party last night."

"I know . . . our society editors covered it."

"Yeah, but according to what the lady over there said"—the fireman motioned towards Betsy Potter who was walking away with a sulky expression on her face—"the police and the paramedics were here earlier this morning . . . took the children away in an ambulance. Mr. Morgan seemed to be hurt, too."

"She just happened to be walking around in the middle of the night and saw all that?" Marvin asked.

The fireman shrugged and continued. "Then Mrs. Morgan tells me she's burning trash, but that's no ordinary trash fire . . . rugs in there."

"OK, thanks," Marvin said, and he walked up to one of the caterers. "Did you see the Morgans bring their rugs out here?" he asked.

"Sure did," the man answered. "They hauled drapes and sheets, too."

"Did you notice anything odd about them?"

"Yeah . . . they were all splotched up with blood."

Marvin moved towards the rear of Pigeon Hill, and he rang the doorbell. Carrie came down and waved him away. He tried the Potters next but got no answer. Marvin went back to his office and decided to start asking more questions.

CHAPTER NINETEEN

Judge Shallaway had treated the Morgan dilemma with constitutional dimension and guidance, both of which provided the jurist with a scheme of rationality. The Clipper understood this, although its import seemed too distant and obscure. There was another precedent folded into the unified decision not to deliver the Morgan family to the juvenile court. Judge Shallaway had said that the rights of privacy predated the Bill of Rights. What also predated the document was Menlo Head.

Had Marvin Eddleman and Sergeant Don DiMaggio understood the closer harmonies of the town's history and that of the state of Connecticut, they might have pursued their causes of truth and justice with more accommodation and respect for Menlo Head's prerogative rule.

Both men were totally out of tilt with the town's past.

Marvin's grandfather had been born in Lithuania, and the Clipper's father had come to the United States from Palermo as a child; thus, there was no particular reason why they would understand the Connecticut tradition.

Many Menlo Head families traced their roots to the original Connecticut Colony; to them, people such as the Eddlemans and DiMaggios were classed as ethnic libertarians, dropped on U.S. shores to enjoy certain benefits and freedoms bitterly fought for by the first families.

Chief Caramati was an ethnic, too, but he was considered a good policeman because he was a quiet, conservative lawman. When Caramati arrived in Menlo Head from Chicago, he realized that there were certain sanctuaries grafted to the history of the state which could *not* be abridged.

On the door panels of Menlo Head's seventeen police cars were outsized words printed under the town's seal: TO SERVE AND PROTECT.

When Caramati first took up his job as police chief, the mayor, a descendant of original Connecticut Trumbulls, told the Italian: "You had better know and understand what you're serving and protecting if you intend to last in Menlo Head."

The police officer had terminated his formal education at the age of fifteen and so had a sense of street acuity and survival.

Caramati got the message. He responded to the signals at once, collecting and studying books on Connecticut history and that of the town he was to serve.

Marvin Eddleman and the Clipper were unaware of the legal intricacies, new and old, which prevailed in the town, and they were not students of the constitution.

The newspaperman went immediately from Pigeon Hill to police headquarters behind the dismal City Hall and looked at the logbook for that morning:

FILE NO. 89067. CALL AT 2:00 A.M. COMPLAINT OF MAID AT 1202 POWDER HILL ROAD, PIGEON HILL. SUSPICION OF BREAKING AND ENTERING—FELONY IN PROGRESS. RESPONSE TEAM COMMANDED BY SERGEANT DONALD DIMAGGIO. UPON INVESTIGATION, NO UNLAWFUL ENTRY FOUND. ENTERED PREMISE UPON ADVICE AND INVITATION OF MAID. DISCOVERED ACCIDENT WITH GLASS INVOLVING MINOR INJURIES TO SEVERAL MORGAN CHILDREN. NO COMPLAINT OR FURTHER POLICE INVESTIGATION INDICATED.

The paramedic report in a separate file was open to Marvin; it read:

RESPONDED TO CALL FROM MENLO HEAD POLICE AT 2:22

A.M., APRIL 22. BREAKING AND ENTERING. FOUND CHIL-
DREN SUFFERING SUPERFICIAL INJURIES BY CONTACT WITH
BROKEN GLASS. FIRST AID ADMINISTERED. TRANSPORTED
INJURED CHILDREN, CATHY MORGAN, AGE FIFTEEN, LAURIE
MORGAN, AGE ELEVEN, TO EMERGENCY ROOM, MENLO
HEAD MEMORIAL HOSPITAL, FOR TREATMENT.

From there, Marvin went to the fire department, housed
in a modern, two-story building constructed in 1965, located
three blocks from the police department. The report, just
typed up, read:

CALL 090890. VIA PHONE, NEIGHBOR, MR. LANE POTTER.
FIRST INFORMATION: FIRE IN CARRIAGE HOUSE, 1202
POWDER HILL ROAD. PREMISE OWNED BY MR. AND MRS.
KENNETH C. MORGAN. FIVE TRUCKS AND BATTALION CHIEF
RESPONSE. FIRE FOUND TO BE TRASH BESIDE CARRIAGE
HOUSE. CONTROLLED IN THREE MINUTES BY HAND EXTIN-
GUISHERS WITH FURTHER IMPLEMENTATION OF THREE-
INCH HOSE LINE. DAMAGE: NONE. INJURIES: NONE. EQUIP-
MENT DAMAGE: NONE. TIME ON SITE: TWENTY-EIGHT MIN-
UTES. RESPONSE TIME: TWO MINUTES TWENTY SECONDS
FROM ALARM. CITATIONS: ONE, BURNING TRASH AND
REFUSE IN VIOLATION OF TOWN ORDINANCE 9081B, AS
AMENDED. PERSONALLY SERVED ON AND ACCEPTED BY MRS.
MORGAN ON SITE. TIME OF REPORT: 9:15 A.M. DAY OF
INCIDENT.

What rippled through Marvin's pursuing mind was the
neighbor's comment that morning, that Mr. Morgan had
seemed to be hurt, too. There was no mention in the paramedic report of Kent having been injured.

He returned to the police station and asked the desk
sergeant about that; the answer was a shrug and a yawn.

Marvin said, "The sergeant who commanded the response
team . . . Donald . . . ah . . ."

"DiMaggio."

"Yeah, that's right. Can I speak to him?"

"He's off duty."

The reporter's next stop was the Menlo Head Memorial Hospital where he had a contact, a fat, redheaded charge nurse who worked in the emergency room. He had taken the woman out for a few beers, flattered her to gain access to medical reports; she had shared a few with him in the past, mostly attempted suicides or overdose write-ups which never reached the paper. The usual policy of news suppression was dictated by the editor, Alex Palmer, who, like Caramati, realized the importance of a subdued approach to the town's problems.

But Marvin pursued the facts because that was his journalistic obligation, or so they had told him at Columbia.

The nurse had not been on duty the evening before, but she went to a stack of reports not yet filed. Marvin read the write-up with wide eyes. The children were *not* superficially injured. Dr. Driscoll had taken a total of thirty-eight stitches in two of the young girls, and they had all been X-rayed for possible rib and skull injuries. The report involving Kent Morgan read, in part . . .

ELEVEN SUTURES ADMINISTERED TO PATIENT, MR. KENNETH MORGAN, IN AREA OF LOWER AND UPPER LIPS. TWO TEETH JUDGED UPROOTED. SOME MOBILITY NOTED. RECOMMENDED DENTAL APPRAISAL AND FURTHER TREATMENT. PATIENT RELEASED. REFUSED PAINKILLING MEDICATION.

"What does this look like to you?" Marvin asked the nurse.

"I'd say he was in an automobile accident . . . or he was beaten up."

"Yeah, reads like a solid punch."

Marvin then drove back to the police station once more and asked to see Chief Caramati, who viewed visitations as a part of his public relations job, in addition to his official duties.

The chief's office was a dark paneled room in the back

of the City Hall annex, overlooking the loading dock for the Safeway Store. On the walls were photographs of the officer with Mayor Daley and various congressmen whom he had guarded during Chicago's political conventions. To the rear of his oakwood desk was a line of cheap bowling trophies which Caramati had earned as the captain of the Chicago Police Bowling Team, four-time winners in national competition.

To reflect the neatness of Menlo Head, the chief's desk was orderly. He usually wore a Brooks Brothers suit with a buttoned-down shirt and regimental tie to mimic the other men in town, but the conservative Ivy League look did not harmonize with his brooding eyes and dark gray cheeks shaded by an abundance of face stubble. (He had gone through fourteen types of razor blades and shaving creams, hoping to lighten the lower reaches of his jaw.)

Marvin, on the other hand, wore no tie and usually went about Menlo Head in blue jeans. (He had been told to dress appropriately for his job by the editor, but he had refused using the excuse that he had seen the city room of *The New York Times* where the reporters wore Levi's. What was good enough for *The Times* was good enough for *The Herald-Statesman*.)

The chief did not like Marvin Eddleman, or Jews in general, and he called the reporter Eddleman, never Marvin or Mr. Eddleman.

"What's it this time?" the chief began.

"The Morgan case."

"Eddleman, there's *no* Morgan case. A case is a case only when there's a complaint filed, and there's no complaint outstanding."

"Forget technicalities," the young reporter said.

The chief paused and felt the wheeze in his lungs churning up. His doctor had suggested a job with the Tucson police for his asthma, but if the chief was slightly out of place in Menlo Head, he would have been an alien in Arizona.

"What do you want?" he said, hoping to get the intruder out of his office as soon as possible.

"There's a conflict in the police report about the Morgan accident early this morning."

The chief studied Marvin through narrowed eyes, but the young man, who earned a pittance at the paper, could not be intimidated; he had very little to lose.

"Conflict? How do you know!"

Caramati belted out his words, knowing that he had edited the report to reflect the unspoken policy of Menlo Head's laundering on all levels of judicial control.

"I'll tell you how I know. I went over to the hospital and looked up the emergency room log. It said that Mr. Morgan had eleven stitches in his mouth, and his teeth were half knocked out."

"So what?"

"But the police and paramedic reports don't mention Mr. Morgan's being beaten up."

"Who says he was beaten up?" the chief asked.

"I concluded that."

"You did, huh? Maybe the police report didn't have it because Mr. Morgan might have tripped and fallen in the hospital parking lot." The chief said this with little zest, knowing that the lie was too broad for anyone to digest.

"That's bullshit, Chief. You know it. I was at the scene of the fire this morning, and the Morgans' neighbor . . ."

"What fire?"

"Didn't you know?"

"This is the police department . . . we don't handle fires. In case you didn't notice, our cars aren't painted red."

Marvin told the chief about the rug fire and what he had heard from the fire marshal and the caterers.

"All of this doesn't interest me, and I'm busy."

Marvin drew in a deep breath, and he wound up his anger with a rattle of indictments. "What happened to Mr. Morgan . . . who beat him up . . . one of your men?"

Marvin knew he should not have said that. The chief

194

lifted himself out of his roller chair and came around the desk. He stood over the reporter with his large, meaty hands curled up.

"What we don't need in Menlo Head is a Queens kike, shooting off at the mouth. Get the fuck out!"

Marvin jumped to his feet, and when he was a safe distance from Caramati, at the door, he turned with a smile on his thin lips and said, "Maybe we don't need a wop cop . . . one who lies. And I'm going to find out what happened to Mr. Morgan. It's interesting that the paramedic report said the Morgan kids were superficially injured, but the hospital report noted they had a total of thirty-eight stitches."

"Do you know a criminal lawyer, Eddleman?" the chief said, gaining his composure.

"For you or me?"

"You know kosher, Eddleman? Well, going over to the hospital and wheedling your way into confidential hospital reports isn't kosher . . . it's like one of you eating pork five times a day. Worse than that, Eddleman, you committed a crime by fraudulently obtaining hospital reports, however the hell you did it. That's in violation of the laws of privacy . . . interference with privileged information. Two misdemeanors . . . or possibly felonies. Now, if you don't forget all this, which is nothing, anyhow, I'm calling Judge Shallaway for a bench warrant. You just admitted to me that you committed a crime . . . and it could be one year or five thousand dollars, or both. And the hospital has a cause of action against you . . . so when you swing out of Wetherfield State Penitentiary, the hospital will serve a civil complaint on you."

"You can't arrest anyone without a complaint."

"My friend, we'll get a bunch of complaints from the hospital . . . Mr. Morgan and me. Get out and think it over."

"There's nothing to think over. I was only trying to get at the facts. That's my business . . . the *facts*." Eddleman slammed the door.

At that moment, Caramati felt like grabbing the frail reporter and choking him to death, but he forced himself to calm down. Returning to his desk, he put in a call to Phil Cummings.

"Phil? Frank Caramati. You know that little kike Jew . . . Eddleman . . . who works for the paper?"

"I know him."

"Well, the son-of-a-bitch bagel eater goes over to the hospital and finds out Morgan was beaten up last night. We didn't put that in the police report."

"How come, Frank?"

"You know why. The judge told us to fix things. How were we going to explain Morgan's lip . . . say he fell on the glass?"

"I see what you mean. What does Eddleman think?"

"Says we must have kicked Morgan around."

"That's crazy!"

"You're corporation counsel for this town. So what do we do?"

"First of all, no reporter is allowed to recite the police log in the paper except for what's given out as official. If he had access to all files, then all a person would have to do is report a phony assault by someone, and that would be printed up in the paper as an injurious fact. Allegations can only be printed when a preliminary hearing is held . . . that's an open forum. Why do you think I wanted the judge to hold a private session this morning?"

"I understand. Do I start gathering a complaint against Eddleman?"

"Not yet. I'll go over and see Alex Palmer. He might as well know the whole story, and he'll do what we tell him. We can trust Alex . . . he's too weak to do otherwise. The man detests any kind of trouble."

"That's handling it, Phil. Listen . . . did you hear about the fire at Pigeon Hill?"

"Fire?"

"Apparently your client burned a bunch of bloody rugs

196

this morning at his house, and the fire department was called."

There was a sigh from the other end of the phone. "I wish these Morgans would get hold of themselves."

"Phil, I'd have a good talk with them when they get back from the islands. There's only so much the judge . . . and all of us . . . can do. I hope the Morgans realize that."

CHAPTER TWENTY

From the chief's office Marvin Eddleman went to the fire department, asking who wrote the paramedic report. They told him that the responding officer in charge was off duty, and they would not give out the home number. Marvin then returned to the newspaper office.

He knew that Alex Palmer had probably been reached already by Chief Caramati, but Marvin hoped to talk to his editor before being yanked in for calling the police chief a "wop cop."

Alexander Palmer, the editor and publisher of *The Menlo Head Herald-Statesman,* had inherited the paper from his father. He had gone to work as a nonfighting editor at the age of forty-one, after spending some twenty years in Europe as a remittance man and layabout. Alex was the present chairman of the Menlo Head "Old Liners," a prestigious historical society honoring families living in the town who could trace their heritage to pre-Revolutionary days. The Palmer family, originally of Lancashire, England, had arrived among the first settlers from the New Haven colony to the east. It was said, although never confirmed, that Joshua Palmer named his trading outpost Menlo Head, after a spit of land which ran out from the river Mersey in what is now the reaches to the Port of Liverpool.

Alex had graduated third in his class at Harvard, but after five marriages and too many years of drinking, his brain had atrophied; he wore a constant, unmoving smile as if he had been painted permanently by a creator of string puppets. In many ways, Alex *was* a puppet and a cooperative one; all the man desired was a small dose of respect, no fuss and a reasonable income from the paper. He had achieved these minor goals.

When Marvin tried to see Alex, his secretary said that the publisher was in a meeting with Phil Cummings, who had scurried directly over after Caramati's call.

"And I enjoyed that party," Alex was saying now to Phil. "Sorry to hear that it brought on such grief. You know, I heard about Kent slamming his wife. What was this, the return punch?"

"In a way, I guess. They simply drank too much, but they're both back in love again. As I told you, Judge Shallaway wants this kept confidential, and I'm not even supposed to talk to you . . . but we have to bury the story."

"Of course. This isn't news, anyhow . . . it's rag gossip. What respectable paper would print it? The judge is correct. All it would do is embarrass the children at their school."

"I'm glad you see it our way."

Phil Cummings' reference to "our way" could be termed duplicity. He was the Morgans' lawyer and also served as Menlo Head's corporation counsel; he held a voting seat on the town council. He failed to question his own conduct when any other lawyer might have suspected that he was deeply involved in dual advocacy—possible grounds for disbarment in any jurisdiction but Menlo Head.

After he had Alex's assurance that he would handle Marvin Eddleman, Phil asked, "Why is a liberal Jew working for the *Herald*? He's out of place here."

"A couple of fellows asked me the same question," Alex said. "First of all, nobody but an Eddleman would work for our wages. Let's be candid, Phil . . . most of my people are lady dilettantes. Marvin, at least, has some journalistic training, and no one around here—including my managing editor, a gal who can't spell—has ever complained of Marvin's work . . . just his bad breath."

"But getting into files illegally . . . And where does this kid get off going over there and accusing the police of having beaten up Kent Morgan?"

"Phil, I respect you, and I'm glad you came directly to me with this. You know how we've always cooperated."

"Of course."

"And you know how I want to make things right."

"Yes."

"I'll take care of Marvin's story. Why don't we scare him? I'll call him in."

"Just fire him, Alex."

"I don't know. Marvin's a loudmouth. He might hurt us."

Marvin walked into Alex Palmer's office. Phil Cummings looked glumly at the reporter.

"Sit down, Marvin," Alex said. "You know Mr. Cummings . . . our town attorney?"

"Yeah, we've met."

"Mr. Cummings is outraged, Marvin."

"So am I."

"Let me tell you our problem first," Alex continued. "Mr. Cummings is about to have Judge Shallaway arrest you for pulling private files from the hospital. No one on this paper instructed you to do so . . . did they? I didn't."

"I needed to find out certain things, Mr. Palmer."

"But in doing so, you broke the law, Mr. Eddleman," Phil said.

"The law?" Marvin laughed. "Why did the police attempt to hide what happened to the Morgan children and Mr. Morgan's mouth? What about that? Who hit the guy?"

"What's on the police report is the truth," Phil Cummings said.

"A version . . . or a portion . . . of the truth, Mr. Cummings."

"The records contain *all* substantive information. Nothing more is required," Phil answered.

"When a man has his teeth loosened and his lip closed up by eleven stitches . . . that's substantive."

200

"Mr. Morgan wished to have his right of privacy protected, *and* he was trying to protect his children. He fell on a sharp edge in his bedroom. That's how he cut his lip."

"What sharp edge?" Marvin asked.

"It was a door . . . the shower stall."

"Is that what he told you?"

"Yes."

"Well, I think he was slugged in the mouth . . . and that's what the hospital nurse believes."

"Now, Marvin," Alex said, shaking his finger at the young man. "Do you want to be arrested or fired or both?"

"I don't care. But there's something not coming across."

"You're entirely wrong and off base, Mr. Eddleman," Phil said. "I speak as a town council member and town attorney. I've talked to Chief Caramati. All the facts are in. I want you to apologize to the chief. He's a fine man who places the interests of our town and its people far above his own."

"Absolutely." Alex nodded.

"And if I don't, Mr. Palmer . . . will you fire me?"

"You want that, don't you?" Alex said.

"You do run a lousy paper."

"Then pick up your check and get out."

"I wouldn't give you that pleasure. When I find out everything, I'll leave. Not before."

"Pick up your check. I want your desk cleared in twenty minutes. I tried to fight for you, Marvin, but now I'm recommending that the town attorney proceed with your arrest."

Marvin smirked and said, "You two are clowns. First of all, an arrest won't be upheld in Stamford . . . they'll want to know what happened to Mr. Morgan. And by the way, why wasn't a hearing held in court? When the police drag out injured children, it seems to me that someone should ask questions. Who asked the right questions, Mr. Cummings? The folks in Stamford don't like the swells over here, and they might have questions. Maybe I can help steer them in the right direction."

Marvin cherished his own exit lines, and he left the two men gawking at each other.

On the afternoon of April 23, the entire front page of *The Menlo Head Herald-Statesman* carried pictures of the Morgan party which spilled over to pages three and four.

The big black headline, set with three-inch News Gothic, read:

MORGAN PARTY SETS TONE
FOR SOCIAL SEASON

And the subhead expanded the goulash:

> *Over four hundred guests enjoy lawn party at Pigeon Hill; two orchestras entertain; theme of gala is international cuisine personally supervised by Louise Morgan, former Olympian; Mr. and Mrs. Roger Halston honored along with new members of Menlo Head Yacht Club.*

The inscript subhead took the anxious reader further:

> Mr. and Mrs. Kenneth Morgan, the gracious host and hostess of Pigeon Hill, the historic estate on Humble Cove, entertained their closest friends last night with a gourmet supper dance. Under the moonlight and under a gay party tent, over four hundred guests dined on three international cuisines—Oriental, French and Northern Italian—while they danced to the music of Pete Barron's orchestra, which played slowly for the romantic at heart. To entertain the spirited younger set, Mrs. Morgan provided the popular rock group, Deedy and his Dudes, whose new album for Columbia Records is presently nineteenth on the *Billboard* chart of hits.
>
> In the tradition of Menlo Head parties, the Morgan affair, which lifted the curtain on the town's spring social season, was designed carefully for all ages and

all tastes. Veteran Menlo Head party goers and givers told the *Herald* that Louise Morgan's kickoff affair was "sensational," "the best in years." And Louise Morgan, the lovable former Olympic athlete who has beguiled and charmed the town for fourteen years, must be given a top rating for creative party giving, according to all those who enjoyed the elegant hospitality of the unforgettable evening.

This was printed on page one in ten-point type. On page six of the same edition was a brief story set in eight-point type under the heading, Police and Fire Records:

The Menlo Head police responded to a complaint of breaking and entering at Pigeon Hill, home of Mr. and Mrs. Kenneth Morgan. The police reported that no intruder was found.

Two inches down, another item read:

The Menlo Head Fire Department responded to a call phoned in at 8:40 this morning by a neighbor of Mr. and Mrs. Kenneth Morgan of 1202 Powder Hill Road. The Menlo Head Fire Department extinguished a small trash blaze which had been set inadvertently by a member of the Morgans' staff.

The paper reached the Lunsford house that afternoon just after three, and Bunny, seeing the wide coverage of Louise's party, phoned the circulation department and ordered ten more copies. She was the sixtieth person to call, requesting additional copies.

Later that day Louise called her friend from the Virgin Islands, explaining that Kent had whisked the whole family away for a little vacation and to give her a chance to recuperate from the party.

"Well, you sure made the news," Bunny told her. "More pictures and coverage than any party during the last four years . . . that's what Josephine over at the *Herald* told me. Listen to this . . ." and she read Louise the opening paragraph from the paper. "There was just so much to write about," she concluded.

"Well, I'm glad we make news for other people," Louise said, trying to be bright despite an intense hangover.

"How is it down there?" Bunny asked.

"Oh, magnificent. The colors are so beautiful . . . and Kent rented us a private house right on the beach. Bunny, can you keep a secret?"

"I'm a tight lip, you know."

"Well, Kent has his forty-second birthday in three weeks —he only admits to forty, of course—so I decided to give him an extraordinary present. He was such a dear to pay for the party and give us this vacation."

"I can hardly wait. What's the present?"

"A tennis court . . . a grass court . . . just outside the terrace."

"Louise, you're too extravagant. What a present! I wish the General thought in those terms. No one can ever say that Louise Morgan doesn't go the hog."

"Well, it's a once-in-a-lifetime gift. Now, Bunny, I don't want you telling anyone, but when we return from the vacation, I want the whole picture there for Kent . . . absolutely complete."

"Can that be done?"

"I talked the contractor into it. Oh, I know I'll be paying overtime . . . but as a favor, I want you to represent me . . . go over there and see that they do things right . . . especially, Bunny, the schedule. The tennis court *must* be finished by the time we return."

"I understand. So you two are in love again?"

"Oh, yes," Louise said. "I confronted Kent last night after the party . . . and he admitted seeing Babs and having lunch with her and Gwen."

"And you're excusing it?"

"Sure. He told me why he was seeking other company. I guess I just locked the man out of our lives . . . so things

204

are going to be different from now on, Bunny. Big change at Pigeon Hill."

Bunny sighed as she put down the phone, thinking about that "innocent" lunch. She was afraid nothing was going to change.

The Morgans' beach house on the southeast shore of Saint Thomas was settled in a grove of coconut palms. The free-swinging pennant leaves whistled under the constant press of the trade winds, blowing steadily day and night at about fifteen miles an hour.

The shade of the palms gave way to a sugar-white beach, and the turquoise water of the bay beyond was brilliantly clear and warm. Further out, the water turned from pale green to deeper tones of azure blue, reflecting the depth; the magnificent wash of color was continually laced by small whitecaps, but the horizon treated the eyes to more luxury. Eighteen miles away, the verdant mountains of Saint John Island and Caneel Bay sprang up from the sea. In the morning light they appeared blue; during the day they reflected the lush green hues; and towards evening the mountains succumbed to various tones of purple and lavender, finally turning blue-black as the sun escaped the sky.

Above this idyllic scenery, fat cumulus clouds rose to great heights; during the afternoon, when the trade winds blew harder, the wind sculpted their fluffy, white shapes into intriguing representations. Lying on the beach and looking upward, the mind could play extraordinary games with the skies.

Kent had made a decision. He was middle-aged now, settled in his marriage, and he loved his children and his wife, although his affection for Louise was mysterious, more respectful than romantic, perhaps. Whichever, he promised himself that he was not going to take any more inordinate risks with his life. Hawking new romance and acting like a fool at his age ran countergrain to his character. It was poor form. Then another thought slid into his mind. Louise was extremely liberal and forgiving, something he had never quite realized. What other woman, knowing that her husband was having kinky, incestuous sex, would go to a judge's office at dawn and take the blame for the physical altercation at Pigeon Hill?

During the first few days on the island, the Morgan family visited a variety of doctors in Charlotte Amalie. Kent's two mobile teeth were capped; the children's dressings were changed. Luckily, no complications followed, and their pain subsided along with his puffy face.

Kent suggested to Louise that they charter a yacht to take the girls out, since Cathy and Laurie couldn't go swimming until their bandages were removed.

"That's a good idea," she said. "We can get some of those rubber rafts with plastic bottoms so they can look through and see the fish on the reefs."

A fiberglass yacht was towed to the front of the beach cottage and anchored. She was a worn-out, forty-foot fiberglass sloop which had been abused by constant bare-boat charterers. Her sails were stained, her lines half-frayed, and the varnish work—what there was of it—stood in curling blisters. Her upkeep clearly never won over the assaults of the sun and salt. The sloop, in Kent's mind, was a crock. She represented everything he abhorred in a yacht. She was designed to be safe; with a fat, wide underbelly, the sloop could hardly slug her way to windward. She creaked and smelled of residual sweat and rancid food particles which had found their way into the deepest creases of the cabin sole.

Yet Kent took an unusual joy in sailing this bulbous hull.

His yachting was forever an extension of his profession. He had to fine-tune the rigging of his own racing yachts, answer to and placate demanding clients; he never enjoyed the sport for pure pleasure. With the "crock," Kent was suddenly relieved of those pressures.

During the first three days of sailing, he took his family

across the sound to Caneel Bay Plantation for lunch; later they tacked the sluggish yacht back through the waters separating the islands of Saint Thomas and Saint John. But when Kent was at the helm, the children stayed close to their mother, and at times they held onto her.

Unsure of her future and that of her sisters, Cathy came to Louise one night after supper.

"Maybe everything that happened was my fault, Mom," she began. "I went out there and pounded on the yacht deck . . . when it was none of my business."

"Don't feel that way, Cathy. We're down here to fix things up, and I'm going to do everything I can to get us all back on the track. There'll be changes at Pigeon Hill. From now on, we'll do the things Dad wants . . . no more duck shooting and taking care of the grounds ourselves. We'll sail with your father instead of lobstering. Dad says he hates to eat lobster and fish, so we'll have a new menu at Pigeon Hill. And the best surprise of all . . . I've called a tennis court contractor in Connecticut; he's putting in a grass tennis court for Dad. He's always wanted one . . . but don't say anything to your sisters. It's going to be a marvelous surprise when we get back. So, darling, there's nothing to worry about anymore."

Cathy smiled to accommodate her mother. The teenage girl was not certain that a tennis court would solve the problem. Cathy was old enough to understand that props, extravagant gifts to prove affection, were not going to be enough. There was forced friendship, an anxious pretending between Kent and Louise.

Cathy caught the tension, and so did her sisters. Each of the girls felt their mother had changed. Louise's smiles were slight, pushed through with effort, and often she would sit under a coconut palm looking across to Saint John without answering her daughters' questions, as if wads of cotton had been jammed into her ears. The true visible toll of alcohol and drugs, the altering of Louise Morgan's personality, became apparent on the morning when she took the girls for a cruise on the glass-bottomed boat to see the underwater coral gardens.

The seas just west of Charlotte Amalie were kicked up by a strong and freshening tradewind. The old lumbering flat-bottom boat started to wallow, and spray and particles of green water leaped over the bow, ending up in the long, awning-covered cockpit.

The passengers sat up ramrod stiff, accepting the flings of spray as a matter of course, the small discomforts one settles for in order to enjoy something spectacular. The Morgan children had known their mother as a tough bargainer with cold and bad weather, for they had all plunged through icy seas in the winter months pulling lobsters out of Long Island Sound. Here outside the harbor the seas were warm and not too rough, yet Louise became visibly nervous. She sweated and grabbed Jody and held her in her arms.

"What's the matter, Mom?" Laurie asked.

"It's too rough out here for a boat like this," Louise yelled over the roar of the battering waves.

"Are you sure?" Laurie asked.

"Of course!" Louise snapped.

Louise then got up and told the boatman that they were going to capsize. He disagreed, saying he knew his craft and that he had come out in weather like this many times to show people the underwater coral.

"Like hell!" Louise screamed. "All of you . . . this boat is going over. It's going over! We *have* to go back!"

The others looked toward the boatman, who told them that this woman was inexperienced with rough weather, a landlubber. The cruise continued as the passengers reduced Louise Morgan, one of the ablest sailors in the world, to shame and ridicule.

One old lady said, "I know how you feel. My sister is afraid of the water, too. You'll be all right. You'll enjoy the coral . . . everyone says it's really worth it. You just hold my hand."

Louise's children were startled.

That evening the three young girls walked together on the beach, and Laurie broke the silence.

"Mom's changed. What happened?"

"She drinks too much," Cathy answered, "and she's taking pills for something."

"Do you think Mom's really sick?" Jody asked.

"She might be," Cathy answered.

"We should help her," Laurie said. "Dad and Mom aren't the same anymore. I want Mom to be okay. The weather wasn't too bad today."

"Of course it wasn't," Cathy said, "but, listen, we don't want Mom to know that we're worried. Let's not spoil the vacation. We'll wait until we get back to Pigeon Hill before we say anything. We'll see what happens then."

CHAPTER TWENTY-ONE

On their seventh day in the Virgin Islands, Cathy asked her father if she could have her own small sloop, a day sailer, just to fool around in. The next morning, behind a long lanyard, a wooden eighteen-footer was towed over and anchored next to Kent's charter yacht.

The small boat was more fun for Cathy because she could handle it herself. Sometimes she sailed with her sisters and at other times alone. Louise had begun napping again, and there always seemed to be Alka-Seltzers strewn about. She was still drinking throughout the day and downing pills, but Louise promised herself that once she returned to Menlo Head, she'd get ahold of her problem and straighten herself out.

During the following days while the children were out in their day sailer, Kent twisted his sloop back and forth, drinking piña coladas and banana daiquiris. For lunch, he put into a small deserted cove and ate sandwiches which Carrie packed each morning. On his second day of solo sailing, a small cutter with red sails caught his eyes. Kent had specialized in racing machines which in themselves embodied very little charm or the usual lines of a traditional sailboat.

The small cutter, on the other hand—about twenty-six to thirty feet, Kent imagined—was a residual from the past. She had a gaff rig, her topsides were finished naturally with mellowed planks, probably Honduras mahogany, and she was brightly varnished, with a wooden mast which gleamed in the sun.

On the third day out, Kent noticed the red cutter sloshing her way up to windward along the shore of Saint John's island. This time she was closer, and through his binoculars he saw a girl with long blond hair at the helm. He let his own sails out, and the sheets whizzed through the blocks as his sloop tore off on a broad reach, working closer to the cutter.

At that point, the design of the cutter, her blunt, old-fashioned bow and the ancient rig, interested him more than the person at the helm. He closed the distance and saw that it was a teenage girl handling the cutter; she sailed expertly, tacking the vessel back and forth with quick flips of her bronzed body.

"Hello," Kent yelled over.

"Hi."

"Like that cutter of yours," he said.

"Thanks. Dad had it built up in Maine."

"Is she mahogany over oak?"

"How did you know?"

"I'm in the business . . . a yacht designer."

"No kidding."

Kent studied the girl at the helm. She was very young and tall, and her body, almost totally exposed by the skimpiest of bikinis, was an excellent study in proportion. Her breasts were full, and one curve eased into another; yet her arms and legs revealed traces of developed muscles. Kent decided that she must be an athlete.

"What kind of boats do you design?" she yelled over.

"Ocean-racing yachts."

"Would I know any of them?"

"*Starfire* was one of them."

"*Starfire?*"

"Yes . . . she won the Southern Ocean Racing Circuit last year."

The girl brought her cutter closer to Kent's sloop, and they sailed almost side by side.

"Are you Kent Morgan?" she called over.

"None other."

"I'll be damned. What are you doing sailing that thing?"

"I just chartered her. We're down here on a vacation. Couldn't get anything better."

"Would you like to take a closer look at my cutter?"

"Sure would."

"All right. See that headland? Behind it there's a cove and a great beach. I go there every day. We'll anchor."

A strange excitement surged through Kent Morgan. The girl, whoever she was, reminded him of Louise many years ago; her agility and leanness were the same, except that this startling, long-haired blonde was taller. And she looked, thought Kent, the way Candice Bergen must have looked when she was fifteen or sixteen.

Kent hardened up on his sheets, and they made for the headland about two miles to port. In forty minutes both of the sailing craft had their hooks down. Kent inflated his rubber raft and rowed over to the cutter.

"It's great having an important yacht designer aboard," she said, leaning down to give him a hand.

The girl seemed to possess an airiness and innocence not yet clipped by age and experience.

"How are you?" Kent said, shaking her hand as soon as he mounted the deck.

"I'm Sherry Burke from Boston."

"You're a long way from home."

"Our family has a house down here for the winter. Actually, it's only a cottage near Caneel Bay . . . just on the other side."

"How did you get an old pilot cutter?"

"She's really built to an 1890 design of a Cornish fishing boat. We had her shipped down here last year."

She showed Kent the cabin, the small diesel motor, the

212

radio-telephone, and afterwards they rowed over to Kent's sloop for piña coladas.

When they entered the cabin, Kent suddenly wondered if she were too young for midday cocktails, and he asked, "How old are you?"

"Eighteen, Mr. Morgan."

"Don't call me Mr. Morgan. It makes me feel very old."

"You don't look very old to me . . . or too old," she said with a smile.

"Do you go to high school up in Boston?"

"High school? No, I never went to high school in the usual way. Dad's in the export business. I went to various schools . . . in Paris . . . in Stockholm . . . in Copenhagen . . . even down in Lima, Peru."

"Where are you now?"

"At Wellesley. You know," she said after a pause, "I'm a fan of yours. I've followed your career . . . always study your designs in *Yachting Magazine*. You must have the best of all worlds, Kent . . . designing winning yachts . . . and obviously you love sailing."

"I guess I am lucky," Kent said, raising his hand to his mouth with an unconscious gesture.

"What happened to your mouth?"

"Oh . . . a car accident."

"Was anybody else hurt?"

"A couple of my children, but they're doing fine now. We have a beach house over on the cove."

The conversation came to a halt as they stood against the lip of the galley, drinking the piña coladas.

"Well, guess I'd better be going. Thanks very much for the drink, Kent."

"What if we meet tomorrow . . . right here at the cove . . . around eleven?" Kent said suddenly.

She looked at him for a moment and shrugged her shoulders. "Why not?"

The next day Louise took Jody and Laurie into Charlotte

Amalie for shopping and a ride in the glass-bottomed boat. Cathy decided to spend the morning on the beach, reading a new novel, and Kent rowed out to his charter sloop with a pack of sandwiches, piña colada mix and a bag of ice delivered from the main hotel. He sailed out into the "roads" and pointed his sloop for the cove where the red-sailed cutter was already anchored.

As soon as his hook was down and in, Kent paddled his rubber dinghy towards Sherry's yacht. She stood on the deck, waiting for him, and as he looked up at her in the brief white bikini she wore, he thought she had the longest legs he'd ever seen. She was also much prettier than he remembered. He was immediately more excited than he'd been on any occasion with Babs Halston.

During the first hours in the Virgins, Kent had resolved that he would retrim his attitudes towards Louise. He firmly resolved never again to leave home, and he envisioned that their time in the islands would be a second honeymoon, filled with laughter and the excitement of falling in love for the second time.

It never happened.

Louise was hooked and blurred by her addictions, being far more devastated by attrition than she realized. Kent could not carry on a lively conversation with his wife; all she did was sleep and read, and he felt more lonely than he had at Pigeon Hill.

"Hi . . . brought some sandwiches," he said to Sherry Burke. "Thought we might have them later on the beach over there."

She nodded and leaned down to help him aboard.

"Good idea, Kent. I like a man who's prepared. I've got something for us, too. You ever smoke . . . joints, I mean?"

"No."

"Willing to try?"

"Sure . . . I'm feeling adventurous."

She smiled, showing a flash of white teeth against smooth, honey-colored skin. "We're going to have a lovely day."

214

They spent some time becoming light-headed, and finally, with a couple of towels and the sandwiches packed in the rubber dinghy, Kent and Sherry rowed to the scalloped beach lined with swinging coconut palms. After they had drawn the dinghy up and set out the towels, Sherry said, "Do you mind if I swim in my birthday suit?"

It came as somewhat of a shock. Kent had not quite classified the young girl. She was three years older than his daughter, Cathy, but much more developed and mature. She was three years younger than Babs, twenty-two years younger than Louise, and he was suddenly transported back to his youth. He remembered summers at East Hampton many years ago with pretty girls like Sherry Burke.

But he was still young; his body had not yet shown the marks of age—wrinkles, brown spots on the skin, extensive belly flab, balding or the invasion of white hairs at his temples.

Without another word, he stripped off his shirt and sailing shorts. He took her hand, and, both bare, they ran into the light green waters of the cove. They swam slowly back, and in shallow water he slipped his hands about her neck; face to face they talked of nothing significant until she asked him, "Are you a happily married man, Kent?"

"Not exactly."

"What does that mean?"

"Well, I married a great gal . . . Louise Upton, she used to be . . . won a silver medal in the 1964 Olympics for sailing. Did you ever hear of her?"

"No," she laughed. "I was only two years old then."

"My God, that's right. Well, let's not talk about my marriage . . . OK?"

She nodded, and their arms tightened around each other's neck. They were drawn together by an exchange of smiles and their flesh pressing against one another. They studied each other's face, and the looks that lingered were penetrating. Kent felt a certain tranquility come over him; he did not know whether it was the effect of the joints they had smoked or his sudden attraction to a girl who seemed to be something out of a vague dream. She could be described in the language of ultimates without a tinge of puffery.

It happened so naturally. It was not a scene of teasing or tempting persuasion as Kent had experienced in Babs's brownstone, but somehow he was suddenly inside the young girl, and they came together without moving their eyes from each other.

When they were expended, he said, "I love you."

The sound of it rattled his ears. He had not used that sentiment to his wife or any other for so many years that he could hardly remember how to frame the words. But they were true words, and they arrived with no effort.

She smiled and said, "Instant love . . . is that possible?"

"I think so."

"Well, maybe I love you, too, Kent Morgan . . . or maybe we're just stoned. Whatever, I like what you're saying."

They came from the water and went to sleep in each other's arms, stretched out nude on the blanket which they placed in the shade of the palms. They awoke two hours later, and the temperature had cooled.

As soon as they were awake, her haunting eyes, as greenish as a cat's, invited him towards her, and there were no words necessary. He felt his groin going to work, and in a matter of seconds, he slid inside her. She arched her spine and twisted her legs about his back, pushing him deeper and deeper inside her firm body.

It was not sex in Kent's excited mind, but the deepest sensual love in the world. He felt himself being transported to another place; the girl's movements, her smile of ecstasy, her eyes heavy with passion provided the man with a dream. While Babs and her mother had also supplied an erotic vagary with their bodies, he did not love either of the Halstons, only how they performed with each other and for him.

216

Sherry used her body in a skilled way, just as Babs and Gwen; the difference was the deeper meaning. Love. Kent Morgan knew he wanted to spend the rest of his life with this girl.

Over the next six days, Kent met Sherry on the beach at noon every day. He told her his entire story, actually the story of Louise Morgan, and just what had happened during their years in Menlo Head: the inch-by-inch slide of their marriage. They made love as often as possible. Sherry told Kent she wasn't sure what had happened, but whatever it was, she had never been happier, and it was all the more exciting and flattering because her new lover was older than her father.

"We could have a great life together," Kent said. "We're the same kind of people . . . we like sailing . . . we come from the same background. And you've been educated in Europe. You're very sophisticated . . . much older than eighteen."

"You'd divorce your wife for me?" she asked.

"Yes."

"I'm still in college."

"So you can finish up. I could move my design firm to Boston."

She was quiet for a moment. "I enjoy being with you very much, Kent. I think I even love you . . . but getting married all of a sudden . . . and you with a family. What would my parents say?"

"I don't know. We won't try to reach a conclusion right now; we'll both think about it. The only thing I want to know is this. Would you consider it?"

She took his hand and stroked it softly as she spoke. "I'm pretty crazy about you at the moment, Kent, but there are a lot of problems. I'm not one to jump into bed with a man I've just met, either . . . the way it happened with you. I'm usually the other extreme, but something was different this time. And I know it sounds corny . . . but the day I met you . . . the first time you came over to my cutter . . .

217

I knew you were going to be . . . well, important to me. And then when I realized you were married, I thought, 'Forget it, Sherry . . . this is just trouble.' But anyhow, sure, I'll think about it. Maybe we could spend some time together . . . get to know each other better . . . see what happens."

Cathy had seen her father sail away alone for six straight days, saying that he wished to think about new designs, but the young girl knew that this was not like the man; he was not one to take boats out by himself as her mother often did when she had a problem. Just after Kent left around eleven o'clock on the morning of the sixth day of solo sailing, Cathy, driven by instinct and what had happened at Pigeon Hill, pulled up the mainsail of her small sloop. Within twenty minutes she was out, frothing along in the whitecaps of the "roads."

She saw her father's sloop come around on the port tack. The sheets were run out as he drove the vessel behind a low headland of palms into a cove. Cathy beached her boat on the far side of the spit, and after yanking it far up on the beach, she walked barefooted through a dark and dew-dripping jungle, heading towards the flashes of light from the beach on the far side. Then she stopped just short of the foliage break. There were two sloops anchored and two people swimming: her father and what appeared to be a girl younger than herself. She sat down in the shadows of the palms, watching and wondering what was going on. Within an hour, her question was answered; she saw her father make love to the girl on the beach.

Cathy was sobbing almost hysterically as she ran back to her day sailer. What should she do? She had realized that her mother was slipping away from reality a little each day, and in those brief moments Cathy came to the same conclusion that Bunny Lunsford had when she first looked at Rod's revealing blowups. It would be better not to tell Louise what she had just seen on the beach; she had to protect her mother.

CHAPTER TWENTY-TWO

When Kent returned to the cottage after his meeting with Sherry Burke, there was a note for him to call his design office. He got in touch with Buddy Foster.

"Kent, Macfadden called from Chicago. I think he's finally swinging our way . . . but he wants to see *you*."

"Did you tell him I'm on vacation?"

"Yeah, I did, but Kent, this guy is ripe . . . and he's talking about a million-dollar racing machine. We need that commission."

Kent was silent, thinking about the last few exciting hours with Sherry, the promise of more to come; finally he sighed and said, "You're right, Buddy . . . tell Macfadden I'm on my way back."

Kent called Sherry, explaining his sudden departure and promising to contact her up at college in two weeks. Amid the flurry of leaving, packing, paying bills and rounding up last-minute items, no one noticed how quiet Cathy was. On the plane home Louise slept most of the way, while Kent worked on some papers.

The Morgans' private jet landed at Westchester County Airport seventeen days after they had departed. All cuts were just about healed, and the revelatory bandages were off.

"Now I have a surprise, gang," Louise said in the parking lot of the Union Carbide hangar, winking at Cathy. "Here are four blindfolds."

"What for, Mom?" Jody asked.

"Mother has a surprise for Dad . . . and all of you. Now, everyone has to wear a blindfold back to Pigeon Hill. We'll put them on at the corner of Powder Hill Road."

Louise passed out the blindfolds. She drove Kent in the Maserati, and Carrie followed with the children in the station wagon. Cathy sat silently, staring out the window, knowing what was coming. Both cars stopped at the corner some one thousand yards from their driveway.

Louise got out and fastened the blindfolds on the children.

"Does Carrie get one, too?" Jody asked.

"No. Carrie will see later. Now, no peeking. Promise?"

"We promise!" Laurie and Jody chanted in unison.

"Louise, I'm a little too old for blindfolds, aren't I?" Kent protested.

"Come on . . . join the fun, Kent."

"I hate games . . . give me a hint."

"No hints," Louise said, as she drove into Pigeon Hill and stopped. "Everybody out. We'll go elephant style . . . one hand on each other's shoulder."

Louise led her blindfolded family around to the side of the house for the surprise. She hoped that Bunny had had the sign printed and hung over the small tennis house, an afterthought.

Then Louise saw the result of her expenditure. Magnificent! The net was stretched with exactly the proper droop; the tape lines were in; the fence was painted exactly the right hue to blend into the high shrubs beyond; and the tennis house was trim and not too obtrusive. And over it, Bunny had fashioned the sign:

HAPPY BIRTHDAY, KENT!
WITH LOVE, LOUISE.

(Instead of a message printed on a paper sign, Bunny had made one out of roses—red on white—like the blanket of flowers thrown over a winning racehorse.)

220

"Okay! Off with the blindfolds!" Louise cried out.

They jerked them off. There was silence as the younger children stared at the court, remembering that it was once their vegetable garden, their task assignment. They looked at each other and for a moment remained stiff and awed. Cathy studied her father as Kent read the sign and went to Louise with what appeared to be genuine affection on his face. He kissed her and tried to talk.

"I . . . ah . . . don't know what to . . . how did this happen so fast, darling?"

"Influence."

"Thank you, Louise. God . . . a tennis court . . . a grass court."

"It's great, Mom. Can we play today?" Laurie said, jumping up and down.

"Yeah . . . I want to play, too!" Jody squealed.

"It's your father's court . . . he's the tennis master. You must ask him."

Kent was baffled and embarrassed. He had decided to ask Louise for a trial separation after obtaining an assurance from Sherry Burke that they could at least try to live together. Kent was not going to leave his wife without someone on the other end. Now he was confounded; the old Louise, with her brightness and bounce, had come back to him. She rattled along, telling him that Pigeon Hill would go through a renaissance; she would sell *Workboat* and the shotguns and bows and arrows and decoys.

It was the first time in many years that Kent had seen a softening of Louise Morgan. He was not going to come to any fast conclusions. After all, he had two ways to go; each had advantages. Louise was a generous woman. She had her own money . . . and she had certainly been understanding about the business with Babs and Gwen. Perhaps, if he decided to stay with her, he could even continue a little something with the Halston women, discreetly, of course.

Then his thoughts turned again to Sherry Burke. The days they had spent together on the beach seemed almost like a fantasy now, standing in the chilliness of the Connecticut spring. It was a boost to his ego to have a beautiful young girl in love with him. Would he always regret it if he didn't grab a second chance with her? On the other hand, there was an acute difference in their ages. Would she stay with him as he began to get older? She could easily find other younger men if she tired of him. Above all, he did not wish to appear to his contemporaries as a fool.

There was much to consider, and he would think it over carefully. There was no hurry.

The day after they returned, Kent was scheduled to leave for Chicago to meet with Macfadden, the millionaire industrialist who was seriously considering an important design. Kent put in a little time first on his new tennis court, hitting some practice balls with Louise and his daughters, as well as the pro who came over from the Field Club to start the family on a series of lessons. Then he left on a private jet for Chicago.

To Cathy, the new tennis court and what it was meant to express or heal had become a terrible irony. She looked at the perfect turf and almost burst into tears. How could shabbiness be regarded so elegantly? she asked herself. Cathy didn't even try to answer. Instead, that evening she rushed upstairs to Louise's bedroom, and before she lost her courage, she let it all go.

"Mother . . . Dad was screwing a young girl on the beach in the Virgin Islands! She was about my age. I saw it! I saw every bit of it! And he did it every day . . . I'm sure. I'm sorry . . . I'm really sorry . . . but you have to know."

Louise heard the entire story through and then told her daughter not to mention it to anyone else. Later that evening, Louise drove to Bunny Lunsford's and thanked her for the sign and her supervision of the grass court installation. After two drinks, she repeated what Cathy had told her, and Bunny knew then that it was time to tell her friend what had actually happened in the brownstone.

When she had finished, Louise shuddered and said only,

"The bastard. Why didn't you tell me everything?"

"I didn't know if you could take it. Then you had that party, and I was sure I had made the right decision. I prayed I had made the right move . . . please forgive me, Louise."

Louise lit a cigarette and settled back as she told Bunny the events that had occurred on the night of the party: the fight, the trip to the hospital, the session in the judge's chambers where she took all the blame, and the real reason they had departed so hurriedly for the Virgin Islands.

"He's a shit, Louise . . . a shit! What are you going to do about it?"

"I don't know . . . but I'll do something. I'm not going to be treated like the local loony anymore. This is it!"

"You mean a divorce?"

"Maybe." Louise paused, staring at the tip of her cigarette. "There's never been one in the Upton family. We don't believe in 'em . . . bad for the children and all that."

"Promise me something, Louise . . . no more rough stuff. That kind of thing will land you in juvenile court."

"Yeah . . . that's what I understand. Don't worry . . . I'll think of a better way to trim that little prick *right down to size*," Louise said, pacing her words.

Her eyes were full of hate and revenge.

The solution did not come to Louise Morgan until late the following afternoon when Kent called from Chicago. She cloaked her voice in vivacity, a disguise with which she was becoming more and more deft.

"Darling, how is it going?" she asked, while clamping her front teeth down on her lip.

"Fine. Macfadden was very impressed with the private jet . . . and coming all the way out here with sketches for him. I found out that he's a grass-court tennis player, too. Isn't that a piece of luck? I told him I had a grass court . . . didn't say we had just put it in, of course . . . but anyhow, I invited the Macfaddens to Pigeon Hill for the weekend. John and his wife both play. He was flattered . . . half this business is impressing people. Well, I'll bring them in on the jet tomorrow night. There'll be two girls . . . about Laurie's age, I guess, and I just called the Field Club. Rick will have two of his assistants at our disposal for the weekend . . . lessons and easy shots for us to smash back. Now, John likes game birds; he goes over to Iowa a lot to shoot. Get some game birds; call Sherry's in New York and have them trucked out to Pigeon Hill . . . and I want the best selection of wines possible. Include that in the Sherry's order. Tell them I want a complete inventory of Lafite Rothschild '47 and '52 . . . plus a good white wine . . . a 1955 Cheval Blanc . . . and maybe a nice fruity bordeaux . . . say, that '64 Pomerol, Chateau Gazin. The Macfaddens took a wine country tour a couple of years ago in France . . . we'll show them sophistication. I'll leave the menu up to you, darling, but if you don't mind a couple of suggestions . . . perhaps roast pheasant with your apple stuffing . . . wild rice casserole . . . asparagus *chinois* . . . and, oh, we can round it off with a *pomme de savoie* and brie and those delicious little warm puffed biscuits. Can you arrange everything, Louise? I'm counting on you. He wants a seventy footer; that means a hundred thousand in design commission."

"Of course, you can count on me, darling. Carrie and I will get right to work on it. What time tomorrow night?"

"Our Westchester ETA is about six. Now, one other thing that came to mind. Call the tennis court people; see if they can put in some night lights . . . temporary, if necessary . . . so we can have a short game of doubles when we arrive. And tomorrow night we'll serve Maine lobsters on the terrace. Have to run now. Don't forget to call the florist."

Louise's head was going milky from an invading vodka hangover, and the idea of brutal retaliation did not seep into her mind. It bounced in as swiftly as her original decision to install the tennis court.

She made two victorious phone calls: to the nursery owner and to the tennis court contractor, telling each of them to get over to Pigeon Hill immediately. Emergency!

They were there within an hour, and she called both men into the library.

"I'm very happy with your court, Mr. Coleman . . . but I made a mistake. I thought my husband deserved it . . . but I've found out differently . . . and I want the tennis court out of here by tomorrow night."

The two men looked at each other with gaping droops to their mouths and hoisted eyebrows.

"Now, don't be shocked. Things do change in life. If you got it in so fast, I know you can take it out even faster."

"In one day, Mrs. Morgan?"

"In one day."

"Are you *sure* about this, Mrs. Morgan?"

"Positive. Does your nursery have vegetable plants, Mr. Rawson . . . those tomato plants . . . hothouse-grown?"

"Yes, we do, Mrs. Morgan."

"Since my husband detests tomatoes in any form whatsoever, I want the tennis court planted with tomatoes . . . every single tomato plant possible. What you don't have in stock, buy from other sources."

Louise handed each of the suppliers an advance check. They left Pigeon Hill quickly, knowing that the woman was serious and that she had the money to turn her wishes into instant overtime profit.

Louise looked after them and felt the warm pleasure of anticipation; she was very pleased with her creative concept of revenge.

Early the following morning, just after the children left for Country Day, the contractor's trucks rolled into the driveway at Pigeon Hill.

"Mrs. Morgan," the tennis court man inquired once more, "are you certain of this? Have you thought it over?"

"I never change my mind once it's made up, Mr. Coleman. Just get to work, and remember . . . the deadline is five o'clock today. Not a minute past."

Louise made a martini and sat on the terrace overlooking

the work crews. She could not remember a more delicious time in her life, with the exception of receiving the silver medal in Japan so many years ago. She watched every detail: the peeling back of the priceless grass, exposing the drainage rocks underneath; the pulling up of the high fence; the demolition of the seven-thousand-dollar tennis house. Then the grader came in and gouged the soil for the tomato plants, lined up by the side of the terrace, awaiting their new home.

She would have paid a million dollars, if necessary, just to see this and know what was going to result from it. Louise was already planning for her finale that night.

She made a sandwich for lunch. Ignoring Carrie's troubled face and mutterings, Louise looked up the Bank of Milan number in New York, and she phoned Antonio.

"Hello, Antonio . . . Louise Morgan. How are you?"

"Louise, my dear. I'm fine. You've been away?"

"Yes, we went down to the Virgin Islands for a couple of weeks . . . just to sop up a little sun."

"We enjoyed your party immensely. I know Jill called you the next day. There was no answer . . . then we heard you'd gone on a trip. I do hope that little incident on the yacht didn't provoke your husband."

"Not in the least. Antonio . . . I'm driving into the city tonight, and I thought perhaps we could have a little dinner at my duplex on East Sixty-sixth Street. Kent's away. I'm one hell of a game bird cook . . . my specialty is roast pheasant with apple stuffing."

"I'd be happy to join you. You're thinking of dinner for two?"

"Dinner for two. Say . . . eight o'clock? One East Sixty-sixth Street."

Shortly after she'd hung up, Kent called from Chicago to say that he was almost ready to board the jet and that the design contract was as good as signed.

"Dinner all set, Louise? Everything ready? You called the tennis pro?"

"Darling, everything's arranged for you. Absolutely everything."

"Fine . . . we'll see you about six."

With the combination of three martinis and a Valium, Louise fell asleep a few minutes later, after instructing Carrie to wake her in an hour.

Just after lunch, Cathy Morgan complained to the school nurse at Country Day that she had a headache, and the nurse excused her from the afternoon's classes. She was driven home by the school chauffeur, who was often pushed into service when mothers could not pick up their children because of bridge games at various clubs or other activities.

As they pulled up, Cathy noticed the trucks in the driveway and the swarm of men in dirt-encrusted overalls. At first, she thought that the men were putting some finishing touches on the tennis court; she walked out to the terrace to see tomato plants going in. Just as Louise had ordered, there was no indication that a tennis court had ever existed on the flat table of land beyond the bow of the terrace.

Cathy stood there, shocked, for a moment, then whirled and ran into the house.

"Carrie . . . Carrie . . ." she yelled, bursting through the door. "What's going on out there! Where's Mother?"

"She's upstairs resting . . . didn't want to be disturbed. I'm sorry about the tennis court, Cathy."

"But why did she do that?" Cathy cried.

"I dunno, child . . . ask your mother."

Cathy ran upstairs and broke into Louise's bedroom. Louise awoke and put her arms around her daughter.

"Mother . . . Mother . . . I didn't mean . . . oh, it's all my fault again . . ."

"Shhhh, Cathy," Louise said, stroking her hair. "Nothing's your fault, dear . . . but your father doesn't deserve an expensive present. He's been cheating on me all along. You told me about one affair . . . but there've been others."

"Oh, Mom . . . everything's such a mess . . . there's

something wrong all the time now. What about Jody and Laurie? What are you going to tell them?"

"Well, we can't tell them exactly why the tennis court came out . . . they're too young to understand these things. I think I'll just say that Daddy was a bad boy, and they can ask him about it . . . let him figure something out. Cathy, I have to go into New York tonight on some business, and I may be gone a couple of days."

Cathy looked at her mother, bewildered. "What kind of business?"

"I have to see an art dealer . . . I'm thinking of taking up my painting again. Anyway, I want you to help Carrie take care of your sisters . . . and don't worry. I won't be gone long, darling . . . but it's important . . . very important."

If the children had been baffled before by the trauma and chaos at Pigeon Hill, each of them, in varying degrees, now felt that their security and their way of life were being callously withdrawn. Their confusion turned into a mild panic. They all retreated to Cathy's room and locked the door, drawing together in a unit to protect themselves. The oldest girl attempted to comfort her sisters, who seemed to feel they were in a totally alien territory. The strength and providence they had gained from their mother, the assurances in the Virgin Islands that things would settle down, had suddenly erupted into another seething incident. And this time it appeared to be more acute and devastating, for a mocking smile rode on Louise Morgan's lips as she contemplated the ultimate satisfaction of maligning her husband, no matter what the cost.

Kent Morgan had played his role as a talented patrician in Chicago. The stories of his victories in yacht races (when one of his hulls won, he credited himself, not the skipper), plus a parade of name dropping, which included the Duke of Edinburgh who cherished a fast-racing sloop, went on without letup. The Midwestern tool manufacturer, who was extraordinarily rich, and his wife, a bland woman from an Indiana corn farm, were so doused in Kent's fabricated charm and his private jet that they thought some untouchable world had suddenly descended upon Chicago. Riding in a celebrity designer's private jet to Menlo Head for a tennis and business weekend was far beyond the envelope of their hopes. They could afford any racing machine Kent could design, but the industrial client knew that it took more than money to pierce the rigid clique of Eastern yachting.

They brought their tennis rackets, their best clothes and their plump children. As the plane turned onto its final approach for Westchester Airport, Kent said, "John, let's play a quick game of lawn tennis. Five hundred dollars to the winner . . . are you with me?"

"Of course. And be prepared to lose," said the soft-faced manufacturer.

Kent was planning to lose; it was another stroke of patronage in the overall concoction to make the dullard into a yachtsman of standing. And no matter how poorly one sailed, just to skipper a Morgan original, a custom racing machine, brought awe from those who knew what they were doing on the watery racecourses. Part of Kent's sailing tactics was to supply friends of his to break in his yachts; they were really not friends, but paid professionals who made certain that the Morgan hulls performed for their new owners. (Kent was only as good as "his" last silver cup.)

The jet landed. Kent let the client drive the Maserati to Pigeon Hill, while his wife and their children followed behind in a chauffeured limousine. They arrived at the front door, and Louise met them in a black cocktail dress. She shook hands, exchanged banalities and directed Carrie to show Mrs. Macfadden to the upstairs guest rooms.

"Louise, John and I have decided to have a challenge tennis match. Five hundred dollars, John . . . right?"

The big balding man nodded. "I hope you're ready, Kent. I warned him, Mrs. Morgan . . . I'm a good grass court player."

"Did you book a court at the Field Club, Kent?" Louise asked.

"The Field Club? We'll play right here."

"Here?"

"Of course."

"But we don't have a court, Kent," she said with a blank expression on her face.

Kent broke into laughter. "You see, John, my wife has a sense of humor. Come on, John . . . I want you to see the finest grass court in Menlo Head."

Kent took the bulky man by the arm and led him out to the terrace. He froze as his eyes wandered over the rows of tomato plants flipping gently in the breeze.

John looked around amiably. "Where's the court?"

"This is one of my wife's practical jokes," Kent said thickly.

His face was very flushed when he marched back into the house with his now wary client.

"Louise, I'd like to speak to you."

"Oh, I'm sorry, darling, but I'm going to New York, and I'm late already."

"What about dinner . . . the pheasant?"

"Pheasant? You didn't say anything about that, dear."

Kent looked at the poker-faced man next to him, and he tried to smile. He shifted his look again towards Louise, and his face hardened.

"What *happened* to the tennis court?" Kent demanded.

"Darling, what's happening to you? Mr. Macfadden . . . Kent's been very overworked lately, I'm afraid. Did he tell you that we had a tennis court? We could never afford anything like that. We use the Field Club. Well, nice to have met you and your wife. Oh, Kent, there's some baloney and Swiss cheese in the refrigerator . . . and I ordered the bottles of Gallo table wine . . . just as you asked."

Louise spun around and opened the door; then she turned and said, "Enjoy yourselves, gentlemen. Someday, Mr. Macfadden, we might have a grass tennis court. There's always hope, you know."

Kent formed the words with his lips: "You bitch!"

She formed the words with her lips: "You bastard!"

Then she closed the door and was gone.

CHAPTER TWENTY-THREE

Louise's drive into New York that Friday evening was full of glee. She had put her husband down with the swiftness of a well-slung saber, and she had kept her promise to Bunny Lunsford: no violence.

Louise *had* repeated Kent's order to Sherry's: a fresh-killed, corn-fed pheasant was delivered to One East Sixty-sixth Street, along with wild rice. The assistant manager of the building had taken his passkey and placed the bird into the oven. By the time she arrived, Louise could smell the faint and savory whiff of a plump game bird cooking. Each of Kent's wines and champagnes was brought upstairs; she could think of no more complete delectation than savaging his private stock of carefully selected and priceless wines with the eager Italian.

It was to be the first extramarital affair of her married life. Louise wanted each detail, each molecule of pleasure, each salacious second to go by with ultimate pleasure, no stumbles, no crudities.

Louise made herself a drink and looked around the apartment. On the walls were photographs of Kent's prizewinning yachts; there were other pictures showing the silverware being passed out. Upstairs in the library there were burgees of his favorite clubs: the Royal Yacht Squadron, the Royal Ocean Racing Club, the Royal Bermuda Yacht Club, the New York Yacht Club; there was even a highly shined brass telescope at the window, mounted on a light antique tripod.

His walnut and tooled leather desk was actually from the Admiralty, as the heavily carved crown on the foreside indicated. There was a drafting table with a hull model on it in the dining room, which served also as his design studio, and as a final clue, a crumpled pack of Players cigarettes had been discarded there.

In a wild bout of ecstasy, Louise suddenly began to collect each of Kent's props, and she tossed them into the hall closet. Upstairs, she gathered her own museum pieces and hung new pictures up on the walls and scattered about her own yachting awards. On the coffee table, where no eye could miss it, she placed her Olympic silver medal. From another closet, Louise took out several old oil paintings she had done years before: landscapes of the Bay shore, ducks in squadrons flying low over the sawgrass. She placed them about the living room just to show Antonio and others, perhaps, that hers was a compound talent: sports and art.

She finished just as the doorbell rang. Louise swung the door open and kissed Antonio on the cheek, leading him into the room, her room now.

"What a marvelous place. It's *you*," he gestured with a fat, gratuitous smile.

"Just my studio. I do a little painting," Louise said, pointing to the oils, hoping that the suave, dark-suited Italian would not see the nine-year-old dates, dust-coated, beside her signature.

"Marvelous talent, *eccellente!*" he said, shooting his coal-black eyes about the room.

"Thank you. How about a drink . . . wine, whiskey, champagne . . . or one of each?"

"Well, why don't we celebrate our reunion with champagne?"

Louise brought in the Dom Perignon already chilled in the sterling silver ice bucket, Kent's only sailing trophy not remanded to the closet. The Italian's eyes opened wider as he studied the champagne; he dipped his head towards the coffee table where her Olympic silver medal lay.

"You're quite a woman, Louise. You must be proud of this," he said, picking up the medal and holding it in the palm of his hand.

"Luck . . . just luck," she said.

They settled down together on the couch and drank a mutual toast.

"I'm very pleased you called me," Antonio said. "I've never forgotten our brief moment together on the yacht that night."

For some reason, she suddenly began to test the slick humper; maybe it was his cocky eyes which already had her in bed, or it could have been his mushy mouth. Whichever, she decided he was as arrogant as Kent Morgan.

"I have an open marriage . . . you might have guessed that," Louise lied. "And I assume you belong to the same club."

"Club? Club? Sounds common."

She sensed a shrinking of his inflated ego. She smiled and said pleasantly, "Oh, come on, Antonio. We're adults. Both of us like or need freedom now and then. That's precisely why I invited you here . . . and that's *precisely* why you accepted my invitation. Or do you find me the most attractive, irresistible woman west of the River Arno?"

"I find you all of those things . . . certainly, Louise."

It was then she began her under-the-breath review of this man: "You're a liar. I'm not glamorous . . . beautiful."

"You're a very modern woman, Louise," Antonio said, "and your husband must be very understanding."

"Oh, yes. In fact, we talk about our sexual trips . . . we encourage each other's explorations."

"Ah . . . truly sophisticated people. Jill and I were afraid everyone would be too old-fashioned here. We have had our separate lovers for years."

"It's the only intelligent thing . . . marriage can become so boring."

"Yes, yes . . . well, I'm happy my fears were groundless.

And, in fact, your husband might enjoy my wife," he smiled.

"You're not only a prig . . . you're a pimp," she said to herself, continuing her silent assault of this obvious bull-shitter.

"Well, Antonio, we should arrange that . . . discreetly, of course."

"How did you and Kent arrive at the European approach to marriage?"

"We never thought of it as being European. It's just helped our marriage . . . to be free and open."

"Of course . . . I was very reluctant about moving from Milan to Connecticut. I had heard that it was provincial . . . but very beautiful, of course," he said hastily.

"You mean puritanical . . . not provincial," she said to herself. "You don't speak well English, Mr. Lumphead."

"Do you think there can be a happy marriage without outside lovers?" Louise asked.

"Of course, but it's rare. The basic point is honesty . . . tell your partner how it is. We're all sexual animals."

After the pheasant dinner which turned out very well, they retired to the living room with the Napoleon brandy, one of two bottles which Kent had hoarded, believing that a three-thousand-dollar brandy bought at auction in France was just as much a hedge against inflation as the purchase of gold.

"Dear Louise, how can I satisfy your needs? Tell me . . . what are your wildest fantasies? I can deliver fantasies. I happen to know many people in New York . . . passionate . . . beautiful . . . sophisticated people."

"My fantasy is very attractive young men who could make love to me. Not one man, but two . . . and all at once. Like double bubble."

"What is double bubble?"

"It's an American chewing gum."

"You will have your double-bubble experience. Can you stay in town for a few evenings?"

She nodded.

"Then tomorrow night . . . I'll arrange a small party with the right young lovers. I'll attend to it in the morning, but tonight . . . we love."

They said no more. She stood and took his hand and guided the man upstairs without a strain of sexual anticipation or passion, only a mild sense of curiosity. Her head was whoozy with the brandy, which she took along with her. To sip Kent's priceless brandy while being pumped by the lush-talking Italian—a cliché of a man, she thought—was indeed another layer of vindictiveness.

On the way up the curving stairs, she slowed down. Her bravado began to slip; her legs felt heavy, as if she were walking on the carpet of a soggy rain forest. Was she going to bed or going to hell? Louise Morgan was snatched along by her unfiltered hatred of Kent. The removal of the tennis court had settled part of her raw anger, and now she would bear the pain of this sloppy fuck.

She walked faster up the stairs and turned at the top. She knew she would have to pretend the passion she didn't feel.

"Kiss me, darling Antonio."

He embraced her, and she slipped her hand down to his stiffening penis and up again to unloosen his belt buckle.

"I don't know if I can make it to the bedroom," she panted. "We might have to do it on the stairs."

"I have a bad back," he said with perfect attention to formality, not even perceiving the tease.

In the bedroom Louise fondled her breasts, and with no sense of excitement, she ripped her dress off, shredding the old Chanel which she'd never liked, anyhow. His eyes lighted up. She slipped off her panties, spread her hips. By that time his tailored suit was a pile of black cloth on the floor; his tiny penis, which looked like a bean sprout, was as tall as it would ever be.

"You're so big," she exclaimed.

She knelt before him and slid her tongue over his flesh. She tried to shove it as far as she could down her throat.

236

He began to pump, and in unison they moved back onto the bed where he thrust himself into her. She could hardly feel the intrusion of the tiny instrument.

"Oh, I feel you so deep . . . it's all the way. You have the biggest cock in the world. My God!" she screamed out, playing her role.

His eyes signaled the effectiveness of the flattery. She squeezed him in a fake assault of passion, but she didn't feel a thing, or didn't want to, except that something actually quite small was working around inside her. She imagined it was a playful baby snake. Her fraudulent passion, her theatrical performance, rose to a pitch, and she pretended to come and come and come. And then he came in a little pulsating dribble, as if the tiny snake had spit up.

It was over for him. He was small, with no technique, no physical graces. Louise remembered now that the Italian had not been much better with his lips that night aboard the yacht than he was with the tool of his trade.

She started to despise men.

CHAPTER TWENTY-FOUR

There was a faint hint of summer heat in the still air that Saturday morning in Menlo Head. Some boats were already overboard and riding to their tethers in the river before the Yacht Club; sounds of tennis balls being plopped back and forth at the Field Club provided bass notes for the singing birds who were happy because of the unexpected warmth.

At the Menlo Head Country Club, the greens were taking on the deep richness of their summer shadings, having been watered by hose and heaven all that spring.

This was to be Phil Cummings' breakthrough year: the period in his club golf career in which he would finally drop from a six to a five handicap, a barrier he had tried to pierce for almost five years. Phil's lesson was scheduled for nine o'clock that morning. The shoeshine and spike repairer in the locker room picked up the phone, and Kent Morgan asked for the lawyer who was pulling on his new Brooks Brothers golf shirt.

"Sorry to bother you, Phil, but I have to see you right away," Kent said.

"Ah . . . well, I'm just about to have a golf lesson. How about meeting me in my office . . . say . . . at twelve?"

"Now, Phil!"

"You haven't had another Pigeon Hill boxing match? Your lip isn't out of shape, is it?"

"Very funny," Kent said "It's worse than a broken lip. Can I come right over . . . please?"

"We can't talk here. Maybe I can get the governors' room for us."

Phil postponed his golf lesson until later that morning, and Kent met the lawyer in the long, airless room on the second floor of the Menlo Head Golf Club. It was peopled by the faded oil paintings of departed governors; each of them in their various outfits, from funeral suits to golfing sportswear, seemed to look down directly on the lemon-oiled, mahogany table, as if to say no one should sit there but a true governor exercising his puny ex-officio rights.

Kent, realizing the gravity of his decision, had dressed in a blazer of the Royal Yacht Squadron; he wore his newest shoes, had combed his pale blond hair carefully and, above all, had instructed himself to present the facts to his counsel with precision.

"I was surprised to get your call, Kent," Phil said, studying his client for some hint of what was coming.

"Good morning, Phil . . . I appreciate this," Kent said brightly, removing his sunglasses and shaking hands. "I'm sorry that I called you in the locker room, but my home situation is critical. I think you'll agree."

"Sit down," Phil said.

"I prefer to stand."

Kent placed his hands on the banister back of a club governor's chair. He told the story slowly, without once raising his voice, feeling that the installation and immediate removal of the tennis court needed no further emphasis.

He came to the end of his cool explanation, paused and then said, "I was hurt and embarrassed in front of this very important client . . . he's no longer a prospective client. The Macfaddens left my house this morning for a weekend in New York. He thinks the Morgans are disturbed. And my children are still crying; they're baffled. I don't blame them. My wife spent last evening in our New York duplex. She called simply to say she may never come home . . . she told me she's going to 'swing' for a while."

Kent stuffed his hands in his pockets and walked around

239

the room looking into the faces of the old governors; he wondered what their wives had been like.

The soft-faced Ivy League lawyer, a man who was commiserative but out of tune with bizarre realities, said, "I rather thought that Louise was falling away from life that morning in Judge Shallaway's office. And let me tell you something . . . just my opinion . . . but I feel that Louise was trying to inflict serious injury on you that night. It was more than a threatening poke in the mouth. That woman meant harm. She must be critically ill."

"She's flipped all the way," Kent said. "Phil, are your parents still alive?"

"Mother is, my Dad passed away a few years ago. He was a fine man, though . . . Harvard '17."

"Who was in charge of your house when you were growing up?"

"Dad, of course . . . not that he was autocratic, a Clarence Day. My father was a fair man with plenty of compassion."

"And your mother?"

"Wonderful woman, God bless her . . . excellent cook . . . brought us up properly . . . devoted to my dad . . . respected him."

Kent snapped his fingers.

"That's the key! Your mother *respected* your father, and the children respected their parents . . . with emphasis on the father."

Phil nodded. "Mom had her job . . . Dad had his . . . our home was a unit that worked."

"Exactly! Well, at Pigeon Hill, there's been a power struggle going on all along. Louise has been conducting a war right under my nose."

"I don't understand," Phil said, his eyes following Kent around the governors' table.

"Louise Upton stole my authority as a husband . . . as a father . . . as head of the house. I'm a prisoner there . . . a captive in my own home!"

240

"You sound as crazy as Louise. Kent, you're exaggerating."

"I'm *not exaggerating!* Little by little, that woman has taken over . . . undermined me. She's infiltrated our daughters."

"That's absurd."

"I knew you were going to say that. I knew it!"

"What exactly does she do? Your wife's obviously unstable . . . spending good money on a tennis court . . . and then taking it out. I've never heard of anyone doing something like that. What happened?"

"Who knows? If she wants to waste her money, fine . . . it's *her* trust fund. But goddamn it, I don't matter around there. I'm only sweating away at the drawing board, designing big toys. That's what Louise calls my yachts . . . 'big toys.' But, of course, my dear wife was always into the vital things of life . . . lobster fishing . . . farming . . . duck shooting. I'm a nobody. The children won't talk to me at the dinner table. It's Mom this or Mom that. And then they built their own lobster boat, not from my plans. And do you know what my one pride and joy was at Pigeon Hill? It sounds small and simple, but it was *my* thing. I used to go around painting the baseboards. I had fifteen cans of paint in the carriage house . . . each one marked. Now, you would think that the father, the head of the house, could at least be given the authority over the baseboards, but no, she took over. She painted the baseboards one day, and I began to think, 'Why the hell am I here?' So we had a party. Do you think I was consulted? Oh, no. It was *her* party . . . that's what the paper said . . . and that's how it was. And just to bring me down completely, she bashes me in the jaw. I know when a punch is supposed to hurt. That punch was well lined up . . . so well lined . . . she meant to slaughter me right in front of the children as if to say, 'Girls, let me show you what a real modern mommie can do.' She did it! Eleven stitches, and two of my teeth are still loose. I may have to have a total bridge or something. You're right, Phil. Louise meant it, and those girls just loved seeing me go down with a mouthful of blood and a lip that was sliced up. How they applauded their mother . . . no, excuse me . . . *not* their mother . . . *their mother and father both.* She comes as a total package. Completely autonomous. She orders a tennis court because I've always wanted a tennis court instead of that goddamn fucking garden. I hate vegetables . . . tomatoes worst of all. I'm allergic to tomatoes. She puts in the court . . . just to appease me . . . not a way of saying, 'I'm sorry for breaking up your mouth.' Hell, no . . . that woman put in the tennis court with the express purpose of taking it *out* when she knew I had a client coming. And she planted tomatoes . . . on purpose!"

"You're getting out of breath, Kent. Sit down and take it easy. Come on now."

"Do you understand?" Kent asked his lawyer.

"I think so, but why would she do this?"

"She simply wanted to prove who holds the cards at Pigeon Hill. I asked Cathy why her mother took out the tennis court. She said to me, 'You've been a bad boy . . . or naughty or something.' Can you imagine that? I've been naughty."

"Have you been, Kent?"

"No more than any other man."

"You *did* strike your wife one night. Everyone in town knew about it."

"It was just a tap to bring her to her senses . . . staying out there in a storm, laughing her head off while I engaged two expensive tugs. When a man hires two tugs to find his wife, that's true devotion, in spite of all I've been through. Her punch was malicious. Mine wasn't."

"Kent, what do you want . . . an order from Judge Shallaway to have her committed? Maybe that can be arranged."

"I want you to arrange a divorce . . . right away."

Phil Cummings, whose legal work was consumed with estates and trusts, plus some Menlo Head council business, was opposed to seamy domestic problems. And when divorce did occur in Menlo Head, the couples usually departed the genteel old town for other courtrooms.

"Divorce can be ruinous," Phil said. "Think this over carefully . . . maybe try a marriage counselor . . . or talk to someone."

Kent shook his head. "Too late. She is destroying me . . . little by little. I want out *now* . . . and I also want the house and the children."

"You're going to ask the court for custody of the girls?" Phil asked, screwing up his thin eyebrows.

"Absolutely!" Kent said, curling his fists as if to prop up his words.

"Tell me the reason you want those children."

"I'm concerned about them. Louise is *not* a fit mother . . . she's become a total alcoholic. Half the time she doesn't even know what's going on . . . doesn't fix meals anymore . . . doesn't eat herself. And she's gobbling tranquilizers along with the liquor. Even an idiot knows you can't do that. I don't think she'll be able to take care of herself before long . . . much less the children."

"I'm very sorry to hear that, Kent. I had no idea . . ."

"No . . . no one knows just what I've put up with. No more. I've had it!"

"What about Dr. Driscoll? Couldn't he help?"

"He's the one who gave her the pills. Anyway, she doesn't want to stop anything."

Phil Cummings' mind was rattled. It appeared that both Morgans, people he had known and respected for fourteen years, were coming apart at the seams.

"Besides," Kent went on, "I can see what's happening to my daughters. I *don't* want them to grow up like their mother!"

"Christ, I think you two need a shrink . . . not a lawyer." Phil blew out a long breath. "Kent, first of all, there's the tender age doctrine which says that young children should usually be with their mother. Also, just so you know,

Judge Shallaway won't hear the case; it'll go to the Superior Court in Stamford."

"Why? He has jurisdiction."

"This is a community of genteel people, remember? We solve minor problems, but we don't like custody fights . . . ugly domestic disruptions."

"But you know I have a case. Look at my tooth. It still wiggles. Will you defend me?"

"No."

"Why?" Kent blasted out.

"I'm not a divorce lawyer. In fact, I'm against divorce. Most of my clients are my friends . . . and the other lawyers in Menlo Head are my friends. We oppose each other in the courtroom, yes, but we don't carry our grudges around socially. And besides, I know both you and Louise. My advice is to work out a reconciliation."

"I don't want a reconciliation . . . it's way beyond that. Will you help me find a lawyer, then? The nastiest, dirtiest, most treacherous lawyer in the state of Connecticut."

"I'm shocked to hear you say a thing like that, Kent."

"I've been a gentleman too long. Now I want to bring this woman to her knees. I have the money . . . and I know I have a case."

"You also have a confused head."

"Don't talk to me about my head. You haven't lived at Pigeon Hill in the feminist camp the way I have. All I want from you is the Dracula . . . the Attila of lawyers. You owe me that much."

Phil Cummings got up and paced the governors' table, knowing that he could never keep his mind on the golf lesson later that morning. He kept eyeing Kent Morgan, trying to understand him and his wife. How do fine, educated people come apart so unexpectedly? he asked himself.

"I'm waiting for your answer. Don't just walk around the table. Who is my man?"

"All right . . . if you're so determined."

"I am."

"A guy named Robert Booth . . . practices in Stamford . . . known to be a tough divorce lawyer. In domestic relations the man is tops; he'll do anything to win a case. I pleaded a real estate dispute against him one time, and I'll never forget it. Bob's not a Menlo Head type. He's a Californian . . . a Korean War hero . . . a Marine major."

"Where did he go . . . Harvard . . . Yale Law School?"

"No, none of 'em."

"What do you mean . . . none?"

"Booth read for the law in California. That state allows you to take the bar exam without a law degree. They say he passed on the first try. How he was admitted to our state bar is a mystery, but he knows his law. Before you see Booth, though, please think this over again, Kent. You and Louise have too much going to let it slide down the drain."

"Phil, that's easy for you to say. I had pride . . . I want it back. Now, can you call Booth for me?"

"On a Saturday?"

"Why not? I'll drive up to Stamford. I need this man right this minute, Phil . . . not tomorrow . . . not Monday. Today!"

Phil Cummings saw the desperation in Kent Morgan's face. He picked up the phone in the governors' room and asked for Stamford information.

CHAPTER TWENTY-FIVE

Phil Cummings' mind was clouded and disturbed. After he had persuaded Kent Morgan to leave the club that morning, promising to call him as soon as he had contacted Booth, the last thing the attorney wished to do was take a golf lesson. He was not sure he could hold the iron, having been doused with that woeful story. Phil sat at the long table thinking.

He had established in his mind that Louise was in trouble, already separated from sound thinking, but now he realized that Kent Morgan might be unbalanced. His hatred and irrationality in the governors' room had moved the lawyer to grave suspicions. First he thought he should visit Louise to persuade her to seek counseling before it was too late, but that would be interference with a client's wishes. Phil was not certain who was his client: Louise, Kent or both. On thing Phil Cummings knew. He had to toss this mess out of town, send it up to Stamford to the other lawyer, with the provision that the case be heard in that city and not Menlo Head.

When Robert Booth got on the phone, he merely crowed: "Sure . . . I can see the guy today. I'm in the office doing casework. Does he have money?"

"I can guarantee it," Phil said. "He owns one of the biggest houses in Menlo Head . . . must be worth a million."

"Those are the clients I adore, Cummings. Send him over about two. First, call Morgan. Say I want him to write out his dispute in three hundred words or less and tell me just what he's after."

"Why can't he tell you when he gets there?"

"I like the soulful dribble . . gets to accuracy. It also sets the guy up. I have a record of why he came to me and what services he's requesting. And I suppose you want a referral fee?"

"Forget it. Get him out of trouble, and quietly. The fellow's blowing his top."

"Must have a good reason."

"I can't tell."

Phil Cummings transmitted the message to Pigeon Hill. Early that afternoon in the library, Kent began writing a digest of his upcoming complaint, carefully conserving his language to keep the sentences crisp without allowing his emotions to invade the facts.

Lawyer Booth had committed ethical hari-kari years ago. He realized, and correctly, that a man who read for the law instead of attending an accredited institution had about as much chance of an affiliation with a respectable firm as a Sing Sing graduate who applied for a berth in the United States Attorney's office. So the lawyer became a loner, trading upon the miseries of others.

His methods and tactics of prevailing in a case, usually a divorce action, were based upon cruelty, trickery, entrapment, plus a good dose of detailed casework. Even if he were nailed by the Bar Association of Connecticut, all they could do was censure him or, in an extreme situation, disbar him.

As Kent swung his Maserati into the parking lot of a low modern building in Stamford which housed attorneys and a few doctors, he gunned his twelve cylinders to four thousand RPM before he snapped off the ignition, hoping that the lawyer would look out and notice his expensive vehicle.

It worked.

Booth slid back the curtain of his office and saw the red

sports car. He understood exactly what it was and how much it cost.

Kent entered the office and looked at the lawyer, a bulky man in his mid-fifties with a well-formed but grizzled face and a thatch of salt-and-pepper hair. In his short-sleeved shirt, the man appeared tough; his biceps, despite his age, were still limber and firm; he spoke in a throaty voice, not wasting words.

The office was functionally decorated, and the suite was full of computer terminal gear plus a very large copying machine, one which turned typing into what looked like typeset letters.

After an abbreviated hello, Booth drew in his hard lips and said, "Now, Mr. Morgan . . . Phil Cummings says you're financially stable."

"I am."

"All right. Now, let me tell you something about me, if Phil Cummings hasn't."

"He told me a little."

"The man abhors me but respects me . . . or, shall we say, the effectiveness of my work. And I might use him 'of counsel' in this case. You see, Mr. Morgan, I'm a magnificent failure. I'm a prick. No one has ever argued that point. I don't practice the law; I *use* it. After I've read your little essay here, we'll talk. You can decide whether or not we'll get along. If not, we'll say good-bye with a handshake."

Kent waited out in the reception area. Five minutes later the lawyer yanked open the door with such a pull of strength that Kent thought the knob would come off in his huge hand.

"Come on in, Mr. Morgan. Sit down," he said, pointing to a leather chair. He tapped Kent's paper in his hand. "Seems you two had everything going for you . . . money, sailboats, good education. Says here you even spent a year together in England. She studied art while you went to Cambridge . . . very high-class stuff. Sex must have been okay . . . three daughters. She slapped you around a bit

248

and took away your tennis court . . . okay." He tossed the paper on the desk. "What exactly do you want, Mr. Morgan?"

Kent locked his fingers together tightly and stared at the lawyer. "I want a divorce, the property . . . *and* custody of the girls."

"Is that all?"

"I no longer love my wife . . . and the sex *hasn't* been okay for a long time. Louise is a countrywoman . . . wrong for me . . . but worse, she's bringing up our daughters in her image. They spend all their time outdoors in foul-smelling clothes . . . never wash their hair or put on pretty dresses." He paused and then said, "I want control of them before it's too late."

"Too late?"

"Before they're ruined for life by the arrogant single-mindedness of my wife. I love my daughters very much, and I can give them a balanced upbringing. I want them introduced to the twentieth century, to culture, to true sportsmanship, to academics, to cleanliness, to fairness, to God and to a voice other than their mother's."

"Well, that's very impressive, Mr. Morgan . . . but I'll tell you something. It's going to be tough to take those kids away from their mother."

"It's absolutely necessary for their own good. Can you accomplish this?"

"*I* can do it, but a lot depends on you, not *me*. Let's get to the point. You've got money?"

"Yes."

"And you detest this woman?"

"Yes."

"And you want to grind her down to a piece of fleshy rubbish so that even her loose flesh will have nervous hives?"

"That's how I feel."

"And you don't care how you do it as long as she's demolished and you have the kids . . . the property . . . the maintenance?"

"That's about it. I've tried very hard to communicate with Louise, but she's completely dogmatic. She must be taught a lesson. I'm not an unreasonable man . . . I'll allow her the proper visiting rights, but I insist on custody of the children."

"Do you want to be a shit, a prick shit or a prick shit bastard?"

"Whatever is required . . . a prick shit bastard . . . as long as everyone realizes it's *all her fault*. I have an important position in the community. Louise is wrong . . . not me. She's very sick . . . and I want people to understand that the steps we had to take were necessary. None of this is my fault. I've simply made the only decision possible under the circumstances, and now I feel the quicker the whole matter is concluded, no matter what it entails, the better for all of us."

"Well, let me fill you in. In law, it's hard to tell the bad guys from the good guys, and it'll be slimy and rough. I hope you can take it and pay for it."

"I want to tell you something about me, Mr. Booth. I'm not a man to be shamed. My wife has shamed me . . . abused my children . . . loosened my teeth. I am prepared to do whatever has to be done."

"Might still be shocking to you, Mr. Morgan. Anyway, there're three techniques in a highly contested divorce action; one is nasty, and two are abusive. It's been said that a lawyer acting for a mad spouse has a fighting capability which comes out like justified blackmail. If you want to rip this woman apart, the law lets you do it. I'll give you the rules of the game. If you don't have the stomach for it, tell me now, but don't come to me later with bellyaches and a pocketful of antacid pills. Oh, yes, I'm supposed to ask you if you tried everything to avoid a dissolution of this marriage; the answer is everything . . . just everything."

The lawyer worked his chiseled face into a generous smirk.

"That's the answer," Kent nodded.

"Of course," the lawyer said, rocking his large head around his thick neck. "The tactic here is twofold. First, we never let your wife know you're into a divorce. Second, we lead her into entrapment."

"Entrapment?" Kent asked.

"Yes, we encourage her to build our case by committing acts of depravity, child abuse or neglect . . . but we'll detail the tactics later. Without that substantive evidence, you won't get the kids. That attainment, I think, is your way of saying to Menlo Head, 'See, see . . . the court awarded me the children, so it was all *her* fault. The judge just looked things over and decided I wasn't at fault.' This thing about no-fault divorce is a lot of bullshit. If you want those kids, we have to establish fault."

"I'm with you," Kent nodded, beginning to realize the scope of this man's unscrupulousness.

"I'll have you sign a bunch of canned legal documents. Then we'll start building a case against your wife. We'll record tapes and show the court that this lady is a depraved, unfit mother. Step one. With this bundle, we march into court, presenting an order for a hearing. All we need is the judge's signature, and he'll do it because Phil Cummings said this fellow Shallaway was cooperative. Any judge usually signs this kind of an order. The woman is normally the petitioner, but since women and men are so equal, it works both ways these days. Now the order includes a provision that the defendant has to remove herself from the house until the hearing date, usually in a day or two. We don't have to prove *anything* at this point, and we'll hold our big guns until later. We don't require facts. All we have to do is allege that the continuance of this woman in the house would be harmful to you and the children. She's drinking . . . doping herself up. She assaulted you, didn't she? That's what you said."

"Yes, that's true, and Judge Shallaway saw the results in his chambers."

"Very lucky. Phil Cummings isn't so dumb. That doesn't

make him smart, either. All right . . . then I take the order to the sheriff. He serves her one morning right in front of the children, and he tosses her out of the house . . . giving her time to pack up her Kotex, nightie and a toothbrush. The sheriff's not unreasonable. She's got no defense at this point because the court hasn't scheduled the hearing yet. So you win the first round, and it's a good goddamn way to break a person into bits . . . show her that you mean business."

"Then what?"

"We have the hearing and present our side; by the time she engages her attorney, we've constructed our case. The evidence will be there. How's your stomach, Mr. Morgan?"

"Don't worry about me."

"Good. Do you screw around? And don't lie."

"A little."

"You may think it's a little. What does your wife know?"

Kent said there was a girl he had met on vacation in the Virgin Islands whom he had seen briefly, but that there was no way his wife could know about it. Then he told the lawyer about Louise confronting him with the luncheon he'd had with Babs and Gwen at the brownstone. He deliberately withheld information about what had transpired in the bedroom later. He didn't want to appear as some kind of degenerate after just laying out his credentials.

"Well, that's nothing," Booth said when he'd finished. "But she mentioned a skylight . . . did you ever see any photographs?"

"No."

"Did she say she had some?"

"Never mentioned it."

"Would she retain a legal investigator?"

"She might have followed me or had me followed . . . seen me going into the brownstone . . . and seen Mrs. Halston come in. That's all. If some guy had been clanking around on top of the roof with a bunch of photographic equipment, I think I would have known it."

"Not a thing to worry about," Booth said, "if all you were doing was having an innocent lunch with the ladies. Now, she told you she's going to swing a bit . . . is that right?"

Kent nodded. "God knows what she's up to. She took off for our apartment in New York last night . . . hasn't been seen since."

"All right. We'll get a couple of people on this today. They'll be the best, Mr. Morgan. Very costly, but then you appreciate the best. I can tell."

"I also like results."

"Sure, but there're no guarantees from this office. We try, and that's all we assure you. Don't speak about this to anyone. When your wife returns home . . ."

"How do you know she will?"

"If she doesn't, that's abandonment, and we have three-quarters of the case won. But I think she'll blow some steam and come home. At that point, you mislead her. Forgive her for all the terrible things she's done . . . like taking out your tennis court. Make it seem that you're mending the fences. Fuck her a few times, and tell her that you love her. Then you lead her into a subtle low-key discussion about open marriage . . . very subtle. By all means, say that she can bring a few discreet friends to the house. Now we'll pick up our facts, Mr. Morgan; fucking a non spouse at home is *prima facie* evidence of depravity . . . our best grounds. One more thing, Mr. Morgan, if you ever repeat to anyone what I've said here, I'll deny it. Furthermore, I'll get you for slander, and the big house over there in Menlo Head will be mine."

He held up Kent's letter.

"This is why I've got the cards. And this goes in my safe . . . but I don't think you're that much of a fool. Now, I want you to fill me in on this woman . . . all the details. And get a picture to me within one hour. I'll start the wheels. Still with me, Mr. Morgan?"

"Absolutely."

"You'll win, Mr. Morgan . . . you'll win. I'm so sure of it, I won't even discuss fees. That comes next."

Kent Morgan left the office at two-twenty. He drove to Pigeon Hill, satisfied with the results of his appointment.

Bob Booth was the right man. No doubt about it.

CHAPTER TWENTY-SIX

Robert Booth was one of many lawyers who worked on a referral basis with the legal investigation firm of Kirkland & Moore, an outfit established in the late thirties by a group of ex-New York cops. One quick phone call from Booth to the detectives on Saturday afternoon, and the agents mobilized swiftly for the pelleting of Louise Morgan.

At three-thirty that day Kent returned to Stamford with photographs of his wife; these would be delivered later to the Kirkland firm on East Forty-third Street by lawyer Booth's paralegal, a faithful old lady who assisted the attorney without questioning his tactics.

First, however, Booth spent half an hour with Kent, trying to form a profile of their target: Louise Morgan. The more they knew about this woman—her likes, dislikes, habits and personality—the more easily they could make their inroad, or the "puppet plant," in the grammar of legal investigative work.

Bob Booth did not tell Kent right away exactly what he had in mind for that evening—or whenever the first opening presented itself for invasion of Louise's personal life—but the strategy was to find a soft spot and go for the kill. Booth had assembled an image of Louise as a disturbed borderline alcoholic. He also learned that she kept constant company with Bunny Lunsford.

He asked Kent, "Have you ever had any indication of homosexual activities between your wife and another woman . . . perhaps this Mrs. Lunsford?"

Kent stiffened at the thought of it and answered, "No!"

Booth dropped the subject for the time being.

"Now, Mr. Morgan, you told me that your wife's a lush . . . who takes care of things?"

"The housekeeper, Carrie."

"She cooks . . . looks after the children . . . all of it?"

"Sort of. We had a daily maid for a while, but Louise fired her . . . said she wouldn't have a cleaning woman who arrived in a Cadillac . . . or some silly thing. In Menlo Head, most of them do. Anyway, Carrie's arthritic now; she tries hard, but there's just so much to do. Pigeon Hill is a big place."

"I want you to send this housekeeper home on a paid vacation."

"Christ . . . the whole house would collapse."

"That's *just* what we want. And we have to work with lightning speed because your wife is about to do something . . . we don't want her to file before we do. Okay? We're claiming she's an unfit, depraved woman, but these are subjective allegations. Statutory law is vague on the specifications . . . what's considered unfit, depraved, in one instance might be okay in another. The definitions are fuzzy. I've found it isn't safe to rely on one tactic alone. It might be that the judge will ask for the juvenile authorities to come and take a look at the situation. We'll try to prevent that, but if they do, I want them to find a fucking mess."

"It's already looking like hell . . ."

Kent stopped on his words, "looking like hell." He had given up; Louise had given up on the cosmetics of Pigeon Hill; and Carrie couldn't run the house by herself. Months before, the disassembling of a fine home had been helped by nature. A fierce storm, a northeaster, had whipped across the Sound with hurricane-force winds. It had torn at Pigeon Hill, ripping down shutters, breaking windows, gutters with such velocity that shrubs had been uprooted and leaves and muck hurled through the air to land on the already stained and tarnished facade, once spotlessly white.

256

Louise had ordered a cheap cleanup and patch job just to get them through the party, but now a great crack had appeared under the eaves of the mansard roof because the joists were rotted. Kent knew if they weren't replaced, the front exterior wall would eventually open up. One image that Booth did not have to fabricate was that of Pigeon Hill coming apart.

Kent finally spoke. "That'll work against me two ways. I'll be held responsible for sending the housekeeper home . . . *and* for the place looking like a tornado hit it."

"But the maid needs a vacation . . . I wouldn't worry about that. A man provides for his family. You go to work . . . bring home the money . . . and the woman in this case *doesn't* do her job. She won't, I hope. That'll lend us the total picture, Mr. Morgan. I want a foul portrait to emerge."

"Well, I just hope it doesn't smear both of us."

"You came to me for the impossible, Mr. Morgan . . . custody of three little girls . . . all minors. Now, what would really cinch it for us is to have your wife a lesbian."

"No! That's going too far!"

Bob Booth laughed through the phlegm which resided in his upper lungs and throat. "Nothing is ever going too far, Mr. Morgan. You asked for results."

"Yes, but it's the children I'm thinking about. I don't want them hurt. They're very attached to their mother; the idea of something like that would completely traumatize them. No," Kent shook his head. "We can't do this to the kids. Besides, that's not Louise, anyway."

"We'll *make* it Louise."

"Never. You'll just have to go with what you have."

Booth glanced at the photograph of Louise Morgan again. It would be an easy and effective subterfuge, he thought. She was a strong, muscular-looking woman, fully capable of smashing her husband in the jaw; she had spent many hours alone with another woman. Yes, she could very well be vulnerable to one of the soundest strategies of child removal from its mother—homosexuality; more specifically, an affair with another woman in the house. And if that fact could be proved, the next step would be the children's awareness; they did not have to witness the act, just believe it was going on. This would be hard *prima facie* evidence, and it was too good to pass up.

"I'll tell you what, Mr. Morgan," he said. "Why don't you just leave the details of strategy up to me? Trust me to do the best job for you. After all, nobody wants those little girls hurt."

Carl Sheen, a lawyer in his early thirties, handled the Kirkland marital division. Sheen realized that the proper mix of background and emotions was imperative when leading a woman into a homosexual act which would be programmed for video recording of sound and color pictures. It was his idea to employ a stable of unemployed actors and actresses who, for a hefty fee, would present themselves as bait. Using their so-called acting ability, they could gain control of their subjects—influencing them, coercing them, shifting their balance in such a delicate manner that most of the pawns never realized what was happening to them until it was too late.

Sheen received a call from Bob Booth as soon as Kent left the attorney's office. Booth gave him Louise Morgan's profile.

"We can't count on too much cooperation from Morgan," Bob said. "He doesn't want to know what we are up to."

"Well, we'll all be as subtle as possible," Carl answered.

He hung up and started going through his files, searching for a suitable woman candidate. She had to be beautiful, intelligent and interested in sailing. It was not easy; most of the females on Sheen's list were not well-bred or bright. The Kirkland man felt that Louise Morgan would reject the conventional actress-model or see through the ploy, the worst deterrent imaginable in a setup.

Of the 209 women on Sheen's list who were used now and

then for light operative work, as well as for leading both men and women into compromising situations, only three candidates seemed likely. The three women, all of whom had listed sailing as one of their sports on the back of the trumped-up résumés, were called immediately to the Kirkland office. Two showed up; the third girl was away. While they could sail, or said so, their gentility was missing. One blonde who modeled bras spoke with a heavy Brooklyn accent; the second decoy, although not right for the Morgan job, said she knew of a sensuous thirty-four-year-old actress from Philadelphia's Main Line who had graduated from the University of Pennsylvania.

"You see, Mr. Sheen," the woman said, "Julie wants to be an actress. She's been on and off Broadway a couple of times, but her big chance hasn't come up yet. Her family money disappeared, and she hooks a bit, just a bit . . . to make ends meet. She told me one time that her family had a yacht up in Martha's Vineyard and she used to sail in races. I can call her for you."

"Bullshit!" Sheen said. "Why would a girl from a good family have to hook?"

"I asked myself that, too. But things get heavy, Mr. Sheen. People do what they have to do. It's tough . . . but true; look at me. I don't like being signed up with you . . . but I am."

At five o'clock that day, two of Sheen's men entered One East Sixty-sixth Street posing as telephone company employees, with identification papers and test phones swinging from their belts. They proceeded to the cellar, found the outgoing trunk lines and tapped the Morgan apartment with a small transmitter, the hairline aerial of which was led out the window facing the alleyway.

At the same time, Julie Gardiner was taking a cab up to the Kirkland office. The second she walked in the door, Carl Sheen knew that he had found the right person; she had that "rich girl" look. Her light brown hair was soft and shining and turned up just a bit on the ends; she wore an expensive well-cut dress, and her body, while slender, was nicely developed. In her features were years of careful breeding. Her voice was cultivated, her personality pleasant.

"Were you told what this was about, Miss Gardiner?"

"Delores filled me in."

"I suppose you've had relationships with women?"

There was a long pause.

"I'm not a les."

"What's the answer?"

"Yes."

"I'm not being accusatory . . . but it's the nature of this assignment. You must make it with a particular woman," he said, showing her Louise's picture.

"A divorce case?" she asked.

"That's right."

"I think I could score some points."

"Now, what about your sailing background?"

"I raced one-design boats for years . . . Buzzards Bay . . . Nantucket Sound."

"Mrs. Morgan . . . our subject . . . was an Olympic sailing champion."

"I remember her . . . back in '64. Sure, she was all over the yachting magazines. And I'm to make Louise Morgan? What a small world!" she laughed.

"You'll be paid a flat rate . . . two hundred fifty dollars a day, with bonuses if you secure other information. We want you to become her friend; then, at the right time, make your move, but you'll have to coordinate it with our people. Then you'll testify in court. We'll have backup video tapes if needed. But Miss Gardiner, it's important that you *never reveal* that you've worked for us. We'll deny it and come against you if you try to double-cross this firm, or talk about who's paying you and why. Our firm is strong and reputable. Do you understand?"

"I'm supposed to get this gal in bed and perjure myself in court?"

Sheen was surprised how clearly she notched the parts together. That attested to her intelligence.

"If you can't play our game, then leave."

"For that kind of money, Mr. Sheen, I'll play . . . don't worry. I need the job. I wasn't sure how I'd handle the rent this month, and then Delores called. When do we start?"

"Maybe tonight. You see, the lawyer for the plaintiff thinks a quick move . . . very fast strike . . . is necessary. I have men up at Mrs. Morgan's apartment listening to a few things, as you can imagine. I want you to stand by at your place . . . where is it?"

"I live in the West Village."

"When I find out what the scene is . . . maybe a party . . . maybe nothing . . . I'll call you. A proper introduction is the first step."

"I'm an actress. I can handle it. Clothes . . . the bullshit . . . and I can give her a few thrills to boot."

"I'm sure you can. All right . . . here's six hundred in cash on account. You just go home . . . pick out some different wardrobes and wait. I'll call you later."

Kent found Pigeon Hill empty when he returned home. A note left by Carrie said that she was taking the children out for a ride. He had just sat down in the living room with a drink when the phone rang.

"Mr. Morgan . . . Bob Booth. We've found a girl who's going to become a friend of your wife's . . . help us get the evidence we need. Now, the first impression here is important. How the girl meets your wife and under what circumstances is crucial. Do you have a scrapbook of Louise's sailing background . . . some things to fill our person in on?"

"She keeps one in her bottom drawer. Haven't seen it for years, but I think it's there. Want it?"

"Will she miss the book?"

"I doubt it very much."

"We don't know yet what Mrs. Morgan is up to tonight. We have a tap on her phone. As soon as our man calls in, I want you to carry that book to the Kirkland office on East Forty-third Street and talk to their woman. We want to make contact as soon as possible. It might take time to establish the right kind of relationship, and Mr. Sheen . . . he's the head of the marital division at the Kirkland office . . . says that a slow, easy beginning is usually the best, but we can't be sure at this point. We just don't know how much time it will take to crack your wife."

"Louise is half-cracked already, I think . . . what's this woman going to do?"

"Let's not talk about the details at the moment. Just stand by the phone, and have the scrapbook ready."

At five-forty, Booth called Kent, saying that Louise was going to an art opening in the Village, escorted by a man named Antonio; later, there would be a party at the loft of the painter.

By the time Kent arrived at the Kirkland office, Julie Gardiner was already there, wearing designer jeans and an expensive silk shirt which said she was arty and rich. Around her neck was a gold emblem of the North American Sailing Union, a prop Louise would spot in a second.

"Just a couple of rules . . . for both of you," Carl Sheen said, looking at Kent and Julie. "You will never reveal to anyone that you have met. When you do meet, hopefully through Mrs. Morgan, it will be for the first time. Now, Mr. Morgan has brought a scrapbook of his wife's sailing activities. I want you to memorize one race, Miss Gardiner, and say to Louise Morgan that you sailed against her one time and lost."

"No problem. It might be true."

"And Mr. Morgan, you spend about an hour with Miss Gardiner, giving her all the details of your wife . . . her personality . . . small points that Miss Gardiner can use."

Julie went to the art opening and waited until Louise

walked in with Antonio Bianchi. The ground-floor gallery was large and crowded, and in the air hung a pale haze of marijuana. Louise Morgan wore a green velvet pantsuit, and when she was alone, looking at one of the paintings, Julie edged up alongside her. She stood silently, studying the huge acrylic canvas for a few moments; then she eyed Louise with a tentative smile.

"Excuse me," Julie began. "This is rather embarrassing, but . . ."

Louise smiled. "What's wrong?" she asked.

"Do you happen to be Louise Upton?"

"I *was* Louise Upton . . . I'm Louise Morgan now. Have we met?"

"I sailed against you . . . and lost, by the way."

Louise broke out in a wide grin. "Where?"

"At the North American Women's Sailing Championships . . . Annapolis. I had an eye on the Olympic squad."

"What district were you representing?"

"The northeast. I won that area at Marblehead. Our family had a summer home up there . . . sorry . . . my name is Julie Gardiner." She extended her hand and skillfully continued, "Do you sail now, Louise?"

"I do . . . just an old Atlantic."

"They were beautiful boats. Old but great."

"Are you still into racing?"

"My ex-husband was. We had a Bermuda Forty . . . raced around the Vineyard. I'm in New York doing some acting . . . I still go up to the Vineyard. In fact, Dad bought an old boatshop up there."

That remark brightened Louise Morgan.

"I built a lobster workboat one time up in Menlo Head . . . where we live. What does your dad build?"

"He always loved wooden boats. We used to vacation at Bar Harbor, and he'd replace a plank now and then in our Alden Fifty. When he retired from his law firm on Broad Street . . . our family was from Bryn Mawr . . . he settled

263

at the Vineyard with Mom. You wouldn't believe this, but he builds little wooden dinghies for larger yachts. They're clinker-planked from a Scottish design."

"That must be great!" Louise said warmly.

Julie had sprung the right words, and her come-on was effective.

"It's changed the man's life . . ." she continued. "I help out in the summer. The greatest thing is that Dad's sold sixty boats for over twelve hundred dollars apiece. He's making a little profit . . . has four kids working for him."

"I'd love to do something like that," Louise said wistfully. "Do you have children, Julie?"

"One daughter at Foxcroft. How about you?"

"I have three girls . . . seven to fifteen."

Julie sprinkled in just the right information to program Louise. Kent had told her that Louise detested pomposity, the snobbish wings of the "Eastern crowd." Julie played up that point, coming across with the impression that her family worked with its hands, just as the Uptons did—old money but clever gadgeteers, nevertheless. The commonality of sailing, interest in art, age, family background underscored Carl Sheen's premise of like attracting like.

Louise explained briefly to Julie that she was vacationing from her husband at the moment. The Kirkland operative answered: "I know *just* what you mean."

Shortly after, Antonio was introduced to Julie, and Louise suggested that they all go together to the party at the artist's loft.

"I really can't stay long," Julie said, thinking of Sheen's advice to move slowly.

"Come for a little while, Julie," Louise insisted.

They left the gallery, and three blocks down the Soho street, they climbed two flights of stairs to a former warehouse, now the studio of the airbrush photo-realist. "Coke," marijuana and drinks flowed. Louise Morgan was immediately sickened by the pungent smell, and the pain became

264

worse when she was introduced to "her" two young men, a pair of bony, high-voiced dancers from the City Center Ballet Company who had been provided by Antonio Bianchi. Louise faked a quick headache and argued with the Italian about leaving.

Finally she turned to Julie. "Is this your scene?"

"No. Is it yours?"

Louise shook her head and added, "Let's go."

"Fine."

Julie had been told by the Kirkland agency to be prepared to entertain Louise Morgan at her apartment if it was presentable; she assured Carl Sheen that the pad was aesthetic, but she could hardly afford the place without offering it as shelter for her twice-a-week tricks with upper echelon executives from out of town. Kent had informed Julie of Louise's obsessive passion for lobsters—eating them and catching them—and earlier that evening, after Julie had returned to her apartment on one of the best streets in the Village, she had ordered two fresh Maine lobsters from the fish store at the corner. The bill came to forty-two dollars; she quickly peeled off the wad of twenties supplied by the agency, an expensed-out item in addition to her salary. Julie had planned to cook the lobsters Hunan style in a wok, along with sautéed dried string beans spiced with ginger and hot pepper.

Things were moving better than Julie had expected. Just outside the loft, as both women took deep breaths, the operative made her second move.

"Louise, I'm a lobster freak. I just bought a couple of fresh ones this afternoon. How about going back to my place? We'll cook them up Chinese style . . . if you like Szechwan-style cooking . . . that's the spicy side of Chinese cuisine."

"I love lobsters . . . any way at all."

"Let's go, then," Julie said.

"But don't you have an appointment?"

Julie thought fast. "My agent was going to drop off the script of a new play. There's an audition next week, and I just wanted to get up on my lines."

Louise nodded. "All right . . . sounds great."

"What about your friend, Antonio? Do you want to invite him? I have plenty of lobster."

"No," Louise said quickly. "He's enjoying the party. I made it with him once, but he's *not* my type."

"Good lover?"

"Terrible."

Julie Gardiner's apartment on the second floor of a Federal-style brownstone was detailed with elegant architectural flourishes of the period. The ceiling moldings, the pilasters to the sides of the thick wooden doors and the entablatures over the openings were still in place, left over from the days when the building functioned as a townhouse for a wealthy nineteenth-century family. The apartment, decorated in soft beige tones, was cozy and inviting; on the walls were several watercolor sketches of the family yacht and the home in Edgartown.

Louise immediately moved towards a small marine painting.

"Is this yours . . . the Alden yawl?" she asked.

"That's it," Julie said. "Spent many great hours on that deck pulling the strings. Make yourself comfortable . . . I'll get us a drink."

Louise kicked off her shoes and curled up on the cream colored sofa. They sat for a while, discussing love, marriage and yacht racing. Then Julie went into the large country-style kitchen and began cutting up her ginger roots for the spices. Louise cracked open the iced lobsters, pulling out each morsel of pure white meat which she then dipped in a batter of egg whites, soy sauce and cornstarch.

The two women continued their discussion as Julie heated up the woks: one for the green snap beans, another for lobster Hunan style. Louise worked on her vodkas; Julie pretended to keep up with her, although she emptied her vodka down the sink on several trips to the bathroom, hoping to stay alert throughout the evening. This was a job, she kept telling herself over and over.

Slowly, Julie fed in more clues about her college days at the University of Pennsylvania, and Louise came right back with college stories woven around Yale. After the meal, both women settled back on the couch; Louise was just a bit unsteady but still coherent. Thinking that she had made an instant good friend—the Bunny Lunsford of the city—Louise spun the story of Kent Morgan and the blowups at Pigeon Hill.

"Christ, I can't believe that!" Julie said after twenty minutes of silence. "He's fucking a mother and her daughter, and he's making it with some little moppet in the islands. Even my husband wasn't that heavy. Are you going to divorce this guy?"

"Oh, Julie, I don't know yet. I'm very confused."

"I bet he is, too. Putting in the tennis court . . . taking it out . . . I love it. I would have given a thousand dollars to see that man's face when he looked for the tennis court. What a scene!" Julie said, tossing her head back and bursting into a hearty laugh.

Louise nodded. "And here I was . . . thinking I had something to make up to him . . . trying to appease the bastard . . . when all the time he's been fucking his way through the Virgin Islands."

"Men! I heard a great line the other day. 'A woman without a man is like a fish without a bicycle.' "

As Louise laughed at her little joke, Julie realized there was no need for playacting on her part; she liked and related to Louise Morgan. But the question was: Should she make her pitch towards Louise this evening or reserve bait for a second try later on?

Julie did not have to answer her own question. Louise began to cry softly, and she moved closer to Julie, putting her head on the actress' shoulder.

"I feel so mixed up, Julie."

"We all do at times."

"For years I thought I had my life in order. The kids were growing up beautifully, and I thought my marriage was secure. Then Kent just got tired of me. I was getting to be forty. Is that an automatic condemnation for a woman? Does she cross a line, and on the other side there's nothing but a goddamn downhill slope? It's not fair, Julie. A man can attract any young thing he wants to. He buys his love . . . the little girl wants a father image, I guess . . . and the man tells her that his wife doesn't understand him. Oh, what a worn-out line . . . but it's gobbled up each time. What does a woman do? How many ballsy teenage boys are looking for a mother image? Not many . . . if they have any red blood."

"I agree, Louise. The sport isn't fair."

Julie eased her arm around Louise's shoulder in a comforting gesture. "Do you want to stay with me tonight?"

"I'm terribly lonely . . . I need somebody, Julie."

Julie hugged her and pulled her a bit closer; then she slipped a light kiss on Louise's cheek. "You're welcome. I have plenty of room."

Louise smiled gratefully. "You're very nice . . . I feel I've known you for a long time."

"I'd hate to see you go out alone on the streets at this hour. Why don't you just bunk in with me tonight and leave in the morning? I only have the one bed, but it's big enough for both of us, if you don't mind sharing."

"Of course not . . . I . . ."

"Come on, then."

Julie took her hand and pulled Louise to her feet; they walked slowly into the bedroom.

"Now, you just let me take care of everything . . . you're my guest," Julie said as she began to undress Louise who, drowsy with the vodkas and the Valium, didn't protest.

When Julie touched her bare skin lightly, Louise shivered, but her eyes were closed. She swayed slightly, and Julie eased her into bed, kissing her gently on the lips and murmuring as if to a child.

Then Julie quickly undressed herself and clicked off the light. She slid into bed and wrapped her arms around the nude body of Louise Morgan. There was no lovemaking; Louise had drifted off into a deep sleep.

CHAPTER TWENTY-SEVEN

When Kent arrived back home that Saturday night, he called Carrie into the library and shut the door.

"Carrie, I guess you know Mrs. Morgan isn't feeling well."

The old black woman fixed her bulging eyes on him.

"Yes, sir, Mr. Morgan. What's happening, sir?"

"She's temporarily off balance. Now, Carrie, I want to be alone with my family. Perhaps I can bring some sense to this . . . so I'm going to give you a few weeks of paid vacation. You can go down and see your sister in Georgia."

"I'd like to do that, Mr. Morgan, but who'll take care of the house?"

"I will."

"It's a full-time job . . . and things are in such a bad state around here. Sure hate to go at a time like this . . . she needs someone."

"Don't worry. Mrs. Morgan will be as good as new when you return."

The following morning, Kent took Carrie to the railroad station, and then he appeared with his children at the early church service. He stood in front, talking to Reverend Alcott for some time so all could see him.

Roger Halston came up to Kent and said, "Heard you were down in the Virgin Islands, Kent."

"Yes . . . had a little vacation. How are you, Roger?"

"Very well. And my sailing machine's going great. How about coming out with me this afternoon? I want to ask you about the set of the mainsail."

"I have to go to New York for a meeting, Roger, but I'll check at the club for you when I get back."

"Fine. Hey, I heard you put in a tennis court over there . . . must be a lot of money in designing yachts these days!"

"Oh, we started the work, but we've held up the project for a while."

Ogden Barnes also came up to Kent, reminding him of the commodores' meeting later that week.

"Where's Louise?" Oggie asked.

"She's in the city, visiting relatives," Kent answered.

He looked from the side of his eye towards the children. They were stony-faced. Kent had said that their mother was sick, and Cathy had told her sisters that Mom was away on secret business.

On the way back to Pigeon Hill, the two younger children again asked where their mother was.

"She's undergoing treatment in New York," Kent said. "We all have to be brave and hold the fort until Mom comes home."

"But why did Carrie leave us?" Laurie asked.

"She had to go down and take care of her sister in Georgia."

"Will she be back?" Jody asked.

"In a short while."

Cathy was silent; she knew there was no point in discussing the matter with her father.

After church, Kent left for New York, telling Cathy that she was in charge of the children.

The Kirkland agency, meanwhile, had scheduled a debriefing with their operatives working on the One East Sixty-sixth Street premise; the men reported that a tape was jacked into the trunk-line distribution board, along with a radio transmitter. The receiver was rigged in a commercial laundry truck parked directly across the street on East Sixty-sixth, between Fifth and Madison Avenues.

Louise awoke that morning about nine, and Julie served her breakfast in bed. Neither women mentioned the previous night. Julie said she had an appointment with her agent, and Louise took a cab uptown to the duplex; the women planned to talk by phone later that day.

When Julie reached the Kirkland office, she thought how different this private detective agency was from the public's concept of a seedy little office run by bummed-out cops: Kirkland & Moore was big business and fashionable.

The reception area was appointed in modern Knoll furniture; the magazines on the low glass table were *Forbes*, *Fortune* and *Barron's*, plus *Classic*, the journal of the blue-blood horse world. On the walls were original oil paintings; one portrait of Andrew Jackson by Stevens was probably worth one hundred thousand dollars.

After a short wait, Julie was called into Carl Sheen's office which was ringed by law books; he sat behind an antique English partner's desk. Julie shook hands with Bob Booth, also, upon entering; the lawyer was attired in a dark, three-piece funeral suit with a silk tie and a pearl stickpin.

"How far did you get with Louise Morgan?" Carl Sheen asked as soon as she had settled into the plush designer's couch.

"Sexually?"

"Yes."

"We embraced, and she slept with me."

"And?" Sheen continued.

"Nothing more. The woman was drunk."

"How drunk . . . slobbering?" Sheen asked.

"No, but she tossed down six straight vodkas and rambled on about her life and marriage."

"When you were in bed," Booth asked, "what happened?"

"Nothing. We kissed each other good night, and I didn't make another move. I wanted to space it out. Also, she just went to sleep on me . . . in my arms."

"I think that was wise, Julie," Carl nodded. "To go slow, I mean. Now, do you think she's homosexual or bisexual?"

"Neither. The woman's desperately lonely. She hates men at this point, and all she wants is an ear and a hug."

"That's not good enough for our case," Booth chimed in.

"I know that," Julie said. "But I think I can move her into . . . well . . . anything you want, as long as there's no rough or kinky stuff. Louise Morgan isn't that sort of person."

"Will she let you go down on her?" Carl asked.

"That's not the question," Booth broke in. "Will Louise Morgan go down on you? That's what I need."

"It'll take time and work," Julie said. "She has confidence in me, though."

"What else did you discuss?" Carl asked.

"She's not considering a divorce."

"Why?" Sheen asked.

"She thinks that time will cure things, I guess. She's too screwed up right now to think straight, but she did tell me quite a bit about her husband."

"Like what?" Bob Booth interjected swiftly.

"First of all, she knows that he was seeing that Halston girl."

"We're aware of that," Bob Booth said.

"But in the beginning, her friend, Mrs. Lunsford, showed her snapshots that her son had taken of a luncheon in New York attended by Mrs. Halston, her daughter and Mr. Morgan. The pictures didn't amount to a damn thing . . . merely three people sitting around a table, eating. But later, it seems, they went into the bedroom and got into a wild threesome. This kid . . . I mean the son of Mrs. Lunsford . . . couldn't get an exposure because the light was bad, but he saw what happened. The bedroom scene was never made clear to Louise. Mrs. Lunsford thought it might blow her mind . . . drive her over the edge. OK, then . . . so Louise kisses this Antonio, the guy I met at the art gallery, and she feels guilty for clobbering her husband . . . necking with the Italian, etc. So they go off to the Virgin Islands to patch things up. Louise thinks she's getting the marriage back together. The woman puts in a tennis court, one of those grass kind, to prove to her husband that . . . ah . . . well, she wants the marriage to continue. But here's what happens. For the first couple of days down in the islands, things go smoothly. Then Mr. Morgan starts sailing off alone every day on this boat he has chartered. The oldest daughter, Cathy . . . she's fifteen and not stupid . . . begins to wonder where Daddy is. One day she sails her little dinghy out there to chase the disappearing Daddy. What does she find? A fuck scene on the beach. Morgan has found a young girl, and he's screwing her. Cathy's a little traumatized . . . but she doesn't say anything to her mother about it until they return to Connecticut. And there's the tennis court . . . a present to Daddy. Cathy tells her mother about Pop's island humps. Louise runs over to Bunny Lunsford, her best friend in Menlo Head. Then Bunny tells Louise that Mr. Morgan wasn't just eating soufflés with the Halston women that day; he was fucking them both, and the two of them . . . I mean the women . . . were having a little play at incest. So Louise becomes unhinged, as you can imagine. She takes out the tennis court . . . Mr. Morgan brings home a client from Chicago to play on his new court, and suddenly, 'poof,' there's no court. Mr. Morgan goes berserk . . . he's odd, anyway, from what Louise says . . . and, well, that brings us up to date . . . the divorce action."

There was a barren silence in the office. Everyone looked at each other with swinging eyebrows. Finally Carl Sheen spoke.

"Bob, did you know all this?"

"Not to this extent. Morgan didn't level with me. I'll take care of his ass. Miss Gardiner, you've done a goddamn good job . . . getting all this out of Louise Morgan."

She shrugged. "Louise offered the information."

"Does she have any hard evidence besides hearsay . . . from the Lunsford kid or her eldest one, Cathy?" Booth asked.

"I don't think so. If there's anything beyond that, Louise didn't mention it."

"Then we're reasonably safe," Bob Booth said.

"Frankly, gentlemen," Julie said after a pause, "I've never heard of a divorce with this sort of tactics. You people are into some rough stuff."

"Miss Gardiner," Sheen said, "why don't you let us be the lawyers?"

"Well, I bring this up because I don't think Louise Morgan can stand what you're going to do to her. She'll come apart."

"That's just what we want," Booth said with a satisfied smile. "Just what we want."

Promptly at twelve, Kent Morgan walked into the office, saying a polite good morning to Julie Gardiner as he passed her in the reception area.

"How did it go last night?" Kent asked Bob Booth as he sat down in the office.

"Better than we expected. But Miss Gardiner also picked up some disturbing information. Mr. Morgan, you didn't tell me everything. First of all . . . you didn't explain your relationship with the two Halston women. Your wife knows."

"Well . . . I said I was having a little extra duty."

"Do you know when your wife found out?"

"She knew all along . . . she told me the night of our party."

Bob Booth grinned. "No. She didn't know you were involved with the Halston women sexually until after you returned from the islands."

"But Louise told me how they were dressed and the look of the apartment the day we had lunch . . . everything."

Bob Booth spoke slowly, savoring his words. "Mrs. Lunsford had her son follow you. There was no detective. The son took pictures of you and the women at lunch. Nothing more on the negatives . . . but the kid watched you fuck the mother and the daughter. Mrs. Lunsford didn't tell your wife exactly what went on, though."

"Christ . . . you mean Louise was bluffing all the time?"

"Yeah . . . she was bluffing. She didn't know a damn thing because her pal sheltered the facts. But that's not entirely material to our case. Your oldest daughter followed you in a boat on your last day in the Virgin Islands, and she found you making it with some kid on the beach. You're a very busy man, Mr. Morgan. Cathy told her mother when you got home, and that's why the play field was uprooted. Here's the point; this hurts our case. More importantly, Mr. Morgan, you didn't tell me *everything*. I wanted *everything*!"

"Okay . . . okay . . . I didn't think it mattered."

"I decide what matters, Mr. Morgan," Booth said. "This was important information."

"Well, is the case finished? Do I lose at this point?"

Bob Booth got up, moved towards Kent Morgan and sat beside him. He looked the designer straight in the eye, with his stiff jaw protruding.

"It's decision time, as they say. You told me you wanted those kids. Now *you* have to make up your mind how *much* you want them . . . how much you're willing to risk."

There was a pause as both Sheen and Booth stared at the smooth-faced yacht designer.

Kent said, "I'm too far in to back out . . . there's no way Louise and I could patch things up now. I'll do what I have to do."

"Good," Booth nodded. "I'll have Julie get together with your wife again today. And in the meantime, you go back home and play with the kids. Hopefully, we'll be able to persuade Louise Morgan to go back there tonight . . . or tomorrow. By that time, you'll be the good guy and suggest a new-style relationship to your wife . . . anything that will give us the opening we need to move Julie in." There was a brief pause, and the lawyer continued. "Let me call the shots from now on, Mr. Morgan."

"You're talking about the entrapment, aren't you?" Kent said. "Setting my wife up. I told you I didn't want the kids involved. If that woman is in the house . . ."

"She *has* to be in the house for it to work, Mr. Morgan, and so do the kids. But don't worry. I promise to protect the children. Now, one other thing . . . we'll need to install

some electronic equipment in the house for a video taping
. . . backup evidence, you understand. We probably won't
need it . . ."

"I sure hope to hell you know what you're doing," Kent
said grimly as he got to his feet.

After Kent Morgan left the Kirkland agency, Julie Gardiner was given her instructions and a five-hundred-dollar
cash bonus for her good work. For the first time, a faint feeling of self-loathing began to emerge in the woman as she
thought about her part in the conspiracy that was rapidly
building around Louise Morgan.

She came away from the Kirkland office, walking out into
the bright sunshine, thinking that this was no longer a simple
theatrical play, but big business. She was deeply involved,
and there were no discretionary exits at this point.

On the way down to her apartment, Julie realized that a
curtain had been drawn across her life, the promises of her
Main Line upbringing forever banished. Her two ex-hus-
bands were cheats; one was a habitual drunkard, the other,
a spineless con man whose business transactions led him into
civil court as if he were permanently entered on the hearing
docket. Julie desperately wanted to be a good actress and a
mother, too, but because her interior tubes ran in odd ways,
she could never have a baby; of course, there was no daughter at Foxcroft.

That Sunday, her life seemed more shadowed than usual.
She was now committing crimes far more serious than simply
attending to the needs of executives on lonely nights.

As soon as she got back to her apartment, Julie called
Louise, suggesting that they have brunch at the Pierre Hotel,
a few blocks down from the Morgan duplex.

Louise arrived wearing a claret-colored Givenchy; her
hair had been tossed into casual curls which were more becoming than the straight look of the night before, and she
wore expensive perfume. Julie felt that Louise had dressed
up especially for her, and she was touched; nevertheless, the
Kirkland operative kept to her job.

277

"I bet Kent will try to get things back on the track," Julie said. "The last thing he'd want is a divorce. He'd be admitting failure, and your little town doesn't like failures or disturbances. That's what you said, Louise."

Louise agreed; she went on to tell Julie about Menlo Head and how she abhorred the town and its shaky facade. Julie was counting Louise's drinks: three extra dry martinis through lunch; Julie decided to make her move.

"Why don't we go back to your place, Louise? I'd love to see it."

Once inside the duplex, Julie continued with her assignment; but looking at Louise, the flow of her firm body which was now slim and shapely from her loss of weight, and remembering the feel of the woman in her arms the night before, Julie suddenly felt a genuine desire.

They built a new round of drinks, and this time Julie was not tossing them down the sink. Like a few other college girls, Julie had had homosexual encounters; there was a beautiful young girl at the University of Pennsylvania whom she had loved very much. The affair had gone on for two months; then a jealous dispute, a bitter lovers' quarrel, screams and threats, and Julie had started dating men again. She had been involved with three other women on cursory explorations, and once in a while when her clients desired two women, not one, she engaged in erotic, unfeeling play with females.

With fresh drinks and the stereo playing, Julie began to caress Louise's hair; then she moved her hand down Louise's arms in long, rhythmic strokes, brushing the curve of her breasts, her thighs. Louise seemed to accept it all in a misty state. Julie wanted to feel Louise's lips again and her silky hair buried in the gusset between her legs; gently she brought Louise's face towards her and slid her wandering tongue deep inside her mouth.

"You're so lovely, Louise," Julie whispered. "I want to kiss you all over."

Without saying a word, as if in a trance, Julie led Louise

upstairs. They slowly undressed each other in the bedroom, removing one garment at a time, until they were down to filmy silk panties. Then these were tossed aside; all the time, Julie's eyes were fastened on Louise's body. Julie parted her legs while standing up; she guided Louise down on her knees to bury her outstretched tongue in her warmth.

"Keep going, Louise . . . oh, Christ, I love it . . . can you feel me going crazy?"

Louise did not respond as she brought Julie to such a climax that they both fell back across the bed. When there was time for breathing again, Louise spoke finally.

"I never did that before . . . I'm not like that . . . I'm not like that, Julie."

"There's nothing wrong with it, Louise."

"I don't know what's wrong anymore . . . oh, God, I don't know anything."

Julie did not answer. Instead, she brought her hands up along Louise's groin and, spreading her flesh, she flipped her tongue inside Louise. That was Julie's answer.

After a short sleep, both women propped on their elbows to talk.

"Do you realize how good we are together, Louise?"

Louise paused and then said, "I'm very happy with you, Julie. You don't know how much better I feel. I know I shouldn't be saying these things . . ."

"There's no such thing as *shouldn't*. I didn't pick you up last night," Julie lied. "I just saw you and felt something. I'm not a lesbian, Louise, but life is strange. I think we have to take our support and love in the most practical way."

"Well, what happens now? Where do we go from here?"

"Want a suggestion?"

"Sure . . . I need a lot of suggestions."

"This might sound wild, but bear with me. Your husband is kinky . . . right?"

"I'd say so. Incest participation has to rate high on the kinky scale."

"Your husband wants it both ways . . . his marriage and

his position in the community; yet he wants to play."

"I guess so."

"All right. Now, what if you gave him the whole package? You say to him, 'I don't mind you having a little frolic on the side, but it has to work both ways. I slipped a kiss on an Italian's mouth . . . and you went bonkers, but I'm willing to make a deal. You can have your kicks with these other women if I can have mine. I have a friend. She's an attractive woman. I want her to visit us at Pigeon Hill. The children will suspect nothing. You have your ideal . . . I have mine. Equal all around.' "

"I don't know if Kent would buy a woman-to-woman scene."

"He won't approve, perhaps, but at least he can have his fun, and we'll have ours. He's already into a threesie; you said his lady friends enjoy each other . . . so it's hardly foreign stuff to him."

"Where does this lead to, Julie?"

Julie felt a twinge; she knew exactly where it was leading. She caught her stammering voice and said, "We'll just wait and see."

Later that evening Julie phoned Sheen and told him that Louise had agreed to propose the new relationship at Pigeon Hill, saving Kent from the suggestion.

"How did you work that out?"

"The woman's like putty."

"Did you make it with her?"

"Yes. She'll do anything I suggest."

"Who did the work . . . you or Louise?"

"We both did."

"No problems . . . no suspicions?"

"None. Tell Morgan *not* to propose anything. Louise will take the lead."

"I'm surprised but pleased. Is she coming home?"

"Tonight, but get through to Morgan. Don't let him say a goddamn syllable."

"You have a future in this business, Miss Gardiner. When do *you* go out to Pigeon Hill?"

"I'll have to wait for a call from Louise first."

"The sooner the better. Morgan is anxious to serve his wife."

"I don't think he'll have long to wait."

CHAPTER TWENTY-EIGHT

Louise turned into the driveway at Pigeon Hill just as the blush of the sun was dropping. She did not enter the house at once. She was dressed in a smart blue dress; she had spent time on her hair and her makeup to present to her family a person who was together, totally in charge of her own condition.

Sloops and yawls and schooners were wagging their sails as the breeze went down with the sun. Louise looked out on the Sound, thinking that this was a world which had been drawn back into a sealed past. She no longer wanted to sail her sloop at the dock or pick up the leaders from the lobster pots in *Workboat*. Her old life at Pigeon Hill was gone forever, and she could see the changes: rust from the bolts holding the remaining shutters was bleeding over the brick; there were stains and paint cracks along the facade. Wet leaves rotting in the bush beds cast a decayed odor over the lawns, and greenery was creeping up the walls like the fingers of an uncontrolled octopus. Her eyes lifted higher, and she noticed a series of shingles missing from the roof.

Louise entered the house, observing that the disorder of outside was now inside. The girls came flying from all directions as soon as they realized she was home; they gathered in an excited cluster around her, wanting to know how she felt . . . where she had been.

She said, "Fine . . . Mother couldn't be better. I've just been in the city for a few days."

They hugged her and smiled. She told them, "Everything's going to be fine, girls. Now, where's Dad?"

"In the carriage house. He's working," Laurie said.

"I want to talk with him, and then we'll have dinner. Maybe we'll all go out together."

"Great, Mom . . . can we take Chairman Mao?" Jody piped.

"Where's Carrie?" Louise asked them, looking around.

"She went home on a vacation. Dad says her sister is sick." Cathy spoke for the first time.

"I see."

The younger children were confused by their mother's appearance and attitude; she did not seem sick.

Louise entered the carriage house and climbed the stairs to Kent's studio.

"Welcome home," he said, forcing a smile.

He kissed her on the cheek and moved around the room, waiting for the conversation Sheen had told him would emerge.

"Kent, there must be a lot of questions you've been asking yourself."

"There sure as hell are! Pulling out that court, Louise . . . really! My client thought we were crazy. Are we crazy?"

"We might be. Now, let me get to the point. I happen to know that you're making it with Gwen and Babs. Maybe others. I also know you were fucking a little girl down in the Virgin Islands. Kent, I've come home to offer you an arrangement. I want this marriage to continue for the sake of the children."

"So do I," he said.

"But we'll have a trade-off . . . no more standoffs."

Kent turned to look at his wife, wondering just how she would put what he knew was coming. Louise was a direct and facile talker, not one to circumvent a thought.

"Here's the proposal. It's a 'Godfather' deal, Kent . . . one you *can't* refuse."

"Those are the kind I like," he said, taking her hand.

"You get to have your funnies with Gwen and Babs as long as you don't make me look like a fool. I get the same privileges. I happen to like a certain woman I met . . . I want her out here at Pigeon Hill for visits."

"Are you making it with her?"

"That's none of your concern."

"Well, you seem to know how I'm making it . . . so why don't we just square with each other?"

"All right . . . we have had sex. I'm not going lesbo. This person makes me feel comfortable, and I know you'll like her. She comes from a good family down in Pennsylvania."

"What does she do?"

"She's an actress . . . about thirty-five. Very attractive. But one thing, Kent . . . hands off!"

"You have my promise."

Kent crossed to his wife and kissed her.

"It's a deal. Actually, it's a healthy deal. We won't have to keep clobbering each other from now on, and the marriage will go on a truthful path. We each have needs, but why bust up our lives just because we like a little variation now and then?"

"Fine. One other point . . . I want to show the children that we're a family again for about the tenth try. But this time, for God's sakes, Kent, let's be civilized."

"Totally."

"And we'll begin tonight by taking the children to dinner."

Kent agreed. While Louise was changing into jeans for the trip to the Lobster Barge, he called Bob Booth.

"It's all set. She proposed the scene . . . I've agreed."

"I'll get back to Julie right away."

"Tell her to start packing her bags."

The planned razing of Louise Morgan was no longer the act of a man against a woman. It was a slickly organized, totally sophisticated and sharply pronged guerrilla raid. Her husband had engineered a personal strike force.

Julie showed up with three suitcases early Monday morn-

284

ing, May 16; she was introduced to the children as Louise's college friend from the Yale School of Fine Arts. Kent's sham was convincingly pulled off, and he greeted Julie as if he had never seen the woman before. He had been told by Booth that the electronics firm hired by the Kirkland agency needed time to install the equipment; Kent proposed that the family take their guest on an overnight cruise to Port Jefferson that Saturday.

It was obvious to Julie that Louise Morgan's touch with reality was connected by the thinnest of threads. As the once hearty sportswoman continued to live in a twilight of pills and alcohol, Julie often helped Cathy attend to the younger children. Laurie, in particular, seemed to be very tense. The smallest child, Jody, a bright, sunny little girl, had her dolls and Chairman Mao, and Cathy herself seemed almost acquiescent of the situation now. Louise had told Julie during one of their many talks that Laurie was the only one of her girls who as a child had developed a secret, imaginary companion. She had always read a lot, Louise said, and now it seemed to Julie that Laurie Morgan was retreating again into a world of make-believe, even to the point of taking up the imaginary companion which she had discarded so many years earlier.

It was a wrenching experience for Julie, one of agonizing conflict, as she watched Louise meandering about Pigeon Hill wearing a fixed smile beneath glassy, dazed eyes. From one corner of her mind came a pleading: get out of here; this woman needs help. And from the opposite corner, she kept thinking of the look on Carl Sheen's face when he warned her about double-crossing him. Also, her daily fees were adding up to a comfortable amount. Soon the rent would be paid for four months and she would have enough to buy choice steak at the corner meat market. But Julie asked herself: how could she enjoy any of it knowing that she had helped destroy this woman? Julie did not attempt to answer her own question. She couldn't.

Julie slept in the guest room, and although she occasionally touched Louise's cheeks or hands, no sexual advances were attempted. The Kirkland operative had been warned by Bob Booth *not* to pounce too quickly; he reasoned that if Louise suddenly became revolted by obvious and overt sensuous play in her own home, there was a likelihood that she would become an unwilling partner when, indeed, she was most needed.

The weekend prior to Memorial Day was the date chosen for the overnight cruise. The Morgan family, along with Julie Gardiner, sailed out of Humble Cove on a bright Saturday morning and motored Kent's thirty-seven-foot sloop across the Sound to an anchorage near Port Jefferson.

Kent had left keys to the vacant house with Bob Booth. At ten o'clock, after the sloop was over the horizon, a panel truck followed by a car moved into the driveway of Pigeon Hill. The contractor hired by Kirkland began the work of installing a fish-eye electronic camera with a pinhead mike in the bedroom of Louise Morgan.

By four o'clock that afternoon, all of the equipment was in place and tested. The recorder was hidden behind a row of preserves and jams in the cellar closet. On the day, or days, scheduled for the seduction, an operative would be smuggled into the house and remain in the cellar closet until the evidence was imprinted on the magnetic tape. Carl Sheen and Bob Booth figured that this was the riskiest part of the operation; if the presence of the stranger in the house was noticed by Louise or the children, the evidence-gathering routine would be over, and the shift of power, the evidentiary cards, would automatically revert to Louise.

But the trap was baited. They were ready.

On Sunday evening when they returned to Pigeon Hill from the short cruise, Kent went to the cellar and opened the preserve closet with his key. He saw banks of electronic recording equipment and wires leading upstairs through the studding to the second-floor bedroom. It could have been the conglomerate of electronic gear or the trading of looks between Julie and Louise which was becoming more obvious, but suddenly a rush of remorse swept through Kent Morgan.

He called Bob Booth that night and said he had to see him; they met in the lawyer's office just after nine o'clock. Much of Kent's boldness, his combative sense of campaigning was gone, and Booth noticed this immediately.

"What's going to happen now at Pigeon Hill?" Kent demanded.

The lawyer leaned back in his chair, and a knowing smile crept across his face.

"I knew you'd be coming to me with a case of goose bellies."

"I'd appreciate it greatly if you would answer me in plain English."

"You were a big man the first time you came to this office, Mr. Morgan . . . said you wanted to be a prick shit bastard . . . reduce your wife to a babbling lump. And I told you the other day there would be no more hand wringing . . . remember? Now, when we're about to spring, you're not so sure anymore. And didn't I keep saying it was up to you . . . not me?"

"Yes, that's true . . . but I deserve to know what's going on in my own home."

"Isn't it obvious? We're going to roll the evidence, as I said . . . just to have in case Louise doesn't admit to her little act later on. Julie will testify, of course, but one story can be offset by another. What else do you want to know, Mr. Morgan?"

"But the children are going to be right in the middle of all this . . . and they aren't stupid."

"Look . . . we have to put a big bundle together to prove our theory of unfitness, and there's very little that's shocking anymore. The courts are giving custody of children to lesbians every day . . . as long as they can guarantee proper care. Now, do you want us to pull the equipment, discharge Julie Gardiner? Just say so."

Kent was trying to arrange his thoughts. He had come to

this conscienceless lawyer. He had told him what he wanted, and his goal had not changed; he still wanted his children. But now he realized he might lose them, too, by following the lawyer's prescription.

"I want my daughters. Perhaps, for the first time in my life, I'll be able to enjoy those girls the way a father should. I know I can contribute to their proper upbringing, but here's my problem . . ."

"I'm waiting."

"I don't want custody of three mental wrecks. I can't take a chance on the girls seeing their mother in bed with another woman."

"They won't actually witness any perversion, Mr. Morgan."

"I know what you're thinking . . . that I've lost my heart for all this. Well, maybe I have, in a sense. I came here fighting mad . . . I was out of my mind. Actually, I'm a very sympathetic person. I want my wife to get help. I mean . . . there're plenty of good things about Louise. I don't agree with her ideas on rearing our daughters, but I want her to be happy. When this whole thing is over, she can find another man who likes shotguns . . . or ducks . . . but at the same time, I don't want too much on my conscience."

"Conscience?" the lawyer repeated.

"Yes. I want to do what's right . . . what's necessary . . . no more."

"Okay, Mr. Morgan . . . it's getting late. Tell me where to draw the line."

"Just tell Julie to be as discreet as possible and as fast as possible; get all that equipment out of there before the girls suspect something. I don't want my kids involved in dirty movies."

The lawyer got to his feet and opened the door for Kent Morgan.

"Fine, but if you're going to tie my hands, don't complain later. If the judge rules against us and the children go to your wife, *never . . . never . . .* Mr. Morgan, come to me and ask where it went wrong."

"I won't."

"Then good night, Mr. Morgan. I'll inform Julie."

Kent walked out of the lawyer's office, got into his sports car and drove back to Pigeon Hill. He felt better, though not as good as he should have. A strange sense of foreboding still nagged at him, but he told himself that it was out of his hands now. He had done his best.

CHAPTER TWENTY-NINE

The following day the sun rose into a cloudless sky, and the sea was laced white by a snappy wind from the east. After persistent urging, Louise was taking Julie out in *Workboat*; they had invited Bunny Lunsford along, too.

When Bunny arrived that morning at Pigeon Hill, she took in the tarnish which was blushing the facade of the great house. The lilacs, hollies and ivy crawled upwards, sidewards, in untamed spurts, as if the shrubs and trees had suddenly become outraged with the demeanor of their masters. Bunny studied the fat leaves and branches; it appeared to her that the greenery had decided to eat up the house.

It was a rueful voyage for Louise Morgan.

She had not set the traps that spring, and for the first time she went to the fish store on Main Street and purchased three live lobsters at $19.00 apiece. When they reached *Workboat*, pulling at her lines at the end of the finger pier, Louise noticed the deterioration of the vessel she had built with her daughters: sluggish, oil-coated water slopped around the bilges; the topsides were streaked and filthy; and the diesel had to be hand-cranked. Finally it gulped in air, turned over and thumped away, and the bilges were pumped dry. But the muck remained.

Louise, in a feverish bustle aided by the morning martinis, tried desperately to regain a particle of her past: the times she had set the lobster traps with her daughters; the glorious days on the Sound yanking the sea harvest with Bunny; the lunches of fresh lobster and corn cooked in the cozy cabin of *Workboat*.

But the past had reversed itself.

The Bristol-fashioned craft, laid up with their hands and love, now reeked of rotten planks whose opened mouths were taking in huge gulps of seawater as they bounced out on the waves of the freshening breeze. It was sad to have to buy lobsters for a lobster boat, Louise thought, and trying to quiet her own agony, she told a few jokes which somehow fell flat.

Julie was seasick, and Bunny was too depressed to say much. Once she whispered to Louise when they were alone for a moment, "Who is this woman?"

"Just an old college friend," Louise answered.

"Are you all right, Louise? Frankly, you look terrible."

"I'm fine," Louise said, building up a smile.

They threw the hook over behind the island and cooked the lobsters in a pot which was now ruined by rust. The silverware was wet and coated by a green covering of corrosion; the pewter plates had gone to hell, devoured by rust and sea slime.

Each woman drank straight from the vodka bottle. The lobster was tough, and they returned to the dock at four o'clock, wet and disgruntled.

That night in Bob Booth's office there was a final briefing, attended by all those who had contributed to the snare. After the report from each party, Bob Booth turned to Julie.

"Tomorrow is day one . . . go to it, Julie."

She nodded and pocketed without comment the roll of crisp twenties which Carl Sheen handed her.

Tuesday was dreary. The clouds lowered, and the drizzle began just after the children left for school. They were dressed in their wrinkled uniforms by Cathy, who had assumed the role of surrogate mother: cooking, combing their hair, finding lost knee socks, washing and mending. Louise slept late, her unconsciousness induced by four Valiums and a small slug of alcohol for a nightcap. Julie had warned her that the yellow bullets and white juice were not to be mixed, and Louise usually halted her iced vodka about an hour and a half before moving to the plastic bottle. This morning she lay in her drugged sleep until about ten. When she awoke, Louise immediately felt the chill and clamminess of the house. The weather had turned raw. The temperature had slumped into the low fifties, and the crisp wind from the south skimmed the dampness off the Sound, delivering the invisible water particles into every corner of Pigeon Hill. The air-conditioning filters had not been changed that spring, and the dehumidifier system had failed for some reason, leaving the house with a musty, alien smell.

The team had resolved to move just after a martinied lunch if they had a "go" sign from Julie. A right-hand shade in the master bedroom was the signal. If Julie left it up, the setup was on; if the shade was halfway down, it meant there was some doubt that Louise could be manipulated; and if the shade was all the way down, it meant that things were off for the time being—an old and extremely simple visual device.

Julie and Louise decided to cook the Chinese food they had both become fond of, and they drove into town to buy a new wok at Mathews, the overpriced Menlo Head pot-and-pan store. When they returned with the ingredients, Julie suggested that they build a fire in the library to trim down the cool stickiness of the house. Then she built hefty cocktails for them, as much to bolster herself as anything else, and the two women settled down on the soft rug before the fire. They sat in a comfortable silence for a few moments; then Julie slid her arm around Louise's shoulder.

"These have been great days, Louise . . . I'm glad you asked me to come here."

"They're not over, are they?"

"No, of course not. I just wanted you to know that no

292

matter what happens . . . if you and Kent should get back together . . . I'll always remember the times we had together."

"We'll never get back together," Louise said, staring into the fire. "I know that now. I don't even want to anymore, not even for the children's sake. What the hell . . . they're all old enough to realize that Kent and I don't get along. It's funny though . . . even knowing that a thing is coming to the end . . . you think back. You know, Julie, they weren't all bad times. I mean, with the kids growing up . . . it used to be good." She sighed. "You can't help but feel strongly about someone you have lived with for a long time . . . and you remember the good times. They weren't all bad."

Julie looked at the woman's ravaged face, which even the glow from the fire couldn't soften, and she set down her glass abruptly and stood up.

"Let's have some lunch."

When they had eaten, Julie went into the bedroom and yanked on the shade, letting it fly all the way to the top. The electronics man stationed across the street saw it and moved quickly towards the cellar door which had been unlocked. Julie returned to the library where Louise was lying on the couch with a snifter of Courvoisier. She sat down beside her and took her hand. Louise smiled dreamily as Julie raised her hand to her mouth and nibbled at it gently with her full, soft lips.

"Louise darling . . . let's go upstairs. I want to please you . . . make you happy. Come on, darling."

Louise nodded and struggled to her feet.

When she hesitated momentarily outside the bedroom door, Julie said quickly, "Kent's away . . . isn't he? There's nothing to worry about."

There was a pause as Louise seemed to be trying to focus her thoughts, remember. "Yes, yes . . . you're right, Julie. He won't bother us."

The electronics operator in the cellar saw the women enter the bedroom; he moved the lens into focus, pressed the start button and the tape rolled.

When the two women had undressed, Julie took Louise in her arms and kissed her on the mouth, moving her lips slowly and sensuously across Louise's lips. Then she dropped to her knees and worked her mouth around and over Louise's breasts, her tongue flicking her nipples, her hands deftly touching the other woman between the thighs. Louise groaned and reached down to lift Julie up; Julie shook her hand away and continued her exploration into the soft, swollen flesh between Louise's legs, wet now from Julie's tongue and Louise's own excitement.

Then Julie stood and whispered, "Would you please me, Louise? You know, I like it standing up."

(This was a calculated ploy devised by Carl Sheen to bring the action closer to the recording lens so there would be no dispute as to the identity of Louise Morgan.)

Julie spread her legs and caressed her breasts with one hand while she directed Louise to her knees. Grasping the back of Louise's head, Julie guided the other woman's mouth up her own thighs and into her groin.

"Oh, Louise . . . that's so good . . . I love it . . . I love you . . . don't stop . . . do you love me?" Julie nudged Louise's head away. "Do you, Louise?"

"Yes."

"Do you love me more than your husband?"

"Yes."

"You love women more than those bastards, don't you . . . but there're so many other women in your life, aren't there? That's what you told me."

Julie rocked Louise's head in a motion of "yes" and then led her lips into the hollow where no words could be picked up by the three small pin mikes hidden in the bedroom. Louise moved her face and lips up along Julie's stomach, and Julie asked again, "Is it only me, Louise?"

"Of course it is," Louise said in a blurred voice.

Julie guided Louise's mouth back between her legs, and both women reached a climax at the same time. Julie collapsed on the bed with Louise and gathered the woman up in her arms, kissing her breasts; then they pulled the covers up to their necks.

The group assembled again in Bob Booth's office at six-twenty that evening to play the tape on a machine supplied by the electronics firm. The show lasted twenty-two minutes, and Julie sat there feeling very sick as she watched the avid expressions on the men's faces. When the tape finally went black, Bob Booth stood and went around the room, shaking everybody's hand.

"Absolutely beautiful! Julie, you were great. Carl, you have a cunning mind . . . I respect cunning minds. Julie . . . I'll see that you get to Broadway yet . . . did she turn you on?"

"A little."

"How *prima facie* is the evidence, Bob?" Sheen asked.

"Okay, but we want to establish a trend here. Now, Julie, let me be the scriptwriter for a minute. Tomorrow you pull the same act. I want you to say to Louise—make sure she's beefed up with booze, but not so much she can't speak—something like this. Tell her you get turned on by voice suggestions. Have her say to you, 'I'm a lesbian. I love women with real passion . . . I've always been that way. I hid it from my husband . . . no one around Menlo Head knows . . . I've been with women all my life . . .' "

Julie laughed.

"What's so funny?" Bob asked.

"I'll never get her to say that. She's no lesbian."

"Then what have we just seen?"

"She wants to please me, you fool. I'm her friend . . . she trusts me . . . don't you understand? I don't think she even enjoys what she's doing. And if she started making a confession like that, it would be obvious . . . a fake. Good dialogue is supposed to sound real. Let me handle it my way."

"Just make sure I pick up some self-incriminating evidence," Bob Booth said.

"You've got a hell of a lot already," Julie said, gathering up her purse and heading for the door.

The Wednesday tape was not that difficult to achieve. Julie, who was by now the director and dramatist, as well as the actress, was anxious to conclude the whole shabby business, so she devised a plan whereby Bob Booth, the producer, would be satisfied once and for all. It would be a suggestion of transference, the scooping up of a fictitious relationship to achieve the revolting curtain call.

On Thursday afternoon, with the operative stationed in the cellar closet, the two women sat in the living room after lunch. Before Louise could drop off for a nap, Julie said, "You've given me great joy, Louise . . . and I'm very grateful."

"Do you really mean that?"

"Yes . . . you're a very unusual woman. Would you be willing to try something new . . . something different?"

"What?"

"Well, I loved a very beautiful girl one time . . . an Italian girl. She was about twenty-five. We were in Capri, and every time she made love to me, she talked . . . and it turned me on."

"What did she say . . . dirty words . . . that sort of thing?"

"No, she wasn't crude. She used to say over and over that women, not men, were the only thing in her life. She detailed affairs she'd had, and I suppose I gained a new high . . . a thrill . . . through her descriptions."

"Do you still love her?"

"Yes."

"And do you see her?"

Julie sighed. "She was killed in a car accident . . . near Palermo."

296

"Oh, Julie . . . that's terrible. I'm sorry." Louise was silent for a moment, then said, "I think I know what you want . . . the ghost of this girl, or this girl brought back to you. You want me to be this girl for you."

"Yes . . . yes . . . that's it. Does it alarm you?"

"No, it doesn't alarm me . . . but I can't be somebody else. And I'm probably very different."

"That's just it . . . you're not! I love you, and I want you to love me . . . but at the same time . . . remind me of her . . . say the things she did. Don't think you're not enough, Louise. You are, and you're unique. But . . . oh, I suppose it's crazy . . . but it's the memory I'm still clinging to. I want somehow to keep her memory alive."

"All right . . . if that will make you happy. I'll try."

Julie smiled and embraced Louise. "Is it too much to ask . . . would you rather not? I won't force you."

"I know that. No, I'll do anything I can to make you happy, Julie. You've been very good to me . . . when I needed support."

Julie looked away for a moment and then quickly continued, "OK, you be Nicky . . . tell me how you love women . . . your affairs . . . go wild, Louise. Back to boarding school . . . back to Yale . . . anyplace."

They clasped hands and moved into the bedroom. The tape was running; they undressed each other, and Louise knelt at the feet of Julie Gardiner who was standing on the cue markers, never once looking into the grate of the air-conditioning vent where the electronic equipment was concealed.

"Well, there was this Spanish girl," Louise started.

"Show me what the Spanish girl did, darling."

Louise became excited now by her own fantasizing as she talked about loving other women, and she began to make love to Julie. It became a kind of rape, a grabbing of arms and legs, and a wild burst of passionate energy, so moving and hysterical that Julie wondered where Louise was getting her strength. It became slightly rough, and Julie felt that Louise was unleashing on her the terrible anger she felt towards Kent, and maybe all men.

Then it ended suddenly with a violent heave of Louise Morgan's breath, and she fell on the bed in Julie's arms, glistening with sweat.

The electronics operative whistled softly to himself and snapped off the power switch of the video tape recorder. He left the closet with the tape under his arm.

He went to Bob Booth's office that evening and ran the tape on the lawyer's playback machine for him and Carl Sheen.

"That Julie is something, isn't she?" Booth said, notching a cigar into his tobacco-stained teeth.

"Sure is. Either she's a director of enormous persuasion . . . or this Morgan woman has always liked it that way."

"Who cares? We've got what we need," Booth said, "but Morgan wants the equipment . . . everything . . . out of there. Tell Julie to get a sudden audition."

"Not going to stage a grand finale with the kids?"

"Naw. I'd like to . . . just to cinch matters, but I kind of knew Mr. Yacht Designer was going to fold on us. He's a phony. He's got balls enough to play games behind his wife's back . . . but when it comes to doing what's necessary to break her ass, he doesn't have the guts."

Sheen nodded. "I think we have our case anyway," he said, as he glanced again at the tape recorder sitting on Bob Booth's desk.

CHAPTER THIRTY

It has been said that a good trial advocate needs a series of traits: he must have intellectual breadth; he must have desire; he must have an active intellectual metabolism; he must have stomach; he must have combativeness; he must have analytical methodology; and he must be sensitive. Bob Booth had all these traits, except the last.

The lawyer never doubted that he could gain the evidence needed to dislodge Louise Morgan from Pigeon Hill. After an adversary tussle full of steamy rhetoric, the children would be awarded to Kent Morgan, the most senseless, mentally impaired idea he had ever heard of. But that was what the clean-faced yacht designer wanted, and it was a challenge to Bob Booth. He had delivered a few boys to their fathers, but never three little girls, and the idea of it was adrenalin to his ego.

A complaint against Louise Morgan was filed with the clerk's office in Menlo Head Tuesday morning:

CONNECTICUT: IN THE SUPERIOR COURT OF FAIRFIELD COUNTY MENLO HEAD DIVISION

KENNETH C. MORGAN, III
Pigeon Hill
1202 Powder Hill Drive
Menlo Head, Connecticut

Complainant   IN CHANCERY
                               NO. 190897

vs.

LOUISE UPTON MORGAN   **BILL OF**
Pigeon Hill   **COMPLAINT**
1202 Powder Hill Drive
Menlo Head, Connecticut

Respondent

Now comes your complainant, KENNETH C. MOR-
GAN, III, who respectfully represents the following:

1. That on the 6th day of October, 1964, your
complainant was lawfully married in Oxford, Maryland,
to Louise Upton.

2. That the complainant is a resident of the County
of Fairfield, State of Connecticut, and that he has been
so domiciled for more than one year preceding the institution of this suit.

3. That the respondent has been domiciled at the
above address.

4. That three children were born as a result of said
marriage, namely: Catherine Louise Morgan, a daughter, whose birth date is September 16, 1965; Laura
Anne Morgan, a daughter, whose birth date is April 3
1969; and Josephine Naomi Morgan, a daughter, whose
birth date is May 30, 1973.

5. That the respondent has acted under the influ
ence of alcohol and drugs to abuse and neglect her
children and deprive them of moral, physical and paren
tal guidance as to support the well-being of said children

6. That the respondent physically assaulted the
complainant with the intention of maiming him on
April 22nd of this year.

7. That the respondent has engaged in homosexua
acts with a woman guest at above stated premise.

8. That the marriage cannot be reconciled.

9. That the continued presence of the responden
in the household would continue to irrevocably injur

the emotional, physical and moral well-being of the children.

WHEREFORE, your complainant prays that a dissolution of marriage created by the aforesaid bonds of matrimony be decreed him; that he may be awarded full custody of the children of the parties; that he shall maintain full property rights; that no award of alimony is justified; that the respondent shall be removed by court order from the premise; that he shall be awarded maintenance for the said children; that he may have all such further and general relief as the nature of the case may require.

Phil Cummings did not want Judge Shallaway involved in his case, even though his jurisdiction was properly Menlo Head. But Booth reminded his associate that Shallaway was already influenced and prepared for the Bill of Complaint, whereas another judge in Stamford might ask for the *prima facie* evidence to support the allegations.

The two lawyers went together to Judge Shallaway's office at two o'clock that Tuesday afternoon, June 2.

Judge Shallaway read the papers and said to Phil Cummings and Bob Booth, "It's a shame."

"Everyone is regretful, Your Honor," Phil said.

The three men were silent for a few moments; then Phil said, "Judge, would you consider hearing the case in this jurisdiction? You've been excellent in conferencing matters like this; perhaps if all parties talked things out in your office . . . maybe Mrs. Morgan might see the wisdom of giving up her children while she seeks psychiatric care. Of course, Mr. Morgan will be reasonable and allow very liberal visitation rights. Mrs. Morgan will always be the mother to these young girls."

The judge once more looked at the Bill of Complaint.

"These are serious allegations. I hope they are provable." He shook his head. "Gentlemen, this isn't the traditional divorce . . . if any divorce is traditional."

"That's correct, Your Honor," Bob Booth said. "But I can assure you that Mr. Morgan has the well-being of the children in mind."

"In all my years on the bench, I never came up against a case like the Morgans. What happened to these people?"

"Mental illness, Judge," Bob Booth said.

"Then why doesn't Mr. Morgan put his wife in a hospital. What's a divorce going to solve?"

"The gap between these people is too great to close," the lawyer responded.

"Mr. Booth," said Judge Shallaway, "I've heard that you can become a vicious man in court. I want you to enjoy every availability of the law, but if you so much as badger Mrs. Morgan, insult her or break any rule of advocacy or politeness or respect, I'll have you thrown out of court."

Judge Shallaway picked up his pen and signed the order.

The sheriff's car with two deputies entered the front drive of Pigeon Hill at precisely 7:23 A.M. the following morning. Kent answered the door.

"Is this the home of Mrs. Kenneth Morgan?"

"It is," Kent said.

"We have a court order to be served against Mrs. Morgan. Is she here?"

"Yes, she is."

"Would you ask her to come to the door?"

Kent went upstairs and woke his wife up.

"The sheriff is downstairs. He wants to see you."

"Leave me alone . . . get out of here."

At that moment, Cathy descended the stairs in her bathrobe and saw the two officers. She ran back up to her mother's room.

"There's a policeman downstairs, Mom!"

"About what?" Louise asked in a thick voice, covering her face from the light.

"They have an order, Louise," Kent said.

"What order?"

"You'd better come downstairs and find out," he said.

Louise slowly pushed her legs to the floor, put on her robe and made her way down the stairs. By this time, all the children were in the hall, watching the sheriff's deputies.

"Are you Mrs. Morgan?"

"Yes."

"Mrs. Morgan, I have an order signed by Judge Shallaway. It says that you must remove yourself from this house."

"What are you talking about?"

"This order, ma'am . . . it's a bill of complaint for a divorce."

"Kent . . . what the hell is going on?" Louise cried. "Is this some kind of joke?"

"Louise, it's necessary," Kent said softly.

"Why?"

"I won't go into it in front of the children."

"You never asked for a divorce."

"Everything's on the paper."

"You can't make me leave my home because of a goddamn piece of paper."

"I can't . . . but these men can . . . and will."

Louise turned to the deputies. "Get out of here. I'm not going anywhere!"

The children gathered around their mother, holding onto her bathrobe.

"Where are you taking my mom?" Jody said.

"Yes . . . just where am I supposed to go, officer?" Louise asked.

"Ma'am, we don't know."

"Am I being arrested?"

"No, ma'am. The order says you must leave the house. You can only take clothes and personal articles."

"When?"

"Right now. Well, of course, we'll give you time to pack and get dressed."

"I'm *not* going!" Louise shrieked. "This is my house!"

"No, Louise . . . my name is on the deed . . . not yours," Kent said.

"Mrs. Morgan, this is the most unpleasant part of the job . . . but you have to go. We're bound to carry out the orders of the court. They're not our orders . . . but the judge's."

"I'll call Phil Cummings. He's our lawyer."

"It won't do you any good, Louise . . . he's *my* lawyer," Kent said.

"You goddamn bastard!"

Louise made a threatening move towards Kent with her fist drawn back. One of the deputies stepped in front of her and grabbed her hand.

"Mrs. Morgan, calm down. We'll give you ten minutes. You pack up, and let's get this over with."

"I told you. I'm staying."

"Mother, don't go!" Cathy yelled.

Louise turned away and went upstairs; they heard her close the bedroom door and lock it. The children started after her, and Kent put out a restraining hand.

"No . . . wait here . . . Mother will be back."

"What's wrong, Daddy? Why are you letting them do this?" Laurie cried.

Kent just shook his head and motioned the officers into the living room. When Louise did not reappear within a few minutes, Kent escorted the men upstairs and unlocked the door for them. Then he went back to the living room.

The two deputies stood at the entrance to the bedroom.

"Mrs. Morgan, you *have* to go."

"Then you'll have to drag me out."

The officers looked at each other, and one of them said "Better phone in."

"Yeah."

One stood against the doorjamb, while the other man crossed the room and made a quick call to the sheriff's sub station, explaining their problem.

"What the hell are you calling me for?" the desk sergeant

said. "You got the order. It was signed by the judge, and Cummings is representing Mr. Morgan. Get her out of there."

"It's not that easy. She's resisting . . . and there's kids all over the place. They're all yelling."

"Do you want me to send another car?"

"Maybe it would help. This woman is kind of crazy."

"That's what the order says. Okay . . . you got another car comin'."

Cathy clutched Laurie and Jody, both of whom were crying wildly, as two more deputies arrived minutes later and their mother was dragged in her bare feet and nightgown down the stairs, trying to hold onto the banisters and yelling.

"Kent, is this what you want to do to our children? Look at them . . . look what you're doing, you bastard!"

"Daddy . . . stop them . . . stop them!" Jody screamed.

Louise's hand was pulled and unpeeled from each banister as the four bulky deputies dragged her down the stairs little by little. Louise kept screaming and kicking. Terrified, Cathy ran out of the house and across the lawn to the Craigs' house.

"They're taking my mother away. Help us!" Cathy cried.

Both of the Craigs and their children started towards Pigeon Hill. The door was open, and they could hear Louise's screams.

"Hey . . . you can't do this," Don Craig said, pulling at one of the deputy's arms.

"Like hell we can't! Get out of here!"

"What in God's name is going on?" Fran Craig said, nudging one of the officers.

"Fran . . . Don, this is none of your business. Please . . . leave us alone!" Kent yelled.

"You're going to stand there and let this happen, Kent? What the hell is wrong with you?" Don said.

"You don't understand."

As the conversation went on, Louise escaped the deputies. She ran to the back of the house, broke a window and started screaming.

"Help me . . . someone . . . please help me!"

Betsy Potter heard the cries.

"It's Louise Morgan . . . she's screaming!"

"Don't get involved with them," Lane said. "Forget it."

But the screams continued, and Betsy believed that Louise was being raped or attacked. She quickly dialed the Menlo Head police.

"This is Mrs. Lane Potter. Something terrible is happening next door at Pigeon Hill!"

At almost the same time, Fran Craig picked up the phone in the library of Pigeon Hill and called the police; she was even more descriptive.

"There's a riot going on at Pigeon Hill. Hurry."

The four sheriff's deputies had picked up Louise and were carrying her back through the house, towards the front door.

"Listen, I'm not going to put up with this shit!" one of the deputies said. "I'll get a heart attack. The woman is as strong as an ox. Cuff her."

They wrenched Louise Morgan's arms in front of her and snapped on the handcuffs as she tried to bite the officers. Suddenly, with no warning, Laurie and Jody hurled themselves at the officers, grabbing their legs and arms.

"Mr. Morgan . . . for Christ's sake . . . get the kids back . . . get the kids!" a deputy cried out.

One of the officers lost his patience and brought his hand across Louise's mouth, hoping to subdue her. Cathy screamed, seeing her mother struck, and she lashed out at the man with her fist as Don Craig and Kent entered the scuffle, trying to pull the girls off the deputies. Arms and legs were whirling. The children kicked and struggled. Laurie, whose hands were around the belt of one of the deputies, reached down and unsnapped the protective cover of the man's thirty-eight service revolver. She yanked the gun out, raised the barrel to the back of the officer's head and with both hands she pulled the trigger.

The close-range concussion knocked the officer across the hall; he plunged headfirst into the Chippendale table beside the front door. The silver plate used for calling cards careened up into the air and fell to the marble entrance floor with a clang; it seemed to announce the death of the Fairfield County sheriff's deputy—a man of forty-five with two sons and one daughter.

He lay in a twisted lump. There was a gaping, irregular hole in the man's forehead where the bullet, squashed and spent, had come out to lodge itself in the insert panel of Pigeon Hill's front door.

There was a sudden, stunned silence. All motion ceased. The people in the room stared at the man on the floor, and the first remark came from another deputy.

"My God, you've killed my partner."

CHAPTER THIRTY-ONE

Seconds after the thundering explosion in the hall of Pigeon Hill, three squad cars from Chief Caramati's department slid to a halt on the bluestone driveway out front.

"It's too late . . . it's too late!" one of the sheriff's deputies screamed out the open door.

The Menlo Head police entered with their guns drawn; then they recoiled, seeing the dead officer with his head in an expanding pool of blood.

"The little kid's killed Abbot," the deputy in the hall sobbed.

In the pandemonium by the stairs, Louise, barefooted and still handcuffed, reached out and grabbed Laurie. Cathy and Jody saw Louise's eyes signal the dining room. No one noticed them slip out of the house, and once they were on the bow of the terrace overlooking the tomato patch, Louise and her daughters leaped off the curved steps in the direction of the carriage house.

Running along behind the cover of the lush elms and maple trees, Louise and the girls, all in their nightclothes, entered the rear door of the carriage house. They sank to the concrete floor by the Maserati, trying to regain their breath and their senses.

"Oh, Laurie, oh, my poor darling . . ." Louise said over and over, holding onto her daughter's hand and reaching out distraughtly to pat her on the face and shoulders and hair.

The young girl did not respond at all, just looked at her mother with a totally vacuous expression.

"She was trying to help you, Mom," Cathy said, staring at the stark face of her younger sister.

"I know, darling . . . I know . . ."

"We all were!" Jody cried. "Those guys were hurting you, Mom!"

"Do you think that policeman's . . . dead?" Cathy asked, after a pause.

"I don't know, Cathy. I hope not. Your father made a terrible mistake . . . ordering those King Kongs over here at daybreak . . . trying to throw me out of the house. I'll fix him for this. No more playing around with tennis courts."

"What do we do now?" Jody asked.

"God, I don't know," Louise said. "How could I have screwed up so royally? I'm sorry . . . I apologize to all of you . . . I'll make it up to you. Goddamn, I will."

Louise thought for a time, her head buried in her shaking hands. Then she whispered with a deep voice; it was her old spunky tone which had disappeared months ago.

"Okay," Louise said. "First, I'm taking you kids with me. Nothing wrong with that; I'm your mother. And I'll be damned if your father is going to have his way. I don't trust him at all now; if he's capable of a stunt like this, he might do anything."

"We don't want to be with him, Mom," Cathy said, hooking her arms around Louise's neck.

"Don't worry . . . you won't be!"

"Will Laurie go to jail?" Jody whispered to her mother.

"No, of course not. They can't put kids in jail. Cathy . . . grab your father's hacksaw over there, and help me out of these bracelets. Christ, I never thought I'd be handcuffed like a common criminal in my own home."

"But how do we get out of here, Mom?" Jody asked.

"We'll use the Maserati . . . go to Mrs. Lunsford's."

There was the screech of a car coming to a swift halt in the driveway outside the carriage house. Jody looked out between the cracks in the door.

"Too late, Mom! The driveway's blocked."

"All right then, we'll run over . . . through the Potters' yard. Saw these damn things off . . . quick."

A surge of police officers from Menlo Head and the sheriff's department, accompanied by county investigators, had rushed into Pigeon Hill, right past the pool of blood still oozing out of the dead man's head. There were shouts, ringing phones, hysterical outcries from the sheriff's deputies, and in the turmoil no one had noticed that Louise Morgan and her daughters were missing. Some order was restored with the arrival of senior police officers, and then a deputy yelled, "Where are they? Where's the woman and the children?"

No one knew; someone said, "Find them!"

Kent, somewhat in shock himself, said, "They're probably in the carriage house."

"Any guns in there?" one officer yelled.

"Yes . . . ah . . . I believe there are some shotguns."

With the dead officer in the hall and the word "shotguns," a mild panic broke out among the police; orders were given to surround the carriage house.

Chief Caramati stationed himself in front of the door and yelled through his microphone, "Mrs. Morgan . . . come on out now."

There was silence. He repeated the order. Finally they heard Louise's voice. "To what? More handcuffs? You're taking my children away. Like hell I'll come out!"

Mayor Turpin arrived moments later; he saw what appeared to be an army of police officers, some in bulletproof vests, some holding canisters of tear gas, some pointing shotguns at the carriage house.

He said, "Good God . . . what are you people doing? This is no way to handle the situation."

"That Mrs. Morgan is crazy, and she's got the kids in there," an officer said.

"How do you think this looks?" the mayor asked, peering over his shoulder to see a photographer from *The Stamford*

Courier punching off photographs. "I'll go and talk to Louise."

"One policeman is already dead," the officer persisted. "We don't want another killing, Mayor. Let us do it our way . . . tear gas. The captain of the sheriff's department just showed up, and he's so mad he's ready to blast the whole place down."

Walt Turpin shook his head; he approached the carriage house and called out, "Louise, can I speak to you? Let me in, please."

"Why? What do you want to say?"

"Louise, there're twenty or thirty men out here. A sheriff's deputy is dead. Now, I'm trying to avoid more violence, but the officers . . . well, you can imagine how they feel."

"I'm sorry the man's dead, but I didn't bring all this on. Judge Shallaway signed that court order. How can he allow me to be treated like this . . . like an animal . . . dragged out of my own home? What gives people the right to do that?"

"Louise, I honestly don't know, but you're not resolving anything by staying in there, and you're intelligent enough to realize it. You have to come out." He paused and added, "Think of the children."

"Don't talk to me about my children!" she screamed. "My husband didn't think of the children, did he? Oh, Christ . . . what's the use!"

They could hear the despair in her voice and knew that she was ready to give in. A few minutes later, Louise Morgan walked slowly from the carriage house with her daughters. The juvenile authorities, who were waiting outside, took the three young girls one way, and the sheriff's deputies took Louise by the arm another way. The children broke into loud tears and turned back towards their mother.

"So, Kent Morgan, are you happy now?" Louise screamed, shaking her fist as the photographer moved in and snapped her picture.

Bob Booth was eating breakfast in his jogging shorts and sweat shirt when the call came.

"This is Kent Morgan. My . . . my daughter, Laurie . . . just shot a sheriff's deputy. He's dead." There was a silence. Kent continued, "Did you hear me?"

"I heard," Bob Booth said crisply. "What went on? Tell me what you saw."

In stops and starts, Kent related what had happened.

"Then your wife was acting crazy. The police had to subdue her . . and that provoked the kid to pull the gun out. Then she attempted to kidnap her daughters . . . leaving the scene of a homicide."

"Did you hear what I said? A man is dead! He's in my front hall . . . still bleeding," Kent said, gasping for breath.

"All right, Morgan, get ahold of yourself. All this will help our case."

"The man's *dead*."

"Listen to me . . . *listen*. Don't say a damn thing until I get there. I'm leaving right now."

The fact that an officer had been killed did not in the least deter Booth from his goal to win child custody and a total property settlement for Kent Morgan. That was what he was paid to do. He would achieve his purpose. The killing was not central to the case, except that it probably revealed the bottom-line influence of the way Louise Morgan had brought up her daughters.

As Booth drove towards Pigeon Hill, he tried to visualize the next step. He determined that three separate layers of questioning would take place: interrogation of those who were obviously being held at Pigeon Hill as material witnesses; the coroner's inquest; and the hearing of the juvenile division of the Superior Court to establish the custody of the three Morgan children. The first two interrogations would try to establish if the sheriff's deputies had conducted themselves professionally or in any way provoked the shooting. The custody hearing would dwell on the family life at Pigeon Hill and the fitness of each parent.

Laurie Morgan could not be charged with manslaughter or murder; she was under sixteen. However, Booth realized that the Fairfield County prosecutor would be rancorous; he would be listening intently for any disparity in the accounts of all those involved in the conspiracy against Louise Morgan.

When Booth, dressed in a gray three-piece suit, walked in, a blanket was draped over the body of the dead sheriff's deputy, and the house was crowded with county officials.

Bunny Lunsford rushed out of the library. "Are you Kent Morgan's lawyer?" she demanded.

"Yes, I'm Bob Booth."

"I'm Bunny Lunsford . . . a close friend of Louise's. Where the hell do you get off writing a piece of bullshit like this and tossing Louise out of her house?" she shouted, shaking the bill of complaint and the court order in the air.

"I can't discuss the case," Booth said, "and it's none of your business, Mrs. Lunsford. Your name's not on the complaint."

Kent entered the room at that moment, and Bunny exploded.

"You're a goddamn bastard!" she screamed. "I hope you're happy! You've destroyed your wife . . . your daughter's skull . . . and now you've killed an innocent man!"

One of the officials grabbed Bunny by the arm and led her away. Bob Booth noticed that Kent Morgan was very shaken by her attack.

Statements from each witness to the killing were taken. After a long conference between the sheriff's deputies and the assistant county prosecutor, it was established that Louise Morgan should be charged for resisting a valid court order, resisting arrest, assaulting a police officer in the rightful performance of his duty and leaving the scene of a homicide without authorization.

Louise was read her rights and marched out of the house in handcuffs, with Bunny trailing after her.

Just before she was placed in the sheriff's car, Louise

turned to one of the officers and asked, "What's going to happen to my children?"

"They'll be safe . . . under the care of the juvenile authorities. We don't want them on the loose or running after you," the officer said.

Louise was booked and arraigned before Judge Shallaway, who was ashen after he heard about the shooting.

"Tragic . . . this is tragic," he said to those assembled before his bench. "Mrs. Morgan, are you represented by counsel?"

"No. Phil Cummings always took care of our legal problems."

"He's representing your husband," the judge said.

"I just heard."

"Do you want representation?"

"I'll get my own lawyer."

"How do you plead to these charges?"

"Not guilty."

"I'll set bail for two thousand dollars and a hearing one week from today. Do you have the bail?"

"I have it, Your Honor," Bunny spoke up.

Bunny wrote a check to the clerk of the court, and the two women walked out of the courtroom.

The aftershock hit Louise when they reached Bunny Lunsford's home. Had Rod and the general been there, Louise might have been more composed, but she merely collapsed on the couch and sobbed, repeating over and over, "What happened? What happened?"

When Louise had partially cried herself out, Bunny said, "Louise, do you have any guts left?"

Louise nodded dully. "Yeah . . . I guess so."

Bunny grabbed her by the shoulder. "Your husband's responsible for that man's death. That's what I said back at Pigeon Hill, and it's the truth. He's a fucking goddamn shit! You have to fight, Louise! Go in there and *hurt* him. If you don't, you won't get custody of the children or a property settlement. Are you ready to be the toughest bitch in the world?"

Louise raised herself off the couch and nodded again; this time she had a fierce look on her face.

"I'm going to fight, Bunny."

"Good!"

"Now, how do we do it?"

"Your husband found a mean bastard to represent him; we'll find a meaner one. I'll make a few calls. In the meantime, you stretch out and rest. You're going to need every goddamn bit of strength you have . . . so Louise, try to cool the booze and pills, huh?"

"I can do that . . . it's my turn now," she said. There was a pause, and Louise added, "God . . . my poor baby . . . my poor Laurie. What will this do to her?"

CHAPTER THIRTY-TWO

Bob Booth had listened carefully to the tone and texture of the questions being fired off by the edgy Fairfield County prosecutor as he paced back and forth through the rooms of Pigeon Hill. The lawyer was exercising his criminal pulse taking. He felt a dismal foreboding, and he quietly slipped the word to all those involved in the conspiracy and entrapment of Louise Morgan that they were required to attend a strategy and buttressing session in New York City as soon as possible.

Lawyer Booth had his paralegal book a room at the Hotel Biltmore that day. He knew the prosecutor was scratching about for some reason to mobilize a grand jury, anything to atone for the death of the sheriff's deputy; investigators could follow Booth and his client within the county, but they had no jurisdiction in New York City.

Each party arrived at the hotel separately: Carl Sheen, Julie Gardiner, Kent Morgan and Booth's elderly paralegal. Bob Booth poured drinks for everyone and passed around a plate of hors d'oeuvres.

"I'm very sorry this happened," he said to Kent Morgan, who was still stunned and only half-shaven.

"You're sorry? You *caused* it!" Kent bristled.

"Just a minute . . . you came to me with a large order . . . a very deep grudge, my friend. I was acting on your instructions. I have the paper you wrote me. Remember the paper?" Booth said, his bull-like face not reflecting a hint of remorse.

Kent jumped to his feet and crossed to the window; he looked down on Vanderbilt Avenue and across to the Yale Club, where he had dined so often with Louise. Finally Kent spun around and continued, his red eyes strained. "I never asked for this. My God . . . my daughter . . . Christ, how can she go through life, knowing she killed a police officer? Poor Laurie can't even answer the sheriff's questions."

"I had no idea this would happen," Bob Booth said. "Mrs. Morgan was more unbalanced than I thought. For the kid to pull the gun out and fire it . . . does anyone think I would have proceeded on this theory if I had known what would happen?"

There was silence.

"Do any of you think that?" Bob Booth said, raising his hoarse voice.

His mock compassion did not dupe those in the stuffy hotel room.

"All right," Carl Sheen said. "Forget the explanations. What now?"

"I want an agreement among us," Booth said. "Total agreement. That Fairfield County prosecutor's not going to let up; he'll be in there with a jackhammer."

"Booth!" Kent screamed out. "Why aren't we worrying about my daughter . . . the dead man . . . my reputation! Who the hell cares about the prosecutor! What does he have to do with this goddamn mess?"

Booth padded about the hotel room; his face was lowered, and his shadowed jaw was ducked into his meaty chest. He slung his face from side to side.

"Morgan, you're too much. The deputy is dead; his blood is cold. You wanted those kids . . . you came to me for that purpose."

"Not at this expense, for Christ's sake."

"You told me to get results. I'm getting those results . . . but we have a temporary problem."

"I'll say we do," Julie Gardiner said.

Booth stopped and turned on those seated before him.

317

"All of you! *Don't* get lofty with me! Each of you knew the risks. Each of you knew we were breaking the law. Some of you were paid, so don't pull a pious scene with me. There's no one in this room who's not guilty!" He breathed hard, glaring at Kent and Julie. "Listen, you two pharisees . . . all of us could be considered accessories before the fact to manslaughter or murder. At the very least, we'd be guilty of conspiracy if they found out that Louise Morgan was set up."

A long silence followed Booth's assessment of their possible complicity in serious crime. They traded looks, and finally Kent asked, "How do you figure that?"

"Each of us knew of, or was directly or indirectly involved in, the entrapment . . . providing a circumstance for an unlawful act which someone would not ordinarily enter into. It was to prop up a falsified complaint; that's conspiracy, criminal contempt, maybe. The complaint, when served, led to a killing. It might be only a weak link, a very thin thread, but one matter does bear on the other, and it all balances on the anger of the prosecutor."

"And you want us to commit another crime . . . perjury?" Julie Gardiner said.

Booth smiled in his heavy, sardonic way as he flicked his hand over his chin. "If you wish to remain at freedom, Miss Gardiner, you'll be guided by my advice."

"But your advice led to a killing," she said acidly.

"It was something we couldn't predict. Now, do I have an agreement among us?"

"What about my daughter . . . and the dead man?" Kent Morgan said.

Bob Booth exploded. "Forget them! You are on your way to prison . . . we are all on our way to prison. A police officer has been killed; we are accessories before the fact."

"And now we'll be accessories after the fact," Kent Morgan said, his voice shaking and losing all of its Oxonian notes.

318

"Yes," Bob Booth came back hastily. "But we can beat this thing if we stick to the same story. If not, you will never get your children. You can't bring the officer back to life or remove your daughter's fingerprints from the gun. Do you want to make it worse?"

Kent Morgan shook his head. They all followed. Booth smiled; he knew he could daunt them into further complicity. The lawyer then went through each detail of the upcoming testimony; they rehearsed until late that afternoon, with Booth taking the role of a very truculent Fairfield County prosecutor hunting for reprisals.

After about a dozen phone calls, Bunny Lunsford had found Tim Ahearn, another Bob Booth, but slightly more polished and younger. He was thoroughly experienced in the hard-edged practice of cruel divorces. He had, in fact, opposed Bob Booth on several occasions and prevailed, so he told Bunny and Louise when they arrived at his Darien office late on the day of the shooting.

The lawyer looked over the complaint and stroked his dark, well-groomed hair; then he fingered his pin-striped vest. (He was fine-featured and immaculately turned out in conservative custom clothes.)

"You have an uphill battle here, Mrs. Morgan. With an officer dead, they'll be looking for blood."

"Whose?" Louise asked.

"Anybody's. OK, now as to the complaint against you . . . why did you take those kids after the shooting?"

"I wanted them."

"Well, it was poor judgment, but maybe I can get you out of that. You said the officers didn't explain the court order?"

"They said nothing. Just get out."

"All right . . . we might not have a problem there. It's the custody thing. Tell me what's happened so far, Mrs. Morgan."

Louise filled the lawyer in; finally Tim Ahearn held his

hand up and came right to the point.

"You want those kids, and you want a good property settlement?"

"Yes."

"So we have some work to do. Did you have relations with this woman?"

"Yes."

"Are you bisexual?"

"No. It . . . it was the first time."

"She's no lesbo," Bunny said firmly.

"Now tell me how you got together with Miss Gardiner."

Louise took Tim Ahearn through the chance meeting with Julie Gardiner and recalled as much as she could about the relationship; there were gaps and blanks in the recitation, leading the lawyer to doubt the state of Louise's competence during the days she had spent with Julie Gardiner. Tim Ahearn did become highly suspicious of the timing, however; on the very weekend that Louise Morgan left home after having the tennis court removed, by chance, she met Julie Gardiner, whom she then invited to Pigeon Hill.

"This woman just came up to you in the art gallery? What did she say?"

"She said she remembered me from sailing."

"When?"

"About 1962 or 1963."

"So you're at an art gallery in New York . . . this woman approaches you . . . says she remembers you after eighteen years? I don't believe it," Tim said flatly.

"I don't, either." Bunny nodded her head.

"Did *she*, Julie, suggest the invitation to your home?"

"Sort of, I think. I'm so damn confused."

"I understand. And how did your husband find out about your relations with Julie?"

"I told him."

"Why?"

"I don't know."

"Miss Gardiner might have been a setup, if I know Bob Booth."

"What does that mean?"

"It could mean that Miss Gardiner was paid by your husband to form a foundation for unfitness, the depravity count on the complaint here."

There was a long pause as Louise thought about this; then she said, "Well, what about the alcoholism and drug stuff?"

"Oh, I have a psychiatrist who'll testify the way I want. You were obviously disturbed by the conduct of your husband, and that led you into liquor and pills. You were given the drugs by the doctor, so we don't have to worry about that."

"It's the homosexual count, isn't it?" Louise said. "How do I get around that?"

"Mrs. Morgan, anybody can say anything in court. It's not a game of truth; it's simply whom you believe. I've found out one thing about law after twenty years of practice. Law is the art of convincingness . . . nothing else."

"Julie will say one thing . . . I'll say another?"

"But if we can establish this woman as a tramp, her word means nothing. If we can further establish that you were set up, it'll mean trouble for your husband . . . a *lot* of trouble."

As soon as Louise and Bunny left his office, Tim Ahearn called a detective agency in Manhattan; within three hours, he had a report on Julie Gardiner.

"She's a pro, Mr. Ahearn," the detective told him over the phone. "No visible means of support . . . pays the local bills by cash. She's got men parading in and out turnstile fashion. Sometimes she's picked up at night in a Cadillac . . . the long, black kind."

"Did you find any of her clients?"

"I'm working on that. We'll get someone to testify, even if they've never seen her."

When Tim Ahearn had what he wanted, he called Bob

Booth. After the exchange of a few preliminaries, he said, "Mrs. Morgan's going to fight for the kids, Bob. The woman is pissed. You turned on the heavy stuff."

"The heavy stuff was the shooting," Bob Booth said. "How could a kid do that? The juvenile people have packed them all off to the shelter."

"So I understand. Bob, you want a pretrial?"

"Naw, let's just slug it out." He paused. "Judge Margaret Green of the Juvenile Court will probably hear this."

"Why the Juvenile Court?"

"Delinquency is now mixed in with custody. I think we're going to be immersed in a little social revolution along the way."

"Well, it ought to be a good one. Morgan's your kind of client, isn't he? Rich and angry."

"Yeah . . . just like Mrs. Morgan."

The tragedy of Pigeon Hill had crystallized into senseless retribution. Kent and Louise hardened their disdain for each other. They wanted nothing more than to injure the other. The police and prosecutors were searching for justice, which meant a counter-blow, if possible. Of all those who originally saw the portents mounting at the Morgan home, only the Clipper and Marvin Eddleman spoke up, but it was the young newspaperman who had been punished by the loss of his job.

Minutes after the shooting at Pigeon Hill, Marvin Eddleman had his chance in the spiteful sweepstakes. He had gone to work for *The Stamford Courier*, a large daily with a paid-in circulation of 79,000. Having lived and worked in Menlo Head, Marvin was assigned to the Pigeon Hill story. As he walked out of the newspaper office at eight-ten on the morning of the shooting with a photographer, he said to himself: "I'll riddle those bastards in print."

Then he stopped and thought again. "No, I'll just tell the truth. That'll be all I need, if I know the Morgans and Menlo Head."

That afternoon, large, thick headlines were stretched across the top of the *Courier*'s front page:

SHERIFF'S DEPUTY SLAIN BY CHILD
AT LUSH MENLO HEAD ESTATE
Officer Was Attempting to Serve Divorce Order
When Killed by Bullet from His Own Gun.
By Marvin Eddleman
Courier Staff Writer

The peace of Menlo Head, the historic Connecticut town, erupted into a wild West show early this morning, and when the gunsmoke cleared, William Abbot, a twenty-year veteran of the sheriff's department, was dead in the front hall of Pigeon Hill, the waterfront estate of Mr. and Mrs. Kenneth Morgan, prominent Menlo Head socialites.

According to eyewitness reports, four sheriff's deputies were attempting to remove Mrs. Morgan from the premises, acting on a court order. One of the Morgan children, an eleven-year-old girl, pulled out Abbot's .38 service revolver and shot him through the base of the neck. The sheriff's deputy died instantly, according to the Office of the Medical Examiner.

The divorce complaint, signed yesterday by Judge Shallaway of the Superior Court, alleged that Mrs. Kenneth Morgan, a former Olympic yachtswoman, was an alcoholic and drug abuser and guilty of having committed homosexual acts in her own home.

The sheriff's department charged Mrs. Morgan with resisting arrest and attempting to leave the scene of a crime. The young girl who shot Officer Abbot was charged with juvenile delinquency and taken to the juvenile shelter in Stamford with her two sisters, ages seven and fifteen.

The Courier also learned that there has been domestic trouble at the Morgan home before. On April 22 of this year, physical violence erupted at the estate, and two of the Morgan children were hurt, requiring hospital treatment. On the same night, Mr. Morgan was assaulted by his wife. Judge Shallaway, who reviewed the domestic upheaval at approximately 6:15 A.M. in his chambers on April 23, dismissed the case.

The local Menlo Head newspaper failed to carry a full account of the incident, and the town's police records, according to some Menlo Head employees, did not reflect the true events at Pigeon Hill.

William Abbot, the deceased officer, was born in Hartford, Connecticut, and had served with an excellent record in the county sheriff's department since 1960. He leaves a wife and three children.

Arthur H. Bernstein, Assistant Fairfield County Prosecutor, who arrived at the Morgan home shortly after the killing, told the *Courier*: "This is a needless tragedy, and it will require a thorough investigation and full explanations from all parties. It's hard for me to understand how an eleven-year-old girl from a privileged, educated family, who's never been in trouble before, could kill a police officer in cold blood."

Mr. Bernstein was expressing the feelings of many people around the town of Menlo Head, who were stunned by events at the waterfront estate.

"It's like something that happens in the ghetto . . . not in Menlo Head. The Morgans had everything," one neighbor said.

At press time, Mrs. Morgan had been arraigned before Judge Shallaway of the Superior Court, Menlo Head Division, and released on a $2,000 bond. Mrs. Morgan was believed to be at the home of a friend, and she refused comment when contacted by *The Courier*.

CHAPTER THIRTY-THREE

The following morning, the coroner's inquest was held in the Stamford Courthouse, and the facts were reestablished. The prosecutor angrily tried to badger all the witnesses, including Laurie Morgan; the family relations officer, who was now in charge of the Morgan girls, halted the questioning, claiming that nothing new was to be learned by conducting a punitive hearing aimed at a young girl. The Craigs, Louise Morgan and her daughters all testified that the officers had used bad judgment and unnecessary roughness and force at Pigeon Hill. Kent Morgan testified that his wife was kicking and assaulting the officers and denied unequivocally that unnecessary force was being employed by the officers.

The next day, the Juvenile Court, under the direction of Judge Margaret Green, appointed a guardian *ad litem*—or a guardian for the purpose of the trial—to render a report on the emotional condition of the children. Their well-being was material to the upcoming custody case, and how would their rights and interests be protected? Which parent did the children desire to be with?

The guardian *ad litem*, a lawyer experienced in domestic relations, called in a court-appointed child psychiatrist, and throughout one entire week, the State of Connecticut, in assuring the rights of the minors, conducted extensive tests and evaluations of the three Morgan children. Finally, Laurie, emerging from trauma, began to speak a word here and there. The guardian *ad litem* also interviewed Louise and Kent.

During a meeting in Tim's office, Louise said, "Why didn't we talk to people like this guardian before the big explosion? He's decent and very helpful."

"I don't know, Mrs. Morgan," Tim said. "Judge Shallaway should have referred the case to the state. He probably thought you people were too proud to ask for assistance, and I'm sure the judge also felt he was protecting your First Amendment rights. I looked at the witness list; Judge Shallaway is being called."

"Just for a custody hearing?"

"It's gone way beyond that. Judge Green is conducting a full hearing; there will be at least ten witnesses."

"Have you figured out my defense yet?"

"We'll go over everything Tuesday, the day before the trial. In the meantime, I want you to see my shrink, Dr. Childress."

Louise looked thoughtful. "I've never talked to a psychiatrist before. What will he think about this mess?"

"He's heard it all before. Simply tell him that you drank too much because your husband was off pulling sex scenes. Indicate that you are now on the road to positive recovery. They like that phrase . . . positive recovery. You'll clean up your act, in other words."

"And about the homosexuality?"

Ahearn shrugged. "You can't remember because you were too boozed up. Also say you are perfectly normal and don't go for the gals, which you don't."

"But I did."

"Mrs. Morgan, forget what you did! You don't recall. It's blurry in your memory. Just like gauze. You *might* have had a little kiss with Miss Gardiner, but more likely, you didn't."

"I had more than a little kiss."

"You don't remember, for God's sake! That's it and that's what you tell the judge!" the pinkfaced attorney snapped.

Judge Margaret Green moved to hear the case in the Menlo Head Courthouse. That decision sparked an uproar

326

throughout the town. It appeared that the small and proper community was coming to trial, and there were pretrial hints that the cause of Officer Abbot's death went far beyond the Morgan household. Particularly concerned about the case being heard in Menlo Head were the town counsel, Phil Cummings; Chief Caramati; and Mayor Turpin. In a sense, they were on trial, too.

The police chief called the Clipper into his office and asked him, "What's your position?"

"You know I've always been concerned about those Morgan kids. I'm not sure we did the right thing that morning in the judge's office."

"How are you going to handle your testimony, Clipper?" the chief asked, lowering his dark eyes.

"Tell the truth."

"About the reports?"

"Yes, sir."

"You might not have a job here after the trial's over," Caramati said.

"If that's the way it is . . ." the Clipper said, leaving the office.

The first day of the trial started off hot and humid. The Menlo Head courtroom was mammoth, true to the architectural concepts of the twenties. There was a high-raised platform upon which was a huge, leather-backed, deep-red chair for the judge. The walls were paneled, and the windows were bordered with blue velvet draperies.

The session was closed; the records were not to be revealed to protect the children. The only individuals allowed in the courtroom on an ongoing basis besides the Morgans were the judge; the clerk; the court recorder; the bailiff; the guardian *ad litem*, Mr. Burns; counsel for the plaintiff, Bob Booth (his associate, Phil Cummings, had quietly faded into the remote background); and Tim Ahearn, counsel for the respondent. All other witnesses were kept in the jury assembly room and would be called when needed.

"All stand," the bailiff said. "Superior Court of Connecticut, Fairfield Judicial District, Juvenile Division, is now in session . . . the Honorable Margaret Green presiding."

Judge Green walked into the courtroom, looking tired and drawn. She did not wear robes but appeared in a tailored gray dress. She recited her concern.

"This is an unpleasant and agonizing proceeding for all of us. Something quite inexplicable has happened; there has been a gross failure. Because court is sitting to establish facts surrounding the death of Officer Abbot, as well as to come to a decision on the future parental rights of the Morgan children, the court will proceed on its agenda of witnesses, some of whom are here via subpoena. You may begin, Mr. Booth."

Bob Booth pushed his heavy frame up from the table where Kent Morgan was sitting.

"Your Honor, there is little to be said except that Mr. Morgan expresses deep sorrow for the shocking incident which happened in his home. We will show that it was the disturbed actions of his wife which led to this appalling tragedy. Mr. Morgan does not claim he is the perfect parent. He has made mistakes of judgment, as these findings will show. But Your Honor, the man has worked hard to provide for his family. He is a distinguished yacht designer, one of the best in the world, a warden of the local Episcopal Church, Saint James. He is vice commodore of the Menlo Head Yacht Club, where he is in charge of the young people's sailing program. He has always been deeply interested in community affairs, and the home he has provided for his family is one of the finest in the area. But Mr. Morgan is not a psychiatrist or a social worker, nor could he serve the best interests of his children while they were being pathologically influenced by Mrs. Morgan. He loves his three daughters, and for that reason and for the well-being of the children, he prays the court will award him sole custody so that the children may continue in the home that they know and among their friends at the same school. Thank you, Your Honor."

Tim Ahearn then approached the bench.

"Your Honor, our main inquiry is that of your own. Why did this happen? How was it allowed to happen? That's the better question. I believe there were serious influences which led to Mrs. Morgan's temporary breakdown. Mrs. Morgan loves her children. They love her, and they wish to remain with her. Thank you."

Judge Green began with Sergeant DiMaggio, who told the court about his anxiety for the Morgan children that morning in Judge Shallaway's chambers.

"Now, Sergeant DiMaggio," Judge Green started, focusing her tight blue eyes on the witness. "After you had grave doubts concerning the well-being of the children, what did you do about it?"

"I made my thoughts known to Judge Shallaway."

"And were you satisfied that Menlo Head's police and paramedic reports reflected the incident?"

The Clipper wiggled in his chair, crossing and uncrossing his legs while he patted his thick crop of ebony hair. Finally he said, "Ah, well . . . I guess. They attempted to shield some of the facts, but I don't know if they were important."

The judge shook her head, unloosening strands of white hair.

"A simple family dispute with injured people filling up the judge's office at six in the morning? I ask you again, what did you do about it?"

The Clipper paused, trying to understand the jurist's approach.

"I thought I answered that, Your Honor."

"Are you aware that a police officer, a doctor or a citizen, or that matter, may bring information involving the safety and interests of a minor to the attention of the Commissioner of Human Resources? That's the law, Sergeant DiMaggio."

"I've heard that."

"Yet you did not act upon that provision of the law?"

"Not exactly."

"Not at *all*, sir! Was it not your duty, Sergeant?"

"I thought I was performing my duty at the risk of my job."

The judge thumbed through the coroner's report, Kent Morgan's complaint and the bulky papers from the guardian *ad litem* and the psychiatrist.

"My point is this, Sergeant," she continued. "Why didn't you take the matter to the juvenile authorities, despite what the judge said? That shouldn't have prevented you from going further; you saw what happened."

"I didn't think it was my position, or my responsibility. I'm not the court."

"We know you're not the court. You're an officer of the peace and a citizen. That might be more important. Do you feel that if you *had* presented the Morgan domestic problems to the family relations people, it would have helped to prevent this tragedy?"

"I can't say. Well, I suppose so. It's a very difficult question. I can't answer it exactly."

"Thank you, Sergeant DiMaggio."

Marvin Eddleman was called next. He went through his story of examining the hospital records, the talk with Chief Caramati and his termination from the Menlo Head newspaper. Judge Green drifted into the identical line of questioning she had used on Sergeant DiMaggio.

"Mr. Eddleman, you knew the facts here . . . what happened that night. Why didn't you contact the Commissioner of Human Resources or the Fairfield County Prosecutor's office?"

"I got a new job with the Stamford paper, and, frankly, I forgot about the Morgans. I figured it wasn't my business anymore."

"When you heard about the shooting, everything came back to you, didn't it? Did you ask yourself what *you* could have done to assist these people?"

"I was accused of committing a crime just because I looked up the hospital records."

"You might have visited the Fairfield County Prosecutor's office for immunity in exchange for information."

"It never occurred to me."

"So you did nothing?"

"I attempted to do something, and I got fired," Marvin said, beginning to lose his composure.

"You're an intelligent man; what do you suppose went wrong here?"

"I think the Morgans needed help from the beginning. Menlo Head is a very well-oiled piece of machinery. Everybody knows everybody else; it's an 'inside straight' which has worked for hundreds of years, I guess. The judge sits, it seems, for the pleasure of the town and its council. The police chief reports to the mayor who appoints the judge. The newspaper is controlled by the town, and the town doesn't want any interference. The attitude, Your Honor, is 'hands off.' For instance, don't you think, Your Honor, that Mr. Cummings, the town counsel, acted in too many roles? He defended the Morgans, both the Morgans; he influenced the newspaper; and now he is defending Mr. Morgan in this divorce action."

"Your Honor!" Bob Booth was on his feet instantly. "Mr. Cummings is of counsel. I am the chief advocate for Mr. Morgan, and, further, Mr. Eddleman is a disgruntled ex-employee of the Menlo Head newspaper."

"But Mr. Cummings *was* involved. Is that not true, Mr. Booth?"

"He was involved . . . yes, Your Honor."

Judge Green peered at Marvin Eddleman. "Mr. Eddleman, what do we have here? You suggest that Mr. Cummings was acting improperly, on behalf of too many clients, and you suspected that police and medical reports on the Morgans had been altered. Knowing all that and believing that the children needed help, you still failed to act."

"I tried to be a good citizen, Judge. I couldn't get up the

331

first rung of the ladder. I told you that. My only reward was being kicked off the newspaper. I was threatened with prosecution. Maybe I did nothing right, but I did try."

"Yes, you did, Mr. Eddleman. At least, you spoke up. I commend you for that."

Betsy and Lane Potter were called in. The judge persisted with the same tactic. Why didn't they do something if they felt the Morgans were in trouble? They had no answers, even after Betsy told the court that she had seen a lot of blood on the rugs being burned.

Those who had entered the police and paramedic reports were questioned; they informed the court that it was not the practice of the departments to go into details of domestic disputes. They considered their reports "adequate for the purpose."

"What purpose?" Judge Green asked.

"Official records."

Chief Caramati echoed that comment, denying vigorously that he had been influenced by anyone. But the newspaper editor did admit that his decision to fire Marvin Eddleman was based on comments by the police chief and the town counsel.

"Are you always so influenced, Mr. Palmer?" the judge asked.

"No, but Mr. Eddleman had committed a crime by breaking into the files at the hospital."

"That is private information. I don't condone that, but had somebody really moved on the basis of those records, a man might still be alive," Judge Green said.

"That's not my business. I run a newspaper. Of course, I'm sorry it happened."

As the judge continued her line of questioning, there was no doubt in anyone's mind that the court had, for the time being, altered the issues. Menlo Head was, indeed, on trial: its system, its social unawareness, its attitudes and its rule of sedating and controlling problems in a tailored fashion.

Dr. Thomas Driscoll was called next; he elaborated on his

concern for the Morgans and his counseling of Louise Morgan.

"But Dr. Driscoll, you are a licensed gynecologist and obstetrician, I understand," Judge Green said. "Why didn't you refer Mrs. Morgan to a psychiatrist?"

"In my opinion, Mrs. Morgan did not need a psychiatrist."

"And how would you be able to evaluate this?"

"Because I've known all the Morgans for years. I've taken care of the girls since they were born."

"And when you stitched them up that night, did you think of contacting a family relations agency?"

"Ha!" he laughed. "The family relations people . . . my dealings with those civil servants has been disappointing, Judge. They're not trained to handle cases like the Morgans. In fact, I doubt they're trained at all, despite their so-called degrees."

"Then who should have handled it? *You* apparently failed. Did you not consider the children in all this, or were you concerned only with Mrs. Morgan's health?"

"My decisions were my own, Your Honor. I refuse to answer any more of these questions," the doctor said, tossing his head back and looking up at the scrolled ceiling in a show of defiance.

"You're here by subpoena, Dr. Driscoll. You *have* to answer questions," Judge Green said in stinging terms.

"I do not have to be evaluated on the standards of my practice. The medical board of this state has that authority, not *you*, Judge Green."

"Oh, Dr. Driscoll, you would be surprised what authority this court has. There has been a homicide. You issued a prescription for the drug Valium for Mrs. Morgan on December fifteenth of last year. Is it not true, Doctor, that this prescription can be written one of two ways, so that it can be refilled automatically, or for a specified dosage after which the prescription must be reissued?"

"That is correct."

"March's Drugstore in Menlo Head has refilled Mrs. Mor-

333

gan's prescription fourteen times since you wrote the original prescription, according to their records. During this period did you ever call Mrs. Morgan back to your office to re-evaluate the situation . . . to see if she needed to continue the drug?"

"I did mention to both of the Morgans on the night of their party that a consultation would be appropriate, but they went away immediately after that."

"Dr. Driscoll, I believe at the time Mrs. Morgan consulted you back in December, she was somewhat concerned about her drinking. Was it advisable to issue such a patient a tran-quilizer—refillable at her discretion—in the first place? And did you ever make clear to Mrs. Morgan the dangers inherent in mixing alcohol with the drug?"

"I refuse to comment. I came here without counsel . . . to be helpful. I didn't know that I was going to be taken to task. I've practiced here for twenty-nine years; my record and contribution are beyond criticism."

"You had the right of counsel, Doctor."

"*I* also have the right to say nothing."

"Are you answering my question?"

"No!"

"Then this court will consider contempt proceedings. You are excused, Dr. Driscoll. I would suggest that you retain counsel; this court reserves jurisdiction and the right to re-call you."

Of all those called to testify, only one witness admitted a gross error: Judge Shallaway. He conceded that he should not have released the Morgans that morning in April until a court psychiatrist had been appointed to evaluate the condition of the children. The jurist said he knew the Morgans well; he had attended their party on the evening of the incident. He believed that they were rational individuals, capable of solving their own problems.

"But *how* did you know the extent of the problem?" Judge Green asked.

"I did not know. I should have taken necessary precautions

I don't mean calling the juvenile authorities. The Morgans had sufficient funds for private consultations."

"I want to thank you, Judge Shallaway, for your honesty. Now we come to a secondary matter, no less important. Do you feel that the law is adequate or too broad in allowing the sheriff's department to enter a premise to eject a woman, a mother physically—or anyone else, for that matter—when there is no opportunity for defense until the hearing?"

"I think that is a grave question of statute which should be reconsidered by further evaluation."

"But knowing what was legally open to Mr. Booth and Mr. Cummings, you did sign the injunctive order?"

"I acted within the law."

"I know you did. I'm questioning the law."

Judge Shallaway's bald head drooped momentarily. Then he straightened up and said, "I would have broken the law by *not* signing the temporary order. As a human being, I would not have signed it; as a jurist, I was compelled to sign it. My oath of office says that I must uphold the laws of the state. I did that . . . unfortunately."

"And do you feel that Mr. Cummings was acting for too many parties in this matter?"

"I do. But there is no prohibition against this. Mr. Cummings is not paid for his services to this town; the man has to earn a living by representation."

"Should that be looked into?"

"Yes."

"The court will stand adjourned until tomorrow afternoon. I must caution everyone here not to speak to others about these proceedings. I will say, for the record, that I am deeply disturbed by what I have heard today. There was illness here . . . there *is* illness still. Court adjourned."

CHAPTER THIRTY-FOUR

Bob Booth called Julie Gardiner the following day when court convened. She proceeded to explain how she had met Louise Morgan, and she recounted in some detail her sexual activity at Pigeon Hill.

"Did Mrs. Morgan invite you to her home?" Booth asked.

"Yes."

"Did she tell you that she was a homosexual?"

"She said she had had affairs with other women."

"Did she name the women?"

"No."

"Did she discuss her husband or her marriage with you?"

"Yes."

"And what was Mrs. Morgan's viewpoint of her husband?"

"Louise said she hated him."

"Did you see signs that Mrs. Morgan was neglecting her children when you were at Pigeon Hill?"

"Yes. Cathy, the oldest daughter, had taken over the care of her sisters and the cleaning."

Bob Booth's eyebrows lifted. "Cleaning? You mean this teenage girl was trying to manage the house, too?"

"There was no one else to do it."

"I see . . . and Mrs. Morgan wasn't capable?"

"Objection, Your Honor . . . conclusion of the witness," Tim Ahearn said.

"Sustained."

"Your witness," Bob Booth said.

336

Tim Ahearn walked towards the witness stand; he saw the wary look enter Julie's eyes.

"Miss Gardiner," Tim began, "what is your profession?"

"I'm an actress."

"What was your last part?"

"I'm studying acting."

"What is your means of support?"

"I was left some money by my family."

"How much?"

"Objection, Your Honor," Bob Booth said. "Immaterial."

"Sustained."

"Miss Gardiner, are you a prostitute?"

"Objection. Miss Gardiner is not on trial."

"Approach the bench, counsels."

Each lawyer walked up to Judge Green's bench. She said, "Mr. Ahearn, may I ask the thrust of this questioning?"

"Your Honor, Miss Gardiner has a reputation as a prostitute in the neighborhood. Men come and go at all hours. I can call a witness who will testify that he's a client."

"What is the point?" Judge Green asked.

"I believe that Miss Gardiner was employed by Mr. Booth to set Louise Morgan up and that their meeting was not by chance."

"All right. I'll let you ask the question."

"Your Honor, I object. This woman isn't known to me," Bob Booth said. "She's a friend of Louise Morgan's; they met at an art gallery."

"Mr. Ahearn, can you prove that Miss Gardiner was employed by Mr. Booth?"

"No. But I want certain questions directed to Miss Gardiner on the record."

"I'll let them go on that basis."

Tim Ahearn returned to the table and repeated his question.

"Miss Gardiner, have you ever been paid for having relations with men or women?"

"No."

"Are you sure?"

"Yes."

"Did you ever meet Mr. Booth or Mr. Morgan preceding your meeting with Mrs. Morgan or have any contact with them?"

"No."

"Tell the court how you recognized Louise Morgan at an art show."

"I used to do quite a bit of sailing, and I raced against her one time prior to the 1964 Olympics."

Tim Ahearn paused, then said, "Let's see . . . that would be at least sixteen, seventeen years ago? You have a remarkable memory, Miss Gardiner."

"She still looks the same," Julie Gardiner said.

Kent Morgan smiled.

"That will be all, Miss Gardiner," Tim Ahearn said.

"Just a moment. I have a question," Judge Green said. "Miss Gardiner, did you have relations with Mrs. Morgan before you came to Pigeon Hill as a guest?"

"Yes, I did . . . at my apartment in New York where Mrs. Morgan spent the night . . . and at the Morgans' duplex on Fifth Avenue."

"Thank you, Miss Gardiner. You're excused."

Julie Gardiner stepped down from the stand without looking at either Louise or Kent Morgan.

Louise leaned over towards Tim Ahearn. "I'm not going to be able to get out of this. The judge believes her."

"The judge hasn't heard you yet. For God's sake, just do what we rehearsed; you don't recall these things. Play it by our script, please, Mrs. Morgan."

Immediately after lunch, the guardian *ad litem* gave his report, revealing that Laurie Morgan was in a serious emotional condition. He indicated that he viewed Mrs. Morgan's behavior, brought on by the promiscuous activities of her husband, as highly suspect, and he dwelt for some time on the incident of the tennis court.

The three psychiatrists—Louise's, Kent's and the state's—

all offered routine and highly predictable testimony. Dr. Childress said that Louise had been driven to madness by her husband; Booth's man said that Louise had always been mad, and that fact had driven Kent from his own home; the state's psychiatrist was suspicious of both parents' behavior, but he stopped short of indicating any parental unfitness.

But Margaret Green was reading between the lines.

Kent Morgan was called to the stand; he stepped up jauntily.

With a lead question from Bob Booth, Kent proceeded to tell his side of the marriage and the paralyzing influences at Pigeon Hill. The man spoke in low, contrite tones, employing his dusty English accent which lent authority to what he was saying. Kent freely admitted to the court that he had had extramarital affairs, that at times his judgment might have been impaired because of work pressures and his forced isolation at Pigeon Hill. However, in the end, he came to the conclusion that equal rights for women did not include the splintering of a family. How could it possibly be judged correct for a wife to divide a household, making the husband an alien? Kent had spoken calmly, rationally, using examples to make his points. Bob Booth asked him a few questions; then Judge Green took over.

"Had you ever met Julie Gardiner before she arrived at Pigeon Hill?"

"No, I had not, Your Honor."

"Why did you allow this stranger in your house, Mr. Morgan?"

"She was represented to me as a friend of my wife's. I would have agreed to anything at that point which could have helped Louise."

"Did you ever suggest to your wife that she seek professional help for her problems?"

"Many times."

"Have you ever observed your wife with another man?"

"Yes . . . Mr. Antonio Bianchi . . . during a party held at Pigeon Hill on the night of April 22."

"And what did your wife have to say about Mr. Bianchi?"

"Well, she left home and said that she was going to 'swing.' Those were her words."

"After you observed this incident on the night of the party, did you confront your wife later that evening?"

"I did. She became very belligerent . . . began to scream and shove me. The girls ran in, and I tried to calm them down. Unfortunately, there was an accident at that point; some glass broke, and the children were cut. Louise punched me hard . . . she had a wild look in her eyes . . . she was ready to kill me."

"Objection, Your Honor," Tim Ahearn said. "Conclusion of the witness."

"Sustained. However, the assault is a matter of record. I have no further questions for Mr. Morgan," Judge Green said. "Mr. Ahearn?"

The tall, dark-haired lawyer got up and walked towards the witness stand.

"Now, Mr. Morgan, let's run down your sexual scorecard."

The woman serving as court reporter laughed, and so did the plump bailiff leaning against the paneled door. Their smiles were eradicated by the sharp crack of Judge Margaret Green's gavel.

"Mr. Ahearn! I don't like the tone of that question. There is nothing amusing about this affair."

"Sorry, Your Honor. Well, Mr. Morgan, just to set the record straight, you did have sexual relations with a client's daughter, Miss Barbara Halston?"

"I did."

"And how old is Miss Halston?"

"Twenty-one, I believe."

"And then you had relations with Miss Halston and Mrs. Halston?"

"Yes."

"Together? Mother and daughter? Isn't that what they call incest?"

Bob Booth was on his feet.

"Your Honor, we're not here to discuss incest. Mr. Morgan admitted to these acts. There's no benefit in going into detail."

"I was only trying to show, Your Honor, that the moral character, the fitness of Mr. Morgan, is highly questionable."

"Mr. Morgan's already told us that he made mistakes. Go on, Counsel," Judge Green said.

"All right, let's consider your boxing career. You were captain of the Yale team, one-hundred-forty-seven-pound class?"

"Yes."

"The night that you struck your wife on the dock, did you intend to hurt her?"

"No, I only cuffed her lightly to bring her to her senses."

"For what reason, Mr. Morgan?"

"There was a storm. She was supposed to be bringing her boat around from the yacht club on the advice of the commodore, but she stayed out there on purpose. I thought she was lost, naturally. I hired a tug at a cost of about five thousand dollars to find her. There was nothing wrong. She had merely decided to taunt me. I was upset, and I did give her a little jab. I apologized afterwards, of course."

"Mr. Morgan, at that point, did you think there was anything wrong with your wife's mental condition?"

"I suspected it."

"Did you seek help for her at *that time . . . not later?*"

"I suggested she see someone."

"But nothing happened?"

"All I could do was suggest it."

"And so your wife's condition began to worsen. Did you ever at any time *demand* that she seek counseling?"

"I did, but, of course, Louise never listened to me."

"Now we come to the forcible ejection of your wife from your home on June 3. Did you feel that the officers were abusing your wife that morning?"

"It was my wife who was highly disturbed and abusive. I believe they were only doing their duty."

"If you thought she was that disturbed, why didn't you seek psychiatric care instead of letting an ill woman be dragged out of her house . . . away from her children, by force?"

"I was told it was all legal."

"It might have been legal, but was it the humane thing to do?"

"Your Honor, I must object," Bob Booth said. "That's asking for a hypothetical conclusion. The fact is that the officers proceeded to perform their duty. Are we questioning the officers here, or Mr. Morgan?"

"I am questioning the *right* of the officers to proceed in this fashion. Yes, I am questioning this, Judge," Tim Ahearn said.

"Your Honor, perhaps it's wrong," Bob Booth answered. "But this is not the state legislature. We don't make the laws."

"Mr. Booth, if a law is abusive and if it results, indirectly or directly, in a death, then perhaps we have the obligation to test the validity of the statute."

"I'm sorry, Your Honor. Of course, we must look into this. I'm not in favor of statutory abuse."

"But you used it in this case, Mr. Booth."

Judge Green's eyes drew tighter; her disdain for Bob Booth was evident. She continued to stare the counsel down, then shifted her gaze towards the paneled witness stand.

"Now, Mr. Morgan, how do you sum this up—let me interrupt myself—how could it happen? For two days, everyone we've questioned has avoided responsibility . . . and on logical grounds, I suppose. Where do you think the fault rests?"

Kent looked at Bob Booth, who nodded his head.

"Where do I think the fault rests?" Kent repeated. "Part of it lies with me. I've admitted that I had affairs . . . and for a policeman to be killed in my home . . . well, I never thought I'd see that. You don't know how badly I feel. I'm a human being; I've suffered over this, too."

The judge looked at Kent Morgan with sympathy. "I know how you must feel, Mr. Morgan, but how did all this happen at Pigeon Hill? You and your wife are educated, sensible people; where did it go wrong?"

"I don't have all the answers, Judge, but I think the atmosphere of marriage is just as important as duty and love. Right now, my daughters think their mother's a heroine. Sure, she is. Louise won a silver medal at the Olympic games . . . she built a workboat by hand. I've never built a boat with my own hands. I've never pulled a lobster or shot a duck. You see, Judge, that's how incapable I am, but I'll tell you one thing. I know what a balanced upbringing is all about. It's schoolwork, attention to learning. And these girls should know a few social graces by now . . . how to set a table properly . . . talk to adults. I'm the one to give them a sense of honesty and proportion in their lives. They'll realize that someday . . . oh, they will. It might be too late, but I can try, Your Honor, and I *will* try."

Judge Green took a few notes and she looked at Kent. "Mr. Morgan, have you ever seen newspaper photographs of children who were beaten . . . victims of child abuse?"

"I have, Your Honor."

"Now, Mr. Morgan, when you hit your wife that night in front of your children, was that not abusive?"

"But I didn't hit them, Your Honor."

Judge Green sighed and shook her head. "There are different kinds of abuse, Mr. Morgan. Do you understand mental and emotional child abuse?"

"Yes, I think so," Kent said.

"Well, would you consider what you did . . . striking your wife in front of the girls . . . emotional child abuse?"

"I don't know . . . but I just hit my wife softly. When *she* went at me, four teeth were loosened," Kent said, opening his mouth, pointing to his lower jaw.

"And wasn't that also mental child abuse?"

"I never thought I was abusing my children. I mean, I never considered it." There was a long pause as Kent Morgan stared at Judge Green with sincere, pleading eyes.

"Thank you, Mr. Morgan. You may step down." Judge Green looked out over the room. "Are you prepared to testify now, Mrs. Morgan?"

"I am, Your Honor."

Louise walked slowly across the courtroom. Judge Green noticed that her plain shirtwaist dress was hanging off her frame, attesting to the weight loss of a woman who had partially destroyed herself and, perhaps, those around her.

"Now, Mrs. Morgan," the judge began gently, "this is a fact-finding session, an attempt to gain some insight beyond the coroner's report into the death of Officer Abbot. Secondly, the court wishes to establish which parent should gain custody of the children. First of all, let me proceed on the custody question. Where, in your opinion, did the marriage go wrong? How could all this add up to the death of a police officer?"

Louise leaned over towards the microphone and began in halting tones. Her voice gradually grew deeper, and a rasp crept in as she talked.

"To be honest, our marriage should not have taken place. I know now there was never a chance for its survival, and Kent realized it before I did. The day he came down to my home in Maryland to visit us, he talked about calling it all off. But the engagement notices had already been printed in *The New York Times* and *The Baltimore Sun* . . . and it sounds crazy, I guess, but it just seemed easier somehow to go through with it. But there were too many differences in our backgrounds. As an example, the difference between us was *his* Maserati and *my* Workboat. I come from the kind of people who think the more you are as a person, the less you need. My husband always needed more of everything. We didn't need a house like Pigeon Hill . . . nineteen rooms . . . we couldn't afford it. My husband drove around in a forty-thousand-dollar sports car which got seven miles to the gallon on twelve cylinders. A lot of people in this town need things . . . not ideas, but *things*. We belonged to three clubs: the Menlo Head Yacht Club, which made sense because my husband designed yachts; then the Field Club with tennis courts; and the Menlo Head Country Club. The dues at these clubs cost us over eleven thousand dollars a year. And none of us played golf or tennis, with the exception of the children, and they played tennis at their school. I could see very early that there was no way we could afford this life-style . . . and that's why I introduced guns and bows and arrows. Not only was it fun for the children, but we saved maybe fifteen thousand dollars a year on food bills. I taught my daughters useful pursuits; the other kids were over at the school smoking pot and getting things like a new Mercedes Benz on a sixteenth birthday. I tried to pass on the proper values to my children . . . fundamental things . . . not frippery. Substantive stuff which the girls could use through their lives . . . sailing . . . hunting . . . the outdoors. There's nothing wrong with that. Frankly, my husband hasn't told the truth here. He never suggested that I see a doctor, but I am seeing one now. I know I can get my head together again, and I want my daughters with me . . . enjoying the things we've always enjoyed together. I'll bring them up in the right way."

"I understand," Judge Green said. "And now we come to the death of Officer Abbot. In your opinion, Mrs. Morgan, who is responsible for that?"

"My daughter pulled the trigger, but the law killed him."

"Would you explain that, please?"

"I have some understanding of the law; two of my uncles were attorneys. Why didn't Judge Shallaway call me over to his office and say, 'Louise, here's a piece of paper, and it says you're supposed to clear out of Pigeon Hill until the hearing.' I would have cooperated. That would have been the decent way to handle it, but, no . . . in this case, the law didn't serve justice. In march four heavies . . . they handcuff me . . . the children are hysterical . . . and one of

345

them pulls out a man's gun and shoots him to death, trying to protect me against something she doesn't understand . . . and I didn't understand."

"It's a valid point, Mrs. Morgan, and we're going to be looking into that," Judge Green said. "Mrs. Morgan, I asked your husband earlier about child abuse at Pigeon Hill. When you physically attacked your husband in front of the children, did you consider that you were mentally abusing your daughters?"

Louise looked at the judge and then at her attorney.

"No, I didn't . . . everything happened so fast that night."

"Throughout the deterioration of your marriage, did you and your husband ever sit down and say, 'What are we doing to the children?'"

"I thought of it, of course, but they were emotionally well-balanced."

The judge shook her head once more and stared at Louise Morgan.

"Emotionally well-balanced? Yet one of them killed a policeman . . . another saw you in a compromising situation with a man . . . and also witnessed your husband making love to a teen-ager in the Virgin Islands. Is that what we call emotional balance, Mrs. Morgan? Are flying fists . . . sexual permissiveness . . . your idea of good parental examples?"

"No . . . I . . . ah . . . I guess not."

"All right, one final question. Why did you run out of the house with your daughters after one of them had just shot a policeman?"

"I thought my children were being brutalized by the police."

"Were they?"

"I believed they were."

"Didn't you know that a person cannot leave the scene of a crime?"

"I guess I knew, but I was frightened. I've never been

handcuffed in my life . . . and it was such a horrible thing, dragged down the stairs of my house at seven-thirty in the morning."

"It's also frightening to see an officer killed, don't you think, Mrs. Morgan?"

"Yes."

' Mr. Ahearn?"

Tim Ahearn approached the witness stand.

"Mrs. Morgan, you've read this complaint?"

"I have."

"Are the allegations true?"

"No."

"Have you ever abused or neglected your children?"

"No, I love them very much."

"As to your moral character, did you ever have sexual relations with Julie Gardiner?"

"No. If I did, I don't remember . . . I was trying to escape into liquor at the time."

"Have you ever had sexual relations with any woman?"

"No."

Bob Booth popped to his feet. "May I approach the bench, Your Honor?"

Tim Ahearn walked over and joined the other counsel.

"This woman is lying," Booth said. "We have video tape recordings of Mrs. Morgan in sexual acts with Miss Gardiner. She remembers very well. Mrs. Morgan is a lesbian . . . she says so on the tape."

"Judge, that proves it!" Tim Ahearn said. "It was a setup."

"How did you come to have tape recordings, Mr. Booth?" the judge asked.

"My client suspected his wife and he ordered the tape equipment into the house to prove it."

"And I suppose you assisted him, Mr. Booth?" the judge said, tapping her pencil on the bench.

"I did nothing improper," Bob Booth said, "except assist my client in a role of advocate."

Judge Green looked over at Louise Morgan and then shifted her glance towards Kent. The judge shook her head.

"Where are the tapes, Mr. Booth?"

"In this courthouse."

"Deliver them to my chambers and we'll take a half-hour recess."

"I'd like to see this material, Judge," Tim Ahearn said.

"You're welcome to the shabbiness, Mr. Ahearn. That's all we've had here for the last few days," the judge said.

Then she called out that the court would take a half-hour adjournment and that no one was to leave the courtroom.

Bob Booth walked over to Kent Morgan with a smirk on his face; he leaned down over the table and whispered, "We're going in to view the tapes. Your wife has been caught in a big fat lie."

Tim Ahearn moved slowly across the courtroom to where Louise sat.

"What's the matter? What's going on?" Louise said.

"They have video tapes of you making it with Julie."

"Oh, no!" Louise cried.

"Did you know about the tapes?"

"God, no . . . I would have told you. Damn . . . what are we going to do?"

"Well, let me see what they have first."

The lawyers followed Judge Green out of the courtroom; the bailiff stood by the double doors in the back. Louise sank down in her chair and buried her head in her hands. Suddenly there was a stir at the rear of the room. Julie Gardiner had arrived, and she insisted on seeing Louise. The bailiff phoned down to Judge Green's chambers for instructions, and while she waited, Julie pinned her gaze on the strained, exhausted face of the woman who had been her lover only a short time before.

Julie had felt from the beginning that Judge Green would not believe her testimony, the chance encounter at an art gallery. Her mind had swung back and forth between the

348

meeting at the Biltmore Hotel, at which Bob Booth had threatened them all with complicity in a homicide, and the once strong and resilient woman who was now facing the loss of everything—her husband, her home and her children. The natural affinity she felt for Louise Morgan and her own sense of revulsion finally tipped the scales.

The bailiff hung up the phone and said Judge Green had granted her permission to enter.

Julie moved slowly down the aisle of the small, musty courtroom; Louise sat silently, waiting for her to approach.

"Louise . . . I have to talk to you," Julie whispered.

"You said it all on the witness stand, didn't you?"

"I was paid by your husband's lawyer and a detective to set you up. I'm sorry, Louise . . . I'm really goddamn sorry."

"Why did you do it?" Louise cried.

"Money. I needed the money. All that stuff about my family background is a lie. What can I do to help you, Louise? I'll talk to the judge . . . whatever you want."

"I wish you had developed a conscience a little sooner, Julie; they have me for perjury now. I had no defense."

"I know. Look . . . we'll write a note . . . have it delivered to Judge Green. We'll tell her everything . . . take our chances."

"Might be too late, but let's try."

They asked the court reporter for paper, and the two women wrote a quick note, confessing the lies in the courtroom and the conspiracy against Louise Morgan. The clerk of the court took the note to Judge Margaret Green who read it in the hall outside her office. She reentered the chamber and told Bob Booth to turn off the Betamax machine.

"How did you think you were going to get away with this, Mr. Booth?"

"Away with what, Your Honor?"

"Julie Gardiner just confessed . . . and Mr. Ahearn, you apparently told your client to lie on the witness stand."

"That's not true, Your Honor."

"Gentlemen, I would suggest that you both retain counsel. Very good counsel."

The two lawyers looked at each other with somber expressions. Their impenetrable attitudes dissolved as Judge Margaret Green's fierce blue eyes stared right through them.

CHAPTER THIRTY-FIVE

The judge excused the lawyers and called the sheriff's department in the rear of the building, indicating that officers were to stand by in the courtroom for bench warrant arrests.

Asked who the people were, the judge said, "The Morgans and one other person."

"We'd be delighted to assist, Your Honor," the sheriff said emphatically. "Oh, yes, we can provide that service."

Judge Margaret Green then called Julie and Louise to her office. "You did the right thing by coming to me," she told the two women.

"Will I be arrested?" Louise asked.

"You both will, but I'll recommend leniency. Mrs. Morgan, why did you lie on the witness stand?"

"I didn't want to lie. I really didn't, but Mr. Ahearn thought it was the only chance we had."

Judge Green shook her head. "I would have overlooked the lesbian count. Just last week I awarded custody to a homosexual mother."

"You mean all that stuff about me making it with Louise was for nothing?" Julie said.

"Absolutely," the judge said. "That's the bitter irony of all this."

Sheriff's deputies moved into the courtroom; they leaned against the inset paneling in the back of the large room. Each man wore a retaliatory expression; it was obvious that they were thinking of Abbot as they unbuttoned the small cases holding their handcuffs. The lawyers looked around; they knew well what was coming for their clients and possibly themselves. Booth and Ahearn both glared at Julie Gardiner as she took her seat.

"Thanks a lot, Mrs. Morgan," Tim Ahearn whispered, leaning towards Louise.

At the other table, Bob Booth sat with a blank face. When Kent whispered to him, the lawyer hardly appeared to hear his client.

"Booth, I can't imagine how you manage to stay in business. A man's dead, and I guess I'm going to jail for this. Damn it, you should be in the next cell!"

"Screw off!" Booth hissed.

The judge entered the court, stepped up to her bench and looked at the Morgans with a steely expression. She moved some papers around in front of her; then she lowered her head into her hands, as if burdened by a paralyzing headache. But the agony Judge Green felt was real, and it went right to fundamentals: the Morgans' children and their well-being.

"The court decrees a divorce to Louise and Kenneth Morgan. The property settlement will be continued, based upon further discovery." The judge leaned back and exhaled. "I'm frankly shocked at the way Mr. and Mrs. Morgan proceeded to clear their records as parents. It is the opinion of this court that both Morgans are guilty of flagrant child neglect and child mental abuse. During the collapse of their marriage, did the parents stop to think about the children's rights? What was to happen to these young girls throughout this carnage of fists and sexual adventures? I'm afraid that question was dimmed by the Morgans' 'good time morality.' And that's just what it was. Have a ball and forget the kids.

"Just as serious as those commisions and omissions was their conduct in this courtroom which seems to underline a pattern of behavior which I find contemptible. Both of you were smug, believing you could prevail outside the law. I warned everyone about the penalties of perjury; yet Miss Gardiner and Mr. and Mrs. Morgan entered this courtroom and rendered testimony that was evasive, conspicuously unbelievable and patently false. I am ordering Mr. and Mrs. Morgan and Miss Julie Gardiner arrested at once for perjury. In the case of Mr. Morgan, I am suggesting that a grand jury be convened to hear evidence for possible indictments for conspiracy, entrapment and accessory to murder. The saddest part of this carnival, besides Officer Abbot's needless death, is that the Morgans are rich and educated individuals from distinguished families, and they will probably be out of jail in a matter of hours. They will engage expert criminal attorneys, not the two lawyers they brought into court—they have their problems. The Morgans will mount brilliant defenses and parade witnesses in and out of the court, and I doubt they will ever serve one week in prison. But this court has no jurisdiction in these matters.

"However, within the clear jurisdiction of the juvenile court is the well-being of the underaged Morgan children. In that regard, I have not seen one indication that either parent is capable of rendering the proper example and guidance that these girls require. Therefore, I decree a termination of all parental rights for Mr. and Mrs. Morgan. The children shall be awarded to the custody and care of the state of Connecticut. While the state does not provide for its wards all the amenities it would like to, I will say one thing. A foster home for these children will serve their interests far better than the cruel, affluent life at Pigeon Hill. The sheriff's deputies may now carry out the arrests of those named in the bench warrants."

The deputies came down the aisle and picked up the warrants from Judge Green. They handcuffed the Morgans and Julie Gardiner, and the prisoners were led from the courtroom. The Morgans were so stunned they could not look at each other. Just outside the courthouse where Bunny Lunsford was waiting, Louise broke into tears.

The deputy holding her arm said, "Come on . . . you'll have plenty of time to bawl later."

The Morgans posted bond along with Julie Gardiner. In the weeks which followed, Kent moved out of Pigeon Hill. He was a haunted, exhausted man; he did not have strength to walk past his own front hall or look from the bowed windows of the dining room to see the tomato plants, their bounty rotten and wasted on the slumping vines. Louise moved into Bunny Lunsford's; two weeks after her arraignment, the Commissioner of Human Resources called, saying that her children wanted to visit her for the weekend. Judge Green allowed this, but, at the same time, she issued a stipulation that Louise could not remove the children from the house.

The judge's clerk told Louise, "Mrs. Morgan, I'm sure you'll be correctly advised by your new counsel, but just in case you're not, please understand that any attempt to remove these children will be considered criminal contempt. Your daughters are no longer yours, Mrs. Morgan."

The girls, wan and downcast, arrived at Bunny's for the weekend, delivered in a dusty Volkswagen van from the Children's Shelter in Stamford. Cathy and her sisters were not in the house fifteen minutes when the sheriff's department posted a car outside to make sure that Louise Morgan did not attempt to kidnap her children. That made the visit all the more ominous and frightening; all they did that weekend was peer out the window to see which team of deputies was watching.

On the last day of their visit, Louise took her girls to Pigeon Hill to collect a few of their things; two sheriff's cars followed.

Louise met Kent on the grounds with a real estate woman who had just taken down information for the sale of the house. A light rain fell that morning, and the grayness made Pigeon Hill seem more desolate. A verdant growth rampaged over the facade; on the roof there were shingles missing, and light umber stains of rust from the leaking gutters were coursing down the walls, transmuting the whiteness of the bricks to a sickly, red-brown hue.

Louise and Kent pushed silently through the high, wet grass which had not been mowed for months. Their hatred for each other was gone, burnt out.

"The fall of the house of Usher," Kent commented after a few minutes as they walked out along the paint-peeled dock looking at *Workboat*, half filled with water and about to sink into the mud of Humble Cove.

"Where are you staying now, Kent?"

"At the Yale Club . . . in a little room. I'm going out of the design business . . . selling the old loft. And do you know what?"

"What?"

"Oggie called me over to his house the other night and told me how embarrassed he was. He asked for my resignation as vice commodore."

"Does that bother you?"

"Yes," Kent said.

He thought about that for a while as they came to the gingerbread summerhouse and looked at the rotting yachts hawsered to the float. They both turned quickly and moved through the increasing rain towards the house.

"Oggie said they didn't even want us in the club," Kent continued.

"I don't care because I'm going back to Maryland to build boats. I'm sorry you're no longer a commodore; maybe you'll be a commodore again at some other club. All clubs have commodores, don't they?"

"Sure. Strange . . . people won't even talk to me in Menlo Head. I called Babs, and she told me off . . . and goddamn, that little bitch caused all this."

"Do you really think so?"

"I do. Of course, Bob Booth didn't help . . . that bastard!"

"Why did you go to all that trouble, Kent? I would have given you a divorce."

"I lost my head when I came home with that Chicago fellow and didn't see the tennis court . . . what was his name?"

"I don't know," Louise said. "He was fat. That's all I remember." She paused and said, "I'm going to petition the court to get the girls back."

"Do you have a chance?" Kent asked.

"I think so, but you won't oppose me, will you?"

"No, Louise. I could never really have handled the children in the first place."

"Now you say that," she laughed, half under her breath.

"I was just overcome with madness. It's not that I don't love the girls. I'll always be their father, even if they're in a foster home in Bridgeport."

"Of course you will . . . and you'll see them."

"What does your lawyer say?" Kent asked.

"About what?"

"The charges against us."

"Oh, my man believes I'll be convicted but not sent to jail. What does yours say?"

"He's a damn fine attorney . . . a Yale graduate, by the way, and he belongs to the New York Yacht Club. Well, he claims that Judge Green's termination of our parental rights was arbitrary. If we were poor people, we'd still have the kids. He also says I might have to spend a little time in jail. Can you imagine a Morgan in prison? A former vice commodore of the Menlo Head Yacht Club in with criminals? That's justice; the real criminals are out on the street and me . . . I might go in. I can't believe it."

There was the honking of a horn. A black station wagon with the seal of the state of Connecticut on the door had just pulled into the driveway. Two matrons from the Department of Human Resources got out and stood looking up at the squalid house.

"It's time," one of the matrons said to Louise as she approached the austere women.

356

"Yes, of course. I'll get the girls. They're upstairs, packing a few personal things."

Louise entered the house which was almost bare now, the furniture having been sold. She walked upstairs calling, "Jody . . . Cathy . . . Laurie . . . the car is here to take you to Bridgeport."

When Louise walked into the bedroom, all three of her daughters fell into her arms crying.

"Oh, my babies . . . everything will be all right . . . I promise. We'll be together again soon in Maryland. Dad and I just had a long talk . . . he's not going to oppose me . . . he's changed," Louise whispered, trying hard to hold back her own tears. "We've all changed."

They clung to their mother; their faces were taut with fear.

"I'm sorry about all this . . . so sorry," Louise said, kissing Laurie and reaching out to straighten Jody's hair ribbon. "Your father and I . . . well, what's the use of talking about it? We made some terrible mistakes."

"But what if the court says you can't have us back, Mom?" Jody cried.

"The court will listen. I know . . . my lawyer says so."

"The lawyers were wrong before," Cathy said in a forlorn voice.

Louise didn't answer that. Instead she said, "I love you all very much, and so does your father. Just remember that. We have to go; they're waiting."

They moved downstairs, past the spot on the marble where Officer Abbot had died. Once outside, the three girls looked back at their home and their life. They knew they would never see Pigeon Hill again. The girls kissed their mother and then their father who tried to mumble, "I'm sorry," through his tightening throat.

"Come on, kids," one of the matrons said in a gentler tone now, "we're late. The Espositos are waiting."

The girls shuffled to the station wagon and got in. They

all peered out the windows. Louise and Kent waved until the station wagon was no longer in sight. Then Kent said good-bye; he got into his Maserati and drove away. Louise stood in the rain for a while; then she locked the front door of Pigeon Hill and walked over to Bunny Lunsford's house.

EPILOGUE

Marvin Eddleman wrote one last story about the Morgans on October 10, one year and two days after Kent Morgan first drove his Maserati into New York City to meet with Roger Halston at the Plaza Hotel. It was at that lunch he had discovered Babs.

PIGEON HILL, FAMOUS MENLO HEAD ESTATE, DESTROYED BY EARLY MORNING FIRE
By Marvin Eddleman
Staff Writer

Pigeon Hill, the once elegant waterfront mansion owned by Mr. and Mrs. Kenneth Morgan, burned to the ground early this morning for the second time in this century. The estate, which was for sale, was unoccupied, and there were no injuries. Menlo Head fire officials indicated that the blaze might have been started by vandals; an arson investigation has been ordered. By the time Menlo Head engines responded to the alarm turned in by Mrs. Lane Potter, the next-door neighbor, at 2:45 this morning, the fire was out of control, according to officials.

The original Pigeon Hill was constructed on the same site in 1889 by a New York City politician. It burned to the ground in 1924 and was rebuilt shortly afterwards. Mr. and Mrs. Kenneth Morgan bought the home in 1966 but moved out after the killing of sheriff's deputy William Abbot by their eleven-year-old daughter on June 3 of this year.

During the Morgan custody hearing in Menlo Head, a week after Officer Abbot was killed at Pigeon Hill trying to serve a divorce order, Mr. and Mrs. Morgan were arrested for perjury. It was during this same trial that Judge Margaret Green of the Superior Court's Juvenile Division terminated the parental rights of Mr. and Mrs. Morgan.

In a separate trial, Mrs. Morgan was convicted on one count of perjury and fined $10,000. She was sentenced to one year in the state correctional facility, but the sentence was suspended. Mrs. Morgan subsequently left Menlo Head to establish a small boat-building business in Oxford, Maryland. Three weeks ago, acting upon a petition entered by Mrs. Morgan, the Connecticut Superior Court returned parental rights to her, and the three Morgan girls are now living with their mother in Oxford, Maryland.

After his trial, Mr. Morgan was fined $15,000 and is currently serving a one-year jail sentence in the Bridgeport Correctional Center for perjury and conspiracy.

The ruins of Pigeon Hill were smoldering this morning, and many people who knew the Morgans and attended parties at their once glamorous estate stopped by to see the charred remains. One woman in the small group of spectators watching firemen hose down the embers said, "Pity it all went up in flames. I wish the Morgans were back. They were great people. The only trouble was, they were married—to each other, I mean."